THE SHADOW MASTER

THE SHADOW MASTER

W.R. PARK

SPEAKING VOLUMES, LLC
NAPLES, FLORIDA
2022

The Shadow Master (a.k.a. Overlay)

ISBN 978-1-64540-808-6

*This book is dedicated to my lovely and most patient wife, Genie.
I want to express my gratitude to her, because
without her input, this book would never have seen ink.*

Acknowledgments

I wish to thank Speaking Volumes for their faith in my work—and to bestselling authors James Rollins and Jon Land for their continuing encouragement to write. Write. Write. It paid off.

Prologue

Halfway between the White House and the U.S. Capitol, pressed like an unwanted ugly stepchild hidden among its younger and stronger siblings, stood the small and insignificant dirty gray building called *The D Street Private Library*. A number of years ago, the D.C. local authority and real estate agents representing the U.S. government attempted to purchase the building for their own use, but since the library was privately owned, and the cantankerous reclusive owner refused to budge, it was all but forgotten. Little interest was taken in the library by those who would have normally frequented such halls of literary accomplishment. Its aisles of floor-to-ceiling books were dusty and old. Few books printed in the past twenty years graced its worn shelves. Huge iron-carved doors swung open on rusty squeaking hinges, generally during the hottest days of summer and the coldest days of winter. D.C.'s legion of indigents found it a welcome haven to repose without fear of being hassled.

The D Street Private Library, with its peeling Corinthian columns, chipped marble steps and blacked-out windows, had become almost invisible to those who shuffled past every day. Two blocks from the FBI building and hemmed in by the FTC headquarters, National Archives, Court House, and U.S. District Court, the lesser library appeared not to exist. It had become just another unnoticed barren tree in a petrified forest.

Hidden in plain sight. General Rubin Brock, Chairman of the Joint Chiefs of Staff, smirked as he sat snug in the back seat of a bulletproof stretch Lincoln—one block from the library. All these years and no one ever suspected. "Right under the noses of the fucking FBI suits," he whispered between sips of his only known vice: 21-year old Chivas Regal Royal Salute Scotch Whiskey. West Point's most noted fullback had climbed the ladder of Army success these past thirty years, having served in every so-called war and armed skirmish he could volunteer for. Three purple hearts and a mountain of medals adorned his dress uniform. Today, his intimidating six-foot, five-inch, two-hundred and thirty-five pound muscular frame was clothed in brown heavyweight corduroy slacks, topped with a bulky gray turtleneck. A pair of always-alert blue-gray eyes, short-cropped white hair, and a row of pearly teeth were accented by a deep-tanned, square-jawed, Jack Armstrong, All-American face. Cleft chin included.

Tiny pellets of ice relentlessly tattooed the outside of the ice-encased automobile. Winds howled through the nearly empty canyons of the nation's capital. General Brock had been lounging in his warm plush surroundings for well over an hour; the only time he took his eyes off the library was to refill his glass. Angry with having to give up the only Saturday he'd had off in six weeks—and tired of wiping the steamed-up window, he extended a finger of the hand cradling the precious liquid and pushed the DOWN button; the window lowered a crack—enough to see out but not enough to let in the bone-chilling wind.

A cab stopped a block and a half in the opposite direction. It was difficult to identify the bundled-up passenger who exited. After the cab drove away, the man drew the scarf about his face, leaned into the wind and quickly headed for the library steps. The slight limp gave away his identity.

Expelling a breath of frustration, the chairman glanced at his watch. "That makes eight," he said. "The Secretary of Defense, Director of the CIA and his Director of Special Projects, Chiefs of Army and Navy Intelligence, Chairman of the Foreign Intelligence Advisory Board, the Assistant to the President on International Security Affairs— and me. All here but one. What could be keeping the Secretary of State?"

He was well aware that with any such clandestine gathering there would be, by design, numerous emergency exits. Perhaps the secretary had arrived unseen and used another entrance. It was five minutes to three. Tapping his watch, General Brock decided to give it five more minutes, and then he would join the others as he had nearly three months ago to the day.

"If the secretary shows any more of those idiotic black and white war films, I swear I'll strangle the bald-headed fat bastard and leave," he said, recalling the events of their last gathering.

***

The whirling grind of the ancient sixteen-millimeter film projector and the flickering imaging lights in the darkened room would have acted as a mantra if it had not been for the Secretary of State's raspy voice interrupting the action on the screen. "Those attack dogs," he said, "like the ones you see, were a vital part of our armed forces. Brave but vicious. There was a time, after they fulfilled their tour of duty, when we wanted to reward them by returning them to society." He poked at the screen. "But as you can see by their intensive training, that dog nearly tore the padded arm off the portrayed enemy soldier during the exercise."

Taking another splash of Scotch, Brock peered out the car window chuckling to himself as he proceeded to recall that earlier meeting and the CIA director's whispered remark as he leaned toward the general in the dark. "You don't think he's going to present each of us with a German shepherd, do you?"

Neither man knew if the secretary had heard the comment, because he continued as though he were the only one in the room. "The United States did make a failed effort to deprogram the dogs. We learned the hard way. It wasn't possible." Right on cue, the screen displayed a newspaper headline featuring a sub-headline that read:

Boy's pet attacked and killed a neighborhood friend as they played war. When the dog's owner cried out—attack, something inside the dog's memory triggered its response. It attacked. The boy was dead.

Secretary of State Thomas Cline flicked on the lights, walked over and silenced the projector. As his handpicked audience blinked and waited for their eyes to adjust to the light, he mopped his head with a handkerchief and dabbed at the trickle of perspiration at each temple. The upstairs library room was extraordinarily warm. In recent years, gravity, along with a propensity for food rich in saturated fat, had elongated his jowls and sagged his already puffed cheeks. Along with losing his hair, his eyebrows and eyelashes had also deserted him. Smallish black eyes set in such a large round hairless face gave him the appearance of a human pig. Behind his back, the nickname, *The Grunt*, followed him around the beltway. This was Thomas Cline's second tour as Secretary of State. He had held that position in the Grayson administration eight years ago. Anyone who thought him a pushover would find themselves nose-to-nose with the wisest, shrewdest and most powerful man in Washington.

Eight years ago, at the beginning of President Grayson's term, succeeding a single term *'head-in-the-sand'* president whose policy of *'openness at any cost'* placed the United States in a dangerous and vulnerable international position—a small group of five influential government officials were gathered to protect their country's interests.

Grayson had tightened and strengthened border and homeland security, as well as U.S. property abroad—once again allowing freedom of movement and action by America's various governmental defense agencies—including necessary covert operations.

Recognizing that the current president, President Willard Rhoades, would lead another weak administration—perhaps undoing Grayson's tough policies—four more powerful men were asked to join the covert group, including Steven Heywood, Assistant to the President on International Security Affairs. Heywood was believed to be their weakest link, and to be watched, but necessary for keeping informed of the reigning president's future course of action. Absent was Samuel Ross, Director of the FBI. It was he and the president preceding Grayson who had crippled America's ability to adequately defend herself from unscrupulous forces from within.

"Light your cigars, gentlemen," Cline said, turning his back to face a row of windows. He could clearly view the White House in the distance through the treated one-way glass.

Matthew Johnson, the Secretary of Defense and the only non-smoker, noisily dragged his chair across the timeworn wooden floor to distance himself from the others. In his mid-sixties with rather nondescript features, he normally had his slight tick under control during televised press conferences and interviews—but the aggravation of sitting through a meeting he had no interest in and was forced to attend—and now a smoke-filled session, was more than he could endure. His left cheek twitched without warning. Added to that, the stifling heat caused his glasses to frequently cascade down an elongated nose, further provoking his irritation.

Secretary Cline, tiring of his view of the White House, took his place behind a wobbly ancient desk and looked at the group of highly placed Washington insiders seated before him in a semicircle of hard wooden chairs. A bank of lights at the back of the musty smelling room and the crooked desk lamp were the only source of illumination. Cline had apologized earlier for the lack of lighting. It seemed the remaining banks had blown fuses. To the secretary's left sat Max Carlton, the capable Director of the CIA. He and Thomas Cline's governmental careers paralleled each other. Both had served under President Clifford Grayson. Max's dark brown eyes reflected a man of very little patience—always eager to get straight to the point. *Don't try and bullshit the head bullshitter*, he was known to warn. He scratched at his short-trimmed dyed hair and pulled on a drooping mustache, obviously annoyed with Cline's nonchalant demeanor.

The secretary remained silent, allowing everyone the opportunity to light up and enjoy their first few puffs. General Brock blew a smoke ring and challenged the man behind the desk. The old wooden chair the general squirmed in was getting the best of his bottom. "Look, Mr. Secretary, no disrespect intended," he swept a beefy hand around the room, "but we have other vital duties to attend to; why did you summon us on such short notice?" He took another long draw, filling the air with a heavy stream of smoke. "What does the fact that those dogs were later put to death because of their inherent danger to society have to do with our special group?"

Cline frowned, his small eyes squinted. "Just like my old colleague, Max—you always demand an immediate answer, General," he said, hesitating. "But I guess that's how you've both survived—and succeeded. One cannot deny that—it's why you both have my respect."

Steven Heywood, Assistant to the President on International Security Affairs, the youngest of the group, pushed for an answer to the general's question. "Yes, Mr. Secretary—why are we here?" The others joined the chorus.

Somewhat ruffled by everyone's lack of patience, and the smothering combination of heat and smoke, Thomas Cline leaned forward and spat out the words. "Because we need witnesses. You," he pointed to each individually, "are all witnesses to the successful rehabilitation of one—Mr. Rance Colby."

"And who in the goddamn hell is Rance Colby?" shouted Matthew Johnson from the shadows where the air was less suffocating.

Everyone grumbled in accordance, except Alan Oakley, the CIA Director of Special Projects. He removed his glasses and ran fingers through thinning strands of light brown hair. "I'm in charge of all covert operations, and that name is new to me, too," he said, turning toward his boss.

Secretary Cline sat back in his chair and smiled. "You wouldn't have heard the name, and neither would any one of you in this room."

His grin widened as he proudly announced, "I recently baptized him with that name."

Senator James Cochran, Chairman of the Foreign Intelligence Committee, stood up to speak. He was a robust, no-nonsense black man, who had already taken off his jacket, his muscles testing the strength of the shirt's fabric. "As Brock said, no disrespect. But if this is some kind of joke, and if you've caused me to miss my daughter's ice skating party, the administration's going to have one hell of a time getting anything through my committee." He sat down with a thud on the plain wooden chair. But he wasn't finished. "Now—before my naturally curly salt-and-pepper hair turns completely white—please explain."

Cline threw up both hands. "Everyone's so damn inpatient. Mr. Rance Colby is not the man's real name," he said, appearing somewhat embarrassed. "We're not certain of his real name. You see—for eight years his code name was UCON. It's an acronym for *Untouchable— Covert Operation Nullify*." Before anyone could ask the obvious, he raised a hand for silence. "I'm not authorized to explain the meaning— so don't ask."

"Okay, so what in hell has he to do with us, and why are we considered witnesses? Witnesses to what?" Admiral Lester Michaels, Chief of Navy Intelligence demanded to know. His counterpart, Major General Craig Tomasic, Chief of Army Intelligence, nodded emphatically.

"The man in question was—emphasis on *was*—our country's most successful covert operator. There has been no other like him in foreign intelligence, for any nation—nor will there ever be—we hope. He's a man with no background as far as our intelligence has been able to determine. A photograph of him never existed until recently. It would not have mattered; he's a master of disguise. We have no idea of where he lives, although we understand it's somewhere in the D.C. area. He has no friends, as far as we know. No government record can be found of his existence. Bottom line, gentlemen," he emphasized, "we know very little about this man selected personally by former President Clifford Grayson."

He stood, placed both palms on the desk and leaned forward. "This much we know. He's a trained killer. He's the most lethal human being on the face of the earth. There's not a weapon he hasn't mastered, including his hands. This man," he said, pointing to a closed door, "possesses a photographic mind—and speaks dozens of languages fluently, as well as various dialects." He sat down and wiped his brow.

"It's uncanny the way he always slipped past the most elaborate security measures of foreign governments. That's why the president nicknamed him '*The Shadow Master*'."

Both Carlton and Oakley leapt to their feet. The Director of the CIA shouted angrily. "I've never heard of this Shadow Master character!"

Alan Oakley waved his arms, stood erect and pointed at his director, then the secretary. "Code name UCON, my ass! Neither one of us has heard of him—or it!"

General Rubin Brock was unable to hide his delight. "Well then— I'd say he performed his job quite successfully," he said, then turned to catch the eye of the others. "Wouldn't you all agree?"

Craig Tomasic, the Intelligence Chief, looked-Army, even when dressed in a worn multicolored tweed jacket and dark wool trousers. Normally handsome features twisted with an expression of disbelief. He brushed back thick black strands of hair that had fallen across his forehead and raised his voice to be heard. "Brock! This isn't something to find glee in. If this guy is for real, he's a walking time bomb."

"Aha!" The Secretary of State interrupted. "That's just the point of our unhappy gathering this afternoon, gentlemen." He made a gesture for Max and Alan to be seated. "Ex-President Grayson thought it was time America repay *this man* for services rendered. Otherwise, it would be necessary for him to be terminated," gesturing to the portable screen, he went on, "just like those heroic dogs."

Pushing back from the desk, he stepped to the window and looked out over the nation's capital, now slowly disappearing from view in one of the heaviest snowstorms in recent years. Without turning around, he said, "James, I think your daughter's ice skating party is about to be canceled, if not already." He turned and pointed a thumb at the window behind him. "The snow's snarling what little traffic there is. We all need to get home, so I'll make the remainder of my story as brief as possible.

"At our Sanctuary Clinic, a team of medical doctors with mind-bending—or should I say—mind-sterilizing drugs and sleep-induced memory-sensory technology, first wiped his memory clean—and then, with what is considered a revolutionary but dangerous technique, programmed a new memory."

He glanced quickly at the closed door and continued. "The man you are about to meet, as my witnesses, has a memory of being a retired college professor whose wife, children and parents drowned off the coast of New England five years ago. He was the only survivor. He is under the impression that much of his memory is sketchy as a result of the trauma. He has been programmed with flash-memories of those he lost—grammar school and college incidents, unnamed friends and places—even the name and description of his first girlfriend. And to add to his confusion, a number of cities where he may have grown up are included. In conclusion, his new memory is like a videotape with indiscriminate blanks throughout the tape. There simply is nothing there for him to ever remember—except what we wanted him to recall."

His eyes nervously stared at a closed door, and then coughed. "The name, Rance Colby, was my little grandson's idea. While visiting my daughter several weekends ago, he disappeared in the kitchen and reappeared out of breath. He said—'Grandpa, I *rance* all the way.' Then holding the cold can of beer, shivering he said—'*coldbe.*' He was trying to say he was cold but transposed his words. Instead of coming out 'me be cold'—it sounded like Colby. Thus the name Rance Colby."

"I must protest, Mr. Secretary," Steven Heywood sheepishly chimed in. His young pale freckled face blushed, matching the shade of his shock of unruly red hair. "President Rhoades never advised me of a man such as you have described. And what you have portrayed is totally out of bounds—*legally.*"

Thomas Cline's cheeks puffed out, his eyes piercing. "Well now," he said, "Mr. Assistant to the President of International Security Affairs—that's because your boss has no knowledge of this man's existence. Only two people did—until now. Myself and President Grayson—and now all of you." Two index fingers pointed at the group. His grin grew menacing. "As for your concern of legality—that was never our concern. What we were faced with was a man that, up until reprogramming, possessed not only knowledge of undisclosed clandestine activities that could become politically embarrassing if revealed, but of potential future covert operations that could utterly destroy America's creditability in the world.

"So you see, young man—since this man has no known pattern of predictability, we had two choices. Terminate or reprogram. President Grayson chose the latter." He looked at Matthew Johnson, seated closest to the door the secretary had been anxiously eyeing. "Matt, would you please tell the gentleman in the other room that we're now ready for him to serve coffee."

The loud clatter of the cart being wheeled over the uneven floor unnerved Admiral Michaels. Silent until now and staring uncomfortably at the man Cline described as the most dangerous person in the world, he stood and made a loud gruff sound. Nearly as tall as the general, he rolled his brow and unconsciously, with the palm of his hand, brushed the hair circling a bald crown. Thin wire-framed glasses hung tenuously at the end of a bibulous nose. Scowling, he flung his leather vest over the chair back and angrily demanded, "Mr. Colby, or whatever your name is, leave that damned noisy cart where it is. You can serve coffee from there."

The upstairs library room grew deathly silent. All eyes flashed from the Chief of Navy Intelligence to the man standing by the cart, then to Secretary Cline. Holding his last breath, Cline's eyes were riveted on the man called Rance Colby. The person who bore the brunt of the navy chief's outburst appeared to wince, then became expressionless. He looked at no one. Steven Heywood stepped behind his chair, struggling with his thoughts. *My God, from what Cline told us, he could kill us all.*

Rance Colby stood a little over six-foot tall—and weighed perhaps no more than one hundred and seventy-two pounds. General Brock estimated him to be between forty-two and forty-nine years of age and in the physical condition of a much younger man. Light brown, nearly blond hair, with a few streaks of silver, was combed back at the sides—a handful brushed his forehead. If he were to smile, both dimples would deepen from laugh-lines to his chin. Denim-blue eyes seemed not to focus on any one thing, locking onto no one's gaze. Senator Cochran would later comment that what he saw in the man's eyes chilled him to the bone in an uncomfortably warm room. They appeared to be empty. Completely void of emotion.

"I'm terribly sorry for the noise," he said. "If I have offended anyone, please accept my apology." The man named Rance Colby spoke for the first time. His voice was deep, soft and gentle—almost soothing.

Damn—wouldn't that voice disarm the enemy?—the DCI thought to himself.

A slight New England accent was at once discernible—but his words flowed in monotone, without expression. "If you will all be seated, gentlemen, and one by one tell me what you take in your coffee, it will be my pleasure to serve you individually."

Secretary Thomas Cline, pleased with himself, sat back, sipped his coffee, and watched eight of the United States' most influential and powerful men sit mesmerized by the man called Rance Colby.

Chapter One

Echoes of General Rubin Brock stamping the ice and snow from his boots reverberated, bouncing off fake marble walls, raising eyebrows of a dozen dozing lost souls who loitered, yet were very appreciative of their safe, warm shelter. Noting fresh puddles soaking into porous time-weary wooded floorboards, evidence of those that preceded him, he removed his heavy corduroy jacket. Flapping it like a matador defying a crazed bull, he added to the tiny pools reflecting the library's gloom.

Grasping the jacket's collar, he flung it over his left shoulder and strode toward the far right corner only to hesitate alongside a tattered sofa where a man wrapped in a grease-stained army fatigue jacket, baggy faded jeans, and a pair of heel-less combat boots lay sprawled on his left side. His right hand clutched the jacket to his chest; the visible sergeant's stripes clung by a few loose threads. A paint-splattered NY Yankees ball cap hid his face but for a lengthy stubble of white whiskers. Brock bent over to read the faded nametag. The odd angle of the man's head on the sofa's arm and the wrinkled jacket hid all but the first three letters—PAR.

Cradling his jacket in the crook of his left arm, the general dug into his pant pocket for a wad of money and removed a crisp fifty-dollar bill. Folding it in half, then half again, and twice more, he gently slipped the thin sliver into the jacket breast pocket below the unbuttoned flap. He froze as the man stirred, licked his lips, made a smacking sound with his mouth—then relaxed. The Chairman of the Joint Chiefs ignored the remainder of the bedraggled temporary residents. Alice, the nearly blind elderly librarian, was unaware of his presence—as well as the others sprawled in tattered and malodorous, once plush, chairs and sofas.

Glancing back before entering the last aisle, the general smiled. *Sarge— you're going to have one hell of a stiff neck when you wake up.*

MAINTENANCE ROOM - EMPLOYEES ONLY - KEEP OUT

General Brock ran a finger over the timeworn, partially peeled warning that had been stenciled on the paint-impoverished door sometime during the building's lengthy history. Only a covert few possessed the knowledge that behind the electronically locked door, an elevator waited faithfully for its clandestine passengers. That corner of the library was well hidden by placement of dented cabinets stacked one upon the other and ceiling-high bookshelves. The closest dim light bulb hung two rows away; the door, without a knob, stood in near darkness.

Barely visible in a shadowed corner, fifteen feet above the floor, was what appeared to be a security camera. General Brock stood before the door, pressed the third rivet to the left of where the doorknob should have been, activating the camera, then looked up at the device, forced both eyes wide and stared, unblinking. A faint beam of blue light focused on his right eye reading his retinaprint, simultaneously displaying his image on the Secretary of State's laptop computer. At the sound of the click he entered, securing the door. What the general and the others would soon learn would profoundly change their lives forever.

***

When the elevator door slid open, Secretary Cline had his back to the gathering, his hands clasped behind. "General Brock—you are late," he said, in a voice drained of emotion.

"I had to stop and help a buddy." *If it's any of your goddamn business!*

Cline remained facing the White House, his attention seemingly drawn to the thin streak of blue slowly rising from the horizon. Winds continued to howl, but the freezing rain had finally stopped. As once ominous dark gray clouds were methodically nudged from Washington's skyline, Cline's thoughts focused on the widening field of blue. *If only what I'm witnessing is an omen—and my problems were as easily solved.* He suddenly spun on his heels. "Gentlemen," he said, smacking his hands together, "thank you for coming again on such short notice." The eight men seated before the desk had been in idle conversation, waiting for Mr. Secretary to explain this hastily convened gathering. His attempted failed smile fooled no one, and the circles of gray under his eyes spoke volumes. They all sensed it—whatever he had to say, they would regret.

General Rubin Brock had yet to take his seat, eyeing the empty chair closest to the elevator. Flinging the jacket over the chair back with fanfare, he stood defiantly with hands on both hips, facing the silver screen. He pointed a finger, first at the secretary, then at the portable screen, and said, "Thomas—if you brought us here to watch movies again—so help me…."

"Damn it!" shouted the Secretary of State, losing control for the first time in the group's collective memory. "Damn it, Brock—sit down and listen!" He waved his hand from left to right. "All of you. Not a word, until I'm finished." He slumped heavily behind the desk, placed his gaunt face in both hands and looked up. "This very moment—we're faced with one of the most monumental, potential disasters in our country's recent history."

Steven Heywood, President Rhoades' special assistant, seemed not to grasp the gravity of Cline's words. He looked at James Cochran, sitting next to him, and pointed to the bank of lights overhead. Senator Cochran ignored his gesture. Secretary Cline noticed the extended finger, and said, "Heywood—you have the same limited attention span as your boss. If you must know—after our last meeting I had all light banks replaced. Only three banks are on for a specific reason, which I'll explain if you'll grace me with your undivided attention." He smacked the desktop with a palm. Heywood visibly shrunk in his chair.

Cline nodded to the darkened back of the room. "The lights at the back are out for a reason that will become clear—if I'm allowed to proceed without any more asinine disturbances." He hesitated, waiting for the rumble of snickers to subside. "We have two guests with us today." Again, rumbling from the group—but this time they were angry protests. He raised both hands. "Stop! One has known about our gathering from our conception. The other, out of necessity. I'll explain." Again he lost their attention.

All eyes turned to the shadows at the back of the room. A well-polished pair of wing tips were visible, as well as the bottom cap of what appeared to be a cane. A brief glimpse of the second intruder stimulated their male imaginations. Below a black and white plaid skirt was a crossed pair of perfectly sculpted, well-rounded calves and a delicate ankle, adorned with a tiny rose tattoo.

Often impatient and now indignant, the DCI, Max Carlton, stood and snapped at the group. "Why don't we all settle down and provide Secretary Cline with our attention. I, for one, am anxious to hear what this damned new threat to America is." He gestured for Cline to continue.

Max acknowledged a nod of thanks. Cline walked to an overhead projector and slid it into position before the screen, and said, "Heywood, make yourself useful. Flip that light switch—the light from my desk lamp won't bother the projection." He turned on the overhead and placed the first of several clear acetate film sheets on the projector's flat surface. Loud gasps and groans filled the room.

A clipping from a Colorado daily newspaper flashed on the screen. Cline read it aloud. *"Two men identified as International Security Agents were killed yesterday on an icy mountain road."* He continued to read the editorial copy. *"The contents of the auto and footprints in the snow leading away from the accident site have led police to suspect a third person was also involved. Due to an overnight snowstorm, the alleged injured person's prints disappeared. There has been no word of a sighting in the area of the third accident victim. A search continues. Inquiries to the U.S. State Department have not been acknowledged. Colorado State Police will continue their investigation as to the actual cause of the incident, although inclement weather is the suspected cause."*

Now he had their full attention. All were aware that Rance Colby was being escorted to a small town in Colorado, where he was programmed to begin his new life as a gentle mountain recluse. Thomas Cline left the overhead on. Clutching several loose sheets of film in his hand, he slowly walked into the dim light of the desk lamp. His gray circles had darkened over the past few minutes. "I'm certain there are questions," he muttered almost to himself. "But allow me to go on."

"Go!" shouted the confused CIA Director of Special Projects.

"From what has been pieced together from the crash scene—one agent was driving; the other was napping in the rear seat. He would eventually spell the driver. Apparently Mr. Colby was sitting in the front passenger seat—and for whatever reason, did not have his seat belt secure. He was thrown through the windshield. Both agents sustained broken necks. The driver also had a crushed chest. It can only be assumed that Mr. Colby, injured as he was, unconsciously staggered off." Matthew Johnson, the Secretary of Defense, raised his voice. "That newspaper article was dated nearly three months ago. Why weren't we alerted before now?"

Cline's expression darkened. "I take full responsibility for that error in judgment," he said. "I've had teams of people searching for the missing man since then. Because he had not been seen by any of the local mountain community residents—we had assumed he must have died, and his body would soon be discovered. It has not. It's impossible to speculate the extent of this man's injuries. However, due to recent international events, we can safely determine his present state of mind." He took a deep breath. "I felt it unnecessary to inform you about this—until now." His voice faltered. *"Until now."*

***

The man called Rance Colby dozed in the passenger seat. Special Agent John Murray shook his head, attempting to loosen cobwebs from a very tired mind. For the past hour he had begun to envision, through the noisy wipers, imaginary images dashing across the ice and snow-packed highway. Clyde, his partner of five years, slept in the back. He'd let him sleep for another hour. Then they'd switch places.

Murray glanced to his right, wondering what nightmares caused his passenger to continually turn, groan and strain against the confinement of his seat belt. The man's past and future were unknown, but he seemed to be likable enough. The agent had a transportation assignment. He was the carrier, his passenger—the package. All else was not his to know. His chest hurt from a death grip on the steering wheel and from straining to peer through headlights nearly obscured by blowing driving snow. Physically, the constant pressure on the brake pedal and twisting of the wheel to navigate the mountainous curves began to take its toll. His nameless passenger's body tossed back and forth. Finally he reached across and released the seat belt buckle. Now perhaps the man could get comfortable and maybe enjoy a deeper sleep.

Gripping the wheel with both hands, Murray pulled himself closer to the windshield; straining to see, his chin rested on the wheel. The brief moment of comfort was all it took for his heavy eyelids to close. Agent Murray never saw the curve. Within seconds he and his partner would be dead, and their assignment ended as they left the road in silence, airborne. They would never hear the heavy thud and crunching of impacted metal as their vehicle came to a sudden halt, wedged between a large boulder and a huge hundred-year-old pine.

When Rance Colby regained consciousness, he was bleeding profusely from a deep gash over his right eye. His right leg collapsed as he attempted to stand. He winced and cried aloud when broken ribs come in contact with a thick layer of ice blanketing the snow. Finally managing to sit upright, he looked around, his eye smeared with blood. Wiping it with his sleeve, he shook his head. It didn't help. Without being aware, he had staggered over two hundred yards from the wreck hidden behind a thick corpus of trees. His mind was blank. He had no idea why he was hurt or where he was. Or who he was.

The man called Rance Colby instinctively packed snow against the open wound and found a handkerchief in his pocket to clear the blood blocking his vision. The billfold gave him a name—but not a memory. Flexing the leg he feared was broken; he discovered the pain was from a badly sprained knee. Standing but weak, he took several steps, grabbed at his side, and fell. The bleeding had stopped but his head throbbed, and shooting pains shot from one temple to the other. He closed his eyes. A child's face exploded within a flash of light, and then just as suddenly, the vision of a man's bullet-riddled body plunged into a swirling river. Once more, silence and a blank slate. Without warning it happened again. In a burst of color he could see an older couple smiling on the deck of a small boat. Another splash of color and he saw people at a cocktail party and the surprised expression on the face of a man wearing a fez. There was a soft spitting sound, and then a tiny black and red hole appeared above and between the man's eyes. There were screams and shouts. The vision ended abruptly. Then nothing. He tried to think, but there was nothing left to think with. Rance Colby would have no knowledge of how long he sat waist deep in the snow, reliving bits and pieces of his true past, empty moments, and programmed memories. They all ran together, going nowhere. He wanted to get up and run, but to where? The only thing he knew for certain was that his head hurt like hell. "Who am I? Why am I here?" he screamed in confused rage.

***

Secretary Thomas Cline, the once energetic, unflappable statesman, shuffled toward the overhead and with stooped shoulders placed another clear sheet on the overhead flat surface. "Senator, you were once in the Air Force's Strategic Air Command, were you not? As I remember, you were a pilot on a B-47 Stratojet Bomber. Correct?"

"Correct, Mr. Secretary."

A shaky hand laid a sheet on the flat. "Look at the screen, Senator. Tell me what you see."

"That's an aerial photograph of the eastern coast of the United States." In thought, he put a hand to his chin. "Appears to be from Savannah, Georgia to New York City—from the eastern seaboard, west to Memphis, Tennessee. I'm correct, am I not?"

"Your memory serves you." He laid another sheet over the aerial photograph. "James, tell everyone what you now see."

His grin widened before he answered. "How could I ever forget—I made that practice bombing run hundreds of times." Finding humor in his old profession, he chuckled aloud and continued. "We bombed the hell out of Charlotte, North Carolina; they never knew what hit them."

Cline raised his hand to silence the murmuring remarks. "During those days SAC had seventy-five percent of its planes in the air at all times," he said. Senator Cochran signaled agreement with a nod. "Those practice targets over the United States represented what?"

"Those white circles represented foreign targets." As he was explaining, Cline removed the aerial map and replaced it with another.

The practice sheet remained. "Now tell us what you see."

"That's a map of the old Soviet Union. Each sheet you have used is referred to as an *Overlay*. The practice-bombing run over Charlotte—when lifted and *overlayed* on Russia—coincides with Moscow. When we were targeting and hitting Charlotte—we were bombing Moscow. If the order came, we knew without hesitation—our bombing run."

Max Carlton, although he found the information interesting, wanted to know what all of that had to do with the disappearance of Rance Colby.

"We too, had an *Overlay*," came a soft but stern voice from the shadows. "Have a seat Thomas, I'll take it from here. After all, it's my responsibility." As the man with the wing tips and cane walked into the light, everyone jumped to their feet. They immediately recognized him, although he looked older, due to a recent mild stroke. Standing by the overhead projector, ex-President Clifford Grayson waved everyone silent—and Secretary Cline to his desk. Relieved, Cline handed President Grayson a new set of sheets

The placid face of the man called Rance Colby filled the screen. "This man, as you are all aware, has been missing for nearly three months. Much has been happening internationally during most of that period." He replaced Colby's photo with a flat map of the world. White circles were visible, scattered throughout. "This, gentlemen," he gestured with a hand to the back of the room, "and lady—is an *Overlay* conceived eight years ago by myself, my Secretary of State, Thomas

Cline—with input from," he held up and rattled Colby's photo, "UCON—my Shadow Master. U meant he was untouchable. Once he was given the green light to act, he had free reign to accomplish his goal by whatever method necessary. CON stood for Covert Operation Nullify."

Major General Craig Tomasic sat with arms crossed and interrupted without moving a muscle. "Nullify what?"

President Grayson jabbed a finger at the screen so hard it shook on its pedestal. "Nullify those!" he said with a raised voice, poking at every white circle. "Nullify those governments."

"All those governments?" Alan Oakley whispered aloud in bewilderment.

"Yes, if it was deemed necessary—beginning with the selected regime's Ministers of Defense." He caught the eye of Matthew Johnson, the current Secretary of Defense, and winked. "You see, eight years ago the United States was threatened in two ways. Attack by unstable rogue governments whom we assessed to possess both biological and nuclear weapons—and second, economically. Powerful governments who, during the past few decades, have become manufacturers of goods American citizens rely on daily. U.S. companies, in an effort to survive unreasonable union wages and maintain profits, went overseas to produce nearly every conceivable commodity. America has become an information, service-producing nation." He removed his suit jacket, folded it neatly, and laid it on the desk. Giving his suspenders a tug, he went on.

"Add to the scenario outlined—gas, oil and electricity we import." He pointed a finger at each man before him while asking—"What do you think would happen to this country we love if a number of powerful countries banded together, even the rest of the world, to force us to our knees by initiating an embargo, halting all shipment of goods to the

United States? Farfetched? Yes—but strategically feasible. We had to prepare for both events if either occurred. Thus—UCON was born."

Senator Cochran stood and stretched. "You may have been slightly paranoid—excuse the choice of word, Mr. President. I, too, am concerned that America is economically vulnerable—as you so correctly profile—and believe that government and business should have seriously addressed this vulnerability years ago. But what I don't understand," he glanced at the other faces, "and you have yet to explain—is what role was this man we now call Rance Colby to have played in your scheme?"

A very tired-looking ex-president leaned back against the desk for support. "Forget our nuclear deterrent and anti-terrorist capabilities. This man," he shook the photo over his head, "was America's contingency plan." He began to shout. "He could accomplish what a whole squadron of bombers and twelve platoons of soldiers could not. He's proved it to us," pointing to himself and Cline, "time and time again."

The memory of those clandestine operations, unauthorized by Congress, yet initiated and sanctioned by the president, flashed in Cline's mind. Before Grayson could continue, he quickly leaned across the desk and tapped his president and whispered. "I don't believe it would serve us to go into details."

Without another word, Grayson walked to the overhead and placed a clear sheet over the map of the world, displaying targeted white circles. He aligned both sheets. Four of the white circles were now replaced with red circles. "Defense Chiefs in all four countries, depicted in red, no longer live. Each died within the past three months. Each had a different type of accident—all possibly assassinated. To UCON's credit, neighboring countries are accusing the other of the deeds. It's *his* MO as one could call it. He's a master."

Before he could say another word, they were all on their feet. Max walked to the screen and shook it violently. "You mean to stand here and tell us that this son of a bitch, Colby, assassinated all four men? Why? Damn it. I don't care if you were president—we all demand a quick straight answer."

Grayson, seventy-nine and ill, grasped his cane, ready to defend himself from the irate DCI. General Brock stepped between the men and shoved Max so hard he knocked over a chair. Carlton had fire in his eyes, but the tall imposing general bared his teeth and mouthed—*'Don't you even think about it.'*

Cochran had Max by the shoulders and roughly sat him down and spoke for everyone. "We're all well aware that if what is alleged is true, it steps on the CIA's toes while breaking every international rule in the book." He then glared at Grayson. "What makes you believe *your man* is responsible for these deaths? I thought it was assumed that he died in the mountains of Colorado!"

Cline had convinced the ailing ex-president to sit and that he would explain. "Colby, for lack of a better name—remember, before I named him he had none—was our *OVERLAY*. The *Nullify* operation was programmed into his photographic memory. The sequence of assassinations," he looked at the screen, "corresponds exactly with that of the program—step-by-step." Blowing out a breath of air, he continued. "His hypothetical fingerprints are all over it. There can be no doubt."

Grayson shouted, waving his cane. "He must be stopped!"

"He's right," Cline agreed. "Obviously, Colby survived the crash, and the trauma re-ignited a memory. A distorted memory of the beginning of Covert Operation Nullify. Somehow he believes he was told to execute the project. The poor man is only doing what the President of the United States asked of him."

"Okay, let's say what you have outlined is true. What in the hell do we do now?" asked Steven Heywood. "Do we contact every head of government and say that an American-sanctioned killer is on the way to assassinate their Defense Minister?"

Admiral Michaels had been fairly silent up until now. "Heywood, you're about as much of an idiot as the man you work for. There's no way on God's earth that we could alert any government that America has sent an assassin into their country."

Grayson slammed his cane on the desk to get everyone's attention. "That's not the worst fear. Overlapping with phase one—the elimination of the ministers, is phase two—the assassination of the presidents of those nations." He appeared to be on the verge of collapse. "In one month, the President of the New Republic of Russia is targeted—and next on his schedule, is the Chairman of the Republic of China."

The room fell silent. Their minds were shocked into gear, searching for answers. The Chairman of the Joint Chiefs spoke first, taking charge. "It's getting late. We're all mentally exhausted. What we must do is clear. This Rance Colby must be dispatched immediately. No one but the eleven of us," he said looking toward the back of the room, "can ever know the reason." He slipped on his jacket. "Let's take what knowledge we've learned, analyze it, and meet again in four days with a plan. We're too tired and confused to make rational decisions now."

Cline held up a hand. "If anyone would like to discuss their thoughts, call me at home on my sterilized phone line." His finger swept the room. "I'm sure I don't have to remind any of you that if you call, it's necessary to do so from an isolated public phone."

No one offered an alternative, so Brock headed for the elevator. Turning, he reminded them. "Last one in, first one out, as customary." Then added, "Everyone leaves at ten minute intervals. Right?"

The library was empty as a tomb. His passkey let him out. Funny, there was no visual evidence of exhaust rising from the tailpipe. *If that lazy SOB fell asleep and let my car get cold, I'll have his ass cleaning*

Pentagon latrines for a month. Once alongside the car, he rapped on the driver's side window. Nothing. He knew the driver was in there; he could see his silhouette through the darkened glass. The door was locked so he used his own key. The driver's body slid sideways as the door opened. "Goddamn it, Hank, if you're asleep…"

Hank groaned. Brock lightly slapped him on the side of the face. Then harder. Hank shook his head, blinked his eyes, and stared at his boss. "What in the hell are you doing, General?"

"Waking up your goddamn ass, Sergeant-Major—and if you don't watch your mouth—you'll soon be Private-Major." Brock physically yanked him into the street. "Now tell me you weren't asleep!"

"General, I wasn't asleep. So help me. I heard a tap on the glass. I could see a sergeant standing outside, so I rolled down the window two inches. I heard a slight hiss—and the next thing I know, you're slapping me around."

General Brock flung open the back door and lunged in, expecting to find the indigent soldier lounging in the back seat. Nothing. On the middle extended armrest lay his unrolled fifty-dollar bill. He snatched it up, shoved his startled driver aside and sprinted for the library. He met Alan Oakley in the foyer, grabbed his sleeve and dragged him to the elevator without explanation.

All eyes quickly turned to the two men in the doorway. One appeared confused and angry, the other wild-eyed, shouting, "He's here!"

Cline, already strung tight and further ruffled by being shouted at, yelled back. "Who's here?"

"Your damn Shadow Master—you sneaky bastard!" he bellowed, waving the fifty-dollar bill overhead like a winning lottery ticket. "Your master of disguises. Goddamn it! Colby's here!"

General Rubin Brock slammed the bill on the table. "Look! Look!" he demanded. Pushing and shoving, they rushed to gather around the desk. The unfolded fifty-dollar bill had three large black letters freshly printed across its face.

BOO

Cia Director Max Carlton was giving his drooping mustache hell, tugging on it unconsciously and glaring at his Special Projects Director. Alan Oakley sat quietly, listening to Max's unrelenting ranting and fist pounding. Alan had ceased hearing the tirade minutes earlier. His eyes and mind wandered throughout the DCI's nearly barren Langley, Virginia office. Of course the director could have had his choice, an office with floor-to-ceiling windows in a corner overlooking the courtyard and fountain—but in his own words—*'I want nothing, not for a single moment, to distract me from my job.'*

Oakley made momentary eye contact, and then focused on a handful of black-framed photographs behind his boss. One was of President Clifford Grayson and the director. He had been in the office a hundred times before but had never paid attention to the faded writing in the corner of the photo. Adjusting his glasses, he squinted and read the inscription. *You have my complete confidence and appreciation for your faithful support.* Considering the recent library revelations, he could only imagine what the president had meant at the time. Next to that photo was one of Max and Secretary Cline smiling at a state function, drinks in hand. Of the two remaining photos, one was of a group of young soldiers in full battle gear—the other was of Max and a shapely blonde behind a large boat wheel, wind blowing her hair. Oakley knew Carlton to be a bachelor and an extremely private person; it was all part of the job, so he had never ventured to inquire who she was. The four eight-by-ten frames appeared lost on the large beige wall—almost out of place—as though all the other photos were missing. The only other photo was next to the door. It was of a smiling President Willard P. Rhoades. All government offices displayed the current president's picture. It wasn't necessary for

Oakley to turn and look; he knew why it had been strategically placed. Max had told him that he wanted the president's picture where he could see it at all times—as a reminder to always be vigilant. There was no telling what the lame-brained idiot might do to put all their feet to the fire. And—when Rhoades' term was up—Max could easily toss it out the door.

"And where the hell have you been the past two days?" The director raised his voice an octave or two higher, startling Oakley. Before he had the opportunity to reply, Max continued. "I've been looking all over this damned building for my man in charge of Special Projects—covert projects—like this maniac, Colby." Carlton crossed his arms and stared at the man across his desk—waiting.

Alan Oakley raised a finger and inhaled deeply, stalling for a few seconds more to concoct an acceptable answer. His boss' head snapped to the right. The computer resting on the corner conference table chimed. "Hold that thought," Max barked. He continued talking as he walked to the computer. "I've been waiting for a response from the Colorado State Police. They promised to e-mail me a copy of the coroner's report on our two dead agents."

Oakley watched Max's expression change from one of mild interest to complete dismay. The DCI's right hand rested on the mouse, his left elbow on the chair's arm, fingers tightly pressing his lips. "Well I'll be a son of a bitch," he muttered. Glancing at Oakley and slowly shaking his head, he said—"You won't believe this. If this isn't a kick in the butt. We've been had."

"That was fast," Oakley mumbled to himself.

"What did you say?"

"I said you got it at last."

Ignoring whatever Oakley had said, the director angrily snatched the pages from the printer, walked over to his subordinate and flung the report in his lap. "Read that, damn it!"

The Director of Special Projects read aloud. *"Early yesterday morning a suspicious fire broke out in the Gilpin County Coroner's Office. The coroner perished in the blaze. All records were destroyed, including the autopsy report on the accident victims. Both bodies were burned beyond recognition. Fire Marshal Bagwell suspects arson. The dead agents had been removed from their cooler-cabinets and torched. From the appearance of the ash remains, only a flame thrower could generate such scorching heat. An investigation is ongoing."*

Oakley's features paled as he read the balance of the report. *"The perpetrators neglected the agent's personal effects in our properties room—which included an eighth-full coffee thermos. Today's analysis of the contents showed heavy traces of sleep-inducing drugs."*

He stopped to wipe his brow, swallowed hard, and continued. *"Based on the thermos' contents, it is now my opinion that the crash and ensuing deaths may not have been the result of an accident—but rather a calculated homicide. Contact me as to how you would like us to proceed in the murder investigation."*

"Damn it, man—that report opens a can of worms. And you look as though you just swallowed the whole frigg'en can," Max said with a puzzled look.

Oakley caught a deep breath. "It's nothing. The—the—shock of the report caught me off guard." He flipped the pages on the desk and leaned closer. "You realize what this report suggests, don't you?"

"You'd have to be deaf, dumb, and blind not to see the implications. One of two things happened. Either someone wanted our agent's package destroyed—or Rance Colby faked his reprogramming and drugged our guys in a failed attempt to escape. He hadn't taken the icy road conditions into consideration. Bad weather foiled his plan."

"What bewilders me—is why they waited so long to do the autopsies? And how come the agents' families weren't notified?" Oakley asked.

"The only rational explanation is that Cline put everything on hold, expecting Colby's body to surface. Remember, we were only brought into the loop three days ago—then he filled in the three-month gap. As far as the families' go—their loved ones will have disappeared in some foreign land as heroes in the service of their country."

"Would you like me to go to Colorado and coordinate the investigation?"

"No. Actually it's in the FBI's jurisdiction—but we don't want their inept noses burrowing into our business. They won't be advised of the incident. I'll e-mail the Colorado officials to proceed on their own and to keep me informed. They won't find anything. Whoever is responsible, Colby or an unknown—the tracks are dry."

The director of covert activities got up and stood behind his chair, choosing to change the subject. "We meet with the others at the library tomorrow afternoon. Have you any earth-shattering ideas?"

"I discussed a few options with the secretary last night and felt like a damned felon sneaking about to use a pay phone to call my parole officer." Max stood and with a wave of his hand, ended the meeting—but had the final word, stopping Oakley by the door. "Wait. This is why I was looking for you earlier. Did you get the list of international targets from Cline?"

"Yes. He anticipated we'd ask and handed me a copy before I left the library."

"Good. Compare the cities on the list with the names of our Station Chiefs and Field Officers in those areas." Snapping his fingers, he added—"Also include the names of those we can trust in British Intelligence MI-6, France's Deuxieme and Surete, the Italian Servizio Segreto, Interpol, anyone left over from the KGB, and the Mossad. And—who do you believe we can rely on from China's People's Liberation Army?—if anyone. Add a few sources you can think of—and have the list for me before we head for the D Street Library."

Alan Oakley made the mistake of making a face. "Don't give me that look," Carlton said. "You would have had two days to compile the list if you had made yourself available." The door slammed shut.

***

"Tommy—Mary, stop playing around and eat your breakfast." Both young children—one ten, the other twelve—took a bite, then poked each other in the ribs and squealed. Their mother, an attractive brunette with short pixie-like hair and humorous twinkling green eyes, shook her head and smiled at her mother-in-law. They were on vacation; why not let them be kids? She and her pride-and-joy were in the below-deck cabin—her father-in-law was knee-deep in the engine compartment working on fixing a fuel problem—her husband was on deck attempting to untangle the anchor line.

The well-bronzed, shirtless man leaned over the stern; his hands touched the water. Not only was the anchor line tangled, it was also hung up on something. He cocked his head and strained to hear his father's shout. "I think I've got it fixed—I'll cross the wires to start the engine from here."

That was the last the loving father, husband and son heard before the ear-splitting explosion catapulted him into the bay. The rented boat splintered in a bright flash of flame. Everything went black.

"Ahaaaaa!" Rance Colby suddenly sat upright in bed— momentarily bewildered. Drenched with perspiration, he held his head—and moaned bitterly.

"Honey—is there anything I can do?" came a velvety soft voice from two feet away. He felt fingertips touch his naked thigh. It startled him at first as his mind tried desperately to identify the voice. Then he vaguely remembered—last night at the noisy bar. Lowering his hands, he turned to face one of the loveliest creatures he had ever seen. He was torn between what fascinated him the most—her large fawn-like brown eyes with long fluttering lashes—or firm breasts that swelled in size with each breath—beneath her clinging gown. She gazed at him longingly; her eyes glistened with moisture. Touched by her expression of genuine affection, he realized that she truly cared and could sense the deep pain of the stranger whom she had allowed to share her bed.

Colby opened his mouth, but words failed him. He couldn't believe it—her beauty had literally taken his breath away. Inhaling deeply, he tried again. "Thank you for caring. You have no idea how much I appreciate your kindness." He hesitated and whispered the only thing that came to mind. "God—you're beautiful." She blushed and whisked aside a strand of long thick dark brown hair that had fallen across her breasts. *And I need you in the worst way.* Rance thought to himself.

"I'm sorry if I scared you—but I had a terrible nightmare. One of many." She nodded a silent understanding gesture. "May I hold you?" he asked. She smiled and held out her arms. As he moved closer, she lay back down and leaned toward him, both breasts pressed together by her arms. Scooting down, he placed one arm around her waist and buried his face into two plump pillows of soft flesh. He was immediately entranced by the fresh female scent that engulfed him like a warm and fragrant ocean breeze. For the first time in months, he felt free. Safe. He lost himself in her—completely. She had blocked out the confusing world of his torn and troubled mind.

They lay entwined; time no longer had meaning. She had sensed how much he needed her and had asked nothing of him in return. He stirred. She felt the passion rise within her and responded with a gentle rhythmic pelvic movement. He withdrew his face and looked up and whispered. "No. Not yet. Please."

She purred back. "But I thought I felt something awaken—throbbing."

Rance chuckled to himself. "*He* has a mind of *his* own. May I enjoy this comfort and no more?" Smiling, she leaned forward and kissed him on the nearly healed scar over his right eye. Some minutes later, after he had fallen asleep in her arms, she quietly slid out of bed and tiptoed into the bathroom.

One eye opened when he heard the bathroom door. It had not been just a pleasant dream—a tall, shapely angel had indeed entered his tormented life. Each gliding step she took was deliberately choreographed for his benefit. She slipped under the sheet as he slid out the other side. "I need to freshen up, too. Don't go away," he said.

As he self-consciously strolled to the bathroom, her eyes followed his naked body. She sighed, noticing the dark red indent scar on the inside of his right thigh, as well as a similar one on his upper left shoulder—and a long thin scar across his right chest.

Minutes later he walked out humming. She wore a wide grin and giggled. "I see *he* once again has a mind of *his* own."

Colby pulled back the sheet. Sliding across her body, he stopped, brushed away her hair, kissed her neck—and breathed into her ear. "This time *he* and *I* are both of one mind."

***

Rance Colby's hand reached out. Her side of the bed was empty. The muffled whining sound of an electric hair dryer emanated from behind the closed bathroom door. Rolling on his back, he opened, then closed his eyes. *This brief sleep without a wrenching dream has been a blessing. I could become used to her—but I can't. It wouldn't be fair.*

Stepping though the door, she interrupted his thoughts. Spinning on her toes and extending her arms, she displayed her ruffled white blouse, short red skirt, and matching high heels. Then playfully curtsied. "I'm off to work. You like?"

He absorbed the vision for the longest time. "How do I put this?" he asked without expecting an answer. "You look as lovely with clothes on as you do in the buff." She blushed, closed her eyes, and nodded a thank you. "You shouldn't be going to an office somewhere; you should grace the cover of a fashion magazine."

She pointed to a poster on the far wall. The headline read—*'Molly MacWinter voted fashion's model of the year.'* "That was several years ago," she admitted. "I've been a model since my twentieth birthday—eighteen years ago." She made a face and showed both palms. "My days of modeling are about over—as you can see."

Rance rose up on one elbow. "In my eyes, you're still twenty."

"You're sweet to say so, but I have to run. I have a shoot at one P.M. but will be back by six." Pointing to the next room, she continued. "You're welcome to help yourself to breakfast. There are eggs and bacon in the fridge, bread for toast in the bread box." Molly leaned over, lifted his chin with her fingertips, and tenderly kissed his lips—and whispered. "By the way, you can call me Mac." Before he had the opportunity to respond—Mac was out the door.

He lay back, searching the ceiling—feeling heavyhearted—like a heel. Nothing could ever come of their chance meeting—not with his baggage. She deserved far more. He planned to be gone well before

Molly Mac returned. There was no other choice. No other alternative. Yet, for the first time that his puzzled mind could remember—he felt completely at ease with a woman. They had known each other for less than twenty-four hours, but there spontaneously appeared to be a lifetime of understanding and affection between them. Somewhere deep inside, he knew that their relationship would work, given the chance, but he couldn't afford to take that chance. Not with her. Not with Mac

Those beautiful, expressive, searching eyes seemed to question him as he studied the poster. His photographic memory etched a place in his mind; he would forever picture her silky thick brown hair, wide eyes, high cheekbones, deep twin dimples, full inviting lips, and quirky trusting smile. Colby wanted always to remember the lovely woman that had released him from the nightmares—if only for a moment in time.

"Let's get out of here now!" she had shouted, dragging him by the sleeve to the exit of the Blue Heron Bar and Grill. Rance envisioned how they had met, two blocks from Mac's apartment. He had been sitting in a rear booth when a woman entered and sat at the bar. She ordered a drink and was in conversation with the bartender when three men got up from their booth. One stood directly behind, the others on either side, crowding her. The woman shook her head at something one of them had said and attempted to rise. They blocked her attempt.

Mac later explained why she had yanked him from the bar. "I had never seen anything like it," she said in wonderment. "Within seconds all three jerks lay unconscious on the grimy floor. The bartender was already punching numbers on the phone, most likely calling the police."

He had come to her rescue and she to his. Glancing at the clock, it was noon. The TV remote was on the nightstand. Plumping up the pillows, he leaned back and turned on the Noon News. His mind wandered around the typically feminine bedroom—there was nothing of interest on the tube at the moment. He liked the pale yellow walls and rainbow colors of the flowered drapes. With the filtering light, the room glowed with sunshine. *Just like Mac.*

Suddenly his eyes snapped back to the television as he heard the commentator's words. "The Defense Minister of Iran died in his sleep. His body was discovered late this morning when he failed to arrive for a scheduled meeting." As he continued, the screen displayed a flat map of the world. Five red X's showed the locations of various countries where defense ministers had died within the past few months. "Governments around the world are speculating that neighboring factions are eliminating each other's ministers in preparation for planned invasions."

Rance Colby's body stiffened. Instinctively recognizing the pattern, he sat up; his elbows rested on bent knees—thumbs pressed his cheeks—shaking fingers dug into his throbbing forehead. His brain was on fire. *'Nullify! Nullify!'* The word ricocheted through every corner of his mind.

"It couldn't have been me!" he cried aloud. "Or—could it?"

***

"Hello! Hello! I'm home. Anybody here?" Molly MacWinter closed the door to her apartment and took a deep breath. She hadn't wanted to admit it to herself, but somehow she knew. He wouldn't be there when she returned. Her knight in shining armor was gone. The only man she had ever felt that close to, had freely given her soul to, was gone. She dropped her purse and slid down the kitchen wall, sobbing uncontrollably. "Why? Why?" she asked between breaths. "You felt it too. Damn it! I know you did."

Blotting the flowing tears, her blurry eyes focused on a sheet of paper taped to the refrigerator. Excited, she flew to the note. At first glance, her heart fell. But as she read Rance Colby's farewell letter—in spite of her sorrow—her heart swelled with the joy of a newfound lasting love. It was an enduring love. Neither time nor absence could diminish the fullness of meaning or fade its memory. She crushed the note to her chest—then read it again—and again, and again.

'Lovely lady—you know me not. But know this. I have fallen in love with you. You will remain my love—forever. I had no choice but to leave—and it will tear at my very being until the day I die.

'For one beautiful shining moment—you brought light into the darkness that has consumed me. In your arms—I was free. I was safe for the first time. That moment will remain with me—will sustain me in whatever lies ahead. There is no other—there has never been another woman in my life. Now there's you—the one I will always cherish.

'Believe and remember this. If I had a choice—I would have stayed and held you in my arms the rest of our lives. Please think of us that way. Remember me as I will you. I too, felt your love. Remember……..

'Good-bye…my love.'

***

The Driver Raised an eyebrow to the rearview mirror. *What now—iron britches?* General Rubin Brock tapped loudly on the glass partition. "Open the window, Sergeant-Major!" he shouted to be heard. "And," he went on, holding up a half-full glass, "I'm out of Scotch."

Sergeant-Major nodded and shouted back. "Affirmative!"

Brock often found fault with Hank, the Sergeant-Major—but from experience, was well aware that when the chips were down, there was no one he would rather have protect his back than Hank Sheehan. The man, regardless of his maddening foibles, had been at the general's side in half the fights on the battlefields—and in more bars than he cared to count.

A quick glance at his watch told him it was time. Brock swallowed the remainder of Scotch, held up the glass for Hank to see, and pointed at its emptiness. A reminder of what he had relayed earlier. *I'm out of Scotch.*

As he had done four days ago, he entered the dreary library. His eyes immediately darted to the figure sprawled on the nearest sofa. His pulse quickened. In six giant steps he was before the man dressed in an army sergeant's fatigue jacket and ball cap. He grabbed the sleeping man by the lapels and yanked him upright in one single motion. Shaking him, he bellowed. "I've got you—you son-of-a-bitch! I've got you now!"

Every dozing figure noisily leapt to his feet—a few sprinted for the door. Even poor old Alice was startled and blindly stumbled into a cabinet. No one was more startled than the man in the vise-grip of the Chairman of the Joint Chiefs of Staff. The violent shaking loosened his cap, knocking it to the floor. General Brock unceremoniously released his hold. "What the hell's gotten into you, dude?" gasped the young baldheaded teenager stumbling back onto the sofa.

With no thought of an apology, Brock stood with arms crossed, overshadowing the frightened vagrant. He demanded to know. "How did you come by that jacket and New York Yankees' cap?" His eyes pierced those of the youngster.

"I got them several days ago, dude," he slurred, having difficulty focusing his eyes.

"I'm not your dude," the general barked. "Explain!"

The troubled young man wiped his mouth on his sleeve and pointed outside. "As I just said the other day. Don't ask me how many—I can't always remember." A shaking hand brushed the naked head that appeared to have recently lost its hair. When the involuntary twitching subsided, he continued. "I was cold and huddling in a cardboard box in this here alleyway two blocks from here—when this here dude tossed his

jacket and cap at me and said, 'It's warmer in the D Street Library.' "
The youngster's eyes moved wildly from side to side, then to the man
before him, then to the floor. Suddenly he seemed to calm down and set
the cap on his head, crossing his own arms in defiance, he went on. " 'There's a
place for you on the first sofa'—was the last thing this here dude said."

The general studied the man for the longest time, and then unfolded a
crisp new bill, tossing it in the kid's skinny lap. "Get yourself a pair of
earmuffs." With that, he stormed off toward the elevator—but not
before angrily waving everyone back to their sofas and chairs.

Secretary Cline was engaged in a conversation with Max Carlton
when the elevator door opened. He interrupted their talk but refused to
turn toward the general. "Brock. We could hear you way up here. Next
time we'll sell tickets and invite the entire world in on our dirty secret."
The gathered group had a hearty laugh at the general's expense. Brock
wasn't smiling. He glared at each one individually, holding Cline's stare
before taking his seat. Throwing both hands up in disgust, he silently
motioned for the secretary to get on with the meeting. He was in no
mood for idle chatter.

Max Carlton held up his hand, effectively silencing the secretary's
opening comment. He glanced around the brightly lit, musty-smelling
room. "Hold on. Where the hell is Michaels?"

"Admiral Michaels is obviously not with us," Cline answered, with a
tinge of sarcasm. "His Achilles' heel is well known."

Secretary of Defense Matthew Johnson contributed his thoughts.
"His nose could guide ships away from a rocky shore on a moonless
night." He turned left, then right. "Let's not kid ourselves. Both he and
his wife were always treetop lushes. Ever since their only kid was killed
in a freak sporting accident, they've drowned themselves senseless every
night." He flicked a wrist at Cline. "I don't care what anyone here

thinks. Lester has to go. He can no longer be trusted as a member of this group."

While Cline loudly chastised Johnson for what he felt to be unkind treatment for a man who was not present to defend himself, Alan Oakley silently caught his boss' attention. The DCI locked onto Oakley's stare. Both understood the other's mind. The Director of Covert Operations mouthed the words—*'I'll take care of everything.'* Max Carlton nodded agreement.

General Brock jumped in with both feet. "Yes…yes. I painfully concur. I'll have a heart-to-heart with Lester." He set his square jaw firmly. His eyes blazed with a stare that demanded of the secretary—*no more nonsense*—and gestured with his hand to move on. "What's our strategy to stop your Shadow Master, Rance Colby?"

"Since our last meeting, all of you, with exception of Lester, have provided me with your thoughts." He pointed to Max Carlton. "The director has a consensus of our best thinking. Max, the floor is all yours." The director of the CIA stood and walked slowly to the front. Before speaking, he deliberately but briefly made eye contact with each individual, then turned to the Secretary of State sitting behind the desk sporting a puzzled expression. "Speaking of missing people—where is ex-President Grayson and the rose tattoo?" Carlton asked.

"I believe he's under the weather," was Cline's only answer.

Alan Oakley, much to Cline's displeasure, offered his own interpretation. "Yeah, and the rose is probably pressed under Grayson."

Max Carlton, displaying a slight sneer of satisfaction, continued. "As we all agreed at the last meeting—we cannot divulge to any nation that a rogue assassin from America is on the loose without restraints. We can, however, alert many of your past and present international Counterparts like MI-6, Surete, Deuxieme, Mossad, Interpol, Servizio Segreto, and old KGB contacts, among others—explaining that we have sketchy information that an individual of unknown origin may be responsible for the recent deaths of ministers of defense.

"Alan, cut the bank of lights directly overhead and turn on the overhead projector. The *Overlay* is in place." Though CIA Director Carlton was his direct supervisor, Alan had always resented performing menial tasks, especially in front of such an august group.

Max nodded thanks. "You can see for yourself, gentlemen, the ministers of Jordan, Iraq, Syria, Iran, and Saudi Arabia have all met an untimely demise within the last three months. Up until now, no one has perceived their deaths to be suspicious—with the exception of rumors that one country or another in the Mideast is responsible, and perhaps preparing to invade." He walked to the screen and poked the white circle indicating Cairo as a target. "Gentlemen, according to Colby's schedule, if he follows the original *Nullify* target timetable, the Defense Minister of Egypt is next in line for assassination." Once the grumbling subsided, he went on. "Observe those five targets." He gave them an opportunity to note the *Overlay*. "Yes. We must do everything in our power to abort the impending assassinations of the heads of the Soviet Union and China—but there's another even more pressing problem."

"Israel!" shouted Matthew Johnson, the Secretary of Defense.

"Right!" Max shouted back. "You're ahead of me." Hesitating, he glanced over at Cline, then frowned. "What do you think those five countries surrounding Israel will assume when the Israeli Minister of Defense is spared?" He provided time for the obvious to be absorbed. "You all know the answer. Israel will be blamed for the deaths and accused of preparing for war."

Johnson added his thoughts. "The entire area has been relatively peaceful in recent years—each country tolerating the other. The Mideast could explode like never before. All Arab nations banding together in a united effort to defeat Israel."

General Brock spoke up. "And you know what that means? Such a maddening scenario would undoubtedly involve the United States." He stood and addressed Carlton directly. "Goddamn it! We can't let that happen! What do you intend to do about it?"

Not waiting for an answer, he whipped around and pounded a fist on the desk, startling Cline. "You and that paranoid hawk president are responsible. If we go to war because of any of this—you are both accountable!" He leaned over the desk close to the secretary's ear. "And you'll both pay. That you can place money on. No. Belay that. That you can place your life on." Cline sat silently with his elbows on the desktop, one hand holding his chin. An angry Chairman of the Joint Chiefs of Staff sat down, folded his arms, and looked to Max for answers.

Senator James Cochran, Chairman of the Foreign International Advisory Board, was quiet as usual, but observed all. "Max, we're all aware that you have a nearly impossible assignment. You'd have better luck trying to find the proverbial needle in a haystack than you have finding the assassin, Rance Colby." He stood and walked to the back of the room to stretch his legs. "What can we do to help?"

"Nothing," Max replied with a sweep of his hand. "No one here can achieve what the CIA can. You simply do not have the manpower or international contacts necessary for this project to succeed. Immediately after our meeting, Alan will provide our Station Chiefs and Field Officers in all targeted countries with the assessments of CIA Senior Analysts. Our most experienced Langley operatives will be assigned to the project." He turned briefly to observe the secretary's expression. Nothing had changed. Cline appeared to be drained of emotion.

"No one outside this room, with the exception of Grayson and his tattooed lady friend—whom I intend to learn more about—will be fully aware of the true nature of our pursuit." He aimed a finger at Oakley. "My covert projects director will alert our overseas people and contacts.

I have already assigned a team of internal agents to begin a wide sweeping search of Mr. Colby. If he's still in the D.C. area, we hope to discover his whereabouts and nullify *him*."

President Rhoades' man, Steven Heywood, offered a suggestion. "We have a photograph of the man, and we know that he's a master of disguise. Why not utilize the computer to change his appearance into as many disguises as possible, and prepare copies for your sources?"

Max Carlton took a deep breath and blew it out. "Let me get this straight. You want us to develop an album of hundreds of photographs—from an old man to a pregnant woman and every possible alteration in between and send them to our contacts around the world." Heywood beamed and nodded. Carlton failed in his attempt to stifle his indignation.

"So you're suggesting that our agent in Cairo should carry a heavy multi-page mug-book under his arm, and when he spots someone suspicious, he would begin flipping pages to see if that person is represented among the hundred or so other photographs?" He waited for a reply. Receiving none, he continued. "Don't you think that while the agent is performing this asinine task, the suspect would have disappeared into the crowd?"

Heywood's face reddened as he became the brunt of ridiculing laughter. He stood up slowly and jabbed a shaking finger at the Director of the CIA. "Obviously, our learned and experienced director is not familiar with the computer techniques of facial profiling." Steven Heywood continued lecturing a fuming CIA director as he walked to the front of the room to face his opponent. "What I'm suggesting is that each of your agents be supplied a camera connected by satellite to a master computer in Langley. When they lock on to a face in the crowd, the computer, in split seconds, filters through your album of possible Colby disguises. If the facial features and measurements match, the agent will have an answer within seconds. The result may not be the subject, but at least you have a reasonable possibility. Then act accordingly." Heywood turned on his heel and headed for his chair. Looking over his shoulder, he added—"Give that some thought, Mr. Director."

The others in the group debated whether to applaud the man they had thought to be their weakest link or laugh at the director's discomfort. All eyes searched Max Carlton's blank expression. It had been less than thirty seconds since Heywood sat down, but it seemed much longer. Alan Oakley enjoyed witnessing his boss' humiliation. He knew the feeling. For once the tables were turned.

Finally, Max lowered his chin, tugged at his drooping mustache, and grinned as he lifted his head. His palms came together in a soft clap, then harder. He was applauding Heywood's idea. "I know when I've been beaten. I stand corrected. Steven, your recommendation is brilliant. Let's you and I get together immediately after this meeting and get me up to speed on your facial profiling concept. I like it. We'll do it."

"Gentlemen," croaked Thomas Cline. "Nothing further can be accomplished at this meeting." He struggled to stand. Once upright, he looked directly at General Brock. "Rubin's right. I and President Grayson are solely responsible for the eventual catastrophe." He swayed on his feet but securely gripped the desk for support. "But placing blame will serve no purpose and solve nothing." Cline's color turned ashen as he fell back into the chair. "This meeting is adjourned. Max, please keep me within the loop."

Chairman Brock's hasty footsteps echoed throughout the D Street Library's empty aisles stacked high with dusty, seldom read literary accomplishments. He barely glanced at the young man snoring on the sofa closest to the exit. Sitting unnoticed in a ragged plush green chair in a far corner, an old man hunched forward in a black ankle-length tattered overcoat, a rainbow colored knit cap stretched down over his ears. Clear and alert blue eyes followed the general to the door. When it swung closed, a bright smile widened the man's grin and deepened elongated dimples. The smile suddenly faded as his body stiffened and twitched—hands clawed at his face—a blinding flash of color bursting within his head. The image of two children, struggling and gasping for breath beneath the waves, flashed in his mind, then disappeared.

Chapter Three

"Dammed wall switch! Must have blown a fuse." General Rubin Brock stumbled in the dark of his study, feeling around for the desk lamp's switch. His large hands knocked a glass over on the thick Berber rug. "I hope to hell that was an empty glass," he laughed aloud.

"The lamp is hot, General. Switch it on." A soft deep voice came from the pitch-black corner.

Startled, Brock jumped back, then quickly pulled open the desk drawer, letting out a surprised howl. "Settle down General Brock; we don't want to awaken the wife, now do we? And the pearl-handled forty-five is no longer in the drawer. It's in my possession for now."

"Who the goddamn hell are you? Get out before I call my aide."

"You mean Hank? He's fond of my little can of spray. Sit, General."

Brock, not used to taking orders, and certainly not from an unknown intruder—snatched up a paperweight and charged the man in the darkness. He swung wildly at the black silhouette. Rance easily stepped aside and with an upward blow, jabbed a hard thumb into the brachial plexus nerve bundle under the general's right arm. Momentarily paralyzed, the crude weapon fell to the floor.

"You son-of-a-bitch!" he cried out, holding his limp arm with his left hand.

"I'm sorry I was forced to do that, General. I hold you in the highest regard and mean you no harm. I need your help. We need to work together. Please sit down; I'll explain."

Angrily and in some pain, Brock shouted back. "I'll be damned if I'll listen to a common thief!"

"You have no choice, General. I've got the gun, and we don't want a family witness, do we?" Silence. "Good. Now pour us both a drink and let's get down to business. The business of UCON." He hesitated to observe Brock's reaction. General Brock sat speechless, rubbing the circulation back into his arm. While Brock's mind searched for words, Rance reconnected the wall light switch bathing the room with light.

"You!" he gasped.

"Yes. Me. Whoever *me* is," Rance frowned. "One minute I'm a man on a mission, then wham, in a painful flash of light, I'm a man who watched his family drown." Wiping his brow with a free hand, he firmly gripped the pistol in his other. "...a family I never had. But that's my problem. I'm here to talk about your situation. Operation Nullify."

If a glare could kill, the man holding the gun would have been dead. "You've got the weapon, assassin. You talk, I'll listen. And I'll be goddamned if I'll pour the likes of you a drink."

Colby was about to place his life in the hands of the man who at this point hated his guts—and would prefer to see him dead. "We've met before, General," Colby announced in a soft monotone voice.

"At the library," Brock said. "I gave you a fifty-dollar bill—that you returned—and earlier when you served us coffee upstairs."

"Long before that, General Brock. Think back some ten years. It was in the Algerian desert, at the foot of Mount Tahat. You and your team of rangers covertly flew into Tamenghest to observe and destroy a terrorist camp. The vehicle you had commandeered bogged down in the sand several miles from the alleged camp site, and you had to hoof it the remainder of the way." General Rubin Brock sat captivated, reliving a tale only the president was authorized to know about.

"How in the hell..." Colby placed a finger to his lips. Brock never finished his sentence.

"Bear with me, sir. I have always been impressed with your leadership style. Against the president's best counsel—you were advised not to accompany the team, but as always, you led by example." The untouchable Shadow Master chuckled softly. "Perhaps your celebrated stubborn streak had much to do with it. But I digress. Once at the foot of the mountain, you deployed the team to scout the rocky cliffs to the east while you remained as the lone observer—with only moderate cover. Not a wise decision for a general with your tactical reputation."

"Forget the bullshit, Colby. Someone had to command the effort by radio. I volunteered myself. Proceed, smart-ass."

"Approximately fifteen minutes had passed without any sign of a terrorist camp when you came under direct fire from above—your men nowhere in sight." Rance stood, the gun aimed in the general's direction. "That's when we met for the first time, General Brock." He took a step forward. "And that's when I saved your life."

Brock's eyes narrowed as he struggled to remember. "That crazy bastard was you?"

"Crazy maybe—but one hell of a shot. Wouldn't you say?"

The general leapt to his feet and shook a finger at the man before him. "You. You were that maniac galloping on horseback—dressed like Lawrence of Arabia—standing up in the stirrups while firing away with your rifle. At first I thought you were aiming at me, and I was a goner." Brock's finger was still wagging as he continued. "Goddamn it, man—as I remember it—you fired four times and four Arabs tumbled from the cliffs high above me. Shit. You underestimate yourself, Colby. *One hell of a shot.* I had never seen the likes of it, nor since then." He lowered his hand and stared at the troubled man before him. "Yes. There's no doubt. If you hadn't appeared out of nowhere, I would have been dead. They had me pinned down. You saved my life, then quickly disappeared into the desert."

Both men faced each other. Neither spoke, lost in their memory of that moment in time. Rance Colby broke the silence. "I saved your life,

General—now it's your turn to save mine." Saying that, he tossed the pistol to the general, who caught it in midair, finger cradling the trigger.

Brock cracked a smile and walked to his desk and sat down. "Either you're an arrogant madman, or the bravest son-of-a-bitch I've ever had the pleasure of holding a gun on. Either way—I'll pour you that drink— and we'll talk. You first, Colby," he said. With the gun barrel, he motioned to the chair in front of the desk. "Sit."

"Madman? At times, I wonder. Brave? We'll see, once this conversation is over." Brock poured three fingers of Scotch—sliding the glass across the desktop with the point of the gun. Colby took a long swallow before presenting his case. "We both know what UCON is all about. Cline and Grayson displayed the *Overlay* and explained the ex-president's covert operation to your little group of heavy-hitters."

Brock sat up straight. "How in the hell did you know about that? Who in our group is your informant?"

"General, I'm not called the President's Shadow Master for nothing." He downed the drink and shoved the glass back for a refill. "I'm a mite thirsty tonight." He noticed the grandfather clock in the corner—it was now early morning. "It's getting late, and I'm booked on flight to Cairo tomorrow." Remembering that the Defense Minister of Egypt was the next scheduled target, Brock cocked his head and tightened his grip on the weapon. Colby showed both palms. "Don't get edgy, sir. I'll explain."

Over the next hour and a half, Rance Colby provided the chairman with a full accounting of his last three months—as much as he could recall. From a hidden compartment in the D Street Library's upper room, he had heard and observed the group's last two meetings. "So you see, General, I could not have assassinated the ministers, as everyone assumed. An elderly lady, looking for her lost chickens, found and nursed me back to health. At least part of me. She had no radio or television to learn about the crash and search for a third passenger. And her cabin was far too isolated to be noticed.

"It took me nearly two months to recuperate—and for a while—I wasn't certain who I was." He pressed his forehead with both hands. "At times now, I'm confused." This time he swallowed the Scotch with one gulp and motioned—no more. "One day, drowning my sorrows in a mountain-town tavern, watching CNN, the picture on the screen wrenched open a memory. The memory of UCON. It was happening. The *Nullify Overlay* was there before me. At least the beginning schedule. There was no denying the programmed scenario. Defense Ministers were dying, either of natural causes or in accidents. Bullshit!" He cried out. "I knew different. You know different. They were assassinated. And the Egyptian minister will be next unless I can stop it. If I fail, the assassin or assassins move on to bigger game in Russia and China. I need your help. You're the only one I can trust."

Looking for an answer, General Rubin Brock's eyes searched the face of the man before him. *Should the man that saved his life—a possible assassin—be trusted?* As he weighed the alternatives, his eyes turned to two large bookcases stuffed with military strategy volumes and a wall hung with dozens of photos of war buddies and accomplishment awards. *There's no reason for him to have contacted me—except to risk his life in an effort to abort the operation.* Brock stood and extended a hand. "I didn't get where I am today by being indecisive. Your story is believable." They shook hands. Brock sat down and leaned across the desk, palms down. "Do you have any idea who's behind this? Who's initiating your Nullify assignment? Imitating you?"

Rance rubbed his temples. "Only a guess and I'm in no position to point fingers at this time. Not just yet. You'll have to trust me until I get back from Cairo. If I get back." He forced a smile. "Assuming I do, I'll report to you immediately. In the meantime, you must keep our meeting and my intention between the two of us. Agreed?"

"Agreed. How can I help?"

"I've left a note in your upper right-hand desk drawer. Read it carefully. My success might just depend on how well you follow orders."

"You're a cocky bastard, aren't you? You figured all along that I'd play ball."

The intruder flipped the general a casual two-fingered salute and turned to leave. At the door he looked back, displayed a crooked smile, and tossed a magazine clip to Brock. "I might well be mad. Brave? Questionable. A survivor? Yes. What I'm not—is dumb enough to stand in front of you with a loaded gun in your hand."

The general's eyes widened in surprise. Then he roared with laughter. "I like you, Rance Colby, or whoever you are. Be careful. Report back."

Just before the door shut, Colby added one more bit of information. "If you haven't seen the late-late news, both Admiral Michaels and his wife were found dead this evening in their home, apparently a double suicide. Neighbors heard the shots."

***

Bloodshot eyes lifted from the reflection in half-filled glasses to an old man shuffling through the door of the Blue Heron Bar and Grill. He paused and pulled the collar of his long black coat up around his ears, searching the room. With fingerless gloves, he tugged at his ragged but colorful knit cap. Unable to decide whether to sit in a booth, he shuffled his way toward the bar, choosing a wobbly stool three down from a shapely woman with long thick brown hair. Deep in conversation with the bartender, she failed to notice the old man. Her sole purpose in being there was to ask the man behind the bar—wearing a badly stained apron and a lecherous grin—if the man who had come to her rescue had been in the Blue Heron since the disturbance. She was determined not to let him slip from her life—explaining to the bartender that it was her intention to return every Wednesday (the day they had met)—in hopes that he too, might return. Turning to pull a draft for his new counter customer, he nodded to the first booth, reminding her of the damage her friend had caused his long-time patrons.

Their conversation had ended on a sour note; the three men in the booth chuckled loudly. Ignoring their lewd jeers, Molly MacWinter, always hopeful, nursed her cocktail. Each time the door opened; her eyes gazed to the reflection in the mirror across the bar. Two men dressed in dark suits entered and removed their thick-rimmed sunglasses. The sun had long since disappeared. One straddled the seat to Molly's right, the other, three stools away, elbowed the old man aside. No apology forthcoming. The old man simply grunted, yanked his cap further over his ears, and moved two stools down.

"Miss," the man showed her his ID and then a photo. "Have you seen this man or had any contact with the suspect?" Molly was thankful that the bartender had left for the storeroom to get a replacement keg. The photo was of Rance Colby.

Her brief acting classes proved helpful. Expressionless, she answered a disinterested, "No. What is it he's supposed to have done?"

"That I'm not obliged to divulge." He motioned his head toward the door; his partner flipped a five-dollar bill in front of the old man, and both left. Outside, the inquiring agent grabbed the other's arm. "I'm sick and tired of this assignment. We've talked to over a dozen tasty-looking broads in as many bars and have had no luck, and I'm getting thirstier and hornier by the minute."

"What did those two ugly-suits want?" inquired the bartender, struggling with the weight of a fresh keg of beer.

"They're looking for some guy, nothing serious." But her mind was running a mile a minute. *That was him. But he's too gentle to have done whatever they want him for. I just know it.* Molly's mind justified the situation. *They probably want to question him about someone else. Nothing serious.* Convincing herself that she had to maintain faith in the man she had known and come to understand that night, and fallen in love with, she downed the last swallow and walked out into the night. Her thoughts were of him. *I wish I could help him if he's in trouble.* The door hadn't closed completely when the old man slid off his stool and headed for the exit—just in front of the three laughing men—bent on finishing what they had started a week earlier.

"Which way did she go?" asked one of the tipsy trio swaying under the corner streetlight.

"You want some nude photos of your wife, fat boy?" came a voice from the alleyway.

Spinning around, the heavyset man was poked by his howling friend. "He must be talking to you, Harry."

The third man was in hysterics. "I'd pay to see those myself."

As the three entered the dimly lit alley to teach the man behind the voice a lesson, the old man managed to circle them as they did him. Now they faced the streetlight's pale glow; the old man stood in the shadow. The moment they lifted their feet to take the first step, the old man moved swiftly, catching their stride in midair. His right foot found its target. Harry screamed in pain; his testicles crushed. Within the same fluid motion, he grabbed the throats of the other two. Twisting them back-to-back, he brought both skulls crashing together. They fell in a heap on their squirming partner.

Leaning over the fallen groaning threesome, Rance Colby spoke in a menacing whisper. "One time I'll be an old man, another a banker, or a construction worker, even a biker. You'll never know who I am or where I'll be." He leaned closer. "If you ever look at that woman again, or if I learn any one of you has approached her, talked to her, I'll be in your faces and so help me God, I'll tear out your hearts with my bare hands." He straightened up and waited for a reply. "Do you understand me, tough guys?"

"Yeah," moaned the two, holding the back of their heads. The fat man's hands grasped his crotch; he barely gasped a word.

Rance kicked the man's shoe. "I'll take that as a qualified yes." Turning, he disappeared around the corner. His final words shouted over his shoulder, burned into their minds. "I'll be watching you!"

***

When the sleepy hotel desk clerk turned to place a message in a guest's mailbox, the old man slipped unseen around the corner and stepped into the men's room. Convinced he would be safe—no one would be there this time in the morning—he stuffed the cap and gloves into the overcoat's pocket. Removal of the coat revealed an expensive dark three-piece pinstriped suit, with a red power-tie. After washing off makeup smudges, the man called Rance Colby combed his hair straight back and nodded approval in the mirror. Folding the coat over his arm, he left the lavatory, waved good-bye to the clerk, and stepped into a morning chill.

"Taxi! Taxi!" The only visible taxi, parked at the corner, hadn't moved. Tired, and now frustrated. *There's so much to do before leaving for the airport,* he thought. Rance walked up to the car, placed his foot on the bumper and pressed down hard, rocking the chassis. Blinking awake, the driver raised both hands and motioned his customer inside.

"Sorry, sir. It's been a long night," complained the taxi driver. "Where to?" Responding to the address given, he raised his eyebrows, searching the rearview mirror for his customer's face. Maybe he was a congressman or a senator—someone important in the government. He recognized the address of an exclusive and expensive townhouse location. Traffic was light, and after passing through a gated security entrance, they arrived in front of a stately residence within half an hour. The guard, recognizing the taxi's passenger, waved, and warmly welcomed him home after a long absence. Smiling at his generous tip, the driver made a U-turn and drove off into the early morning light. His passenger pressed a button on his door key—there was a long moment of silence—and the door swung partially open. Had a muted alarm sounded, he would have been alerted to a recent break-in and would have taken appropriate action. Colby sighed from weariness and walked up the whitewashed stone steps. Once inside the marble foyer, he shoved the door closed on an empty house, and lit the overhead chandelier. It was then that the thought struck him. *How wonderful it would have been if Molly had been there to greet him home.*

To his immediate left was a large oil painting of a brooding Italian olive grove. Still holding the door key, he pressed the button twice. The painting slid up exposing a number of small TV screens. Each monitor revealed the view of a strategically placed video camera. Had there been any movement during his absence, the photo of that scene would have been displayed on the screen. A solicitor that had slipped by the gate guard, and had disturbed the front door, was the only sign of movement. Under the circumstances, he felt mild relief.

The room behind the painting wall was his study. To his right was a large formal dining room, and straight from there through two swinging doors was a massive, fully stocked modern kitchen. Passing three marble columns, Colby headed straight for a high-beamed great-room. A brick fireplace to his right, a matching brick circular wet-bar to his left. Pushing a set of buttons on the wall, the fireplace roared to life as did the soothing sounds of the '40s and '50s, and the room was bathed in a dim glow. A marbled foyer led to the master bedroom beyond the great-room. The mirrored wall at the far end of the foyer reflected the blazing fire, providing the illusion of a second fireplace.

Pitching the overcoat on a sofa, he impatiently tore at his collar. Yanking down on the tie, a collar button flew. Ignoring the mishap, the general's new cohort shed his suit jacket and stepped behind the bar. A fiery Bloody Mary would be a good way to begin the day. *Sal, the bartender at the Mafia-owned bar, told me that three drops of garlic juice would blend and mellow the flavor.* "Haaaa, he's never been wrong. Delicious as always."

The once-untouchable covert operator owned two other residences—one an apartment within a few blocks of the FBI headquarters—the other in one of Washington's seedier neighborhoods. All three locales had a purpose. Each was home to a very different appearing tenant. Of course their owners were unidentifiable, hidden in blind proprietorships. Untraceable. Just like several well-stocked, offshore bank accounts.

He shook confusing visions from his head, as well as the tendency to nod off. *I can sleep on the plane,* he convinced himself. *There's far too much to do. Too much to prepare for.* Tired eyes focused on the bucket of decorative firewood, never to be used in the fireplace, yet practical. Removing the birch logs, Rance unhinged the false bottom. Inside were a dozen or more passports and visas—all with his face in varying disguises. Straightening up, he pressed a brick just below the mantel. The right- hand end of the huge redwood mantel log sprang open, exposing a long metal container. Stuffed inside were several stacks of fifty and one-hundred dollar bills—more than enough for his trip to Egypt. Before dressing, he would strap on a money belt lined with bills.

Taking a fresh drink with him into the master bedroom, Colby shaved and showered. After drying his body and hair for the necessary transformation, he removed a lamp from one of the end tables. Flipping over the hollowed-out tabletop, he removed a small black suitcase. Within were various tools of his trade—various jars and tubes of makeup, which included what he would use to transform himself into an Egyptian courier. Once his hair was dyed black, he would apply a skin-darkening gel pigment that would last for at least a week. In the early days he had made a rookie mistake and had only dyed his face, neck, and hands. It had nearly cost him his life. He applied the gel over his entire body, leaving no area untouched. *One never knows.* Next came the mustache. and goatee. Removing the black crepe-soled shoes, he tossed them on the bed—a necessity that could travel in his carry-on luggage. He would have Arturo Testaccio assemble everything else in Cairo. A.T., as the man now called Rance Colby had affectionately called him, lived in retirement in a high mountain villa in a remote region of Italy. Colby chuckled to himself, thinking of how he had often shamelessly ribbed A.T. that he was named after Monte Testaccio, the ancient Roman city dump that reached one hundred and fifty feet high. Arturo was only five feet seven inches in height and nearly as wide, but strong as a bull. A.T. and a man named L' Ami were the only people besides Molly that Rance had allowed into his private life.

Picking up the phone, the suave-appearing Egyptian sat on the edge of the California king-size bed and dialed a series of numbers on his sterile phone, then one last set of digits. After a dozen rings came a booming, questioning voice—*"Come si chiama?"* Colby's dark face grinned. A.T. would know exactly who was calling. He wouldn't need to ask. He wanted to play *the game.* Rance played along.

"Signor Trash Pile, I have a problem. When I get to heaven, how do I get my coat over my wings?" He struggled not to laugh.

"*Mi displace*—but that is not your problem. Your dilemma is how are you going to get your hat on over your horns." The password phrase in place, they both bellowed with laughter.

"My dearest friend," Arturo asked, "how in the hell are you? I assume that you're calling from either a phone booth in some dingy bar, or on a sterile line."

"This call has been routed, relayed, and scrambled through enough foreign cities that it would take whoever would attempt to intercept our call a full fifteen minutes to even come close. Does that answer your stupid question? I need your expertise."

"*Si* to your question, and *Si*, I am prepared to assist my old friend. Emphasis on *old*. How can I be of help?"

"First, my name is now Rance Colby—just in case you happen to hear the name taken in vain. I need you to meet me in Cairo no later than tomorrow evening. You remember the old hotel where we last said *arrivederci*."

"I remember it well, my friend. The hangover lingers, even now."

"You have the contacts in Egypt to obtain what I will need. Airport security is too tight to smuggle my tools. To begin with: a camera with a telescopic infrared lens for night photographs, a night-vision binocular to detect infrared light, an electronic scanner sensitive enough to detect weapons, cameras and recorders within close range, several canisters of immobilizing gas, wire cutters, two knives, and two of my favorite automatic pistols with silencers." He paused. "And if possible, one of those European-manufactured electronic weapons capable of firing three shots with a single trigger pull. Also include a wire garrote. And of course, two skin-tight First Defense bulletproof suits." Stopping to catch his breath, he continued. "This time, purchase a blend-knit long-sleeve black pullover and ski face mask. Not that damned itchy wool stuff you gave me last time. It about drove me crazy."

A.T.'s reply was typical. "I wouldn't have to drive you too far."

"I'm preaching to the choir here. You know what's needed. If you can think of anything else, be creative. Any questions?"

There were more than a few moments of silence, then a loud sigh from A.T. "This sounds extremely serious, my friend."

"The complete success of this, my last mission, will not only save my life, but will also quell a catastrophe that would destroy America's leadership position in the world, and prevent what could become the greatest war the Middle East has ever experienced."

"My friend, that sounds very much like our last mission, and the one before that, and before that." Rance could hear the gurgle of a drink being swallowed. "You know, your call interrupted my gardening, but for you, I'll see you tomorrow evening. *Buon viaggio! Ciao!*"

***

The charman of the Joint Chiefs of Staff, in full uniform, straight-armed the CIA director's bodyguard at the door, and burst into the office unannounced. Slamming the door behind, he demanded to know—"Who in the goddamned hell put out a hit on Lester and his wife?" A powerful fist pounded the desktop for emphasis.

Alan Oakley sat on the edge of a chair in front of Max Carlton. When he attempted to stand, an irate General Rubin Brock shoved him back. "You're not going anywhere, sonny boy. Not until I get some questions answered. Their deaths were too damned convenient. I'm not buying that suicide crap." He glared at the director, waiting for an answer.

Carlton gestured for the general to pull up a chair. "Rubin, we were just discussing this very subject," he said nodding to his special covert projects man. "We too, have suspicions. But under the circumstances surrounding their son's death, and their drinking habits—suicide cannot be ruled out." He held up a hand to close the general's open mouth. "After saying that, we're fully investigating the situation. It's really a local-authority call and could also involve the FBI due to Admiral Michael's government position as Chief of Navy Intelligence. So we must be careful not to ruffle other birds' feathers."

Oakley twisted to face Brock. "I'm personally conducting a covert investigation."

General Brock refused to make eye contact with the man to his right; he spoke directly to Max Carlton. "Look here. Lester worked for me. I need to be updated as to your ongoing progress." Standing to leave, his eyes met Oakley's for the first time. "Have I made myself perfectly clear?"

When the office door shut in anger, the director leaned across the desk, recalling Oakley's mouthed comment in the upstairs library room—*"I'll take care of everything."*

Max tugged at his mustache and with a face made of stone, asked the obvious question. "Just how did you take care of the *Michaels' problem*? You didn't…"

Oakley's chair fell back as he leapt to his feet. "You're not accusing me of a double-homicide?"

Both hands waved Alan Oakley back to his seat. "Pick up your chair and sit down. I'm not accusing you of anything—but you have to admit—it's a remarkable coincidence."

"It was going to be handled by me going over and having a heart-to-heart visit with the family. In fact I did go. I parked a block away so as not to draw attention to my visit and walked around to the back of the house. That's when I heard the shots. On hindsight, I should have broken down the door and discovered for myself what had actually transpired. Perhaps I could have caught the killer if there had been one. Instead, I ran for the car, not wanting a member of the CIA to be found on the premises. That's why I'm personally taking charge of the inquiry. I feel somewhat guilty."

Director Carlton silently stared at his special projects man, his mind conjuring up various scenarios—uncertain if he was being snowed. He harbored suspicions that Oakley hadn't always been completely truthful when it came to reporting on several questionable covert ops. Could this be another incidence? Time would tell. He'd do some investigating of his own. "Go. Form your inquiry. Keep me tight in the loop so I can appease General Brock. I don't want him for an enemy."

As Chairman Brock marched down the hallway from the director's office, he mulled over the significance of Rance Colby's note that was left in his study's desk drawer. Two elements in particular were important.

"Believe me when I say that you should not take anyone, especially those in your library group into your confidence concerning our alliance and conversation. It would not only compromise the mission and place my life in further jeopardy—it may also trigger an attempt on your life. Another convenient accident.

"Gather a team of close associates—those you can trust with your life. It may come down to that. Have the movements of each member of your group placed under twenty-four hour surveillance. Be certain to include President Grayson. And that mystery woman with the rose tattoo. If she can be found."

General Brock pushed the elevator button, planning to reread his new cohort's note once he got to his office. There was still much more to mull over. He had to be cautious. Patting the note in his breast pocket, it would be shredded immediately after it was memorized. Colby wrote that he would provide an update twenty-four hours after arriving in Egypt. The chairman intended to hold him to that promise. The mission had to succeed. Too much depended upon Rance Colby—and the general was determined to provide as much support as he could.

***

Of the several escape routes from his upscale neighborhood estate, Rance chose the spring-loaded patio brick-wall exit—well concealed by a stand of tall thick shrubs. It would be a short stroll through the area's private gardens to the taxi waiting a block away. Two rows of eight-foot high bushes hid the dark-skinned, well-dressed gentleman carrying a black attaché case chained to his wrist and a soft leather carry-on over his shoulder. Slipping sideways between two evergreens, he turned the corner and waved to the driver.

Colby's noon flight from Dulles into London's Heathrow Airport, then on to Cairo International, would provide a fatigued man sufficient sack time to recuperate much needed rest and strength. His time schedule allowed a handful of hours to gather current Cairo street maps and become familiar once again with the immediate area surrounding government buildings and ponder his next move. He intended to be fresh of mind when A.T. arrived at Shepheard's, the grand old hotel.

***

"I believe you have a reservation for Mohmoud Ziwar," said the Egyptian impostor; his dialect was impeccable. Colby's especially designed attaché case, with his disguise-tools, had again passed through security check without incident. Recognized by his expertly forged papers and manacled case of an official courier, he was often obliged to unshackle the cuff and allow the case to pass through the x-ray detector. Hidden in both flat cushioned sides of the attaché case was a wafer-thin sheet of lead. Wedged tight between the lead and the case covering were sheets of paper and single covers of presentation folders—exactly what one would expect when viewing the exterior of a courier's case—no matter which side it was placed on the moving belt.

Clothed in a black long-sleeve Galabaya robe with a touch of cream-colored embroidery—topped with matching cream-colored Khafiyeh that framed his face in folds of cloth held in place by a black twisted cord—the newly arrived guest sat in a verandah rocking chair closest to the long steps leading up to the hotel entrance. After he had gathered his maps and had taken his planned stroll around the government buildings, he had purchased the typical Egyptian attire at a shop two blocks away. A grin widened as a stream of cigar smoke curled from his lips. The loud rotund-looking man exiting the taxi at the foot of the steps was the source of the Egyptian's amusement. "No, damn it!" he shouted, wrestling one bag away from the flustered driver. "You got your blasted tip; now be on your way. There's no more for you. *Capisce?*" The infamous Arturo Testaccio had made his entrance. Removing his wide-brimmed hat, he wiped perspiration from his balding head, and with one finger, shoved wire-rimmed glasses back in place. Dressed completely in khakis, including a rumpled jacket, he looked like the very essence of an arriving archaeologist. With one bag under each arm and one in each hand, A.T. stomped his way to the top of the stairs. Once on the landing, he stopped to take a deep breath and glanced around before preparing to move on. His eyes locked momentarily on the grinning man with the dark mustache and goatee. Nodding a nonchalant hello, A.T. took one-step forward when the dark-skinned man whispered. "Hey fat man. *Effendi.* You like my sister?"

Startled and angry, the bags fell from his grip. Turning to face the pimp, fists readied, he felt the crushing pressure of the man's hand between his neck and shoulder. Immobilized by the compressed nerve, the Egyptian placed his lips next to the stunned man's ear. "I'm in room four-o-four, old friend. See you in half an hour. Cold beer is in the cooler. *Ciao*—Signor Trash Pile." With a swirl of his robe and deep-throated laughter, he disappeared into the hotel's milling crowd.

***

"Defense Minister Merzback Bey Sidky must die in three day's time." Ex-President Grayson repeatedly slammed his cane on the desktop for emphasis. "You claim to be Colby's equal!" he shouted to the only other person in the upstairs room in the D Street Private Library. He ranted on. "What preparations have you made to fulfill your Egyptian assignment?" Grayson slammed the cane again. "And what progress have you made in locating our smoking-gun, Colby?"

He's losing it. His tirades are unpredictable and increasing in intensity. Leaning over in the straight-backed chair—in an effort to stall for time, the woman massaged the ankle rose tattoo. She was called the Arctic Rose by those few who knew her identity—partially due to the woman's cold and calculating methods—and because of her light-blue, almost translucent eyes. Transfixed by her eyes, many an enemy had lost his life hesitating a moment too long. She used that edge to her benefit—hiding behind tinted glasses—until she chose to employ her advantage. Wearing a long redheaded wig, she removed her glasses and stood, staring down at Clifford Grayson. When she was last in the upstairs room, she had been a blonde with short hair and green contact lenses. But not now. The ex-president, on the brink of insanity, blinked repeatedly as he attempted to return her intense gaze.

The Arctic Rose, only in her late twenties, had earned the reputation of someone twice her age. Born into a Greek family of freelance assassins living on the remote island of Thasos in the Aegean Sea, she had been raped repeatedly by her father and two brothers, as well as assassin associates. The family business and its demanding life hardened Rose into a formidable foe. She learned the craft well by watching and listening—biding her time. At sixteen she had killed her father and older brother, allowing her younger brother, the one she had grown fond of, to live. They remained lovers until a botched assignment ended his life. Bitter and twenty years old, she left the island. With her family's established worldwide network of contacts, Rose began anew as a high-priced and successful, in demand, freelance assassin.

"Clifford, sweet man," her cheek close to his, "your questions will be answered, but I resent your demanding attitude and tone of voice." She eased back into the uncomfortable chair before the desk. "Two of Germany's most prolific and reliable assassins have been assigned the immediate elimination of the minister." She crossed her legs and touched the tattoo with perfectly manicured fingertips. "And as you ordered, the Egyptian will be dealt with, not as a questionable accident or health-related incident—but as a blatant assassination. This time, there will be no doubt."

Ex-President Grayson wiped his lips, and nodded satisfaction. He said, "In no time at all—Arab leaders will come to the joint conclusion that while Defense Ministers are mysteriously dying in countries surrounding the Israeli nation, and their minister remains as healthy as a pig—Israel must be preparing for war." Laughter caused a coughing fit, but he managed to continue. "Of course, America will come to their aid in the form of supplying massive arms, planes, tanks, ammunition. My manufacturing associates will be pleased. There's nothing like a good old-fashioned war to stimulate a sagging economy—and to line an enterprising fellow's pockets." He pointed a gnarled finger at the Arctic Rose. "And then it's on to Russia and China."

If it weren't for the fortune he's paying me for this assignment—I'd do the world a favor—and break his scrawny neck, right now. But the world owes me. The female assassin stood and paced back and forth as she spoke. If it were not for the tattoo and eyes, she would be inconspicuous on any street corner. A little less than medium height, and although not considered homely, her features were as nondescript as the girl next door. She stopped at the center of the desk and pointed a defiant finger inches from her benefactor's nose. "Colby remains missing. Nearly every allied country has been alerted that a man matching Rance Colby's description is wanted by the United States—although the reasons provided are purposely vague." She threw up her hands and turned her back. "Hell! What little I know of what you did to his mind, he could be squirming in a corner of an old, abandoned building, foaming at the mouth." Spinning around, she poked another finger in his direction. "But I wouldn't bet your balls on that scenario. My international army of freelancers are also searching for your golden Shadow Master." She swung her arm in disgust. "Your creation."

* * *

The hotel's rickety old elevator shook from side to side and slowly labored from the second to the fourth floor, Arturo Testaccio's mind wandered to the first time he had met his close friend. It was nearly nine years ago this month. Due to a back injury, A.T. had forcibly tendered his resignation to the Italian Servizio Segreto. Although he had planned to continue his covert intelligence service duties for the Italian government after a complete recovery, they had thought differently. So after having received Italy's highest honor, and meager pension, he was happily vacationing in Zurich.

The girl blushed as he smiled and stroked her hand across the table. It had taken Arturo the better part of two hours, plying her with four glasses of wine before she had finally agreed to join him in a weekend ski venture. The side-street tavern was both noisy and crowded full of weekend skiers. At first, no one noticed the tall burly man swagger toward the corner table. Arturo sat with his back to the door, unaware that the girl's angry boyfriend had entered and picked up a wooden chair, about to crash it across his head and shoulders. Her wide-eyed look should have been a warning, but it came too late. A scream cut through the smoke-filled room. Her weekend date lay helpless, stunned on the floor. A hunting knife flashed as the sunlight peeking through a parted curtain glanced off the long serrated blade.

As death poised aloft, a loud shout from the next table snapped the boyfriend's head around. "Hey shit-head, try me first!"

Turning to slice the loudmouth, he was kicked in the shin by the grinning man before him. The strength of the blow bent the would-be slasher over in pain. As he went to clutch his shin, a short, yet powerful right-cross dislocated his jaw. Prone, the jealous boyfriend still gripped the lethal weapon. His assailant stood and stomped hard on the clutching hand. Out of the corner of his eye he spotted the bartender reach for the wall phone—obviously, to notify the police. Reaching down in a single motion, he removed the knife from the groaning man's hand and flung it underhand across the bar, severing the phone cord. Swallowing hard, the bartender disappeared from sight.

The stranger, wearing tailor-made tight-fitting leather gloves, helped a groggy ex-Italian agent to his feet and into a chair. Slapping the man on the back, he whispered, "I admire your hunting technique, but next time check for a crazy boyfriend." As he walked away, he threw one last comment over his shoulder. "And if I were you, I'd blow this joint as fast as my stumpy legs could take me." Then he disappeared into a chilling wind.

Staggering to his feet, the Italian vacationer blew a kiss to the wide-eyed brunette, stepped over her boyfriend, and took the stranger's suggestion. Not being the tallest of men, he jumped up and down to peer over the heads of the street crowd. Spying the top of his target's head turning left at the next corner, Arturo raced to catch up. He wanted to thank him for saving his life.

Out of breath, he managed to catch up outside another bar. Gently but forcibly, he guided the stranger through the doorway, saying, "I owe you a drink for saving my life." Unknown to Arturo, his reflection in the window had also saved his life. The stranger would never have allowed himself to be placed in such a vulnerable position.

Taking a pair of stools in the middle of the bar, Arturo ordered two beers. The man, today called Rance Colby, took an immediate liking to the rotund, yet powerfully built Italian. He found his openness and devil-may-care attitude to be refreshing. The rapport between the two men grew as they laughed about Arturo's lost weekend tryst. Suddenly, a grotesque-sounding shout spun them around on their stool.

Standing by the open door—unsteady on his legs—was the outraged boyfriend. He had followed them. Brandishing a pistol in a shaking left hand, his right wrapped in a bloody towel, he attempted to scream obscenities, but his dislocated and shattered jaw made it both painful and impossible. Without taking aim he repeatedly pulled the trigger. As patrons screamed and ducked, and the mirrored back-bar shattered, the Italian slipped off the stool onto his knees. In a crouch, he rushed the shooter like a linebacker about to make a tackle, burying his balding head into the assassin's stomach, taking the man's breath away. The weapon fell to the floor.

Testaccio continued his charge, shoving the man backward until he pinned the much taller opponent to a large round post. Standing upright, keeping his body close to the man's chest, he wrapped his arms around the post. Slowly, his powerful muscles squeezed tight. The man beat on Arturo's back with his good hand, to no avail. His breath was being squeezed out of him. A.T.'s ear was pressed against the man's chest—hearing the cracking and snapping of ribs and breastbone and air escaping his lungs. The ex-Italian intelligence agent stepped back; the body slid down the post—its jaw hanging at an odd angle—its eyes bulging, staring in disbelief. The man was dead.

Arturo turned to see his new friend still sitting on the stool—a blank expression on his face—a thin trickle of blood running from a crease high on the left side of his forehead onto his eyelid. "Are you all right?" he asked, taking a clean wet towel from the bartender. Dabbing the blood away, he repeated, "Are you okay? Snap out of it."

Much to his surprise, his new friend began to shake his head and laugh. "After all these years of being in range, I nearly get wasted by a jealous boyfriend. And I didn't even know the woman." Now holding the cold damp cloth to his wound, he smiled at Arturo. "Yes, thanks to you I'm okay, but I'm certain to have one hell of a headache in the morning."

"That makes us even."

"No. You're one up on me. Time for me to buy you a drink." He glanced at the bartender who was shaking his head. "But not here."

***

The elderly lady, clutching a small yapping dog to her breast with one hand, used the other to poke an umbrella through the elevator's open scissors-gate to get the passenger's attention. "Young man, you simply must get off. This is the last stop." She shook the ancient sliding gate. "Besides, we must find a patch of grass soon."

She stepped back in shock as the passenger picked up the two satchels and rolled a deep frown in her direction. Passing her, he momentarily paused and barked aloud at the frightened dog. Suddenly, the need for grass had passed. Its bladder had been emptied. Outraged, she swung at Arturo with her umbrella, but missed. Angrily stomping off to change clothes, her agitator continued in the opposite direction, searching for room four-o-four.

Rance had shed his Egyptian attire—including brown-colored contacts, mustache, and goatee—in favor of a comfortable white tee shirt and lightweight tan slacks. At the sound of the rap, he peered through the peephole, released the security latch, and opened the door. Unceremoniously, Signor Trash Pile dropped the bags at his friend's feet, roughly shoved him aside, and headed for the bar. "You better damn well have enough *birra*," were his first words.

"Well kiss my ass, too," Rance shot back, slamming the door closed. "We haven't seen each other in over two years. What the hell kind of a friendly welcome is that? And if you drink all my beer, I'll deduct it from what you're owed for the goodies you brought."

Arturo, opening a bottle, made a gesture with his fingers, brushing off the bottom of his chin. *"Accettate el carte di credito?"*

Catching the beer bottle thrown to him in midair, Colby laughed aloud. "I'd even have cash that you give me checked out for forgery—never mind credit cards." They raised their bottles in a silent toast to each other, and took a long swallow. "Now what seems to have you all in a lather?" Rance asked with amusement.

A.T. cracked open another brew. "Your timing stinks! That's why. I was at my villa preparing to prune a few flowers when your damn call interrupted me."

"You mean like the little bar-flower that wilted when the boyfriend showed up?"

Arturo slipped around from the back of the portable bar; a wicked grin spread from ear-to-ear. Opening his arms to embrace his old friend, he chuckled. "Yeah—something like that."

"The years haven't changed you one bit," Rance said, breaking loose. Clasping his friend's still outstretched arms, he marveled. "Those muscles are as powerful as ever."

"I have to keep in shape for your next call. How many times in the last nine years have you asked me to watch your back and save your ass? When will it ever end? I'm not getting any younger—and neither are you, old friend."

Rance Colby thought before answering, blew out a breath, and looked the Italian in the eye. "It's time for both of us to retire permanently—and settle down." He slapped A.T. on the shoulder as he stepped behind the bar in search of another beer. "You need a little Arturo Junior running around that huge mountaintop villa before you run out of seed to plant in your garden."

Arturo slammed an empty bottle on the bar. "When's the last time you heard of an Italian running out of seed, gardens, or flowers? No. No little Arturo. Not until we hang up the going-out-of-business sign."

"That's just what I'm suggesting. After this last assignment—we're both going-out-of-business. We have more than enough money stashed away to live comfortably the rest of our lives." A serious expression crossed A.T.'s face as he reached over the bar for a third bottle. Rance was already sitting quietly in a plush armchair, fingers firmly massaging his temples, a half-empty bottle by his foot.

A.T. plopped himself across from his friend; the serious look remained. "Something's wrong. I could always read you like a book. Confess to Father Trash Pile."

Rance reached down for his beer and took a long slow drink before answering. "Something happened that you would have no knowledge of. There were times these last few months when I couldn't remember who I was. A master spy—or a man whose entire family drowned before his very eyes." He spent the next hour explaining to his friend what the present United States Secretary of State and ex-President, and a covert group of scientists did to mentally alter his mind. Everything was included: the crash, his initial identity crisis, the old lady's healing process, viewing the TV broadcast of mysterious Defense Minister deaths, recognizing the *Overlay* pattern, secretly spying on the D Street meetings, and the weighty decision to take into his confidence the only person in the group that he trusted—General Rubin Brock.

Arturo placed the empty bottle on the floor, squinted his eyes, and leaned forward. "Let's start at the beginning. Why in the hell did you allow them to brainwash you in the first place?"

Rance rubbed his forehead with one hand as he leaned forward to answer. "I was lied to, plain and simple. They had explained that blood tests were necessary because I had last been in a country that was experiencing a health epidemic. The last thing I remembered was being injected—then awakening while being thrown through a car windshield in the middle of a blizzard.

"I learned about the event and what they had attempted to accomplish as I listened in—without their knowledge—on their clandestine library meeting." He leaned back into the chair, hands clasped on his lap. "The sad part was that they thought they were doing me a favor. Because of what I know about Cline and Grayson's illegal covert operations—it was either death or rehabilitation—for me.

"I also learned that someone had initiated Covert Operation Nullify, a future assignment that I was programmed to carry out at Grayson's orders. When and if he ordered it. Since it was explained to the library group that I was missing, and that I was the original operative to conduct the assignment, it was assumed that it was I who had carried out the assassinations. And would continue, until I either killed everyone on the projected list, or had been eliminated, myself."

Arturo scratched his bald spot, stood, and headed for the bar, holding up two fingers. Colby nodded. A.T. handed his friend a fresh bottle and asked, "If we're all doing a lot of assuming, I assume that you are on the international most-wanted list. Right?"

"You assume correctly. That's why I must rely on my disguises. Steven Heywood, President Rhoades' man in the group, came up with the idea of programming all possible disguises into a computer and making the results available to participating international intelligence services. It's based on the facial-profiling of measurements, but I have a method of beating the system. It's imperative that I succeed in taking out whoever is nullifying the ministers. The Defense Minister of Egypt is the next to be assassinated two days from now if the original schedule is adhered to. Then the heads of Russia and China are next, in that order. You see how serious this is?"

A.T. held the cold bottle to his forehead. "Do I? Goddamn, the whole world could come apart at the seams." He squirmed uncomfortably in his chair. "But, as always—you can rely on Signor Trash Pile to protect your back, and for any help he can render. You know that."

"That goes without asking. We have one ace up our sleeve. They don't know that I'm aware that I'm targeted. We'll use that to our advantage by making me appear vulnerable. We'll flush out the new Nullify crew by using me as bait—with you picking off the hunters. The general is working to keep me up to date on what's happening in Washington and with the D Street Library Gang."

Testaccio thought the plan workable but wore an obvious worried expression. "What's troubling you, my friend?" Colby asked.

"Something you said earlier. Settling down. Going-out-of- business. Retirement. Seeding the flower garden. Kids." He paused and stared at Colby for the longest time. "There's something you're not telling me." He shook a finger at his friend's nose. "You've found a woman—you old son-of-a-gun. Tell Papa Bear all about the lucky lady."

Rance answered with a sheepish grin. "Her name's Molly MacWinter." He explained in detail how he had come to her rescue at the Blue Heron Bar and Grill—and how, in her kindness, she had taken in a mentally confused stranger. "You see, even though I had come to the reality of who I was—I still had blackouts and visions of who they had programmed me to become. That night in the bar, I was having one of those identity spells." He stood and looked out the sheer-curtained window, then turned. "When I saw the men place their hands on Molly, something snapped. Years of honed instincts took over. Before anyone knew it, all three lay at my feet.

"That night at her apartment, she offered me her bed. She sacked out on the couch. When she heard me crying in my sleep—I was dreaming about my lost family—she slipped in bed to coddle me as a mother would an injured child. She seemed to feel my pain and comforted me, a stranger. I felt something I had never experienced before with any woman. Complete peace. We had an instant bonding—she and I. It was the beginning of love, I'm certain." Sitting down, he ended with a sad tone. "But—I had to leave."

Arturo reached across and smacked his friend on the knee. "That sounds great. I'm happy for both of you. She sounds like a wonderful catch." His smile washed away. "But you do realize that you've lost your edge for this business. You have never been this susceptible to danger. For the first time you have a reason to live, and it could get you killed, my friend." Rance Colby smiled grimly. "I'm fully aware of that." He returned the knee slap. "That's why I have you here, *Signor*. Your job is to see to it that I survive and return to Molly's tender affection."

Chapter Four

Chairman of the Joint Chiefs General Brock sprinted from the kitchen to his study to answer the old-fashioned black dial-phone, his sterile line. Inhaling deeply to catch his breath, he reached across the desk and pressed a button that would garble any incoming conversation if security happened to be breached and lifted the receiver to his ear. Circling the desk to sit down, he said, "Brock here."

"This is a sterile line—right?"

"As sterile as my vasectomy. Speak to me."

"This is your new friend, General. I'm calling as promised from a rerouted pay phone in Cairo. Don't have much time. I've formulated a plan and will provide details during our next conversation—if opportunity permits. No promises this time. Have you learned anything new from your end?"

Brock still wasn't one-hundred-percent sold on this new alliance, but with the stakes so high, he had little choice. "An aide assigned to stalk Grayson followed him to the library earlier today. When my man entered, Grayson had disappeared. Obviously, he had used the hidden elevator. My man waited, pretending to look for a book. An hour later, the target appeared with a woman close behind. From her description, it was the same female that had accompanied Grayson before. Although we hadn't seen much of her that one time, he did notice an ankle tattoo." Brock paused to reach for a cigar. "He was particularly taken by her eyes. As she and the ex-president were about to leave—she put on sunglasses, but not before he noticed her eyes. They were cold as ice. In fact, he said they were an ice-blue color. Hardly any color at all."

Colby stole a concerned glance at A.T. standing guard outside the booth. "That's helpful data, General. Anything else?"

"No," came the reply from the palatial home in the rolling hills of Virginia, just outside Washington. General Brock heard a click and dial tone.

Exiting the booth and shoving Arturo toward the hotel, Colby explained. "We're got a formidable foe. A woman sporting an ankle rose tattoo, with colorless eyes, met with Grayson. He's guilty by association. The ex-president is behind the execution of Operation Nullify—and the Arctic Rose is his executioner."

Testaccio stopped in his tracks, grabbed his friend's arm, and spit out the words. "You mean the Arctic Bitch, don't you? She and her band of international assassins are on every wanted-list. She's as dangerous as they come."

Rance placed a hand on his friend's shoulder. "Look on the bright side. Don't you see? That's edge number two. Now we know who's behind the assassinations—and running the organization. And we know in advance who the targets are—and the time schedule."

Grayson's Shadow Master had a plan. Sitting on the hotel room's balcony overlooking the Nile River as it flowed under the Tahrir Bridge, they spread out a map of Cairo on the large outdoor table. Pointing, Rance began to unravel his scheme. "Here are the group of government buildings, and Defense Minister Merzback Bey Sidky's office is located on this corner." A.T. followed the finger's path. "If memory serves me correctly, this is the first of the murders thus far that will be a wet-kill. There will not be another accident or natural death." He forcibly jabbed a finger on the map. "No, this time it will be perfectly clear that the Egyptian Minister of Defense was assassinated."

"I would imagine the security measures at all entrances would be on the highest alert—especially with the recent suspected murders of his Arab counterparts," A.T. said. He placed a finger on the building across from the one housing the minister's office. "Did you have the opportunity to case this building? Could a shooter set up shop here and take him out as he arrives for work?"

"Since the building is situated on the corner and his office is located deep within the structure, not an outside-window office, an attempted hit from either angle would be fruitless." Colby sat back in the chair, stroked his chin, and looked out over modern Cairo. "No, my friend, a long-range hit from outside will never happen, and the inside building security is too tight to attempt. His bulletproof car drives him in and out of an equally secure underground parking tunnel. So that's out, too."

"You're right," A.T. said. "Her track record is impressive. No member of her group has ever been caught. She's too careful. She doesn't take unnecessary chances. Very seldom have her wet-kills been taken down up-close; the risk percentage is too high. Strict discipline is part of her success." He thought for a minute and added, "With exception of the random accident or natural death scenarios."

For the next few minutes they enjoyed the scenery in silence. From the fourth-floor balcony they could see the Hilton directly north, as well as the Television Building. Unseen, behind them and to the northeast stood the Egyptian Antiquities Museum, Sadat Station, and the American University. They had a good view of both the U.S. and British Embassy to the south. Directly in front of them, across the Tahrir Bridge, was the beautiful Opera House.

Colby smiled and gestured due west. "There, my friend is where our assassins will attack. The Opera House."

"And what, pray tell, makes you think that?"

"Smoke and mirrors, old friend—smoke and mirrors." Colby shoved a box of cigars in front of A.T. and invited him to light up. "Before leaving Dulles, I made another purchase. Two cartons of cigarettes."

"You don't smoke cigarettes—only expensive cigars."

"That's correct, but the security guards outside the Defense Minister's building do. Dressed as you first saw me on the verandah, I stopped to shoot the breeze with the two guards, introducing myself as Prince Mohmoud Ziwar, a close friend of the minister. I pulled out the two cartons from my robes and gave each a carton of American cigarettes—explaining that Minister Merzback Bey Sidky had requested that I bring back the gifts for his two most favorite guards."

"You're shameless."

Colby took a long draw on his own cigar, amused at his own cleverness. "They opened up like the Nile dam. One was so impressed with the gift, he volunteered that they both had been chosen to guard and accompany the minister to the Opera House—two nights hence." He slipped a single sheet of paper from under the map. "Here's a floor plan of the Cairo Opera House. They hand them out as part of their promotional package. It's a white-colored complex of buildings—an architectural masterpiece of Islamic design." Using a finger as a pointer, he continued to explain his plan. "There are three theaters. Two are closed halls. The third, a theater the target will attend, is the thousand-seat open area. It's here that he will be most vulnerable." Switching to the large map, he pointed to the Opera House's location, then stopped to point out the closest building. "Here is the most logical site to set up shop. Here's where we'll find our targets."

Arturo leaned across the table and studied the map. Using his cigar as his pointer, he asked, "That's the closest position?"

"That's the only building that has a clear view of the open-air theater. And hear this. I talked to the building manager. There were only two available office spaces left—until today. The one on the top floor facing the Opera House was rented only yesterday. And we've rented the other—one floor below the assassin's."

"You've been busy since you arrived, Master."

Colby let the *Master* zinger pass without comment, but A.T. knew by the raised eyebrows that his friend was too involved with the seriousness of the situation to be humored. So, as always when they discussed a plan, Arturo played the devil's advocate. "We get in, do the job, and out fast. Where are the backdoor routes?"

"First of all, we do the job, but we don't get out fast. Remember, these guys will have backup looking for me. As we discussed, they'll assume I'm in the vicinity and that I'm not aware of their presence. So, we'll stick around as long as it's safe. I'm the sacrificial goat, and they're the prey."

"And I'm the great white Italian hunter in hiding, waiting to save the mangy goat's flea-bitten hide."

Both eyebrows flew up again. "Basically you're correct, but do you have to put it so graphically?" Colby pulled the cigar box back to his side of the table—hugging it to his chest as a gesture for A.T. to watch his mouth—'or *no more cigars.*'

Arturo raised his own brow and frowned in jest. "You're a mean master, Master." He drew Rance's attention back to the city map. "Now show me our possible out-routes."

"Well, there is a slight problem. The office building has various exit routes. I want to be there from early morning on, prior to the assassins arrival to study the blueprint of the building." He pointed to a large rolled-up sheet and winked. "I have that, too. After we conclude our assignment, there are only three basic exits. Across the Tahrir Bridge, east to the hotel, or west over the Al-Gala Bridge. The Opera House, located on an island, poses a bit of a problem. We could always go a few blocks north and become lost in the nighttime crowds in the Cairo Tower—then east across the October Bridge to the hotel."

Arturo raised a hand, stopping his friend. "I'd like to make a suggestion." Rance sat back, rolling the cigar in his fingers, and nodded.

"While we're again assuming, let's assume that Rose's gang is aware of our present accommodations, and we quietly check out of our hotel under the cover of darkness. Say about three in the morning. My contacts will re-register us into a hotel on the outskirts of Old Cairo—and will watch our backs." Colby was about to object, and A.T. knew why. "They know me but have no idea who else is involved. One of your many disguises will cover your identity."

Rance covered his mouth with a hand and mumbled. "Yeah, and I'd have to disguise myself as a woman to maintain your macho image with your *contacts*."

Straight-faced, A.T. answered. "Sounds good to me, but if you think we're sharing the same bed—you're crazy. Your beard itches." He ducked a discarded cigar butt. Grinning, he made one last suggestion. "We have the opportunity for yet another escape route. A fast boat anchored at the tip of the island, ready to whisk us south—three kilometers down the Nile to our Old Cairo hotel hideout."

Colby laid the cigar box down. Using the rolled-up Opera House map, he shoved it back within A.T.'s reach. "That, my friend, wins you another smoke. I knew I had brought you along for something other than the *Master's Court Jester*."

***

Before the sun began its daily sweep of the eastern-sky—on the day of the scheduled assassination of Egypt's Defense Minister—a short, heavy-set archaeologist and his white-robed assistant entered the office building closest to the Cairo Opera House. Each carried a single black canvas bag as they ascended the stairway to their third-floor rented office. As Colby noted when he had surveyed the building—if the German assassins climbed the stairs as they had, and he assumed they would, they would have to pass the third-floor exit just outside the door where he and A.T. waited.

Rance Colby removed a laptop computer from his bag while Arturo entered the stairwell and set up a portable digital surveillance camera disguised as a small emergency light fixture. Now they could monitor the movements of anyone on the stairway outside their office door.

When A.T. returned, the building plans were spread on the floor. "Look here," Rance said. "Here are all the stairway exits, elevators, and a dumbwaiter shaft for moving heavy objects. I checked it out when I rented the office space. From its appearance, it hasn't been used in years, and all floor exits to the shaft have been boarded up." He grinned as he continued. "As I walked the building, I loosened the shaft coverings on all floors and the basement exit. If we need the shaft as an escape route, it will be operable." He shoved the blueprints in Testaccio's direction. "Thoroughly familiarize yourself with all probable exit routes."

Getting up from his knees, he walked to the floor-to-ceiling window. "All offices facing the outside have this type of window." Using a corner of his billowing robe sleeve, he cleaned a spot. "They'll have to cut a hole large enough to insert their silenced sniper-rifle with night scope." Turning around, he shook his head. "They'll have a clear direct shot into the outdoor theater. Merzback Bey Sidky won't stand a chance—without us."

A.T. looked at his watch. "We checked out early this morning. Our bags, including your attaché case, are safely stored on the moored escape craft, and my friends are on guard. I'll take the first nap; you keep an eye on the laptop. We'll switch in three hours. If you see anything suspicious on the stairway, wake me."

It was getting late, and he was beginning to wonder if he had been wrong about where the assassination was to take place. But this is where he would be stationed if he had been the assigned shooter. The beauty of

Cairo's darkening skyline stimulated the memory of Molly. He imagined seeing her smiling reflection in the window against a backdrop of a deep-red sky—casting a pale blood-colored hue over the slow-moving Nile—as city lights glowed like golden fireflies on the horizon. Hundreds of large billboards atop surrounding buildings, in spite of dim spotlights, disappeared in the darkness. A movement on the monitor broke his concentration. Two figures dressed in black, with duffels over their shoulders, passed before the camera and swiftly headed upstairs.

Rance nudged his partner with his shoe. "They're late. But they're here. We're in business." Both had changed into black shoes, socks, slacks, gloves, pullover sweater, and a knit cap. The cap would be pulled down to cover their faces, leaving their eyes exposed. Under it all was a skin-tight bulletproof suit. It allowed freedom of movement and maximum protection.

A.T. jumped to his feet, stretching to loosen his muscles. "How much time do we give them to set up?"

Rance looked out of the window and then at his watch. "The show doesn't start for another hour-and-a-half, and only a few people are now trickling in. Merzback will be arriving last to make a grand entrance. So said his two favorite guards. Let's give them forty minutes. No more." Turning back to Arturo, he changed his mind. "But, to be on the safe side, we'll start edging upstairs in twenty. The building's empty by now. Colby's mind wandered as he kept a vigil on the laptop. It was getting late. We'll camp outside their door and listen." He pointed to a miniature stethoscope around his neck. "If we note readiness, we'll enter quietly," he said, holding up both office-door keys.

Arturo threw up his arms. "Damn, but you never cease to amaze me. You didn't manage to steal the landlord's shorts too, did you?"

"If they had been black to match my wardrobe, I'd have them, too." He slung the bag over his shoulder. "Let's kick some ass."

A.T. quietly closed the door behind them. Earlier in the day, Rance had oiled both office doors, as well as the exit door to the stairway, and the fourth-floor entrance-exit door. Once in the stairway, he removed the planted surveillance camera and slipped it into his bag, waving A.T. upward. Crouching outside the assassin's door, they used hand signals to communicate. Colby placed a finger to his lips behind the black knit mask and pointed to his ears. Pulling the mask up far enough to insert the stethoscope ear-piece, he positioned the head against the middle of the door and listened. Tearing off the stethoscope in silent panic, he tapped Arturo on the shoulder—pointing to the second office door. A.T. nodded his understanding. Obviously, something was about to happen inside. This office was larger than the one beneath—and they had already planned that A.T. would stand by outside the second door while Colby would enter the first. Once A.T. was in place, Colby showed five fingers, meaning he would enter in five seconds. Counting as he inserted the key, he prepared himself for the confrontation.

Kneeling next to the sniper-rifle, set on a tripod, was a man whose sole concentration was on his target far below. In six long, silent strides, Clifford's ex-Shadow Master knelt behind. His right hand slipped under the man's chin, coming to rest on his left jaw. Simultaneously, Colby's left hand coiled around the would-be assassin's right forehead. The entire action took three seconds. With one powerful twist, the man crumbled to the floor—dead, his neck snapped.

Rance barely heard another man approach from behind, but experience prevailed. He only had time enough to raise one hand as a thin wire looped over his head. The second German had been sitting to the side of the door, dozing—unable to assist his partner—but now was about to avenge the death with his wire garrote. Normally, the weapon would have sliced into Colby's wrist, but was protected a by fine chain-mesh cuff on his wrist.

As the assailant jabbed a knee in his back for leverage and grunted in his attempt to tighten the loop, Rance managed to slip the other wrist inside the deadly wire. With increasing strength and the aid of the cuffs, he was able to inch the wire away from his neck. Finding sufficient space to move his head forward, he brought his head back—shattering the assassin's nose. Howling in pain, he released one side of the garrote. Colby immediately bent over, and between his legs, yanked the man's legs forward. Helpless, the assassin fell backward. In one fluid motion Rance spun around, bringing the full force of a palm-chop to crush his opponent's larynx.

He was startled to hear the spit of a silencer—then froze at the sound of a gurgling shout of pain from behind and a short burst of gunfire followed by the shattering of glass. Taking a quick glance up, he saw Arturo with a smoking pistol in his hand. Turning his head, he glimpsed the body of a third assassin crashing through the shattered floor-to-ceiling window to the parking lot below.

A third assassin had been in the bathroom, ignorant of the office death-scene. Arturo had stepped in just in time to see the man begin to raise and fire his Uzi. A.T. managed to get off one shot; it pierced the man's throat, exiting the back of his neck and shattering the window. Stumbling back, the assassin's reflexes pulled the trigger. Bullets harmlessly dug into the floor before momentum forced him through the window.

Yanking off his ski-mask, Colby used it to wipe perspiration from his face. "Thanks, friend. I must have missed the third one in the laptop monitor." As they quickly changed into body-length soiled robes and wrapped their heads to resemble everyday Egyptian locals, he continued. "We had better get the hell out of here. Fast! The noise and falling body will bring on the authorities."

Arturo Testaccio had already dressed. With his swarthy complexion, he could easily pass as one of the men on the street. "What the hell are you doing?" Rance shouted from the doorway as his friend searched the pockets of the two dead assassins. "Leave their possessions! Let's head for the dumbwaiter shaft. It's the fastest and most direct way out of the building. If any of their associates were waiting for us, they'd be long gone. The racket would have run them off—although they could be hiding close by."

Sprinting close behind, A.T. shouted back. "I wasn't robbing the dead, you Caucasian SOB! I was searching for anything that they might have on them that would be helpful to us. And I found something interesting."

Tearing off the dumbwaiter covering, Colby was flushed from the effort and his own embarrassment. He owed his close friend an apology, but not just now. Pitching in his bag, he motioned for A.T. to follow with his—then jumped into the cramped space next to the Italian. Giving the old rope pulley a mighty tug, the platform shuttered and began a slow decline. In an effort to move faster, they both pulled frantically. As they passed the second floor, the ancient rope broke, plunging them downward. Luckily, they fell less than a floor, but the sudden jar knocked the wind out of them. Colby was the first to retain composure and amid the smothering dust, kicked loose the loosely-nailed cover to the dumbwaiter portal. They both rolled onto the basement floor.

Snatching his bag from the shaft, Rance pointed to the exit door to his left. "Hurry! This last key will let us out." He held it over his head, grinning from ear-to-ear. "Then we had better get lost in the nearest crowd—before *we* draw a crowd." As he turned the key, he had one last warning. "And keep an eye peeled for anyone that might remotely look like an accomplice of our fourth-floor dead friends."

They walked briskly without stopping until they safely reached the property of the Giza Sheraton. Standing in the shade of a low hanging tree, well hidden from the hotel's bright lights, Colby started to apologize for not realizing what A.T. was about when searching the dead assassins' pockets. His friend stopped him with a raised hand. "Let's not waste time with foolish sentiment." He pulled a crumpled sheet of paper from within his robe. "Here, read this."

The man called Rance Colby read it silently, raised both eyebrows and reread it aloud. *"Once you have successfully completed your assignment, proceed directly to the Great Pyramid at Giza for further instructions. There you will be met and provided information on your next target—and given transportation tickets, passports, visas to that destination."*

***

A.T. cupped his hands and whispered aloud into the darkness surrounding a number of moored boats. *"Marhaban! Wayn aqrab garaaj?"*

"You're asking the way to a garage?"

Arturo frowned at his friend. "It's our password."

Rance rolled his eyes and shook his head in disbelief. "You couldn't be any more creative than that?"

"Don't scoff, my friend. Don't forget our 'wings' and 'hat' password."

Before the bantering could continue, a voice cut through the darkened night air. *" 'As-salamu alaykum."* "Hello, peace upon you."

Once aboard the boat, A.T. gave Captain Abdullah, one of his Egyptian contacts, instructions to head for the Sharia Al-Ahram Road, three kilometers south. That short stretch of a road would take them to the Giza Pyramids and their rendezvous with the assassins' contract-agent.

Abdullah used a small, nearly silent, outboard motor to leave the mooring so as not to attract attention. Once in the channel, he switched to the more powerful inboard. The two friends sat in the bow, caught up in their own thoughts. Both men were aware that the message could have been planted for their benefit in the event that the assassins had failed—and that they must stay alert. It could be a trap.

Abdullah switched back to the smaller motor as they approached the landing spot beneath the Salah Salim Bridge. He carried two bicycles forward, bowed and bid them farewell. *"Ma a salama."*

As they peddled silently down the road, Rance looked over his shoulder. " 'Go without fear'—is easy for him to say. He's staying behind where it's safe."

It would be a twelve-kilometer bike-ride to the plateau, home to the only surviving members of the Seven Wonders of the World—Giza's monumental pyramids. Closed for the next six months for restoration and repairs, they stood majestically and mystically under a black velvet blanket sky—infused with thousands of twinkling diamonds. The faint glow from Cairo's night-lights cast an eerie illumination, outlining the three massive structures on the horizon. Both travelers immediately noticed that the security lights normally surrounding the royal burial grounds had been extinguished. The possibility of being heard by anyone hiding in ambush was reduced by the near-silent bicycles. While darkness was an added advantage, it also worked in favor of an unknown enemy.

A dip in the road afforded them only a glimpse of the peak of the Great Pyramid. Just as Colby stood on the pedals to gain power to push up the incline, he released the handlebars, groaned aloud, and grabbed his head with both hands. The wheel turned sharply to the right, pitching him into a large sandbank.

Startled, A.T. assumed that Rance had been hit by sniper-fire. Not bothering to put on the brakes, he leapt off, landing in a cloud of dust alongside his friend. "Speak to me! Where are you hit?" he shouted, attempting to pry Colby's hands away to inspect the wound.

"Goddamn it, man! Keep your voice down. We may as well paint a target on our backs," came a disgruntled groan through a mouthful of sand.

Angered by Colby's response to his frantic concern, A.T. reached down and grabbed his friend by the front of his robe and with a powerful display of strength—flipped him on his back. "Don't goddamn me," he growled, yanking Colby's hands away from his head and tearing off his head-wrap. "I thought you had been shot, you blooming idiot." Finding no trace of blood, he sat back in the soft sand, took a deep breath, and glared. "What in the hell happened to you?"

Rance Colby pressed both palms to his temples until his mind cleared, then sat upright, and whacked A.T.'s thigh. It had just dawned on him that the Italian's perception was that his partner had been shot by a silent sniper. With a sheepish expression and an apology, he provided an explanation as to what had caused him to lose control of the bike.

"You're already aware of what Grayson's people did to alter my memory, and the initial confusion I suffered, rendering me unsure of my identity. What I didn't disclose were numerous attacks of pain and flashes of colors that hit me without warning." Wrapping the cloth around his head, Egyptian-style, he continued. "I become momentarily incapacitated. But the encouraging thing is that the events are becoming less frequent and are shorter in duration."

A.T. stood, brushed the dust from the seat of his pants, and offered his hand to help his friend to his feet. "I don't have to warn you that any such event—as you call it—could occur at a most inopportune time— thereby forfeiting your life."

Colby, straightening the handlebars, gave A.T. a serious nod. As he threw his leg over the bike and prepared to peddle forward, he added to the Italian's concern. "Yes, and endangering yours, as well."

They whispered as they peddled slowly, side-by-side, approaching the outskirts of the Giza Plateau. Rance held up his hand and signaled to dismount. Laying the bike flat, he knelt down by the edge of the road and pointed to the pyramids. "The note specifically mentioned the Great Pyramid. There's less cover advancing on our target from the front. We had better leave the bikes here—circle around on foot—and slip in from behind."

A.T. gestured to his left. "If we can make it undetected to Abu al-Hol, The Sphinx, *the father of terror*, as the Arabs call it—there's a causeway trench extending to the Khafre Pyramid. The trench will hide us part of the way. From that vantage point we'll be directly behind Khufu's pyramid."

"Agreed," Rance said, as he sprinted in a widening circle toward The Sphinx. A.T. followed close behind. Minutes later, leaning against the massive stone paw, they rested to catch their breath. Rance looked at his friend and nodded. A.T. nodded back and grinned. He was ready.

Hunched over, they scampered along the edge of the trench. Colby's sudden stop caused a collision. Elbowing A.T. aside, he pointed to the colossal structure to their right. "Did you see that flash of light? It came from somewhere up on the pyramid."

"Hell no! My attention was elsewhere. I was trying not to run up your ass in the dark. You don't run as fast as you used to, you know."

"I wonder if the Arctic Rose's lackeys are as humorous as some un-named over-the-hill Italian covert operative?"

Arturo sputtered an indignant reply. "Lackey…?" Colby was up and over the edge and dashing for the pyramid before A.T. had the oppor-tunity to finish.

Their legs paid the price of lugging a heavy bag across their shoulders while racing along the uneven desert floor. Rance fell to his knees ten feet from the base. A.T. immediately joined him. Both breathing heavily. Gasping for air, A.T. shook a finger in Colby's face. "Once this assignment is over, should we survive, we'll finish that conversation."

Rance, unsuccessfully, attempted to stifle his humor. "Let's stash our bags. It could get slightly cramped inside. Take what you might need with you. Weapons. Knife, revolver—you know the drill."

As they rounded the base of the pyramid, A.T. stumbled and fell. "Quiet, you clumsy Italian ox," Colby whispered in jest. Leaning over, he helped his friend up.

"Clumsy, hell. See for yourself what I fell over."

Rance knelt and felt the body of a guard who had had his throat slit. He stood and looked around, barely able to see. Although the moon was bright in the Egyptian sky, they stood in the shadow of the Great Pyramid. "Chances are there are more dead bodies around here, just like this poor devil. And we can be sure that our target is lurking around, waiting to add two more notches on his pig-sticker." Placing a hand on his friend's shoulder, he gave it a reassuring squeeze.

"That note was a plant after all," Arturo said. "They expected us to take the bait, but this body gave them away. Now we know for certain what to expect."

This time they both spotted it. A brief flicker of light—no longer than a second—flashed above them. Colby muttered under his breath. "If I remember correctly, that's just about where the old entrance is located, but it's been boarded up for years."

Arturo grabbed Colby by the arm. "Wait. Let's think this thing through." He pointed to where they had seen the flash of light. "There's little room for error up there. Those passageways are narrow and dangerous under the best of circumstances." He released his grip but continued his warning. "Chances are slim-to-none that we catch this assassin—or assassins. The odds, up there," he pointed again, "are stacked in their favor. My gut tells me to pass and fight another day—when the playing field is level."

"I can't fault your logic, my friend. But either I face what's up there now and eliminate the danger—or forever look over my shoulder. Canceling one or more of Rose's team members now means one less to worry about in the future. That's Colby's logic."

"Ex-tempore."

"You've switched from Italian to Latin, have you? My logic may be 'for the moment'—and as you're well aware—it changes to fit the situation."

"Yeah. And it's nearly gotten us killed on several occasions. But lead on McDuff. As always, I'm right behind you—Master."

Luckily, the huge pyramid building-blocks had century-worn foot and handholds. After reaching the fourth level of stones, the remaining city lights filtering across the desert from Cairo bathed the structure with an eerie pale cast. They could finally see where they were going. Barely.

Calling upon his photographic memory, Colby closed his eyes to study the page he recalled from a book on the Great Pyramid. "We've still got a decent way to go," he said, extending his hand to assist Arturo up to his level. "The original opening, as I said earlier, has been closed for ages. It's located about one-third the way up. Approximately where we saw the light. Appears that our throat-slitting friends reopened the old entrance." He nodded in the direction from which they had come. "There's a visitor's entrance below that the Caliph Maamun created in 820 AD."

Arturo slapped his brow with his palm. "If there's a goddamn opening below—why in the hell are we breaking our balls climbing this godforsaken mountain of stone?"

"Because that's where the bad guys are." Not waiting for a reply, he hoisted himself upward, leaving the grumbling Italian behind.

Although both men were in top condition, by now their legs were feeling like jelly. Rance Colby stopped, peered down, and waved his climbing partner forward. "If you weren't so damned short, you could reach and pull yourself up a lot easier."

Squinting his eyes, he gave Colby a sly look. "Don't you worry about me being short, my friend—I'm long where it counts when I'm gardening." He paused and went on. "And that's exactly where I should be right now. Relaxing in a flower bed."

Colby knew better than to explore that scenario. "I was right. Look. Someone's opened the blocked entrance just below those v-shaped supporter-stones." With an automatic weapon in one hand and a small flashlight in the other, he scrambled up to the entrance and whispered. "You armed? Got your light?" A.T. nodded and showed his tools. "Good. Then let's go get the bad guys."

I don't like this—not one bit. It's a trap if I ever saw one. It's one of the most dangerous situations we've been in these past nine years. These and many other thoughts crossed A.T.'s mind as he found himself on his belly wiggling through a very tight opening.

Surprisingly, they were at the bottom of a long passage that sloped upward at an acute angle. The walls were smooth; each giant stone-block fit perfectly. Standing upright and reaching for the sides with both outstretched arms, they could touch neither wall. The ceiling was so high, it could only be seen with the flashlight pointed up. Arturo rolled his eyes. "My God, I swear the walls are moving in on me. I don't like this one damn bit." He placed a palm on the wall. "It feels damp, and it smells musty like a damn tomb."

"You're quite observant, my friend. Now that you've discovered that we're in a tomb, so let's move on."

With that deserved sarcastic remark, keeping well to the left, Colby began a slow climb upward. Leaning into the incline, he held a steady beam of light before him, his finger firm on the trigger of his weapon. A.T. walked a few steps behind and to Colby's right, placing his friend out of the line of fire.

Testaccio raised his voice above a whisper. "You know, this goes against our discipline of always identifying and having several escape routes in case of an emergency." The only reply from Colby was a grunt.

Although the ceiling remained at a constant height, the beam fell on a solid object ahead. The shaft was blocked at the far end, but a small doorway was cut into its base. Rance bent over to enter the next space as A.T., still grumbling under his breath, played follow-the-leader. They now stood in a small chamber. The floor was flat, and the area equal in width to the shaft they had just climbed—but there was a small alcove to the right with space enough for three or four men to stand comfortably to one side.

"There're handholds on the back of the stone that blocked the shaft passage." A.T. observed. He handed his gun to Colby and placed the end of a small thin flashlight between his teeth. Using the handholds and reaching the top, he held on with his elbows and shone the beam before him. "It's another long shaft angling up, but the ceiling is much lower this time."

They both heard it at the same time. Colby shouted. "Did you hear that rumbling sound?"

Arturo bellowed. "Holy shit!" and fell backward. Hitting the floor, he rolled over and jumped to his feet, startling Colby, then yanked him into the alcove as the rumbling became an ear-splitting roar.

Not having witnessed what Arturo saw, Colby shouted to be heard. "This damn pyramid stood for over six thousand years, and now it's collapsing. Isn't that just our kind of luck?" Both men turned their faces to the wall and covered their ears with their hands, choking on a cloud of thick billowing dust.

Chapter Five

It's strange what goes through a person's mind when they're about to die. The man now called Rance Colby had inhaled deeply and now attempted to hold his breath as his tortured mind conjured up flashes of a past long forgotten. He was only two years old when his missionary parents' single- engine plane had been shot down over a remote jungle in the Philippines. Both parents were killed in the crash, but the young boy wrapped in a thick blanket had been thrown free in the impact, and miraculously survived. Luckily, the armed mercenary guerrillas hadn't bothered to search for the downed craft.

When Song Lee found the youngster wandering about the crash- site, he appeared to be in good physical condition—although extremely hungry and thirsty. Master Song Lee buried the burned bodies, and after giving the boy a drink of water, carried him to his hideout on a thickly wooded mountaintop.

Master Lee had been China's foremost and celebrated martial arts authority until his wife and three children were mistakenly murdered in a raid on an upstart religious cult—and Lee retaliated in kind. Nine soldiers and three high-ranking government officials were killed before the master's rage was quelled. To save his own life, he escaped his homeland and made his way to the Philippines. Unobserved by the outside world for the past six years, Master Song Lee lived a quiet meditative life, cached in an old abandoned and forgotten vine-covered monastery. Suddenly—after investigating the sound of a fiery crash—he found himself with another family. At least one member—a small healthy Caucasian boy.

For the next nineteen years, Master Lee tutored the youngster in the use of martial arts and weapons. Being a linguist himself, and with the assistance of stacks of books he borrowed from a library, he home-schooled the boy he named Adam on every subject a normal youth would need to know to compete in the world outside—including various languages and dialects. Much to Lee's amazement, Adam possessed a photographic memory. As the years flew by, the boy absorbed written knowledge like a sponge. And in time his self-defense skills surpassed that of the master. On Adam's twenty-first birthday, Master Song Lee, the only family the muscular young man had known, made a startling announcement. An old man by now, Lee planned to return to China to die on his home soil. Adam was to leave the security of the mountaintop and slip unnoticed into America—the birthplace of his parents.

Following Song Lee's instructions and fortified with a healthy American bank account Lee had hoarded for twenty-five years, the two said their tearful father-and-son good-byes. Master Lee, before he had escaped from China, had been a wealthy man. Just prior to fleeing his homeland, he had managed to transfer well over a million dollars into American currency. That money, plus interest, now lay in an account under the name of his adopted son, Adam Lee.

Adam found it an easy task to enter the United States, and with Master Lee's letter of introduction and legal bank documents, equally easy to establish his identity. Following his father's instructions, and with the influence money can buy, he obtained fake social security identification and driver's license. He would learn to drive later.

Adam soon learned to adjust to America's social scene, but after several years of aimless wandering, his sense of adventure drew him to enter the first-ever, American Iron-Man Decathlon Competition, held in Miami, Florida. There he drew the attention of Mr. Thomas Cline. After five days of grueling land and water sports, he led on points. Two events remained—weapons and self-defense. Cline, who had been attending a fund-raising dinner in Miami, was informed by an aide that he might be interested in remaining in town an extra day to observe the unusual physical talents of a most interesting young man.

When the weapons event was completed and the scores tallied, the crowd roared with amazement. The upstart newcomer had accomplished an unprecedented feat. A perfect score. Thomas Cline sat glued to his seat, his devious mind in full gear.

Although Adam was over six feet, his opponent towered over him. They stood face-to-face—the referee barked out the rules—then smacked his hands together. Both men stepped back and bowed. Adam's hands gripped the sides of his thighs, his features noncommittal.

The taller man assumed an offensive stance, hands, and fingers at the ready. He hesitated for a moment, somewhat bewildered by Lee's lack of readiness. Cline couldn't believe what he witnessed. From a relaxed standing position, Adam Lee's bare feet flexed, springing him straight up at least four feet in the air. His left foot shot out as though spring-loaded, striking its mark on the opponent's chin. The much anticipated self-defense match ended within seconds of starting. Adam Lee's Iron-Man competitor lay sprawled on the mat. Unconscious. Much to the disappointment of the screaming spectators and the chagrin of the event's management and backers, their champion walked away and disappeared into the darkness of a humid Miami evening. Cline, one of the country's most influential and powerful men, ordered his aide not to lose sight of the new champion. It was imperative that he have a conversation with this unusual man. Cline was preparing for his anticipated reign in the White House. "Bring him to my hotel room tonight. Tell him who I am—and that his country can use his talents."

Curiosity brought the two men together, and for a number of years Lee worked covertly for Mr. Cline—until he became the Secretary of State. Then Adam assumed the role of President Clifford Grayson's elusive—Shadow Master.

***

"Rance! Rance! Are you okay?" A.T. shook his friend until his shouts were acknowledged.

Colby brushed A.T.'s hand away. "Give me a few minutes. I was thousands of miles away and more years in the past than I want to count." Picking up the flashlight he had dropped, he turned and illuminated the huge block of stone before them. "We're still alive. The blasted pyramid didn't fall in on us after all."

"It might as well have." Arturo leaned over and touched the stone that had come sliding down the shaft toward them. "The damn thing has blocked both our paths, up and down." He pulled on his right earlobe. "And I could swear that I heard a high-pitched laugh—like a woman's." Colby thought before replying. "If you're insinuating that the Arctic Rose is here in Egypt and is part of this," he kicked at the stone block, "then you're dead wrong. It's not her method of operating. She'd never chance getting her hands dirty."

Arturo Testaccio turned to face his friend to capture his full attention. "If it meant getting rid of you—she might risk it."

Rance Colby chose not to comment, but rather gave the stone another kick. It was wedged solid, blocking the way they had come and the passageway above. There was an opening at both ends but too small for a person to crawl through.

"Since it doesn't appear that we're going anywhere, anytime soon, would you mind answering a question?" A.T. asked. Rance sounded a great sigh and nodded his head. A.T. had his opening. "You mentioned that world authorities had been provided a facial-profiling system to identify you. I'm aware of all your disguises, but how could you avoid detection with this system in operation?"

"Simple. Facial-profiling is based on known facial measurements. I simply altered those measurements with makeup elements. My cheekbones were raised and made fuller—the distance between the eyes were widened as well as nostrils, and the jawbone lengthened to a more pointed feature. Their facial identification technique was rendered useless."

"I've got an idea," A.T. said, taking the light from Colby's hand. "Look," he aimed the beam at the edge of the small enclosure, revealing a sizable space. "The stone took a large chunk out between us and the block." On his knees, he peered over the side. "And there's the flashlight I dropped trying to get out of the way before I was crushed to death.

"Hold my feet," he said, now on his stomach and stretching to reach his small flashlight. Rance anchored his friend. Arturo, due to his girth, had to wiggle back and forth to squeeze closer, his fingers straining to grasp the object. "Got it. Haul me up."

Huffing and puffing, A.T. displayed a wide grin. "I think my idea will work. We're as good as out of here."

"Don't tell me. You plan on squeezing down there," Rance said sarcastically, pointing to the small opening, "and lifting a stone block weighing two tons?"

"Yeah, wise guy. Ye of little faith. Something like that. Follow my thinking. Somehow the villains had a large block in place, and using some kind of leverage, they released it down the shaft ramp in our direction."

"I figured all that out by my lonesome. Now what?"

Arturo flashed the light in his friend's face. "You're not the only smart guy on this team, you know. I'll tell you what. I'm going to get us the hell out of this scrape." He turned his attention to the task at hand. "When we stood up after climbing out of the bottom shaft, we stepped into the alcove that later saved our lives. Once we got in, I scrambled up the structure leading to the next shaft, using handholds, and that's when I saw that goddamned block sliding our way."

Rance, still shaken by the harrowing experience and the memory of Master Lee, impatiently motioned with his hands. "Get on with it. Tell me something I don't know."

The Italian made a gesture, using the back of his hand and chin. "There are hand and footholds on both walls, and in the middle of the structure. It's constructed in a chevron pattern, using both slabs of stone and wood." He lifted his robe and reached in his cargo-pant pocket. "If I plant this in the right spot and ignite the fuse—the structure should collapse—and the giant block of stone should fall another few feet, providing sufficient room for us to slip through the opening above."

Arturo flashed a smile of satisfaction. Colby nodded slowly. "That just might work," he said, producing a cloud of dust as he slapped A.T. on the back. "Provided the plastique C-4 charge is large enough to do the job—and not so large as to blow us up with it."

Muttering aloud, "Ye of little faith," as he molded the substance— A.T. lay flat on his stomach and silently jabbed a thumb over his back— a signal for Rance to hold his feet as he hung over the edge to plant the charge. Holding the slim flashlight in his mouth, he struggled to insert the C-4, primer-cord, magnesium switch and fuse in just the right spot to cause the maximum amount of stress. "Damn!" he shouted, biting down hard on the light.

"What is it?" Rance shouted back.

Removing the flashlight, A.T. called for Rance to pull him back up. "What's the matter?" Colby demanded to know.

A.T. appeared somewhat sheepish. "I forgot the goddamned match to light the fuse. And don't give me that look. Just hand me a match. This time, once I'm in place, grab hold of the belt under my robe, and when I yell pull!—pull like hell. The charge is secure, but I've got a short fuse." He knew the moment he said it, he should not have phrased it that way. On his belly, he looked over his shoulder and snarled, "And don't say another word, Yankee."

"Pull!" Rance Colby pulled as hard as he could, yanking his friend across the dusty floor and into the safety of the alcove. As the explosion rocked the foundation and deafened their ears, Rance covered A.T. with his body. Bits of stone showered down. A thick cloud of dust filled their nostrils.

"Get the hell off of me, you big lug! You're squashing me to death!" cut through the noise and debris. A.T. continued to yell. "Aim your flashlight at the top opening. Did it work? Is there enough space to crawl through?"

"It worked. There's even enough space for your stomach to fit through." Rance aimed his light at the base of the stone block, reporting that the structure had indeed collapsed, and the stone had fallen another few feet, now fully blocking the route below.

Colby handed A.T. his gun. "If you're ready, big guy, let's scale this baby and climb up the shaft. There has to be another way out. We'll leave the same way the bad guys did." Drawing his own weapon, he glanced back at A.T. "I figure they're certain we're either dead or trapped—but let's not count on it. Keep a keen eye open."

The air in the shaft, what there was of it, was far easier to breathe than the dust-filled death trap below. The man called Rance Colby paused at the top of the shaft and closed his eyes. His photographic memory scanned the pages of books on The Great Pyramid of Giza. A computer-generated interior of the pyramid filled his mind. Striking a match, he watched the flame bend. "There's fresh air coming from that direction," he announced, pointing to his left. "The breeze is so slight—

it's probably coming from one of the air shafts. They're symbolic paths for the king's soul to ascend to the stars."

"Try another, facing the other direction," A.T. suggested. He glanced around and shivered slightly. "It's early morning outside. It's always dead night in here. The silence in this tomb is unnerving. Get me the hell out of here."

Rance took several steps and struck another match. This time, the flame flickered, and bent in one direction, and then the other. Arturo looked to his friend for an explanation.

"Either the air flow is coming from the King's Chamber up ahead, or from the entry that was later built for visitors to come and go. Since Khufu's chamber has been empty for an estimated twenty-three hundred years, and he's not home to receive visitors—I would think our second choice is the best bet." He looked back at A.T. with a blank expression and continued. "That is, unless you would like to take the time to investigate the unfinished underground chamber at the pyramid's base."

Arturo gave Colby a mighty shove forward. "Cut the bull and get our sorry asses the hell out of here."

The shaft angled downward, resembling the one they had originally entered with the high ceiling. A cool steady breeze was refreshing, but in time, turned into a stuffy waft of heat. Without turning, Rance observed that they were approaching the exit. "Let me do the talking. I can hear voices outside."

Squinting to adjust their vision in the new morning sunlight, Rance went into his act. Shouting at the top of his lungs in a perfect Egyptian dialect, he jabbed his finger at the three gawking armed soldiers— startled to see two men emerge from the pyramid. "I tell you, and you inform your superiors and the antiquities authority, that I, Prince Mohmoud Napoleon Bar, will never go in that," he swung his arms toward the entrance, "death-trap again. During my archaeological investigative assignment for the Egyptian government—a giant block dislodged—nearly crushing this exalted person," he gasped and clutched the front of his robe with both hands, displaying a look of complete distress.

Not allowing the stunned men an opportunity to reply, the prince smacked his assistant on the back of the head, and roughly shoved him toward the back of the pyramid. Once out of sight, Arturo spun around. "You enjoyed that—you SOB," he said, painfully poking Rance in the chest.

Colby placed a hand over his heart, and in a weak humble voice, explained. "I had to make it look authentic. As Prince Mohmou…."

The angry Italian cut him short. "Don't give me that bullshit. You enjoyed every blasted minute—especially that smack on my head."

Colby quickly changed the subject. "Evidently the guard's body had been moved and hidden, or we would have been detained. Rose's people did not want to bring attention to the killing. It may have induced the authorities to search the pyramid, and someone may have found us still alive."

Arturo was on his hands and knees, digging their dirt-covered bags out from the small ditch where they had been hidden. He looked up at Rance with a disgusted expression. "I've had my fill of dirt. From now on I'll even refuse to clean the kitty litter."

"You've never cleaned kitty litter." Rance slung the bag over his shoulder. "Hell. You don't even have a cat."

"That's beside the point," came the reply. "I wonder if our bikes will still be there?"

***

Just as Arturo suspected, their bicycles were missing. It took them longer than expected to hitch a ride to the base of the Salah Salim Bridge. For some unknown reason, the Nile, normally a busy waterway this time of morning, was as smooth as a sheet of dark glass. From the shimmering heat waves, the day would soon become a sauna without the slightest breeze. A.T. grabbed Colby's arm, pointed, and grinned. Abdullah was sound asleep with his back resting uncomfortably against the bridge support—a rope from the boat's bow tied to his ankle.

Arturo quietly snuck up to his Egyptian friend, winked at Colby, and gave the rope a tug. *"Sheffar!"* "Thief!" Abdullah shouted—leaping to his feet—a long sharp blade instantly appeared in his hand. He took a blind swipe at the intruder.

"Qeff! Qeff! Qeff!" Ducking the blow, A.T. stumbled backward, nearly plunging into the Nile. "Stop!" he shouted repeatedly. "It's me— Arturo,"—pointing to himself. The blade fell from Abdullah's grasp. He stared wide-eyed at the man he had nearly sliced open. Rance Colby bent over in hysterics. The indignant Italian glared at both.

"Afwan," my friend, Abdullah pleaded, picking up his weapon. "I'm truly sorry. I thought you to be a thief." Jumping aboard the moored boat, he turned around and motioned for them to follow.

"There has been a murder and you must hide. Inside my cabin— quickly—I have urgent information." They weren't moving fast enough for him, so he raised his voice. "Quickly, before *bolis* spot you!"

The Egyptian's mention of police served as the needed incentive. The three men hastily huddled inside the cramped and fishy-smelling on-board shack Abdullah called a cabin. Colby found the only chair and sat down as he questioned Arturo's contact. "What's this about a murder? Is that why there's no river traffic?"

Abdullah frowned, mildly angered that the American had comman-deered the cabin's only seat. "Defense Minister Merzback Bey Sidky's wife and two children were killed last night. Returning from the opera, their car was blown up."

Puzzled expressions crossed Rance and A.T.'s features—as the Egyptian explained. "The official report is that the minister's men surprised and killed three would-be assassins in a building overlooking the outdoor opera stage. Unfortunately, the assassin's confederate, who *bolis* are now searching for, had planted a bomb under the minister's car as a backup in case the building shooters failed. Sidky never used his private vehicle—only his family."

"Christ," the man called Rance Colby cursed under his breath and angrily smacked his hands together. "Rose planned for every variable. If we had failed in subduing her assassins, the minister would have been shot. If we were successful—which she anticipated—she had a contingency plan. The car bomb."

"Either way," Arturo chimed in, "it would appear to the Arab nations that Sidky had been assassinated like the others. But instead, three innocent people were murdered."

"Either way," Rance said, mimicking his friend's words. "Either way, the Arctic Rose won this round."

"How so?"

"The Egyptian authorities announced to the world that they had foiled an attempt on their Defense Minister's life, and with the deliberate murder of his family—it's further proof of an assassination plot." He glanced at Testaccio. "The noose tightens around the Israelis."

Arturo took hold of his friend's arm and led him just outside—away from Abdullah's hearing. "But they're not the target of *Overlay*. The heads of Russia and China are next."

"It's called peripheral damage. Only Russia and China are the prime targets. If Israel falls as a result—so be it—it's called lagniappe. Something extra. Frosting on the cake as far as Rose is concerned."

Colby walked in and touched Abdullah, who sat securely on the chair, on the shoulder. "Getting us safely to our hotel accommodations in Old Cairo is worth a bonus." He looked over at A.T., whose head was hanging low. "He and I both need several hours of rest, a change of disguise, and a long flight home."

***

The normally jovial Mike O'Reilly, manager of the Central Intelligence Agency's motor pool, had witnessed agency directors come and go every few years during his twenty-eight year reign. He knew Director Max Carlton by reputation only—and that was fine with him. O'Reilly's face matched the color of his hair. He had been summoned to the director's office for an eight P.M. meeting. "Eight o'clock! Damn it to hell," he muttered to himself in his underground parking and maintenance office. "Tonight's my wedding anniversary. Mary's going to kill me, for certain." The phone rang.

"O'Reilly, here," he growled. "Director Carlton!" His tone changed abruptly, surprised to receive a personal phone call. It had never happened before. "Yes. Thank you. That sure would help. One in the morning? Most unusual. But, yes, I'll be there."

Well I'll be a monkey's uncle. He's not so bad after all. Mike was all smiles. Director Max Carlton had called him personally to say he'd heard that tonight was Mike's anniversary, and that he didn't wish to interfere with the celebration—but considering the seriousness of the meeting, would he mind stopping back at one in the morning. Carlton went on to explain that the unusual hour would mean they wouldn't be interrupted and would be alone. After all, it was a sensitive matter.

The Irishman thought aloud. "What could he want with me about a sensitive matter?" His full cheeks flushed. "I had better stay sober. That'll be an anniversary first. Mary will be amazed—and suspicious."

115

Chapter Six

Rance Colby mulled over the disturbing events of the past few days as he sat behind his suburban Washington, D.C. townhouse bar—nursing a dirty martini. He enjoyed the delicious blend of gin, vermouth and three small splashes of olive juice—accented with mouthwatering imported marinated queen olives. Three per martini, of course.

Arturo Testaccio's appearance was long overdue, and that was troubling. They had spent their last night in Old Cairo hiding from the local police and the Defense Minister's swarming forces. Abdullah's place of concealment, the cave below the Church of St. Sergius, proved to be a good choice. Twice they had heard the heavy boots of searchers on the tiled floor above them. Rance would later admit that it was an eerie sensation hiding above the cave where legend says the Holy Family took refuge during their flight from Egypt. St. Sergius was built on the spot in the 5th century A.D. The crypt, now known to be flooded as a result of the rising water table, was never searched. Rance and A.T. rested the night on a wooden floor suspended over the flooded cave.

Rance Colby, in the disguise of a courier, had boarded Lufthansa's Airbus to Frankfurt, then flew to Washington's Ronald Reagan Airport without incident. Cairo International Airport authorities had waived him through the check-in area after studying his diplomatic papers—while he carried the chained attaché case. A.T. was to depart St. Sergius Church two hours later and planned to meet him the next day at Rance's estate home. Arturo's estimated arrival time was twelve hours ago. Colby mixed a second martini and became lost in thought. *What in the hell could have happened to that Italian? If he's been picked up by the Egyptians—I have no way of knowing and Abdullah would not know how to reach me.*

The doorbell rang, disturbing Colby's musing. The security monitor behind the bar displayed the grinning face of Signor Trash Pile. Rance shook his head—grabbed an imported beer from his bar cooler—and headed for the front door. On the way, he debated over chewing out A.T.'s butt for being late and not checking in or being thankful nothing drastic had happened to his best friend. He opted for the latter.

"Here's a brew," Rance said with gusto at seeing the ever-smiling face. "Give me one of those bags and make yourself comfortable. Then you can explain why you're so damned late." He couldn't resist.

Walking through the tiled foyer, A.T. followed Rance past the study to the far bedroom to drop off his luggage. Returning to the great-room, Arturo plopped into a large rustic-looking leather chair, placed his feet on the matching ottoman, and sighed deeply. He knew he was in trouble, but he couldn't care less. It had been worth it.

Rance remained behind the antique-brick circular bar and downed the remainder of his drink. As he savored the last tasty olive, he raised his eyebrows. "Well? What happened?"

Showing a mouthful of strong pearly-white teeth, A.T. began. "I could lie and say that I enjoyed Abdullah's company and couldn't tear myself away. Or, that I had been detained by the Egyptian authorities." He motioned for Rance to pitch him another brew. "Truth is, that I had remembered that I had some pruning to do back at the villa. So—as much as I hated to, I made a necessary detour." His grin widened. "Believe me, friend, it was a much-needed pruning. If my flowers are not pruned occasionally, they tend to bloom elsewhere. *Capice?*"

Rance couldn't decide whether to strangle him—or to kiss his reddening baldhead. He merely laughed out loud and mixed another martini. Soft jazz filtered through the room, relaxing the host as well as his guest.

"Now that I'm off-the-hook," A.T. said, "what's our next move?"

Rance climbed into the tall director's chair next to the fireplace and studied the water painting of a Native American pueblo behind A.T.'s chair. "It's imperative that I reach General Brock. He needs to be made aware of Rose's latest venture. And I need to know what he's been able to uncover here in Washington."

"Thought you said he could be reached on his sterile home phone."

"There appears to be a problem with the line. It's been busy each time I called. Phone company verifies a cable was cut during excavation work. I considered stopping by his home in disguise but felt that I needed to remain at home just in case you showed up alive."

Arturo considered saying he was sorry, but he knew he wasn't. "So what's the plan?"

"I'll go to the main library, use their computer, and send an e-mail message."

"And that's safe?" A.T. looked puzzled as he got up and walked to the bar. "Don't you think the CIA, FBI, or any international hacker could lift the message?"

"Not the way I type," Colby answered, stretching his arms, and wiggling his fingers. "Brock and I had a contingency plan in case of an emergency such as this." He leaned to his right and pressed a button. The fireplace came to life. "I've had the heat turned off and there's a chill in the house."

"I'm perfectly comfortable—as long as you don't run out of beer. Continue."

"I'm to e-mail him on his personal office computer…"

"Oh, that sounds secure," A.T. interrupted.

"Will you allow me to finish, wise-ass?" Rance snapped. "We worked out a plan. I'm to assume the role of a defense contractor requesting to schedule an appointment with the Chairman of the Joint

Chiefs. The bogus message will be double-spaced. The real message will appear between the lines."

"And the bad guys won't read that part?" Arturo chimed in sarcastically.

"No they won't. Remember when you were a kid, and you wrote invisible messages in lemon juice, and the message would become visible when applying heat to the paper?"

Arturo nodded. Rance continued. "Same principle. Before I type in-between the lines—I click the *set font color* box, then click the white block for font, and type my message. It won't be seen. At the other end—the General highlights those lines—then changes the font back to black. Presto," he snapped his fingers, "the real message can be read. We'll meet tomorrow evening at eleven o'clock in a seedy bar two blocks from the D Street Library. You're an unknown in Washington. You'll arrive a half-hour ahead of time to observe—and watch my back."

Arturo rubbed his dome. "You never cease to amaze me."

***

Seedy? That was an understatement. It had been some years since Arturo had frequented a dive as rank as the Golden Eye Tavern. In fact it had been a waterfront bar in Chuanchow off the coast of the Taiwan Strait between southeastern China and Taiwan. Rance Colby was on an assignment to defuse a nasty dispute between the President of Taiwan and a powerful rogue Chinese warlord bent on seizing the island as his own property, and challenging Beijing's authority. When the warlord mysteriously came up missing, the situation cooled. Now, just as then, the Italian was present to cover the Shadow Master's behind. Stepping over the drunk passed out on the doorstep, A.T. took a deep breath and wished he hadn't. Quickly exhaling the stomach- wrenching odor of days-old stale spilt beer—a heavy layer of cigarette smoke and the undeniable acid-smell of urine—he slowly groped his way through the darkness to the second booth. Checking the booth seat facing the door for any unwanted leftovers, and signaling the barmaid wearing what A.T. suspected was the apron she had been born in, he ordered a pitcher of beer. *Damn—Colby will owe me big time for this one! It'll take me a month to rid myself of the smell that would otherwise wilt my dainty flowers.*

His eyes hadn't yet adjusted to the dim illumination, and he was forced to squint to locate the door. The barmaid parted and swirled the fog of thick smoke as she slung her hips in his direction, hoping to impress her new customer. *How in the hell can she see through that waterfall of stringy dirty-blonde hair covering her face? It's just as well. I can see several missing teeth through the twisted grin.*

"Here's your pitcher, sweet thinggg… If there's anything else—you want—just to ask, strong man," she slurred in a voice that could grate cheese, then clicked her tongue. Arturo lowered his head and shivered at the thought. *I couldn't get that drunk in a million years*—he was tempted to say.

Between gulps of brew, he eyeballed the door. There were only a few people clinging to the bar for fear of falling off their stools. The remainder of the patrons appeared to be fast asleep in booths too dark to be noticed. Remembering Rance's proclivity for locating all escape exits in case of an emergency, he glanced at his watch. It was twenty minutes before contact time, and although it was apparent Colby was familiar with the bar, A.T. had time to search the premises for himself.

A quick tour took less than three-minutes. The puke-splashed restrooms had no windows. There was an illegally padlocked backdoor and an opened doorway from the rat-infested kitchen to a foul-smelling dark alleyway. When A.T. returned, he noticed the first booth was now occupied. He could have kicked himself for having left his post. A large man sat with his back to Arturo, facing the entrance. He wore a tan leather golfer's cap pulled forward, and from what A.T. could determine from behind, the man had a full white beard. He had hung a tattered leather jacket on the post between the two booths—revealing an equally worn black turtleneck sweater. As the barmaid turned to fetch his order, he smacked her on the rear and laughed aloud with a booming voice, stirring several sleeping beauties. Ms. Golden Eye giggled and skipped like a young bride all the way to the bar. *What a little flattery won't do— even if only a passing smack on the butt. The old buzzard bears watching. It'll pass the time till my master appears.* He chuckled inwardly at the self-deprecating humor.

As usual, his mind had drifted to his flower garden, when a down-and-out veteran stumbled through the door. A.T. strained to get a clearer look at the man wearing a misshapen paint-splattered NY Yankees ball cap cocked at an angle over a face twisted in pain. Scratching at his stubby gray whiskers, he licked his parched lips and pulled the collar of his fatigue jacket snug around his neck. Staggering slightly, he appeared to search the darkened tavern for a familiar face. Teetering in one spot for several minutes, he zeroed in on the bearded gentleman in the front booth. *This I have to see,* A.T. mused.

The man in the turtleneck stiffened as the ex-soldier limped over to the booth, and placing both hands on the sticky tabletop, leaned over. "Buy an ex-army foot-soldier a beer, hey Cap?"

Turtleneck grabbed the vet by the front of his jacket and roughly slung him around the other side of the booth. "Where in the hell did you get that cap and jacket? I thought you gave it away to the hippy kid?"

Before the questioner could release his grip, the vet had hold of a thumb in a painful death grip, paralyzing the larger man who gritted his teeth and listened. "I must warn you, General, do not ever lay a hand on me if I'm not aware of who you are. Otherwise I'll not be responsible for your broken neck." Rance Colby abandoned his grip and sat back smiling. "Now, how about that beer before I answer your question and we talk seriously?"

General Brock shouted his order. "One pitcher of suds and another of these," he said waving his glass. "Scotch, my ass," he complained, "it's a mixture of crankcase oil and turpentine."

Colby remained silent until the pitcher arrived. The barmaid was obviously incensed because someone had captured the attention of her assumed pigeon. She spilled foam over the vet's grease-stained fatigue jacket. He shook the flap, spraying the foam in her direction and turned to answer the general's question. "Yes, I gave the cap and jacket to the kid because I no longer needed it—and he did. This morning, I returned to where I found him, and traded it for a new and much-warmer one. I needed it again so you would recognize me in this...." He gestured with a hand—then fell silent—locking eyes with the man across from him.

The Italian in the next booth was unable to discern all the words, but heard enough to recognize his friend's voice, if not his appearance. A.T. had been in the tavern long enough to become accustomed to the light-starved room and began to assess possible danger, sizing up each patron. Earlier, when searching the exits, he had evaluated the snoring five at the rear. They appeared to be just what they were. Drunks. That left the three at the bar. One was an old gray-haired woman—the other two were men in their forties. Arturo had been watching the man on the left who was having trouble keeping his elbow on the bar. It kept slipping. Twice he had nearly fallen from the stool. The last man looked suspicious. His clothes didn't quite fit the establishment, and although he appeared to look drunk, he had been nursing his draft for the past half hour. This one bore watching.

Brock sat in silence while Colby filled him in on what had transpired in Egypt—including eliminating the shooters and the unfortunate death of the minister's family, and that it was probable that the Arctic Rose was involved in his near death in the pyramid. He purposely avoided any mention of Arturo Testaccio—his ace in the hole.

Rance shoved the pitcher aside and leaned across the table. "We have twenty-six days before the President of Russia is assassinated—if they adhere to *Overlay's* original schedule." He leaned back, downed his glass, and filled it again. "I intend to tie up some loose ends in Washington—then head for Moscow—allowing myself three weeks to establish protocol." He pointed a finger at Brock. "What have you learned on your end, General?"

"Not a hell-of-a-lot, to be frank." He hesitated and nodded his head at the man across from him. "Before I go into what little I found, I recognized you because of the way you're dressed. How in God's name did you pick me out so easily in this black hole of humanity?"

Colby grinned. "Easy. The *smell of army* was stronger than all other fragrances polluting the air. You were the only body that didn't appear intoxicated, and you're not as ugly as the gent in the next booth," he said raising his voice. "And," he went on, "the right side of your fake beard has come loose."

General Rubin Brock failed to find humor in Colby's assessment. Pressing the beard to his face, he grumbled, "Goddamned disguise."

Colby couldn't resist. "Your tailor, General. Who's your tailor?" He lovingly stroked Rubin's hanging leather jacket.

"If it's any of your business, Goodwill." He attempted some humor of his own. "If you like, I'll give you the name of my tailor."

"General, we live at opposite ends of the pendulum, but by coincidence, we shop for clothes at the same store."

"Enough of this bullshit!" the general spat. "Let's get back to why I'm in this snake pit with a hired killer…."

Before he could say another word, Rance Colby reached across and grabbed Brock's wrist in a viselike grip. "Let's get it right the first time, General Brock," he said with a grim expression. "*Your* killer." He released his grip. "And to remind you—you didn't hire me, I volunteered to save your wide ass. And everyone else's ass. Including the U.S. of A." Taking a deep breath to relax his tension, he added, "Now what do you have that would assist me—if anything?"

Armed Forces under the general's command had always liked the man for two reasons: his strength and his fairness. He sized up Colby with a burning stare. "I apologize and stand corrected. You had placed your life in danger dozens of times for the President of the United States and now again for those who have wronged you—and are presently attempting to take your life." He downed what was left of his glass, was about to order another, but thought better of it. "Rance Colby, or whatever your real name is, I promise you this…if you're successful in saving all our assess and survive…you can ask *any* favor of me. And whatever it is—you'll have. That's a promise you can stick in your faded jeans."

"Thank you, General. I'll be sure to look you up. Now, what have you learned?"

Brock had little to offer. Max Carlton was conducting his own personal investigation into the cause of the car crash that took the life of the two agents escorting their package to a Colorado mountain retreat. Max suspected, although could not substantiate, that the Michaels' so-called suicide was actually premeditated murder. And had his suspicions. It had been confirmed that the woman called the Arctic Rose had indeed left the country, but her destination was yet to be determined. The other members of the library group, shadowed by the general's aides, appeared to be acting normally—with the exception of the person they all assumed to be their weakest link, Steven Heywood. Even though he was a special assistant to the president, he was spending an exorbitant amount of time in private sessions in the oval office. He was targeted as someone to closely observe.

"What's the latest fallout on the Arab Defense Minister assassinations? Has the CIA picked up communications linking an Arab coalition to punish the suspected Israelis?" Rance inquired.

"Max is right on it and has been keeping me up to date every twelve hours." He frowned, picked up the pitcher, and took a swallow. "Yes. The Israelis are the likely culprits in the eyes of the Arab world. Defense Ministers have died in countries surrounding the state of Israel. From what we can piece together, it's a wait-and-see game. If time passes and their man is not attacked, that will be all the proof needed to point the finger, in this case, pointed rockets."

"It would be to Israel's advantage to have their minister assassinated. It might avert a war."

Brock scoffed. "Be serious, Colby."

Rance checked the pitcher. It was empty. He scanned his watch. "This meeting is over, General. I have some catching up to do." Half standing, half leaning over the table, he added, "I am serious, General. Dead serious. Until all this is over, all the Israelis have to do is to stage the assassination. He doesn't have to die—just disappear until I succeed in completing my mission. The kill is not on the *Overlay* schedule, but at this point, it doesn't matter. Five days from now would be good timing. If I were you, I'd talk over the event with their ambassador." Rance stood next to the table and whispered. "I'll be in touch before I leave for Russia," and staggered away, shouting over his shoulder. "Thanks for the beer, Cap! Next time I'll buy," he cackled.

General Rubin Brock hadn't heard the vet's final words; he was too deep in thought. *Son of a bitch. No wonder he's been so successful. That was a brilliant concept. The Israelis should jump at the idea—and they could pull it off.*

Arturo watched his friend leave the tavern and immediately focused on the man to the right of the bar. On the count of ten, the man pitched a bill on the counter and hurriedly headed for the exit. A.T. was hot on his heels. Once outside, he spotted the man standing under a lamppost, peering around for his target. Dodging a taxi, the man crossed in the direction the vet had been last sighted.

From habit, A.T. had walked the surrounding streets prior to entering the tavern and was aware of the alleyways and darkened doorways. He dashed down one of the alleys in an effort to intercept Rance's tail. Turning a street corner and slipping into the closest doorway, he wished he were a younger man. He was getting too old for this but would never admit it to Colby. Within seconds, the man from the bar walked within arm's length. Two powerful arms reached out and all but lifted the startled man off his feet. He was spun around and shoved against a creaking door.

Arturo's face was a nose away from the other's. His beer breath bellowed. "You got a light, Mac?" The man attempted to sidestep the shorter man, but it was like dislodging a fireplug. He wasn't about to move.

"Get the hell away from me, you drunken sot!" the man from the bar shouted back. Still the fireplug remained anchored to the spot.

"Not until I get that match, guy," A.T. slurred. He shoved the man harder against the door, and it gave way, propelling both into a dark abyss. The drunk's dead weight pinned the other to the floor and after a minute of wrestling, A.T. allowed the man to free himself and flee. Rance had plenty of time to disappear into the night.

***

Her playful humming was like honey to Rance's tired ears. The click of the lock woke him from a light nap; the sound of her voice brought a smile to his face and calm to frayed nerves. In various gym lockers throughout Washington, Rance kept changes of clothes. Shaved and showered and dressed in a pair of light tan slacks and two-toned brown silk shirt, he lay atop Molly's bedspread, hands folded behind his head. Closing the apartment door, she wearily reached for the light switch, but failed to connect. Dropping her handbag on a chair, she shuffled toward the bedroom in the dark, kicking off one shoe at a time. It had been a long photo-shoot, lasting well into the night. Completely exhausted, she wanted nothing more than to collapse into bed, clothes, and all.

This time she managed to flip the bedroom light switch just as a soft deep voice said, "Hey babe. I've been lonesome ever since the day we met." She muffled a scream born of fear at hearing a man's voice, then gasped aloud from the pleasant surprise. Rance, fully awake and craving to hold the bundle of soft femininity in his arms, pointed to her dresser. A dozen roses, half-red and half-yellow, awaited her attention.

Taken completely by surprise—and forgetting that she had a water-bed—Molly ran and leapt into his waiting arms. If she hadn't clung to his shoulders, Rance would have been propelled six feet into the air and out of bed, as the impact caused a wave powerful enough to pitch him upward. They both laughed hysterically, locked in a firm embrace.

Molly pushed herself away and kissed Rance on the cheek. "I need a shower, and you've got too many clothes on. I've missed you, too. I began to wonder if I'd ever see you again." She stood, brushing a tear aside. "And I've got a basket full of questions."

She opened the bathroom door, turned, smiled, and blew a kiss. The shower noise drowned out his reply. "I may not have the answers you're looking for." *I can't recall when I've laughed so freely,* he thought, as he stripped off all his clothes and slipped under the covers.

It was a night he'd remember the rest of his life. They fell asleep in each other's arms, drenched in perspiration and utterly exhausted. Rance woke first. He looked down. Molly's head lay on his shoulder; her long silky hair blanketing his chest. *How can I tell her? I can't. I don't want to leave, but there's no choice. Until this is done, I shouldn't risk seeing this lovely creature again. It would place her life in danger. Damn. What a predicament. Damn Clifford Grayson. Damn the general. Damn. Damn.*

Molly began to stir. Her smile brightened his dismal mood. Kissing the top of her head, he suggested, "Let's take turns in the bathroom—you go first—then we need to talk." He paused. "Unless you have other ideas," he winked.

She turned on her stomach, kissed his chest, and slowly slid out of bed, but not before playfully nipping his thigh. She giggled as he let out a yelp. Just the reaction she had planned. "Don't you disappear on me again, damn it!" she said, before closing the door, her voice cracking with emotion.

One long shapely leg was exposed, the remainder of her body squirmed mischievously under a pale-blue sheet. A well-manicured finger beckoned him to bed. As much as he wanted her again, he knew they must talk. Arching her back forced her breasts to rise and fall with each deep breath—swelling against the taunt sheet. Standing naked beside the bed, after taking his turn in the shower, he squeezed his eyes shut. *What the hell. We can talk later.*

Between sips of coffee, Molly grinned at her lover. She was draped in a red silk pajama top; Rance wore nothing but one of her fluffy robes.

She thought he looked adorable. He couldn't care less. He was where he wanted to be—and was having difficulty thinking of anything else but their future together. The roses were now on the kitchen table. She tenderly touched the vase. "Yellow for friendship—red for love." Looking at him approvingly, she whispered. "They would have been my choice, too."

It was time; he couldn't delay it any longer. Rance reached over and took her hand in his. The look of his arms protruding from the frilly sleeves made it hard to remain serious. "First, I want you to know how much I love you. And my wish is to spend the rest of my life in your arms. But there are circumstances. Circumstances beyond my control."

She pulled her hand away and looked him squarely. "Does this have to do with the men who were asking around about you? They said they only wanted to talk to you. Nothing serious, they said."

Rance ran his fingers through his hair—his eyes pleading to be believed—to be understood. "You said that you loved me, too. I'm being perfectly honest when I say that I'm one of the good guys,—and telling you any more than that my real name is Adam—would place your life in grave danger. And I won't do that—even if it means losing you. I love you too much."

He held his breath. She looked at him without expression, then reached out for his hand. An audible breath of air left his lungs. "Tell me only what you feel is necessary. No more. You have my complete trust."

A heavy weight left his shoulders. He could leave now—do his job with the knowledge that she would be waiting to welcome him with open arms. Then they could head for points unknown to start a new life together. As Brock had said: *"Ask any favor of me—it's yours."*

Before Adam left, and as they embraced for the last time, Molly whispered in his ear. "How'd you get in the apartment without a key?"

Between an ear nibble and a kiss, he whispered back. "Trade secret, my love."

"And I'm to believe that you're one of the good guys?" she said guilefully.

In the hallway, he flashed a satisfied smiled and shouted through the closed door. "And—the best there is!"

***

Colby had given A.T. the combination to both door-entrance keypads and alerted him to additional security-system booby-traps. Once inside, Arturo could take his friend's suggestion and make himself at home. Even before punching in the numbers, Colby could hear the combined voices of Pavarotti, Carreras, and Domingo filtering through the front door. His dearest friend was sound asleep in the leather chair, his bare feet on the ottoman and five empty beer cans neatly lined up on the floor. A thought forced a wide grin to Colby's lips.

Without making a sound, he walked to the bar and opened the cooler. A bar towel helped him hold a large chunk of ice between two fingers. Tiptoeing to the chair, he knelt down and gently rubbed the ice against the fleshy under-part of Arturo's big toe. As the sleeping man began to stir, a faint smile appeared on his face. Lips curled as he moaned. "Oh. Oh. My little flower…that feels so…"

Rance's laughter woke A.T. with a start. The sudden loud explosion of Italian phrases rocked the trickster backward. Rolling on the floor, Rance pointed at his embarrassed and angry friend. "Oh, my little flower…"

Before another word left Rance's open mouth, a well-aimed shoe glanced off his shoulder. Beer cans flew everywhere as A.T. leapt to his feet, heading for the bar. He spun around, aiming a shaking finger at the sprawled figure. "You. You ruined a…beautiful dream. My villa garden…was bursting…with a rainbow of blossoms…pleading to be harvested." He threw up his arms, all anger dissipated. He bared his teeth. "You want a martini, master?"

For the remainder of the day, the two friends discussed plans to avert the assassination of the Russian president. Brock had offered no knowledge that would be of help. They were on their own—as usual. Both men preferred it that way. All too often, intelligence agency's op information proved to be either wrong or incomplete. Too often, it had placed their lives in danger. *Winging it*— as A.T. put it—*was a hell-of-a-lot safer.*

Arturo was to meet Rance at the Hotel Rossiya in Moscow in ten days. Colby explained: "The hotel is on the doorstep of the Kremlin and the Duma. I'll become inconspicuous—hiding in plain sight—among throngs filling over three thousand rooms, including many Russian and international politicians." Remembering his last unauthorized visit, he chuckled. "The old KGB building is a five-minute walk—Red Square, a two-minute stroll."

Colby, in disguise, would be checked in under the name of Andrei Zakharov, a little known, but wealthy eccentric poet from the village of Kropotkin, eight hundred kilometers south of Moscow. "It's near the Turkish border. I'll sneak across from Turkey and take the train directly to Moscow. The better part of two days of travel will give me time to formulate a plan and make adjustments."

Devouring a once frozen, microwave pizza, Arturo looked puzzled and pointed to himself. "You, my Italian friend," Rance said, "will spend a few days with the FBI." With that startling information, Rance flipped him a set of keys. Now Arturo appeared even more perplexed. "Those are the keys to my apartment two blocks from the FBI building. Spend a few days sniffing around the local pubs agents frequent. Buy drinks.

Make friends." He nodded and lifted his brows. "They do have FBI agent flowers in bloom." Showing both palms, he continued, "You know, my friend, pillow talk."

Wiping pizza sauce from his chin, A.T. nodded back thoughtfully. He had been forced into that situation on occasion. That could be handled.

Rance winced as he bit down on an olive that should have been pitted. "Before I leave for Mother Russia, we'll meet back here to compare notes. In the meantime, I plan on doing some snooping of my own at the CIA and the West Wing—if I can slip through security as easily as the last time." His smile faded.

***

The last two stars on the Central Intelligence Agency main foyer wall-engraving—-honoring those who had lost their lives on behalf of their country and the fifth from the bottom—were particularly familiar to Rance Colby. Before approaching the information desk, he had stopped to pay his respects. One of the stars represented a man who had sacrificed his life without his knowledge, enabling Colby to accomplish his mission. On several occasions, the president's man had found himself in situations where the agency or another country's intelligence operator was in the position to compromise a situation. In such instances it often caused an abrupt change in plans, sometimes placing an agent in the line of fire. This time, CIA Agent Curtis Bromm had lost his life by being in the right place at the wrong time. Bromm's wife and children received the standard CIA letter of sorrow, without explanation. One month later, Ms. Bromm opened a letter from an offshore bank confirming a three hundred thousand dollar account in her name—with no explanation.

Rance raised his head from a prayerful position and took a step toward the smiling female receptionist. Suddenly he clutched his head, groaned aloud, and crumpled to the floor. Those in the foyer crowded around the fallen man. The woman shouted for guards and punched a button, alerting on-staff medics of an emergency. By the time two guards turned up, Colby was in a sitting position, cradling his head. The medics arrived moments later. "I'm all right," the man insisted, attempting to get to his feet.

A burly medic grabbed Colby roughly by the chin and looked into his eyes. "Your eyes appear dilated." Motioning his assistant to take the man's other arm, he ordered, "You're coming with us to the downstairs infirmary. We'll check your vitals. If you're all right, you can continue to wherever you were headed."

Unsteady on his feet, Rance nodded agreement and walked between the two medics toward the elevator. *My head hurts like hell, but my luck's holding out. I couldn't have planned it any better. But A.T. was right. These spells could get me killed one day.* Once inside the elevator, he stumbled headlong into those already on board. Colby and the medics apologized for the mishap, but not before he had pocketed CIA identification badges lifted from two unsuspecting, grumpy three-piece suits heading for the parking garage, and a normal two-hour lunch break.

Five minutes after arriving at the infirmary, the medics were summoned to another emergency. An auto mechanic had a severed finger. Once both men were out of sight, Colby headed for the nearest elevator and the third floor where Agent Tim Johnson's office was located. Johnson's ID tag allowed entrance by sliding it through the electronic security panel. Rance was in luck; everyone was out to lunch. He found the computer on the desk, proudly displaying a photo of the agent with his wife and four children.

Colby's fingers flashed across the keyboard. He could allow himself two hours before the agents returned—but if anyone cut their lunch short—he'd be discovered. And if either agent noticed their badge missing, they'd be back on the run. He needed to find the information, print it out—and disappear. Fast.

***

"I don't give a goddamn if we don't have badges!" the baldheaded agent shouted to the guard on duty. "You know us both. We played on the same office softball team last month, for God's sake!"

Red-faced, the guard answered the only way he could. "I don't make the rules, Agent Johnson. Sure I recognize you and Agent Murphy, but my standing orders are no badge—no entrance," he said with force. "Director Max Carlton wouldn't get past me if he weren't wearing his ID. That's that." Murphy ran fingers through his salt 'n pepper curls. "Look, damn it! We believe our badges were stolen when a man we couldn't identify was brought on the elevator with the medics." He slammed a fist down on the guard's desk. "If we're right—we've been compromised." He waved a hand in a wide arch. "Christ, man! This entire facility may have been compromised." He leaned across the desk. "You want that on your record?" Neither man gave an inch. Murphy backed off and pointed. "Get on that damn phone. Call the director. He's there. He never takes lunch. And let me talk to him. Now!"

"Holy shit!" Max Carlton shouted into the phone. "That's all I need! Let me talk to the guard, and both of you guys get to your offices immediately. I'll be in Murphy's office in two minutes."

Murphy's electronic record indicated no exit or entrance within the past forty-six minutes. They ran to meet Johnson who had just reviewed his security printout. Sitting dumbfounded, he looked up at his boss.

"Someone spent twenty-five minutes in my office, and we missed him by two."

"Look around, damn it. Is anything missing?" Carlton ordered. Agent Johnson's eyes swept the room and came to rest on his computer. He glanced at the computer, at the director, and back to the computer. The light was on. "I know damn well that I turned it off when I left the office. I do it purposely. The perp used my goddamned computer!" he shouted, throwing up his hands.

Max Carlton pushed the emergency button on the phone's intercom. His voice echoed in every office and hallway. "This is Director Carlton. This is a shutdown. I repeat. This is a mandatory shutdown. Activate all exits and entrances. No one, I repeat, no one is to leave this building. Anyone attempting to leave is to be automatically detained. I'll be in the main foyer in three minutes.

"You," Max jabbed a finger at Johnson. "Get on that computer and pull up whatever it is this perp was searching for."

Johnson punched all the right keys. He spun around on his chair and with a blank expression exclaimed, "Nothing."

Carlton was running out of patience. "Nothing. What in the hell do you mean…nothing?"

"I mean I get nothing. Other than the ON light indicating power, nothing happens. The computer's dead."

Murphy opened a desk drawer and tossed a cross-point screwdriver to his buddy. "Tim, pop the hood on that mother."

Johnson slumped back into his chair. "I'll be damned," he gasped and pointed to the computer's innards. "He tore out the damn hard-drive and took it with him. We'll never know what he was after."

"Oh shit," Max said, yanking on his mustache, "and he's got whatever national security information was stored there." He ran for the door and turned. "We're in deep, deep shit, gentlemen. Follow me."

Frustrated and impatient with the slow-moving elevator, the director slammed his hand against the elevator door. "We need new elevators, damn it! The stairs would have been faster."

When the doors slowly opened, the three men dashed toward the reception desk. Carlton came to a sliding halt. "Bring up the surveillance tape of the man who earlier collapsed in the foyer." He nervously drummed his fingers on the console top, peering over the guard's shoulder.

They studied the flashing images. "Here's the best frontal view," the guard offered. He clicked a key several times. "And here's a close up shot."

The director squinted. There was something vaguely familiar about the man on the screen. "Transfer the close-up to the profiling monitor."

Black, gray, and white wavy lines merged and formed a clear image of a man with a thin black mustache, straight dark hair, elongated sideburns, and dazed-looking deep-brown eyes. Max squinted again and shook a finger at the screen. "Lose the mustache and sideburns. Okay. Now make the hair light-brown and his eyes blue."

The CIA director slammed a palm down on the countertop. "Goddamn it! It's him!"

He spun around, surprised by the two voices behind him shouting the name in unison, "Rance Colby!" General Rubin Brock and Special Projects Director Alan Oakley were staring in disbelief at the monitor.

Agent Tim Johnson appeared puzzled. "Who's Rance Colby?"

"Only the most-wanted and sought-after man in the world," Oakley blurted out.

Carlton needed to squelch any reference to Rance Colby. He looked at both agents. "It's all on a need-to-know basis." He scowled. "And neither of you need to know."

Murphy nudged his partner and whispered aloud. "Must be a renegade that strayed from the reservation."

Angered, Max Carlton shot back. "He never was on the *Res*."

He turned his attention back to the guard. "When's the last time you saw this man?"

"Just minutes before you ordered the lock-down." He pointed to the doors. "He left just as Agent Oakley and General Brock were coming in. In fact, he passed them, then he got in the same cab." Gesturing to Oakley he continued, "that he arrived in."

Carlton ran to the door, shook the push bar, and pounded on the glass with his fist. Outwitted by ex-President Grayson's untouchable, he shouted over his shoulder. "Open this damned door!" He knew the cab would be long gone—but he rushed outside anyway. Max knew there would be no reason to trace the cab. Colby, being the crafty covert operative, would have changed into at least three cabs within the first fifteen minutes.

Dejected, he tugged at both ends of his thick handlebar mustache and caught Brock's stare. All in one breath he instructed the guard to lift the lock down—asked the general what he was doing in Langley—and suggested that Oakley go have his eyes checked.

"This Colby fellow has rattled your brain, my friend," Brock said, slapping the director on the back. "We have a one-thirty get-together. Remember?"

Alan Oakley was standing nearby, and his ears perked up. "You want me in on this meeting?" he asked.

The director's head snapped sideways. "No!" was his curt reply.

***

Arturo had just turned on CNN when Rance entered the room. A.T. tossed him a beer and pointed to the screen. "This is a repeat of what I heard on the radio."

A map of Israel appeared superimposed with a photo of the Minister of Defense and a badly demolished vehicle. The TV anchorman explained. "At nine-thirty in the evening Israel time, it was reported that Defense Minister Mishmar Bet Guvrin was killed when his personal vehicle was demolished by a suspected terrorist bomb attack. The Israeli government is calling it an obvious assassination." Rance clicked off the television. He took a long pull on the bottle and smiled. "Good deal. They took the general's suggestion," he paused. "Actually, it was my idea."

A look of confusion crossed A.T.'s features. "You suggested that the Israeli Minister of Defense be assassinated?"

"Well, in a matter of speaking, yes," Colby answered and held up a hand to close his friend's open mouth. "In the next booth you couldn't hear all of the conversation I had with General Brock, and I failed to fill you in when we met back here at my pad. Sorry." He removed a beer from the cooler and handed it to A.T., then sat in the opposite chair.

"Follow my thinking. All ministers in the surrounding mid-eastern countries had been murdered, except Israel's. One needn't be a rocket scientist to assume—since the Israeli minister was still alive—that the Israelis were behind the killings and that they were preparing for war." He pointed to his head. "Wouldn't it be smart to have the Israeli Minister of Defense assassinated to take pressure off the Jews?"

Arturo nodded in agreement, but he still looked perplexed. "Isn't that a little drastic? Murdering your own man?"

Rance leaned forward in his chair. "He isn't really dead, old buddy. It was all staged for the benefit of getting Israel off the hook—for the time being."

"That was smart—for the time being— but fraught with an inherent danger."

"Being?"

Arturo leaned forward to focus on his friend's eyes. "If he's recognized by anyone, the entire ruse will blow up in their face. That's all the proof the Arab nations would need. They'd see through the deception and assume the worst. Israeli would be attacked from all directions. The Middle East would become a powder keg."

Colby took a deep breath. "You're right. Hopefully, they changed his appearance and flew him out of the country under an assumed name to a remote location. If he can remain incognito long enough for us to put a stop to Rose's madness, the United States can release their findings of a rogue source behind the assassinations, and of that source's demise."

"Without implicating you or the United States," A.T. added.

"Precisely."

Colby sat back in his chair and gave his friend the once-over. "You look pretty spiffy this evening. I thought there was something different about you." He leaned forward again and sniffed loudly. "My, but you smell good, too. New shirt and slacks, and a shiny dome. What's on the agenda?"

"Cline's doctors really must have done a job on your mind for you to forget my pillow-talk assignment."

Colby hadn't forgotten. It was his attempt at light humor to soften the mood. "Speaking of my mind—I had another of those spells today— at CIA headquarters."

As Colby explained, A.T. shook his head in dismay. He got up, took the empty bottle from his friend, and headed for the bar. "What the hell am I to do with you? With your broken noggin, and your new love interest—you're becoming more vulnerable every day." Colby felt a twinge of resentment at A.T.'s mention of Molly. That was his business.

His future. But he bit his tongue and remained silent. Plopping down on a bar stool, he took the beer from Arturo who was playing bartender. "You know, good buddy, there was a time a couple months back when I wasn't sure of who I was. I've explained most of it before—but not all."

"If this is confession time, old buddy? Wait till I get my collar on and you can address me as Father Trash Pile."

Colby shut his eyes, hesitated, let the moment pass, and continued. "Those visions of my family drowning. Losing a father, mother, wife and two great kids was almost more than I could bear. That, thought-to-be-true experience, along with all the other life-experience facts they filled my head with—all appeared real to me. So real, that at one point, some time after, even when I began this *Overlay* mission, I thought perhaps *this* was not real. I wondered if what I was doing as Grayson's Shadow Master was a product of my imagination and was not real. Was I in reality the college professor whose entire family drowned?"

Colby suddenly grabbed A.T.'s wrist and asked, "Are you real?" When A.T.'s face lit up with a startled expression, Rance laughed out loud. "No. Someone as ugly as you would appear only in the darkest nightmare. And Molly MacWinter's in this dream. This must be real."

Arturo was anxious to be on his way and tired of Rance's having fun at his expense. "Can we get on with the debriefing? What did you find out at Langley?"

Rance Colby was toying with his friend. But there *was* a point during the last two months when he had questioned his sanity—as he had explained to A.T.

"When I got into Agent Johnson's computer, I pulled up and printed out all the names, responsibilities, personal photos, and profile data of CIA personnel in Moscow and Beijing. Now I know who to look out for, where their offices are located—as well as individual residences." He picked up the bag he had carried with him and flipped it on the bar counter. Not saying a word he motioned for A.T. to inspect the contents.

"I'll be damned." He held up the bag's content. "It's a computer hard drive. You didn't...?"

"Yeah. I did. I lifted his hard drive. I couldn't let Carlton discover what else I had stolen." He stuffed it back into the bag. "This goes into the vault until this is all over. Then they can have it back." He let the bag fall to the floor. "And before you ask—no I didn't slip into the White House. There was no reason to push my luck. I have all the information I need with the CIA printout."

"Okay. It's my turn. Wish me luck in the local FBI watering holes."

"Happy pruning, old buddy."

***

From five o'clock on, A.T. had swaggered into bar after bar within walking distance of the FBI building. Though crowded, the first two were frequented mostly by run-of-the-mill government office workers. Jackpot. Jake's Place was crawling with FBI types. *I can spot them a mile away. Their arrogance precedes them.* He stood at the door, surveying the bustling scene. A.T. had the uncanny ability for scanning a room in seconds and identifying his prey. There were a dozen or more women scattered about. Five at the bar were in heated conversations with male counterparts. The remainder was seated at tables in clusters, gossiping about the women at the bar, he mused.

Spotting a single vacant bar stool at the far end, he squeezed in and ordered a draft, swiveled to face the scene, and settled in to observe. His plan was to read the patrons—those who appeared accessible. Body language, facial expressions, posture, voice inflection, general disinterest in immediate interplay with associates—all would influence his next move. Luckily, the corner bar was surrounded with floor-to-ceiling windows, and the fading sunbathed the room with soft illumination. He would have to make his choices soon before the bar darkened. Overhead indirect lighting would soon cast a shadow over the faces of Arturo's unsuspecting targets.

***

"I nearly lost my Scotch when I saw your face on the CIA profile screen. Have you lost your mind?" General Rubin Brock caught himself. "Sorry, Colby. I forgot what those bastards, Cline, and Grayson, did to your head."

Rance Colby had called an old contact phone number in Paris which triggered a series of rerouting calls across the globe—ending with the general's private sterile line in his den. This was not the time to be careless. Leaning against the wall of an isolated telephone booth, he gently closed his eyes and excused the general's unintended slip. Brock refreshed his drink with two more ice cubes and a healthy splash of Scotch. His voice roared. "And to top it off, you SOB, you stole a CIA top-priority hard drive crammed full of highly sensitive data. Some potentially dangerous. Hell. It's all dangerous in the wrong hands. What do you mean to do with it?"

The line went silent. "Damn it, Colby. Are you there?"

Colby let a group of people pass before answering. "I'm pleased that your sterile line is operative. We can't chance being seen together. That would surely compromise our covert relationship." He was stalling for time—time to come up with a believable answer to Brock's pointed question. Outside of A.T., General Brock was his only collaborator. He decided the truth would do.

"General, as you're aware, President Alexie Velichkin is next on the *Overlay* schedule to be assassinated. I'll soon leave for Moscow and need to know whom the CIA has stationed there. Their data was lifted from Agent Johnson's computer, as well as that of their local Russian informants. While in, I extracted similar data on those in Beijing. Assuming my mission is successful in saving Velichkin's life." Another group passed the phone booth. "Obviously, I couldn't leave the hard drive behind for the CIA computer guys to discover what information had been lifted. The hard drive is secure and will be returned when we've accomplished our mission. God willing."

"Damn, you're a piece of work," the general said. "I'm sure glad you're on our side." He changed the subject. "The reason I was in Langley today was to confer with the director. Max and Senator Cochran are the only ones I trust right now."

"Trust?" Colby spit out.

"Don't get your testicles in an uproar, Colby. I don't trust anyone enough to confide in them. Hell. I'd be cutting my own throat. My position would be compromised. I'd be useless to you. Not that I've been of particular help so far."

"Okay, General. What did you learn from Carlton if anything?"

"Max is nearly convinced that there's a mole at Langley. He doesn't believe the individual, or individuals, are in the grasp of a foreign force. There's no evidence that points in that direction, but rather someone with an ax to grind with the agency or him." This time the pause was for a long swallow of Scotch. "He's conducting his own investigation into the crash that took the lives of two agents and nearly yours. As well as into the twin suicides of the Michaels. He suspects that they were both murdered and made to appear like suicides."

"Does he suspect anyone in particular?"

"He wouldn't commit, but from what he said, I gather that his Director of Special Projects, Alan Oakley, is high on the list. He learned from the motor pool manager that it was Oakley who gave the agents driving you to Colorado the two large thermoses of coffee to take with them."

"He thinks they were laced with drugs?"

"They know the coffee had been drugged. Whoever trashed and destroyed the Colorado coroner's office missed the thermoses. Max mentioned that when Oakley read the report, he acted somewhat strange, even startled. Max began to question in hindsight: was Oakley surprised at the drugged coffee, or that the thermoses were not destroyed? He also acted suspiciously when hearing of the Michaels' suicide."

"Alan Oakley's one of the library group and privy to everything. He could be extremely dangerous and needs close observation." Colby hesitated, and added, "Or he could join the Michaels. If you get my drift."

General Brock nearly choked on his Scotch. "Yeah. I catch your meaning. But let's not get trigger-happy. Besides your own actions, everything depends on the secrecy of your mission. The man could be completely innocent. Let's give Max a chance to clean his own coop. Depending on the outcome—we'll consider wringing the pigeon's neck.

"There are two puzzles in the equation. Puzzle one. Those two thermoses would never have lasted a three-day drive from D.C. to Colorado. They would have been refilled along the way. Puzzle two. Everything, including the bodies, was destroyed. And if both coffee containers survived—why had they been wiped clean of fingerprints?"

Colby's mind was in motion as Brock spoke. "Let's assume for the sake of argument that Oakley is the culprit. The coffee could have been drugged in anticipation that the crash would have occurred at any point along the route to their final destination. They would not necessarily have to crash in the mountains of Colorado. All major roads throughout the heartland were treacherous that week. If the drug was lethal enough, even a small dose of residue at the bottom of the containers could affect the refills. Remember, the drug could have had an accumulative influence on the men as they drove across the country. With both men taking turns driving, they might not have noticed as a single driver would have. I have no recollection of the trip—so I can't help there."

"Sounds plausible. How about the lack of fingerprints?"

"Obviously, a second party wiped the lethal thermoses clean sometime before whoever torched the office and bodies."

General Brock cleared his throat. "Alan could be clean; I only have a gut feeling. Nothing more at this time. He'll remain under internal surveillance until Max is certain he's not the mole. I'm attempting to trace his movements and whereabouts the final hours before the Michaels' alleged suicide." Rance could hear a swallow. "Enough about Oakley. What are your plans? Off to Moscow?"

Colby glanced in both directions and lightly rested his finger on the phone's cutoff lever. "One more day or two and I'm off to save President Velichkin. I'll be in touch."

Prior to hanging up, he tossed out one final thought for the general to chew on. "Before we end this contact—remember that Grayson brought the Arctic Rose into the picture. Consider the possibility she might be behind the crash and suicides, and the puzzlement regarding the cleaned thermoses—hoping to manipulate Max into accusing his own man. Oakley."

Rubin Brock heard the click, replaced the old-fashioned receiver, and poured another round of Scotch. Lifting the glass, he made a toast. "Here's to your success." *I'm beginning to like and appreciate this guy by the minute.*

***

A soft buzzing woke Rance out of a sound sleep. One eye stared at the wall monitor. Someone had inserted the code and opened the front door. The sound alerted Rance that the entrance had been breached, but he was in no immediate peril. The smiling face thumbing his nose into the security camera was a surprise at two o'clock in the morning. *He's got the key to my other apartment. What's he doing here? Don't tell me A.T. got shot down tonight. This is a first. This I have to hear.*

By the time Colby had climbed out of his California king-size bed, slipped on a robe and slippers, and run fingers through his hair, he could hear his friend digging around in the refrigerator. Unnoticed, he crossed his arms and leaned against one of the thick bedroom foyer columns. Arturo sensed a presence and spun around. Colby was grinning like a Cheshire Cat. "What?" was all A.T. could manage at the moment.

Rance grinned. Obviously annoyed at the grin's inference, A.T. turned his back. "Don't you ever have anything to eat in this damned fridge except an occasional pizza?"

"Crow."

"Cut the bullshit. You weren't there. But if you'll find me something to fill an empty stomach and wipe that damned smirk off your face. I'll begin the debriefing."

A large glass of cold milk and a double-decked pastrami sandwich did wonders for the Italian's disposition. He glanced around the brightly lit kitchen and waved his hand in a circle. "You could fit a fifty-piece orchestra in here."

Colby leaned back on his kitchen island stool and frowned. "Quit stalling, old buddy. Let me hear all the gory details. Or should I begin singing the first chorus of *'Signor Trash Pile Bites The Dust?'* Or *'Shot Down In The Old FBI Corral?'* Speak up. I can't hear you."

Arturo lowered his head. "It's the first time in my life that I'm truly ashamed of myself. Well, almost."

He ran a finger over the Spanish tile that matched the sink area and commented on the wallpaper. "You really must like the Southwest. Your wall treatments in the kitchen, master bedroom and bath all have that motif." Noticing the look of frustration on his friend's face, Arturo continued his explanation of the evening's exploratory venture. "Okay so I'm stalling. I'm not proud of what I did to that sweet young thing."

Rance's grin turned to a grim frown. "You did what?"

"Don't look at me with that holier-than-thou expression. It's not what your demented mind is conjuring up. Actually, if you want to be technical—it's all my damned father's fault." He washed that stretch of imagination down with a large gulp of milk. "In one of his drunken stupors, my old man gave me advice on how to pick up a woman in a bar. He said it worked every time. 'When it's late in the evening and you've struck out—zero in on the most lonesome looking signorina or signora in the bar and ply her with unbridled attention. Never fails.' " A.T. threw up his hands. "Great advice to give an impressionable twelve-year-old snot-nosed kid."

"It's late and I need rest. Get on with your assorted tale of woe," Rance moaned wearily.

"Jane looked to be bored stiff, sitting with four other female FBI types. They were all jabbering away, paying little attention to their timid- looking co-worker at the corner of the table. Those few times she tried to join the conversation, she never got a word in edgewise. She mostly spent her time looking around, crossing, and uncrossing her legs, looking at her watch and sipping on her drink. It didn't take long for me to follow my dad's advice. Jane became the target.

"When the small table next to her opened up, I muscled two guys aside and sat down, challenging them to make a fuss. *Non-capisco* I said, showing my palms, claiming ignorance, while giving them the evil eye. They backed off. Laughing out loud and waving for the waitress, I had hoped to attract Jane's attention. So as not to be conspicuous, I waited a few minutes before making my move. Leaning back in my chair, I made eye contact with the target. She couldn't resist the infamous Arturo smile and returned the polite gesture. Turning slightly, and in a thick Italian accent, I explained that I was new at the Italian Embassy, and that this was my first time in Jake's Place. Her smile brightened as she explained that it was her first time to join her office workers."

Arturo stuffed the last piece of sandwich in his mouth and went on with his story. "My standing bow brought a genuine smile to her thin lips. Placing my hand on my chest, I told her that it would bring much pleasure to a lonely Italian's heart if she would honor him with her presence and allow him to offer her a drink. She looked at me, then those at her table, and nodded.

"Her name was Jane. Wisely, that's all she would disclose in the beginning. A waterfall of words would soon follow. She was attractive, in a simple way. A long oval face was topped with brownish-blonde hair set in a bun. As the night went on, her green-eyes brightened with amusement." A.T. looked pleased. "Jane laughed at my jokes. She appeared to have a slim frame, but when she excused herself to go to the restroom, I noticed a pair of long shapely legs."

"Speaking of rest," Rance said, "if you don't get to the point of all this, I'm heading to bed."

Without a word, A.T. left the kitchen and returned with two beers. Colby shook his head, refused a bottle, and motioned for his friend to continue. "I introduced Jane to martinis. Dirty martinis with three splashes of olive juice and three olives. She loved the first one—which, unfortunately for her—led to three more."

"Now I know where you're going with all of this," Rance speculated.

"No you don't," A.T. corrected him. "It was she who ordered the last two. Jane loved your special blend of martini. Personally, I hate olives.

This isn't something I would want the Italian olive growers to hear," he joked, taking a long swallow from the bottle. "Granted, by one o'clock, she was feeling no pain—but delightfully happy. And I didn't have to invite her to your apartment to gather information. First of all, she was in no shape. And secondly, I wouldn't have taken advantage of such a sweet naïve young lady." He shook a finger in Colby's mistrusting face. "To prime the pump, I confided in her that I was working in liaison with the Italian government and the FBI—to determine the whereabouts of a suspected American rogue operative. As it so happens, for the last six months, Jane of the FBI has been working in the Oversight Department for Investigating Unapproved U.S. Covert Operations. She catalogues requests from all government security forces. If the FBI or any other organization were aware of *Overlay* and the man called *Rance Colby*, she would have knowledge. She did not. And believe me, if she had known, she would have told me."

"And what happened next?"

"You never give me any credit," A.T. protested the question's implication. "As I had said, she was extremely timid." He looked at Colby with innocent eyes. "*Was*—is the operative word. She explained earlier that the girls had been pressuring her into joining them at Jake's ever since she began work there six months ago. Then when she finally agreed, they treated her like a stepsister all night." Arturo flashed a perfect set of teeth. "I came to her rescue."

"And?" Colby asked, slipping off his stool.

"After a brief conversation with her two remaining girlfriends at the next table, they agreed to be certain that Jane would arrive safely at her apartment. I said my fond adieus and left—a wiser but sadder man. I'm sending her an anonymous dozen roses in the morning."

"Well, I'm proud of you, I think. You obtained the necessary information and controlled yourself by not deflowering an innocent young lady." He stretched his tired muscles and pointed in the direction of a spare bedroom. "Bunk here tonight. We've got much to discuss in the morning before my noon flight to Turkey, and my train trip to Moscow."

Chapter Seven

The Russian countryside zipping by his window reminded the passenger of scenes out of Doctor Zhivago and painful memories of his last covert Moscow mission. Penetrating the secure borders of Turkey and Russia had proved to be no problem for Andrei Zakharov. His piercing black eyes highlighted by darkened circles suspiciously searched the faces of newly boarding passengers at every train stop. Long strands of gray hair hung below his dyed lamb's wool cap, brushing his bushy eyebrows. A classic hawk nose protruded proudly above a disheveled gray mustache and beard. With one hand he clutched his long black cape against the bitter early morning breeze sweeping through opened car doors. The other firmly held a small black case between his body and the window-seat wall.

Rance Colby dozed occasionally. The steady clicking of the train's movement over the tracks, combined with the rhythmic sway of the car, plus the lack of sleep had a hypnotic quality. The monotonous flat farmlands frequently spotted with scrawny-looking cattle and horses began to fade along with the evening sun. A loud blast of air announced their arrival at the next whistle-stop. Colby's chin remained on his chest, but his eyes opened halfway. Moving his head slightly, he observed those who had left his car, and the two well-dressed men who had entered and now occupied seats at the back. *Those two bear watching. They're out of place dressed to the nines in the middle of nowhere. And they chose a perch where they could keep watch on the entire car. On the other hand, I'm probably becoming paranoid. They could be bureaucratic farm officials checking out rural communities.*

Another slow-moving hour had passed, and Colby was becoming antsy, bored, and stiff from sitting. Tightening his grip on his tools-of-the-trade case, he slid off the leather double-seat and headed for the open platform separating the next train car. He was amused when a small boy crawled between his legs in the aisle and noted his mother's look of disapproval. To keep in character, he frowned at the woman and proceeded toward the door, unaware of the movement of two suspicious men.

Still clutching the case, both arms hugged his heavy cape against the cold stream of air. The top half of the platform side door was open. It happened as he leaned out for a better view of a lone farmhouse whose lights had just appeared. Distracted, the sound of the car door opening was muffled by sounds of the racing train. Simultaneously, one man grabbed the case's handle while his accomplice's powerful arm encircled Colby's neck from behind and began to squeeze.

Refusing to relinquish his grip on the black case, Colby tightened the muscles of his neck to withstand the pressure. He was limited in his ability to retaliate. There was scant room to maneuver. The head of the man who had him in a death grip was close to the left side of his own, making it impossible to use his head as a weapon to crush the man's nose. Ignoring the man behind for the moment, he concentrated attention on the one in front. Colby yanked on the handle, pulling the assailant toward him while lashing out with his left foot. The man cried out in pain as the point of Rance's shoe found its mark. Releasing the case, both hands clutched crushed testicles.

Colby's left hand held the case; his right was clamped firmly onto the forearm of the man behind. Quickly releasing his grip, he grabbed the case with both hands and slung it over his left shoulder, smashing it into the man's face with all his might. The arm around his neck went limp. Spinning around, Colby grabbed the man's throat with one hand, the other slipped under his crotch. In one mighty surge of strength, the man was lifted in the air and hung precariously out the platform door, hanging over the side of the speeding train.

"Who sent you?" Colby shouted to be heard. As the man pleaded for his life, his arms flaying about for balance, the all too familiar sound of a silencer's spit froze the Shadow Master's breath. He had forgotten about the other man. Losing his grip on the would-be assassin, he squeezed his eyes shut, waiting for the pain that never came.

"Well pilgrim, A.T. was right. You're losing your edge. You've become careless in your old age. And that's dangerous for all of us."

Rance had his back to the platform, his eyes still shut. That distinctive voice. How could he ever forget it? He turned slowly, not believing his eyes. "What in the hell are you doing here?" was all he could think of saying.

"Open the door so I can dump this piece of garbage, and I'll explain over a cup of Turkish coffee."

A strong grip clamped onto the dead man's belt. He soon followed his partner, tumbling and twisting as his body hit the graveled embankment. Colby swung the door closed and faced an old friend. "You've saved my butt more than once, and if I remember correctly, the last time was right here in Russia. And you were quite ill at the time. I'm glad to see that you survived. Thanks again," he said, offering his hand in friendship. Instead of a handshake, he received a rib-cracking hug. His friend stepped back, his deep-set black button eyes twinkling with mischievous amusement, ever deepening a cluster of laugh lines. Alvin L' Ami had always reminded Colby of the actor Sean Connery: his physical appearance and mannerisms, even his speech patterns. Conversely, where Connery was balding, Al proudly displayed a thick head of tousled salt and pepper hair, matching his equally thick mustache and beard. A black wool knit cap miraculously clung to the back of his head. Over a blue and white plaid shirt and faded bib overalls, he wore a heavy three-quarter length, leather-trimmed, denim jacket. A pair of soft leather, black crepe-soled shoes completed L' Ami's outfit.

Rance followed the man who had just saved his life. To his surprise, most of the train cars on their way to a near-empty dining car were less that half full. Neither man spoke as they moved through car after car. Colby's mind raced into the past six years ago. His assignment was to retrieve the designs for a non-nuclear weapon of mass destruction that Russian agents had stolen from a secret U.S. facility. A.T. was recovering from a serious bout of the flu, and Rance needed back up. Alvin L' Ami was his second choice—available and familiar with the territory. Once as mysterious and elusive as Colby, L' Ami was one of a handful of shadowy unacknowledged agents who had walked away from their clandestine world of intrigue—alive. It was rumored he had threatened that an existing diary would be revealed upon word of his unnatural demise. Little protection, but effective, it appeared.

"Okay Al, Arturo must have contacted you. Why? And what are you doing in Russia? On this train?"

"Impatient as ever, aren't we friend," came a crusty reply. Al waved to get the waiter's attention. "Two coffees here, if you please."

"Well?" The pointed question accompanied a no-nonsense glare.

"As I recall, you were more than delighted to see this handsome smiling face when I reached down and yanked your ass out of the elevator shaft a few years back. Just before the elevator was about to squash that skinny ass—I might add."

Colby's cursed memory never let him forget. He had had the stolen plans securely taped to his body, and he and Al were attempting to leave the Russian government security building when their presence was discovered. All hell broke loose. An intermittent shrill whistle blared aloud, and men with weapons scattered in all directions. Al took to the stairs. Colby pried open the eighteenth-floor elevator door, and with the help of a pair of welder's gloves, began a slow slide down a greasy cable. He had made it as far as the tenth-floor level when he heard the echoing blast—felt the sting in the fleshy part of his left shoulder and heard the whine of the elevator motor. They were coming for him. If he didn't move fast, he'd be crushed. With his remaining strength, he lunged for level ten's landing. Hanging on for dear life, he struggled frantically to pry open the doors. The elevator was two levels above when they sprang open and Al's grinning face appeared—then his welcome hand.

With a grunt and a heave, Colby was pulled to safety as the elevator plunged down, narrowly missing him. Both men dashed for an open window and disappeared down an enclosed fire tube and into the night. This was the first time that they had spoken since separating on a dark and blustery Moscow street corner.

Colby took a sip and swallowed hard. The coffee was strong. His pulse rate had returned to normal, and he began to relax. "I'm really pleased to see you looking well, friend. It's been a long time." L' Ami said nothing. "Now it's time for you to answer my questions," Rance said, glancing at seven noisy people at the far end of the car.

"Arturo called me early yesterday morning." He understood the questioning look in Colby's eyes. "Yes. We both were on rerouted public phone lines and discussed the situation," he paused, "at least some of it, in our own adaptation of a predetermined cryptic code. There was no way for him to reach you. There's been a fire at his villa. Apparently it occurred under very suspicious circumstances. He immediately left for Italy—concerned it may be connected to his association with you and your mission. He added that he wouldn't put anything past the ice bitch—the Arctic Rose."

From the large sterling-silver pot left by the waiter, L' Ami poured a stream of thick black liquid into bone-china cups. "A.T. knew of my familiarity with Russia and that I had old contacts here, contacts he did not have. He also explained that he would have called on me even if he hadn't been distracted. It wouldn't be the first time the three of us worked together." He laughed softly, keeping the source of a fond memory to himself. "What he didn't explain was the assignment. All he said was that you needed my expertise, and if you chose, you'd explain fully. That's all I needed to know."

Rance Colby was thankful for his friend's loyalty but concerned by the news of Arturo's misfortune. Was Rose's organization behind the blaze? It was farfetched, but if A.T. suspicions were correct, her thorny stems were far-reaching. "When are you to hear from him next?"

Al pulled back his jacket cuff and checked his watch. "Two hours ago," he said, with a deep frown. He reached into an inside pocket and showed Rance a GlobalPhone. "I have a scrambled site and his villa phone is, or was, a sterile line. Should I risk it?"

"Go ahead."

Al L' Ami punched the buttons and waited. His black eyes grew larger the longer he waited. The phone was ringing but no one answered. Just as he was about to flip the phone closed, someone picked up. "Tell him it's the fox." For the next three minutes, he listened without saying a word. Nodding to himself, he closed the unit. Colby's expression demanded an answer. "That was one of A.T.'s flowers. She was expecting my call. She said that the villa had been attacked by three assassins an hour after A.T. arrived to assess the fire damage. All three of Rose's men are dead. She said the last one took longer to die. A.T. learned from him that they had been sent by the Arctic Rose—and..."

Before he got the next word out, Colby demanded to know, "What about A.T.? How come he wasn't on the phone?"

L' Ami's eyes said it all. "He was wounded in the scuffle." Al raised a hand. "But he's okay. A knife thrust to the side glanced off a rib, slicing the flesh. It's not serious, she assured me. A.T.'s resting and gave her instructions that if the fox called—to provide me with details, and to say that he'd contact me soon after he woke."

Colby blew out a breath of relief and downed the remaining coffee. "It's suicide to underestimate that bitch. But the more she exposes her international reach, the more we understand the enemy's capability, and the better we can prepare ourselves." The pot was empty. Picking it up, he held it above his head to get the waiter's attention. "If I'm to be attacked, shot at, stabbed, blown up, I might as well go down full of pond sludge."

From his wizened appearance the old man might have been the original server when they laid the tracks. He excused himself from a friendly conversation with the gathering crowd at the other end of the dining car. Holding the large pot by the handle with both hands, he slowly paced himself down the aisle of the swaying train. Before setting it on the table, he stared at both men, then frowned at the coffee stains on his crisp linen tablecloth. They returned his stare and shrugged their shoulders. L' Ami reached into his pocket and shoved a gold Euro coin to the table's edge. The old man snatched it up, bowed politely, and shuffled away.

"You do the honors," Rance said, removing his v-shaped wool cap. He ran fingers through long strands of hair, pushing it back out of his eyes. "Damn, that cap's hot," he complained. Nodding thanks for pouring the coffee, he took a sip and winced. "The more you drink, the stronger it tastes. Now let's talk about that little incident on the platform. Was that a mugging, or do you think they knew who I was?"

"They were searching for you, and they knew who and what to look for. In fact, I had heard that you were bound for Russia even before A.T. contacted me." He observed the look of puzzlement on Rance's face. "I, and possibly dozens of freelancers, was contacted by Rose's operatives.

She has an organization, but it's not large enough to locate and take out the target. *You.*" Before continuing, he removed his jacket and flipped it on the next chair.

"While you were basking somewhere in the Caribbean, in between one crisis or another, A.T. and I had to make a living. We worked several assignments together and were never contacted directly. We always used numerous in-between messengers, each unknown to the other. The last individual on the totem pole knew nothing except the assignment code and phone number that I was to call. Last week I phoned the given number. The poor bastard provided me with more information than he should have without first finding out if I'd accept the job. I got the impression that he was under pressure and desperate. The guy was still cussing me out after I refused and hung up.

"In the past, those who we had called back to see if there was something of interest, never knew who we were, and we never accepted assassination assignments. This was obviously one of those. I have little doubt that dozens of men and women are spread throughout Russia, watching all avenues into Moscow. It's no secret that the target—*you*—will be in disguise. The one thing they are told to look for is a tall man carrying a bag that he never lets out of his sight. He might even have it chained to a wrist. Clutching that black case like you do, made you a target for those two would-be assassins. It would make little difference if they were wrong. It was worth their risk."

Colby grinned at the thought. "I guess that means that tall men carrying small cases are now being mugged in airports, bus, and train stations, all across Russia. That's a lot of muggings. I can see the newspaper headline now. *Mugging epidemic spreads across the Mother Land.*"

"I've got a suggestion. We'll soon be making a three-minute stop in Millerovo. It's a small hamlet. There will be at least two passengers boarding—two of my trusted contacts from years past. Once we finish our pot of pond sludge, you place the case in one of the onboard lockers and give me the key. You'll no longer be a target. When we get to Moscow, you pick up your luggage and head for your hotel. By the way, where will you be staying and under what name?"

"Rossiya Hotel. Andrei Zakharov from Kropotkin."

"After you're off the train, I'll open the locker, retrieve the case, and leave with two armed escorts—then meet you early that evening in your hotel room. Agreed? Good. And you can buy me dinner. I know just the place," he said with a sly grin.

Before parting and giving Al the key, Rance apprised him of the mission to save the life of the Russian President, Alexei Velichkin. He'd go into detail over dinner—leaving out the part as to why the president was targeted for assassination.

For the remainder of the trip, Rance Colby stayed comfortably in his seat, leaving only to stretch, relieve himself, and for quick bites of food. The noisy little boy and his mother had gotten off at one of the small stations, leaving the car silent but for the rhythm of the train. He sat quietly, contemplating a scheme to smoke out Rose's assassins before they set up their deadly apparatus. For that, he would need Al—a crew of his contacts—and time.

***

Amid the snarled crush of buses and taxis, Andrei Zakharov tapped the taxi driver on the shoulder, instructing him to pull over and stop at the curb. From where he stood with his luggage, atop the Vasilyevsky Ulitsa Slope, Andrei recognized the enormous Rossiya Hotel with its four twelve-story wings. The northern hotel wing featured a twenty-three-story tower in the shape of a ship's bridge. Before walking down the slope to Varvarka Ulitsa, the street where the hotel is located, he paused to absorb the remarkable mixture of architectural styles. Old churches stood next to neo-classic structures, in contrast to the modern Rossiya Hotel poised at the edge of the Moskova River.

At the bottom of the hill, he stopped to buy an apple from an old lady whose fruit stand consisted of a table covered with a worn green rug and two cardboard cartons of shiny red apples. Her son sat on the corner of the table smiling at passersby—playing an ancient-looking brass flute. Andrei flipped a coin to the youngster, motioned with his head to the smaller of the two bags, and then to the hotel entrance a block away. The boy grinned and glanced at his mother who nodded approval. The grin changed to a look of fear as they approached the entrance and he saw the uniformed doorman. Taking a step backward, he handed the bag to Andrei and was about to bolt, when the stranger grasped his collar. In perfect Russian, the generous man in the black cape smiled and said, "There's nothing to fear. Do you and your mother sell your fruit every day at that location?"

A frightened squeaky voice answered, "Yes, sir. But not on Sunday."

The smiling man smoothed the boy's jacket hood and handed him another coin. "I can tell you're a good son and a smart boy. How would you like to make extra money working for me while I'm in Moscow?" The little head bobbed with enthusiasm. "Good. My name's Andrei. If you're not around when I come out later today, I'll talk with you tomorrow. How's that?"

This time the voice answered with confidence. "I'll be watching for you, sir. Yes I will, Mister Andrei. I'll be watching."

"And that's just what I'll want you to do for me, son. Watch."

Colby smiled to himself as he watched the boy race back to his mother, the long tongues of his sneakers flapping in the breeze.

"U minya zakazana m esta. Minya zavut Andrei Zakharov." The reservation desk attendant frowned as he slicked back a greased mus-

tache with one slender finger and checked the list of scheduled guests. Colby removed his hat and brushed hair from his eyes, then frowned back. "Does there seem to be a problem?" he said. The attendant's eyes searched a computer printout without looking up. Suddenly he made what Rance assumed to be a happy sound.

"Yes. Yes. Yes. Here you are. Zakharov from Kropotkin. You have reserved a second room for an Italian." He looked over Colby's shoulder. "Is," he reread the roster, "Signor Pascucci from Rome with you?"

"No. Unfortunately, he has been detained for a few days. However, if you have a double room available with a view of the Kremlin, as my single, please reserve it for a Monsieur Bayeaux who will arrive later today from Paris. When Signor Pascucci shows up, he can share a room with Bayeaux." Colby stood tall and peered down at the shorter man. "We are all poets and will attend a conference at the end of the week. In the meantime, we plan to sightsee in your marvelous city."

The poet Zakharov folded a few bills and shoved them across the desktop. Bribery will get you everywhere and anything in Russia. "That will be acceptable," the attendant said, clicking his heels and smoothing out a mustache that appeared to be slicked down with a thick glob of bear grease. He was about to call for luggage assistance when Colby placed his hand over the shiny bell.

"Just the key, please. I have a very strong back." A pair of indignant eyes became mere slits as he nodded acknowledgment. He would be losing his share of the bellhop's expected tip. After he reluctantly handed Zakharov his electronic key, another fold of bills forced a perfect smile. Colby had made a friend. As long as the money held out.

***

Raised voices carried across the calm of Chesapeake Bay just offshore of the U.S. Naval Academy. "Goddamn it, Clifford!" the current Secretary of State Thomas Cline shouted. A heavy palm slammed down on the small deck table, spilling the ex-president's gin and tonic. Cline's face was flushed with anger. He glared at one of Clifford Grayson's serving deckhands standing within earshot, who got the silent message and joined the crew below deck.

Normally, Cline enjoyed the cruise down the bay on Grayson's luxury yacht, but not today. Not since that fateful gathering months ago in the D Street Library. When he heard the hatch close, he returned to the subject that brought him on deck. "Who was that tattooed broad you brought to our meeting? That had to have been one of the dumbest things you've ever done, in or out of the presidency. You exposed the group and the *Overlay* debacle to a perfect stranger."

Grayson seemed not to hear his old friend's tirade. He silently sopped up the spilled drink with a napkin and took a swallow from an empty glass, without acknowledging Cline's question. The secretary stared in disbelief as the ex-president began to hum a baby's lullaby. His left hand fell into his lap—the glass rolled off the table and onto a crisp pair of blue and white seersucker slacks, and dribble fell from a curled lip staining Grayson's navy-blue, double-breasted sport coat. Searching, empty eyes slowly turned to Thomas Cline as if pleading for help. His grotesquely twisted mouth moved—but not a sound was heard. The Secretary of State leaped to his feet and ran for help.

***

Andrei Zakharov, alias Rance Colby, moaned, tossing, and turning in bed. The renovated eighteenth-floor room overlooking the brick-walled fortress of the Kremlin had been furnished with modern furniture: three chairs, a desk, small table, TV, telephone, refrigerator, fan, and a private bath with bidet. Prior to falling asleep, which he hadn't planned on doing, Rance had arranged for the refrigerator to be stocked with beer in honor of the anticipated arrival of Signer Pascucci. Since Monsieur Bayeaux preferred Jack Daniel's and Colby the makings of a martini, a bottle of extra dry vermouth, their best gin, and a jar of olives accompanied the order.

Removing the tight wig, he lay down, closing weary eyes. He had intended to spend the hour plotting the team's next move. Instead, frantic cries of help filled an unwanted deep dream. The explosion, the sounds of splashing water, and those awful screams—daddy! honey! son!—tore into his subconscious. He woke with a start, drenched in perspiration, head throbbing with pain.

It wasn't until the knocking became louder that Colby regained awareness. He retrieved the 9mm Beretta from under the pillow, slipped off the bed, and wearily approached the adjoining-room door. Standing off to the non-hinged side of the door, he asked, *"Khto?"*

"It's your savior from the train, Monsieur Bayeaux. Your next-door neighbor. And he's as thirsty as an aged French whore. Open the damned door."

Colby was surprised and pleased that both Al and A.T. would be close by, making for easier communications. "Come in, you old reprobate. Whisky's on the table and there's ice in the fridge."

Al closed the door, turned, and stared at his friend. "What the hell happened to you? You look as though you've taken a shower with your clothes on." Spying the bottles of gin and vermouth, he didn't wait for an answer, but added, "And for Christ's sake, take out your cheek plugs. Your disguise didn't fool me anyway. I'm reminded of a hoarding squirrel. Besides, you'll never chew olives with those in place."

Colby plopped on the edge of the bed and took a deep breath. "It's the damned dreams and sudden headaches. They'll pass with time." He felt around inside of his cheeks with his tongue and laughed. "You're right about the plugs. It's a wonder I didn't swallow them in my sleep." He paused and philosophically continued, "That would certainly solve all my problems, wouldn't it?"

L' Ami dropped three ice cubes in a glass and filled it to the brim. He saluted the sitting man with his drink. *"Shchisliva!* To the success of our mission, and to you and your lady."

After splashing the mixture of gin and vermouth with three spoonfuls of olive juice, Colby replied, suspicious. "Is there nothing that Italian blabbermouth didn't tell you?"

Al drew back the double set of curtains, exposing a panorama of Moscow's skyline. "You know, one time we were here to bury Russia as they promised to bury America. Now we're playing footsy with them." He turned and looked Colby in the eye. "No, there's not much that Arturo didn't tell me. Of course, he left out specific details of the mission. He explained what those bastards did to your mind, and the resulting problem you're experiencing—at the most inopportune times. Your situation could place my life in danger. It was imperative that I be aware." Sitting down, he went on. "And he and I both want you to live a long life with your lovely lady. That's why we're both here. To be your eyes in case you can't see clearly." Before Colby's response, he asked, "Any objections?"

"None whatsoever—my friend."

They were both startled by the phone ring. Colby reached over to pick up the receiver and stopped, hand in mid-motion. He shrugged his shoulders, shook his head, and pointed to his unpacked bag. "It's my GlobalPhone."

L' Ami bent over and unzipped the small pocket on Colby's bag resting by his chair, pulled out the phone and tossed it to his friend. Rance glanced at the displayed number and scowled. "It's the General. I normally call him. There must be a problem." He pressed a finger to his lips, signaling Al to remain silent. No one as yet knew that he had enlisted the assistance of two close associates.

"Yes."

"Colby, is that you?"

"No. It's President Velichkin," he answered, in no mood to fence. "Of course it's me. Speak. This must be important to risk a call."

"Ex-President Clifford Grayson is dead." He waited for a reply. After a few seconds of silence, he continued. "He was with Cline on his yacht—suffered a massive stroke, then a deadly heart attack. Considering current circumstances, he's on ice, literally, in a secluded sanitarium. The body will remain there until you've completed the mission. His six-man crew has also been secured. These are risky but necessary precautions. I was afraid that if Rose got wind of his death, she would no longer be bound to the original *Overlay* schedule and become even more unpredictable." He paused again. Rance could picture Brock swallowing a mouthful of Scotch. "And to put your fears at ease, I'm using the latest electronic scrambler."

"I've got the feeling that's not the real reason you contacted me."

"Not the main reason, no. Max's people picked up a garbled transmission from Russia to an unknown location off the coast of Greece. The message was too broken to comprehend, but when Max read it aloud as I sat in his office, I nearly fell off my chair. It was a communiqué for someone named Rose. She must have left the country and relocated somewhere in Greece. With all his immediate pressing issues, the name Rose escaped Max's attention, so he disregarded its importance."

"You saved me a phone call, General. Having played football, you know that the best defense is a good offense. An hour ago I decided to go on the offense. Now I know where to begin." He humorously snarled into the phone. "It's about time you made yourself useful, Brock. This information is invaluable."

L' Ami stood up and threw his hands in the air when he heard that Rance was going after Rose. Colby motioned for Al to sit back down and mouthed the word—*'Later.'*

Spilling his Scotch, General Rubin Brock growled back. "You can afford to be arrogant, Colby. You sure as hell can't afford to take chances. What about her agents in Russia?"

"I've got it all under control, General. Now I need a favor from you with no questions asked." The general coughed. "I need the Russian equivalent to our twin, high-powered engine Sikorsky helicopter, fully armed, combat equipped, and fitted with pontoons, to be ready in four hours at an outlying airfield with sufficient fuel to get me safely to Greece, and a guaranteed return trip when ready. You can arrange it. I happen to know that you and Russian General Mikhail Rutskoy have become great friends. Aren't you his grandson's godfather?"

"How in the goddamn hell did you find that out?" he shouted.

"We'll discuss that another time. Can you arrange it?"

After a long pause, there came a weakened reply. "Yes. I'll get right back to you."

"Have the good General Rutskoy tell his pilot to be looking for an elderly woman, and not to ask questions—only take orders. I'll be in touch." Colby flipped the cover closed. Al raised his brows. He had heard the general's angry shouts from where he sat.

Al downed his whiskey, and squinting at his friend, silently demanded an answer. *Okay, explain yourself.* Taking his time, Colby finished chewing on his olive, stood up and as he walked to the huge picture window, began to explain his plan. "We've got, if Rose stays on schedule, approximately two weeks before the strike. If I can neutralize her, this assassination attempt will likely be aborted, as well as the attempt on the life of the Chairman of the Republic of China. I can't just sit here waiting for them to come to me. You and Arturo will place your local contacts in strategic locations throughout Moscow. They're to listen for rumors—watch for unfamiliar faces within the underground community, and report back to you. I have faith in you both to sniff out the assassins." He grinned and pointed at the refrigerator. "Just be certain that Italian gardener saves me a beer."

Against Al's better judgment, he listened while Colby outlined his plan. Colby would begin his search in Thasos, the small island in the upper Aegean Sea where Rose was born. He didn't think she'd return to the scene of so much pain, but without additional information it was the only starting point he could think of. He'd work his way forward from there. While he was away, either A.T. or Al would sleep and shower in his room, so that no one would be aware he had left Moscow.

Al went into his room and returned with Colby's black case. "I don't like this one damn bit."

Colby ignored the comment. He opened the black case, then flipped the larger of his two suitcases on the bed. It contained various pieces of clothing. L' Ami closed his eyes, bit his lip, and shook his head as his friend removed an ankle-length heavy gauze skirt, red paisley print blouse, a pair of well-worn black flat heel shoes, and tattered green shawl. The black case held, among other disguises, a gray wig, padded stomach and bra, and the elements to turn Colby into an aged woman. Underneath the disguise, he wore a short-sleeve tan shirt and slacks. Stockings were rolled down to his ankles. In an emergency, discarding the old woman's appearance, he could quickly distort the masquerade. After rolling up his pant legs above his knees, he strapped a Velcro holster to his thigh and inserted his 9mm Beretta. The skirt had a hidden Velcro slit corresponding to the weapon's location for quick access, making it unnecessary to lift the skirt. He slipped the cylinder- shaped silencer in the left-hand skirt pocket. Within forty minutes, the man called Rance Colby became a wrinkled, bent-over, peasant woman.

Rance lifted his skirt and circled the room, waiting for his friend's reaction. Instead of praise for a job well done, L' Ami continued to shake his head. He didn't like the plan one damn bit.

"All right, ye of little faith, while I wait for Brock's confirmation call, I need you to take a short walk. Exit the hotel, turn to the right, and walk one block. You'll see a woman selling apples with a young son. Give the boy a few coins and tell him it's from Alexei, and that he'll be hearing from me within a few days. Assuming I return safely.

"One last thing. Here's a diagram of all hotel-exit escape routes that I drew. Memorize them and have A.T. do the same when he arrives— then flush it."

***

The heavily armed and fortified long-distance helicopter was waiting as promised. Accustomed to carrying out General Rutskoy's requests without question, the pilot seemed not to be surprised by his passenger's appearance. Leaning over from the hatch, he offered his hand. "Grand-mother, let me help you up." It wasn't until the little old woman athletically leapt into the craft and in a deep masculine voice barked orders, that he gasped in amazement. Then laughed out loud. This was going to be an interesting trip.

Colby liked the pilot's initial reaction. In perfect Russian, he addressed his companion. "You appear to own a sense of humor, Captain.

It may serve you well before this assignment is over. Do you know where the Greek island of Thasos is located?"

With the same finger he had raised to imply that his passenger should be patient, he punched buttons on a computer-radar screen. Within seconds the island's image appeared along with its coordinates. He glanced over at Colby, now sitting in the copilot's seat. "We'll fly low and fast to avoid Turkish and Greek radar and arrive in approximately three to four hours, depending on prevailing winds."

As they flew over Russia and rapidly descended as they approached the Turkish border, Colby took notice of the fully equipped assault gear. It was all there: automatic assault rifles, mini-submachine guns, a selection of pistols, scuba gear, wetsuits, black jumpsuits, climbing apparatus, one and eight-man black rubber rafts, and more. For now, in Thasos, he would rely on his old-woman disguise. Finally relaxed, he leaned back in his seat and closed his eyes as the craft cruised, pushing the maximum of 200 MPH.

When Colby had broken into the CIA computer, besides gathering overseas-agent data, he pulled up the Arctic Rose file. His mind absorbed the information. Of special interest were her family background and her real name—Megara Perrakis. Meg, for short. He'd begin by finding the Perrakis family.

"Grandmother. Grandmother." The pilot snickered aloud, "We're an hour away. What are your instructions?" He gently nudged the sleeping old woman.

Colby opened a deeply wrinkled eye to a clear blue sky and matching sea below. In the distance, a thickening haze was visible. "Can you pull up the island's dimensional image on the screen?" Smiling, the pilot poked a button and using the command roller, moved the image to view the Thasos periphery. He leaned forward and pointed to a tiny bay.

Colby cocked an eyebrow at the captain. "What makes me think you've done this before? That's the read I would have made. It's a secluded bay with overhanging foliage to camouflage the craft—and a short stroll to the center of town for an old lady. The hanging haze is an unexpected blessing. Approach low, just above the water. Set her down on the pontoons and I'll make use of the one grandma raft. It may take several hours to gather information. Take a snooze. Just keep one eye open for the local police or an inquisitive fisherman."

Pitching the craft nose down, skimming the tops of small whitecaps, the pilot stretched his neck to relieve the tension of a fairly long and utterly boring flight. "While you're drinking ouzo with the ladies, I'll stay busy draining the reserve fuel tank." He poked a thumb toward the rear. "Did you notice the large black bubble hitching a ride?" Colby nodded. "It's my own invention for an extended mission. It's a little dangerous, but I had hoped we wouldn't be shot at on the way here. Once I drain the fuel into the main tanks, we'll have more than enough to get home and then some. Then your friends can shoot at us to their heart's content." He gently patted the triggers of his twin rotary cannons, grenade, and precision missile launchers. "Of course, I'll be obliged to shoot back." They both shared a grin.

"Besides being your pilot, little grandmother," the captain said, his grin widening, "I'm your official tour guide. After several glasses of ouzo, be certain to visit the ancient city, built in the fourth century B.C., containing the sanctuaries of Theogenis and Agoraeos Zeus. Walking further south you'll come to the Roman conservatory which is a small theater of the second century A.D. Follow the small road and it will bring you to the shrine of Poseidon, also of the fourth century B.C. The Gate of Hermes…." Colby cupped his hands over his ears and shook his head, signaling an end to the tour.

***

"Ya! Kalispera! Ti kanis?" the ancient woman inquired, pulling on the frayed jacked sleeve of one of a group of men gathered in front of a corner bar. The outside bench, the bar, and surrounding building had recently been whitewashed. Even the painters who were filing into the bar for a well-earned refreshment looked whitewashed. The haze had lifted over the town of 2,300 inhabitants. No longer blocking the sun directly overhead, it forced the woman to squint her dark eyes. The entire town appeared to glimmer with blinding sunlight. Actually, it was the colored contact lens that caused the problem. The last man who had had his cuff tugged, stopped, and turned.

He angrily snatched his arm away before he saw the kindly looking figure bent with age, her sad eyes pleading. A frown switched into a smile as he asked, "What do you want of me, grandmother? I'm in a hurry."

She clutched a thread-worn embroidered bag to her chest, her hands trembling. "I've come to visit a family I haven't seen or heard from in over twenty years—the Perrakis family." She noticed his frown had returned, this time with deep furrows.

The worker turned his head away from the woman and spat on the ground. "If it's the Perrakis brood you're referring to, we ran them off the island after the father and brother were murdered." Opening the door, he looked over his shoulder and pointed to a small dirt road leading up a pine-covered mountain. "Their abandoned shack is three miles in that direction. If you see any one of them—run for your life."

Three miles there. Three miles back. Time's not in my favor. Ha! There's my transportation. Someone inside the bar had left the key to his motor scooter in the ignition. *Let's hope he plans to stay a while.* Those few pedestrians who saw the little old lady barreling up the dusty road pointed and roared with laughter. Within a mile, the road turned into a bumpy service track leading to a marble quarry. Holding on for dear life, Colby zipped past an abandoned mine and remnants of several ancient ruins. At the top of a ridge, he slammed on the brakes and came to a skidding halt, creating a billowing, choking cloud of dust. Below, he saw the shack described by the painter, nearly hidden by a thick stand of trees and brush.

Rance Colby rolled the scooter off the track, hiding it behind dense brush, facing it the way he had come, ready for a quick getaway. Undoing the skirt's hidden Velcro, he reached in and pulled out his 9mm. Holding it by his side, he slid down the hill, using the trees as a shield. At the corner of the shack, he heard movement from within. The door opened and a heavily bearded man walked out carrying a long tree trimmer. Turning, he was startled by the old lady standing behind him. A weak shaky voice asked, "Could you tell me, young man, do any members of the Perrakis family still live here?"

Menacing eyes flashed annoyance. Bushy eyebrows met, creating a long black caterpillar, half-hiding dark piercing orbs. He pointed the trimmer in the old lady's direction. Colby tightened his grip on the Beretta now buried in the folds of his skirt. "Get off my land, old one! This is no longer owned by a Perrakis," he growled, spitting on the ground as he warned her.

Tears welled in the eyes of the old lady. She pleaded for information about a family that had owed her money and her desperate need to locate any remaining Perrakis relatives. Now there were two caterpillars. The man seemed to have softened, the trimmer no longer threatening. He reached into his shirt pocket and pulled out a well-worn map of Greece. Stepping closer, he unfolded the map and pointed to a red circle in the middle of the Aegean Sea. "There's a small uncharted island here." He jabbed a dirt-crusted finger at the circle. "I'm told what remains of the dreaded Perrakis family live there. That's all I know. Go now, I have trees that need attending." With that advice, he dropped the map in the dirt and disappeared into the emerald, green forest.

Colby, still gripping the gun, picked up the map, stuffed it in his skirt pocket along with the silencer, and scampered up the hill.

Luck was with him. He placed the scooter in the spot outside the bar where he had found it. Not a soul appeared on the trail leading to where the helicopter was moored, and throwing caution to the wind, he lifted his skirt and ran like hell.

***

"The electronic screen map doesn't indicate an island in that general vicinity," the captain observed aloud. He pressed several buttons until he found what he was searching for. "Here it is!" he shouted to be heard over the roar of the engines and rotating blades. He turned to see if his passenger was paying attention. Colby had been busy changing into a black jumpsuit and selecting additional weaponry to accompany his 9mm Beretta. He had decided to take several grenades and a mini-submachine gun with him when he hit the Perrakis island beach. For the pilot's benefit, and to remain anonymous, he donned a man's black crew-cut wig and mustache.

Tapping the screen, the pilot briefed Colby on the approaching island's terrain. "There's no beach. There are piles of rock on the perimeter encircling the main compound and landscaped area. Some boulders appear as big as a small house and rise straight out of the sea. The housing structure is built in a hollowed out area in the center of the island—unseen from water level. That's to our advantage. If we hug the waves, they can't see us either." Colby's heart caught in his throat as the copter dove, then leveled off just above the whitecaps. Spray from the blades encased the craft.

Reducing speed, they could see what appeared to be a mountain of gray-black rocks and boulders looming before them, extending two hundred yards inland. "Ancient Greek gods must have used the island to dump discarded trash," the pilot said, pointing straight ahead. "I assume you want me to remain out of sight of the house, drop you off just above the first grouping of rocks, and moor just off the drop area?"

"Now I'm sure you've done this before," Colby laughed, becoming more and more impressed with General Rutskoy's personal pilot. "I'd hate to have you as an enemy. We think too much alike. Yes. We'll do just as you suggest. And we'll both hope that I return."

As the craft hovered, Rance double-checked the grenades clipped to his belt, felt for his chest-holstered Beretta, shifted the sling of the machine gun strapped across his chest, and patted his ankle stiletto. He slid the hatch open and dropped two feet to the top of a small boulder—and waved the copter off. He was on his own.

Fit as he was, Colby was forced to stop and catch his breath after five minutes of climbing up and down mounds of various size and shapes of rock. Not yet able to see the house, he had no concept of how far he had come, or how far he had to go. Taking a deep breath, he was off again in the direction his wrist compass pointed. Finally, after climbing one of the larger boulders, he spied the flat roof of a house whose structure seemed to be carved out of light gray rock. His pulse quickened as he climbed closer and was able to see the entire area. Indeed, the house was built into the side of a massive rock formation, and surrounded by a beautiful landscape of flowering bushes, low-lying fruit trees, and row upon row of bright red roses. *'Jackpot! This must be it.'* He mumbled under his breath.

In the twilight, small lights around the perimeter of an Olympic sized pool were on and glimmered in glass-like water. He was initially puzzled by the lack of electronic security, guard dogs, or armed guards. Attempting to rationalize the situation, he concluded that the occupants were probably satisfied that no one in their right mind would attempt an attack after traversing the nearly impregnable rocks. Upon further consideration—something wasn't right. Either security was well hidden—or the compound had been abandoned—though not likely. He had no choice but to proceed, with caution. Choosing to continue to use the rocks for cover, he circled to the right before dropping down to a well-manicured lawn on the darkest side of the house. Remaining statue-like, he listened for any telltale sound. Nothing. Palming his Beretta, he bent low and tiptoed along the edge of the pool and up a stone-carved stairway, overlaid with lush green hanging foliage.

Illumination from flickering candles caused an eerie shimmering glow from within. At the landing, Colby stopped to observe the exterior of the structure carved out of the rock formation. Turkish architecture dominated. Huge open doorways and numerous windows boasted sweeping arches. From what little he could observe through a window, all entrances to rooms were arched. The flooring was made of white marble; the gray walls were carved from the interior of a massive cave. With his back to the wall, he inched his way inside and down a long flight of wooden stairs to a large foyer. With eyes scanning a soaring ceiling, he listened for any sound or movement. Nothing. To his right was a private reading room with a low arched entrance and a matching arched fireplace. The high ceiling was made of dark wooden beams, the same as the fireplace mantel. All walls were whitewashed to match the marble floor. To his left was a well-equipped kitchen. About to step into the kitchen, he heard a faint sound straight ahead. As he hugged the wall along a long dark corridor, the volume increased. No one could mistake the playful giggle of a woman in the throws of passion.

Approaching the room, he crawled on hands and knees to the corner of a huge master bedroom, then lay flat, peering into the candle-lit interior. In the middle of a teakwood floor was an oversized bed hung on either side with sheer gauze drapes cascading like twin waterfalls from the high ceiling. Arched windows were carved out of stonewalls, back-lighted to provide the appearance of muted sunlight. Three body shapes twisted and turned under snow-white silk sheets. Colby glanced around; no bodyguards were visible. Now on his knees, he stretched for a better view, then stood and walked silently to the center of the room—his pistol aimed at the giggling threesome.

Politely, the man dressed in black, cleared his throat. "I'm sorry to break up this little tryst, but I find it necessary." Startled, two naked men, one on either side of the female, leapt out of bed, both tugging at their end of the sheet, trying desperately to cover their bodies. The scene, if the mission hadn't been so serious, would have been comical. Colby noticed that the men were identical twins, and with the removal of the sheet, stared intently at the object of their attention. She leaned over on one elbow, smiled, and clapped her hands. From out of a hidden chamber directly behind Colby, strode two heavily bearded, well-muscled, and well-armed guards—their assault rifles pointed at his back. Now sitting up, the naked woman's smile widened. "Mr. Colby, we've been expecting you." She made a motion with her hand. "Like a good little boy, please drop your weapons."

At the moment, he had no choice, and dropped the Beretta at his feet. A guard removed his machine gun. Both guards slung their rifles over their shoulders and roughly grabbed his arms, one on each side. He purposely struggled, forcing them to tighten their grip—just what he had hoped. Then his legs went limp—causing them to lift him off the floor.

He swung both legs forward, as his hands gripped the front of each man's jacket for balance. The swinging momentum of his legs now behind the men, Colby spread out his legs. As they came forward again with a powerful force, they struck each man's upper calf—buckling their knees from behind. Colby maintained his grasp on their jackets and pulled back as the men crashed backwards, their heads bouncing off the unforgiving floor. The moment they hit, the man in black braced for the fall, then crossed his arms. Flinging them outward in a power move—spread-eagle fashion—the sides of his hands simultaneously crushed both men's larynxes.

Rance scooped up his Beretta, and as he rolled to his right, a slug tore into the floor where he had been laying. Rolling again, he raised the pistol and hesitated. The naked woman was now standing on the bed, still smiling, and pointing a smoking gun in his direction. Having a problem balancing on the plump feather-filled bed, she too hesitated. Before squeezing the trigger, Colby thought to himself—*Those are the longest legs I've ever seen.* Then squeezed. The smile faded as a small red and black hole appeared above her left breast.

I didn't think you were Rose. You were too tall. Examining both ankles, he confirmed his quick assessment. There was no rose tattoo. From what she had said, it was apparent that they knew he was coming and were prepared. He had to leave fast. Not having to contend with the twins, who had since disappeared, he dashed past the bedroom doorway just as something caught his peripheral vision's attention. Something flashing red sat atop a large wooden designer box just inside the bedroom entrance. It was camouflaged when he had entered. One of the twins must have knocked off the draped covering in his haste to leave. Colby took one look and shouted—"Oh shit!" and sprinted for his life down the hall, through the foyer, and up the stairs.

He only had eighteen seconds to get outside and into the pool before the entire complex blew itself into the sea. Willing to sacrifice the compound and the people in the house who were unaware of the planted bomb, the Arctic Rose had taken no chances. Counting as he ran, Colby speculated that he had tripped a laser sensor when he had entered the bedroom, starting the countdown. He reached and sprang from the diving board just as the blast's impact—a billowing gold, red and orange ball of flame and scorching heat propelled him through the air toward the far end of the lengthy pool. Six feet from smacking into the opposite edge, he plunged headfirst, tucking his body like a swimmer making a turn. Both legs pushed off as he headed for the bottom, pulling hard to reach the diving board. Huge chunks of rock and flaming slivers of wood splashed above. Avoiding the sinking debris, he flattened himself against the wall under the board for safety as the sky overhead rained down with what remained of Megara Perrakis' palatial estate. He could still hear the loud roar of flames but falling debris had stopped. Pulling himself out of the pool, he glanced back. Flames reached for the heavens out of a gaping hole where a beautiful house once stood. A burst from an automatic weapon spun him around. Looking over his shoulder as he ran across the lawn, he could count at least a dozen armed men climbing over the last pile of rocks at the far side of the tiny island. Rose was hedging her bet. She wasn't taking any chances. She wanted Rance Colby dead.

Rounds tore into the turf by his feet as he dove for the temporary safety of rocks and boulders. He grabbed his shoulder after bouncing off a large rock. It hurt, but that was the least of his worries. As he climbed and sometimes fell over and around the rocks, heading for where he hoped the captain was moored, bullets ricocheted everywhere. His attackers sprayed the rocks where they assumed he was hiding, hoping a careening slug would hit its mark. He dare not expose himself. The 9mm was no match for that many men and their deadly weapons, and as they had assumed correctly, he had been hit twice. One, a minor flesh wound to his right arm, the other where a chunk of rock had chipped off, slicing his left cheek. He tossed three grenades that the guards failed to remove, one after another, in three directions and scampered up and down the never-ending mountain of rocks.

Nearly out of breath, he was gasping hard, his throat raw. His eyes darted about wildly, searching for the best escape route. Streams of perspiration trickled down his temples, and beads dripped from his chin. The enemy's shouts seemed to be coming closer. Suddenly he heard the deafening wapp-wapp of chopper blades, then a loud whoosh of a missile, followed by a massive explosion from beyond the rocks on the far side of the island. A billow of smoke appeared soon after. The Russian helicopter hovered overhead, its nose peering down into the rock crevasses—rotating cannons cutting down man after man. Rance mustered the courage to stand on a rock to view the slaughter—and thrust his fist in triumph. Grenades were launched at a fresh group of men in an open area on the lawn. Within minutes, bloody bodies lay strewn about the island surface. Not a man moved. The only sound was the welcome noise of the wapp, wapp, wapp. Off in the distance lay the smoldering wreckage of the ship that had brought the assassins.

Climbing up the chain ladder of the hovering craft, Colby collapsed from exhaustion onto the floor. The pilot motioned to the copilot's seat. Following the direction, he sat down and strapped himself in. After they were well underway, he unzipped his jumpsuit to his waist and pulled his right arm free to check his wound. Just as he had thought, he had only been creased, his blood already congealed.

Poking a thumb over his shoulder, the pilot said, "There's a first aid kit in the back and while you're at it—put something on that facial wound—it's beginning to look infected."

Colby stripped to his shorts. After cleaning his wounds and applying a bandage to his arm, he disinfected the deep cheek gash. He removed the old-lady disguise from the large embroidered threadbare carpetbag, but before applying makeup, he placed a strip of antiseptic tape on his cheek. The captain chuckled to himself as the old lady took the copilot's seat.

"Whoever was after you sure as hell wanted you dead in a bad way. That beautiful estate was blown to smithereens, and close to two dozen men lost their lives on that island—as well as their boat."

"You're one fine shot, Captain. That missile was right on target." Rance thought a moment and added, "There were at least five people inside that house, that I know of, who also unnecessarily forfeited their lives." He was through talking. "Wake me when we're home." Eyes fluttered, then closed. The old woman was soon fast asleep.

The attack helicopter skimmed the water and remained low until crossing the Turkish border, then climbed to its cruising altitude over Russian territory. "Wake up grandmother. It's celebration time."

Colby slowly opened his eyes. It was pitch black outside the craft. Inside, the green, white, and red buttons and instruments glowed, illuminating the cockpit. "Are we home yet, grandson?"

"Not just yet. But it is refreshment time. See that white knob to your right on the instrument panel? Turn it and pull down." Rance followed orders, twisted and pulled. There before him was a tabletop with two silver cups in snug holders. Deep inside the compartment was an unopened bottle of expensive Russian Vodka. "That too is my invention. You are old enough to partake?" the pilot grinned.

Colby rubbed his hands together, twisted off the cap and poured. "Your General Rutskoy is a very understanding guy." He handed a cup to the pilot.

"Oh yes, he's the best general in Russia. Perhaps the best the mother country has ever bred." He took a healthy sip of vodka and laughed aloud, pulled off his goggled helmet, and ran a palm over his closely cropped layer of silver hair. This was the first time that Rance had seen the pilot's face, always hidden by the headgear. Above a wide toothy grin, lay a bristly silver mustache. Deep-set icy blue eyes twinkled with humor, emphasizing wrinkled laugh lines that had witnessed fifty or more years of laughter and pain. He lifted his cup in a salute to Colby's safe return.

The salute was returned. "And here's to you for your valuable assistance and perfect aim. I couldn't have succeeded without you, Captain."

A loud roar filled the cabin. Slapping his thigh, the pilot turned to Colby. "For your edification, my American friend—it's not captain—it's General Rutskoy from now on."

Colby's jaw fell open.

General Rutskoy's grin disappeared. "You think I'm too old to be a combat pilot?"

"No. If I had even entertained the thought, your recent actions would have more than proved me wrong. That is, if I had known who you really were in the first place." He filled the outstretched silver cup. "But why you? What happened to your regular pilot?"

A smile reappeared on the well-tanned oval face. "Do you think I would trust a friend of my son's godfather to a mere stranger?" This time, he reached over and slapped the old woman's thigh. Colby knew it would leave a mark. "Hell, I wouldn't have missed it for the world. That's the most fun this old general has had since Rubin Brock and I cleaned out a Spanish tavern of a bunch of rowdy, rude French naval officers. Your general has one mean right-cross."

For the remainder of the flight, Rance silently mulled over the reality that the Arctic Rose and her people had been aware of his plan to discover her whereabouts, and they had relied on his ingenuity to find her if clues were made available. They had purposely guided him along the way. The woodcutter and the map were too obvious, with hindsight. Who is the informer? This he had to discover before it was too late.

Rance Colby jumped down from the helicopter and extended his hand to General Rutskoy, once again thanking him for his help. Turning away, he could barely make out what Rutskoy said over the wapp, wapp, wapp. "When you see that old rascal, give Rubin a great big Russian bear hug for me!"

They're a perfect set of bookends—those generals.

Chapter Eight

Only one member of the committee of nine was missing: the recently deceased Lester Michaels, the late Chief of Navy Intelligence. Max Carlton, Director of the Central Intelligence Agency, sat behind the timeworn wobbly desk on the second floor of the D Street Library, usually manned by Secretary Thomas Cline, but this meeting was hastily convened by Carlton. It was his call. Also absent, but not a member, was Clifford Grayson, ex-President of the United States.

Max Carlton stood up and said nothing, his silence demanding attention. When everyone had ceased their individual conversations, he sat down. "Gentlemen, we can relax now. The hunt of our *Overlay assassin* is over. Rance Colby is dead. It has been reported that a body matching his description was fished out of the Moskva River, downstream from Moscow."

The room buzzed with animated applause and a universal feeling of relief. General Rubin Brock sat stunned, his face carved in stone. Was this true? Was America's only hoped to survive an international crisis dead? "Max!" he shouted aloud, commanding everyone's attention. But before he could ask his question, the director's laptop computer chimed.

Carlton held a finger aloft. "Hold that thought, Rubin; this is the data on the deceased subject that I've been expecting." He read aloud from the screen. "Subject's physical description and features, although badly decomposed due to massive facial bone trauma and expected fish and rodent damage are a perfect match for the sought-after target. However, a check of fingerprints showed that they had been badly distorted by acid prior to his death. From their appearance, it is determined by local forensic experts that the erasing occurred years ago. Luckily, one thumbprint and a forefinger had grown back sufficiently to be readable.

Both were run through our files and Interpol without success. No match was found." Max's original expression of glee turned sour.

Shoving the computer aside, he looked at Cline. "You must have Colby's prints on file—somewhere?" Then he thought about the question and said, "He was just a wispy shadow before you had him deprogrammed—no photographs, prints, address—before that. But surely you lifted his prints while he went under the knife, or whatever you bastards did to him?"

Secretary Cline appeared to shrink in his old wooden chair. "No, we didn't. The scientists and doctors weren't CIA—that wouldn't have even crossed their minds."

"The coffee pot and cups!" James Cochran, Chairman of the Foreign Intelligence Committee, had just remembered the time that Colby served them coffee.

Cline ran a pudgy palm over his bald dome. "No good. Alice would have washed the pot and cups dozens of times since that day."

General Brock could no longer control his anger. He stood, shoved his chair aside, and gestured to the laptop. "Is there someone live at the other end of that damned device?" Max acknowledged that there was. "Good. And are he and the forensic experts present with the body?" Again, Max nodded.

"Well get on that blasted thing and ask them to describe bodily scars." Max's fingers flew across the keys. He hit send and sat back, trying not to lock eyes with the seven stern-looking faces.

Four agonizing minutes passed before the laptop jingled. You could hear a pin drop. Even their breathing was shallow. "It says only one visible scar. A wide three-and-a-half-inch horizontal scar across his left bicep."

"It's not the body of Rance Colby," Cline blurted out. "I was witness to his naked body on a clinic gurney." He walked to the front of the room, pointing to himself, indicating where Colby's scars were located.

"There was a rather nasty red scar inside his right thigh—another on the upper left shoulder—and a long thin scar across his right chest." Slowly walking back to his chair, he added, "There could have been others on his back, but I didn't have the opportunity to view them." He poked a finger at the computer. "That. That dead man isn't Rance Colby."

"Goddamn it!" Max slammed the computer closed. "We're right back to square one." He scowled in the direction of his Director of Special Projects. "Oakley, you stay. The rest of you go about your business."

The Chairman of the Joint Chief's barrel chest heaved a sigh. He lowered his head and said a silent prayer for the man he had come to greatly admire, Rance Colby.

***

Suspicious eyes followed the ancient-looking woman shuffling across the thick-carpeted foyer of the famed Rossiya Hotel. She seemed not to belong but appeared to know where she was going. Stopping to pick up the house phone, a shaking finger punched in the room number. A deep male voice acknowledged the call. She grinned, and whispered, "This is your grandmother, sonny boy—just wanted you to know that I was on the way up to join you—so don't shoot me through the door when I insert the key card."

Grandma was met at the door by a short, round bowling ball, fire-plug-built man, with a breath-squeezing hug. She beat him off, defending herself with her large, embroidered bag. "Unhand me, you Italian thug—or I'll tear out your pruning shears."

L' Ami stood in the adjoining room doorway, laughing himself silly. "I'm happy to see you're all in one piece, including your sense of humor."

As he discarded the disguise, Rance described his unsuccessful attempt to kill or capture the Arctic Rose, including his harrowing escape from the island, and his surprise when learning of the pilot's identity. After stripping to his shorts and removing makeup, he headed for the refrigerator. Leaving the door open and holding up the one remaining bottle of beer, he shot Arturo a nasty look.

The Italian shrugged a shoulder and nodded his head in Al's direction. "He told me that you gave instructions for me to save you a beer." He pointed at the bottle. "So I saved you *a* beer."

Before Rance could react, Al gestured to the open door of the adjoining room. "For your benefit," he grinned, "we moved it all into our refrigerator. There's plenty more where that came from."

Arturo rubbed his stomach. "We haven't eaten dinner yet—too concerned to leave the room until we heard from you. How about ordering room service? Then we can bring you up to date on Al's local contact activity."

"Sounds good to me. I'm famished, too. One can build up an appetite when blown up and being shot at." He walked over and poked A.T.'s solid round girth. "And how's the knife wound? Tell us about it."

Waiting for the food to arrive, Arturo graphically explained his hand-to-hand tussle with three of Rose's assassins. He was certain they were her associates from the questions shouted as they threatened his life—and from the lips of the last dying man. His initial concern was the fire that threatened the villa and the welfare of his flower garden. Damage was minimal, workers were busy with repairs, and the garden was blooming brightly.

Testaccio's face grew dark; he touched his forehead with a finger. "How's your head? Anymore spells?"

L' Ami took a swallow of his whisky and answered for Rance. "Prior to leaving, he had a nightmare that drenched him with perspiration."

Rance rolled his eyes, knowing that failure to respond would result in a stinging tongue-lashing. "You look like you need another beer," he said, heading toward the next room. A.T. answered with a nasty looking scowl. He flipped a beer to Arturo and glared at Al for letting the cat out of the bag. "Yes, I had a dream, that's all." Changing the subject, he explained what had happened to him while being pursued by Rose's assassins on the island, and an unexpected surprise.

"Just after the blast, and as I ran for my life and the cover of the boulders—slugs whizzing all around, I felt it happening again. My head hurt like hell. But as I dove for cover, I slammed into a large boulder with my shoulder." He massaged it and moved his arm in a circular motion. "It's still a little sore and stiff." A raised palm cut A.T. short. "Here's the kicker. The pain I experienced, bouncing off that rock, stopped the spell in its tracks. The normal excruciating headache and blinding flashes immediately disappeared."

Another raised palm shut A.T.'s mouth. He was chomping at the bit to be heard, but Colby continued. "Perhaps when I become aware of the spell coming on, I can exert some form of pain, and master the problem"

Arturo had heard enough. He pushed up from his chair and faced Rance who was standing by the bed. Shoving his friend backward, he said, "Who in the hell do you think you're bullshitting? That's crap! You've got a problem that may get you killed," he pointed to himself and Al, "and us along with you. Face it. You need help. And if you don't seek help after this is all over," he looked out over the darkened skyline of the Kremlin, "I'll drag your sorry ass screaming *I don't want to go* all the way to the shrink."

"And I'll help him," Al chimed in.

Rance sunk back into his bed, an expression of defeat crossing his face, then smiled. "You two are something else. There are no two better friends. Okay. Agreed. After this mission is over, I'll seek professional help, but on one condition." He paused for their reaction. Two frowns and four piercing eyes waited for him to state the condition. "This is the last assignment anyone of us will accept. We'll retire. Arturo and I have discussed this subject briefly. We all have enough money stashed away to last several lifetimes, and let's not kid ourselves, we're getting a little too long in the tooth to be running around getting shot at." He pointed at L' Ami. "And you're older than both of us."

Failing to appreciate his friend's backhanded observation, Al knew Rance was right. He and A.T. nodded to each other, then in tandem, nodded in Rance's direction. It was agreed.

They flinched at the soft knock at the door. A.T. checked his watch and rubbed his stomach for the third time. "Hope that's room service."

The small table from A.T. and Al's room was moved into Rance's and shoved together to accommodate the enormous spread of food that Arturo had ordered. Rance scratched his head. "Are we expecting guests, or is this dinner—and tomorrow's breakfast and lunch?"

Arturo patted his stomach and licked his lips. "I'm a growing Italian boy."

Al nudged Rance with an elbow. "Yeah, we can both see that."

"Hey. We're supposed to be teaming up against him," said Arturo, pointing a turkey leg at Rance and tossing a pork chop at Al, "not you and he against me."

Rance raised both hands. "Okay, enough already. Let's sit down and eat, and I'll tell you what I'll be doing first thing tomorrow. Then, Al, you're on next. Fill me in on where you have your contacts placed."

***

Max Carlton sat staring at his Special Projects Director. The silent stare caused Alan Oakley to squirm in his chair. Max had his suspicions about Oakley's involvement in the car crash, the Michaels' suicide, and now Grayson's stroke and heart attack. Could it have been a managed death? Could Secretary Cline, who was with Grayson at the time of his death, and Oakley be collaborators? It was the CIA Director's strategy to explain what had happened to Grayson and the whereabouts of the ex-president's body, to see if the event would be leaked. That—he could directly trace to his man, Oakley. That's why he had had him remain behind after the others left the library upstairs room. But now, on second thought, he felt that keeping the body's hiding place a secret was far too important to chance a leak. No. He now had other plans. He'd sit and stare a little longer, letting the project director squirm, allowing his imagination to run amuck.

Without a word, Max Carlton rose and walked to the elevator, turned, locked eyes with Oakley, and smiled at his puzzled expression. Max stepped in and punched—DOWN. *Let the crafty little bugger stew in his own juices.*

***

"First thing in the morning, I'm going to frequent Moscow's version of a Goodwill Shop. There are several scattered about to service those in need—which include most of the poor families visible on every street corner and in darkened doorways."

"If you're short on clothes," L' Ami offered, "I'll lend you one of my bib overalls," knowing full well what Rance was up to.

The suggestion was ignored. "I plan on gathering various worn garments, of both genders, from at least six strategic locations throughout the city—along with six small bags to hold each outfit and matching disguises. There should be a bus or train stop, or hotel locker, church, or abandoned building—where I can cache each bag. If I'm spotted anywhere in Moscow, I'll have both the opportunity and ability to become someone else and disappear, blending into the crowd. Perhaps even stalk the stalker." Blue-denim eyes glowed with anticipation; a wide grin deepened his dimples as he brushed back a few strands of light brown hair.

L' Ami performed his best Sean Connery impression. "The thought of hide 'n seek, seek, and destroy, still excites you, doesn't it?"

For the second time tonight, one of Al's comments was ignored. "Let's forget about me and get to the next essential element of a successful mission." Rance looked at Al with a deadpan expression. "How many local contacts have you enlisted, what were your instructions, and what have they reported back? If anything."

"From several earlier clandestine visits to Russia, seven loyal contacts were cultivated and remain available." Al's eyes narrowed as he finished his drink and motioned to A.T. for a refill. "You know my procedure. Only two of my contacts are aware of my identity, and it's money that maintains their loyalty." He gestured with his hand, rubbing a thumb and finger together. "Each of my magnificent seven has mustered five reliable contacts of their own. Within the next ten days, there may be more. Of the present thirty-five, none are aware of who we are or the reason behind their assignment. As before, they'll blindly follow directions. Each team is responsible for an area of the city, spread out in hub fashion. Importantly, everyone is eminently familiar with Moscow's underworld and its players." He shrugged a shoulder. "They're part of it, and that's where they'll be stationed. If an unknown player should emerge, or someone known appear suspicious, it will be brought to my attention. It's too soon for any report."

Rance nodded his satisfaction. "Right on top of it, as usual. Unless otherwise stipulated, we'll all meet in my room every night at six o'clock for debriefing our day's activity." He threw up both hands. "After that, you're on your own. You can't remain monks every minute you're here." He caught A.T.'s eye. "Can you?"

Colby stood, stretched, then pulled out computer printouts from a suitcase hidden pocket. He tossed them on the table. "Here are photos of CIA agents in Moscow, their dossiers, office and living quarter locations. Including personal expertise, habits, quirks, and known Russian informants. Study them; I've memorized the information."

Al and Arturo reviewed the data while Rance walked over to the refrigerator and removed a jar of olives. "This is just what I need," he commented, mixing his favorite drink. Savoring the first swallow, he sat on the edge of the bed and attempted to fold his legs under him. "Oh, I'm too old to sit like that. If I did, it would take both of you to unfold me, and I'd never walk again.

"Tomorrow, Al will touch base with team chiefs and remain available for reports." He snapped his fingers as he thought of something else. "Have the magnificent seven provide you with the names of their men— and compare it with the list of CIA informants. We can't afford a mole in our midst."

Now it was A.T.'s turn. "I want you to play the Italian tourist. Visit the Kremlin for the next few days. Begin identifying buildings, floors, office space, exits and entrances where CIA personnel are located, as well as their haunts, bars, restaurants, barbershops, dry cleaners, brothels, you know the drill."

Colby finished his instructions and chewed on an olive. A dreamy faraway expression appeared as he glanced toward the opened window and the dying sounds of a nearly silent Moscow night. "I know you too well, old friend. If Molly were on your mind, you would have displayed a devilish smile." A.T. said, gathering the computer pages and handing them to L' Ami. "No, you were thinking of that ice bitch, Rose—placing yourself in her spiked heels—attempting to anticipate her next move."

"You're right, trash man. And I'd give anything to know her whereabouts so I could go after her again. Terminating the Arctic Rose would end this here and now." He downed the martini, stood facing his friends, and with a somber tone, said, "Thanks for your friendship and loyalty. God willing, after this is over, I hope we have the opportunity to enjoy each other's company from time to time, under pleasurable circumstances." He grinned and pointed to the adjoining room door. "Will someone please roll the food out to the hallway, and then don't let your room door hit your butts on the way out. I have a special dream programmed for tonight."

***

Two men sat huddled in a small sound-secure room in the West Wing of the White House, the only room devoid of a tape recorder. Hands clasped behind, slightly bent, and deep in thought, the tall slim figure of a man smartly dressed in a navy blue suit paced back and forth. The expression on his face appeared as dark as his full head of black hair. Muscles in a square jaw pulsated. Coming to a halt in front of a man sitting on the rustic leather sofa, he tore off his suit jacket, tossed it on the couch, and roughly loosened a red power tie. He shouted with animation, holding his wrists together in front of him. "Steven, my hands are bound. I can't do a goddamned thing without blowing the whistle on you and exposing this insane business to our allies and the entire world."

A host of freckles exploded on Steven Heywood's blush-laden face. His head resembled a mop from nervously running fingers through his red hair. President Willard Rhoades' Special Assistant on International Security Affairs had been at a loss for words until now. Timidly, he offered an opinion, talking to the floor, unable to face his boss' glare.

"There's an international alert out for this man, Rance Colby—President Grayson's creation. They're certain to find him any day now, before any more harm is done." His eyes remained glued to his shoe tops.

"You can guarantee that?"

Haywood took a deep breath and forced himself to raise his eyes. "No I can't. But…"

Rhoades made a gesture with his hand, angrily waving away Haywood's words. "This entire scenario is crazy, insane. Just like that old bastard, Grayson. Where in the hell is he, anyway? It's like he's vanished off the face of the earth. Why didn't he do us a favor and disappear before he was elected?"

"Cline said that he was on an extended ocean voyage and didn't wish to be disturbed. No one's aware of his route or location. The strangest part is that his ship hasn't been picked up by our satellites. Of course he could be anchored in a remote harbor somewhere. We just don't know, Mister President."

Rhoades resumed walking, his arms flailing wildly as he spoke. "Hell! I can't even talk to my Joint Chiefs. Nobody in government—or I'll blow your cover. I need you at those clandestine meetings, or I'll never know what's going on behind my back. And I can't go public with this; it'll destroy our nation's credibility. The President of the United States is essentially dead in the water. I'm completely helpless, damn it!"

The one-sided, heated conversation continued for another fifteen minutes before they emerged from their secret meeting. President

Rhoades walked briskly toward the Oval Office, followed by a Secret Service agent. Steven Haywood walked slowly, red-faced, toward the nearest exit. Outside an adjacent office stood a familiar figure known to all. Small dark eyes squinted in thought. Sagging jowls and a puffy face tightened in anger. Secretary Thomas Cline removed a handkerchief and dabbed perspiration from his hairless face and crown. *Just as I had suspected. A Judas. There's no doubt in my mind.*

***

"I'll remain in the room for most of the day," L'Ami said, holding up his GlobalPhone, "and insist that my people provide me with a current appraisal of their activities." He looked at the frowning face of Andrei Zakharov and added, "It's scrambled."

Andrei grasped the bottom of his full beard and nodded approval. One finger pointed to the Italian tourist, dressed in tan shorts that fell below his knees and topped with a black and yellow flowered vest over a plum-colored long sleeve shirt. Sunglasses were wedged atop a bald crown; a video camera sat in his ample lap. Rance Colby, posing as the eccentric poet, Andrei Zakharov, raised his eyes to the ceiling. "Assuming that you're not arrested for indecent exposure or creating a fashion riot, and besides the assignment we discussed last night—see what you can discover about President Velichkin's schedule for the next ten to fourteen days." He turned his head to the side and looked directly at A.T.'s exposed legs. "Man, with those calves, you'd never pull on a pair of cowboy boots."

Arturo raised both palms in protest. "Am I on a spy mission or entering a beauty contest?" He pointed back at his friend. "If you lifted your pant legs…"

L' Ami finished A.T.'s sentence. "I know what you're talking about. "I've seen better legs on a piano." Both friends laughed, fingers pointed at their leader.

"Okay, I'm out of here," Colby sneered. "See both of you at six, and Trash Man—try not to get lost."

Rance saw the young boy's mother standing with a red-cheeked smile, holding a flat wooden box of pears for a passerby to choose. Her hands were as rough as any man's. A white scarf circled her face. Under a dark blue, three-quarter length vest, she wore a faded pink long-sleeved shirt; around her waist was a well-worn gray apron. "Hey, Mr. Andrei!" shouted the youngster with the bright blue hooded jacket, floppy-eared sneakers, and a smile that brightened Colby's morning.

Rance purchased a pear from his mother, walked a few steps away, and squatted down to address the boy. "You know my name, but I don't know yours."

"Josef!" he blurted out in excited anticipation of the promised job.

"Okay, Josef. Your nickname is *Joe* while you work for me. Is that all right with you?" Joe's head bobbed up and down like a doll sitting in the back of an old Chevy. "This must be between you and me. No one else." Joe's head continued bobbing. "I've got some errands to do, but when I come back, I'll explain everything." He pulled back Joe's hood and tousled his thick blond curls. Joe enthusiastically waved good-bye.

Rance Colby, alias Andrei Zakharov wrapped in his long black cape, decided to begin in an area around the Bolshoi Theatre, located several blocks behind the walled Kremlin, and then circle back. He was aware of a shop that sold used theater costumes and makeup. There just might be something of interest to add to his kit. In no hurry, he took the time to observe Moscow's mixture of humanity.

Young students found the edges of statues and building steps to sit and read their lessons. An old man sat in an alcove of a church reading his newspaper, oblivious to the black-clad Orthodox monk and nun collecting money on the street corner. The traffic cop, in full dress uniform, complete with shiny black knee top leather boots and matching billed cap, kept one eye on the crushing stream of cars, and the other on the money collectors. His dark green, red-trimmed uniform coat hung down to the top of his boots; red and gold-trimmed epaulets were the final touch to an impressive military presence.

Delicious aroma of coffee swirled on the early morning breeze, reaching out to the wandering poet through colorful sheer curtains of the coffee shop's open window. Peeking in, he saw crisp red and white checkered tablecloths, scenes of old Russia on the walls, and a cheery-looking heavyset woman beckoning him in with both hands.

Colby closed his eyes, held the coffee cup under his nose, and deeply inhaled. The aroma satisfied his senses, cleansing his mind. This was the first time in months that he truly felt relaxed, other than when he and Molly had been together. A mixture of young office workers and older neighborhood patrons filled the small coffee shop. A large slice of black bread piled high with homemade blueberry preserves soon disappeared along with a second cup of coffee. Holding the cup over his head caught the attention of the shop's jolly hostess. Steam poured from the container as well as fresh-smelling black liquid. He held the cup to his nose, laid it down, shut his eyes and leaned back until his head rested against the wall. A dozen whispered conversations became his mantra as he relaxed, blending without notice into a dimly lit far corner of the pleasant café.

His eyes snapped open, alert to the pleading outburst by the plump proprietor. "I told you before; I can't afford to pay you! Please leave me alone. Get out!"

Fully alert, Colby sat upright in his chair. He heard a whispered comment from the next table. "Young Russian Mafia—the bastards."

"Don't, you're hurting my wrist," she screamed as one of three men standing side-by-side in front of the counter, reached across and roughly twisted her wrist. Within seconds, the caped man leapt to his feet and flung his body horizontally, like a football player's cross-body block, collapsing all three men's knees simultaneously. As they were bent backwards, their knees crashed into the counter. Colby rolled away, just in time to see one of the prone men pull a knife from his jacket pocket. A foot quickly pinned his forearm to the floor. The other stomped down hard on the hand grasping the weapon. Everyone in the café heard small bones crack before his cry of pain. The bearded man in the black cape reached across the counter and lifted the coffee pot from its warmer, splashing the other two stunned ruffians with the steaming liquid. One lay on his side grasping his broken hand to his chest. Those scalded moaned and held their faces in their hands, attempting to scramble to their feet. One at a time, a firm foot pinned them to the floor.

"This is only a sample of the hell you'll receive if you ever show your ugly faces in here again." In turn, he kicked each man. "Do you understand?" They wailed in concert. The two red-faced smalltime hoodlums lifted their wounded buddy and stumbled out the door.

Cheers and applause from the café crowd startled the smiling owner's caped hero. First confused by their reaction, he hadn't given the incident any thought; it had been an act of pure instinct on his part. She hugged him with two powerful arms, smothering him with wet kisses. Struggling unsuccessfully to free himself, pleading for help, he peered wide-eyed over the thankful woman's shoulder. *It's a damn good thing this beard is glued on. Let go of me, woman.*

Finally prying her arms loose, he fumbled for his money. "How much do I owe you, *Zhenshchina?* I must be on my way." He didn't wish to bring any more attention to the incident.

A lively stirring of both arms was overwhelming evidence that she was energetically refusing payment. As he backed out the door, she threw him kisses of gratitude and followed him into the street, exclaiming it was she that owed him. Most of the patrons spilled into the street, noisily waving good-bye. Trying not to run and gather undue attention to himself, he briskly walked away, turned the corner, and vanished into Novy Arbat's milling crowd of late morning shoppers.

Novy Arbat is the main western route, connecting the Trinity Gate of the Kremlin with the Kalinin Bridge over the Moskva River. Although barely a kilometer long, the high-rises on either side give it an airy appearance with its wide promenade. Colby noticed that the upper floors appeared to house office space, the ground floor featured supermarkets, department stores, and service agencies. Of special interest to Colby and his associates, on the high bank of the Moskva River, was Moscow's 'White House,' Russia's former Parliament building.

Satisfied he had escaped, Colby resumed a normal meandering gait, even stopping to peruse store windows, ever mindful of the reflections of suspicious forms and prying eyes. He had all day to make purchases and drops; why not enjoy the sights and smells of the city, he had carelessly asked himself. *There's something I've always wanted to do—have my palm read.*

A young woman had just left the bench where a middle-aged man dressed in a tie-less, wrinkled dark business suit and wearing a matching tam, held a giant magnifying glass. His pointed ears reminded Colby of Mr. Spock of the Starship Enterprise. Somewhat amused with the thought, he sat down and showed both palms. The pale-looking man's thin lips parted slightly; nodding, he held the gold-rimmed glass over one hand, then the other. He frowned, then repeating the process, his frown deepened. Glancing up at his client, his eyes widened. Uttering a gut-wrenching grunt, he suddenly bolted away.

Stunned, Colby's first reaction was to run and catch the fool but thought better of the idea. He had enough excitement for one morning, and although he'd swap A.T.'s testicles to know what had frightened the guy, he wasn't too sure he wanted to know. The gray-haired lady occupying the bench across from him caught his eye. She wore a long bright red sweater and held up a large two-toned furry puppy for him to see. Her impish facial expression and round black eyes hinted—*He's for sale if you want him.* Colby smiled back and politely shook his head, speculating that once he and Molly were married, or at least together, they'd have a dog. He had always wanted one.

***

At least two dozen tourists crowded Spasskaya Tower, the entrance to the walled Kremlin. Before leaving the hotel, Arturo had purchased a plum-colored tam to match his shirt and to keep the bright Moscow sun from scorching his shiny dome. He returned the smiles of those who found humor in the way he had fixed it on his head, cocked defiantly to one side.

One eyebrow lifted as he observed two young people waiting in line. *And they thought I looked strange.* The boy wore a black bandana, black leather shirt with an extra wide, chrome-studded belt, badly torn blue jeans, and flaunted a hint of whiskers that when covered with milk, a cat could lick off. His pregnant friend wore a Russian flag dress over a black and white striped long-sleeve shirt. Her black hair was shaved on either side of her head, with the exception of long stringy sideburns, and topped with a golden-colored Mohawk. Both wore earrings. An old man turned to his wife and remarked for all to hear. "Western decadence." The kid playing the 'bad dude' ignored the comment; his significant other stuck out her tongue.

Arturo had spent the morning studying and shooting videos of the office buildings surrounding the Kremlin's walls. He was unable to spot any of the individuals on his mental list and only identified three of their office locations. Two other sites were within the walls. Recalling the story of Napoleon's 1812 mishap, A.T. entered the tower and removed his hat, as did everyone except the bandana-clad kid. Spasskaya Tower was regarded as being holy. Elated by his victory, Napoleon had decided to ride his white horse through the tower in defiance of tradition—not bothering to remove his hat. As he paraded through, his horse, suddenly startled, reared up, nearly throwing his master, and causing him to lose his hat.

Noticing the time on the tower clock, A.T.'s stomach growled its displeasure with the late noon hour. *Settle down, old man. I'll shoot some video from a few angles on those remaining office buildings, find a nice quiet restaurant outside, fill you up,* he patted his middle, *and return to look around for a few more hours.* Of particular interest would be the residence of the President of Russia, the triangle-shaped connecting buildings close to the Nikolskaya Tower.

A short stroll around the wall and across from Red Square was a very appealing small eatery. He could see the Lenin Mausoleum from its entrance. The sharp-angled red and black architecture looked like something Frank Lloyd Wright would have designed. Three soldiers drinking and laughing, sitting at an outdoor table, caught his attention. From their appearance, he assumed that they were on leave or had just finished a shift of duty. All outdoor tables were occupied, but that had never deterred the Italian before. He sashayed up to the table of cheerful soldiers, placed his tam over his heart, smiled, bowed, and said, "*Izviniti.* If I were to purchase rounds of *piva*, might I join you at your table? Italian tourists are notoriously thirsty." He pointed to himself and laughed.

With boisterous shouts of joy, camaraderie, and anticipated free beer, they invited A.T. to become their benefactor. "*Minya zavut*, Arturo Pascucci," he announced with typical Italian fanfare, sitting in the offered chair. In turn, the soldiers introduced themselves in broken English while waving for a waitress' attention. They had finished a twelve-hour security shift and were winding down. Waiting for one of the two servers, A.T. learned that one man was a guard at the Palace of Congresses, another at the Premisses of the Supreme Soviet in Russia, and the least animated of the three, within the President's residence. He also discovered that they made a habit of meeting there every day at the same time. The manager wisely reserved their table.

Arturo learned a few Russian jokes and he told a few, joining in the laughter, but becoming impatient, thirsty, and hungry. Finally, a spindly-figured girl with beautiful features, holding a pencil and pad, approached the table. Beers were ordered as well as plates of cold cuts, cheese, and two loaves of bread. Signor Pascucci jabbed a thumb at the retiring waitress. "She needs some meat on those bones. A body could get cut with those sharp knees and elbows." They all howled and pounded the table with their bottles. He was aware that his next joke would be crass and unkind but would be a big hit with his newfound friends. He drew a finger across his chest. "Know what she has tattooed there?" Leaning forward, they shook their heads. "In case of rape—this side up."

A.T. had been right. They nearly fell out of their chairs. One, looking as though he was about to pee his pants, slapped him on his back and pointed to the door. "Here comes her twin sister with food and drinks."

Twin? Damned if she isn't. But this one was as heavy as the other one was skinny, but with the same beautiful features. In her case there was no need for a tattoo on that ample chest. A billboard for an ocean liner wouldn't fill the space. After depositing two trays filled with food and beer bottles, she turned sharply, nearly hitting one of the men in the face with her right breast. A.T.'s eyes grew wide as he watched her navigate her way between tables. He pointed to the target of the near catastrophe and shouted, "If her bra strap had broken, you would have been knocked clean off your chair, received a concussion, and a pension from the army!"

Tears flowed freely from the soldiers' eyes. Slapping each other on the back, they pointed at their Italian benefactor and laughed hysterically. Arturo's humor received the reaction for which he had hoped. Under much protest, he stood, tossed more than enough money on the table, and begged their forgiveness. "I wish to visit more of your beautiful city before the sunlight fades," he held up his video camera. "But since I've enjoyed your company so much, could I join you tomorrow at the same time? I'm buying." Turning his back among claps and cheers, he wandered back toward the Spasskaya Tower. *Two more days of plying them with booze, and my charming sense of humor, and they'll be eating out of my hand. Who knows? Their cultivated friendship could prove to be most useful in days ahead.*

Arturo had always thought of himself as a spiritual person, but not particularly religious. That was until he had visited the Cathedral of The Annunciation with its five golden peaked domes topped with huge crucifixes. The beautiful Byzantine frescoes caused him to reflect. Especially impressive, he thought, was the oak door covered with sheets of copper, engraved with twenty Biblical scenes and inscriptions made in gold and black lacquer. *'This has to rival the Vatican,'* he whispered to himself in Italian. After pausing to gather his thoughts, he exited the walled area and headed for the hotel.

***

Colby, alias the eccentric poet from Kropotkin, had a productive day. Pleased with his purchase of several items from the theater's used-costume store and stashing of six bags of emergency clothing, he stopped in front of Russia's version of a Radio Shack store. As he watched the TV screen in the window, a reporter began to interview the lady who owned the coffee shop he had frequented earlier that morning. Quickly entering the store, he stood mesmerized. Her comments were obscured by the news anchor's narrative highlighted over the picture and sound.

"Early this morning, Sudarynya Sholokhov, proprietor of a small coffee shop, was threatened by three toughs offering protection for money. Other businesses in the area, having been threatened by this form of extortion, have also come forward. The three men, one whose hand had been badly crushed, the other two scalded by hot coffee, were quickly apprehended by the authorities at a nearby street-side hospital clinic. It appears that a bearded stranger dressed in a black cape, v-shaped wool cap, and whose hair hung into his eyes, dispatched the ruffians..."

Colby, his mind alert to what was necessary, turned on his heels and left the store before he drew the attention of a curious clerk. Two shops down was a men's haberdashery. Prior to entering, he stuffed his hat into a large bag bulging with two theatrical costumes, removed his cape and placed it over his arm. Inside the store, he picked out a pair of rose-tinted, oblong-shaped, wire-rimmed eyeglasses. His next purchase was a Greek sailor-style black cap, gaily embroidered with stitching in red, blue, yellow, and white. Finally, a plain walking cane. After paying the kindly old clerk, he asked permission to use the restroom where he donned the cap, brushed his hair under the bill, reversed his cape from black to dark green, perched the glasses on the end of his nose, and left the building with the assistance of a cane.

Satisfied with the altered disguise, he tapped the cane, seemingly pleased with himself. That all changed when he decided to rest on a park bench to watch an old couple picking apples that had fallen from a stand of trees. Two toddlers ran in every direction, excited to be helping their beloved grandparents gather the delicious booty. Rance Colby sat with both hands atop the cane, his chin resting on his hands. Watching the children with amusement created a chilling sense of sorrow for a life lost to international intrigue. He closed his eyes, filled his lungs with air, stood, and walked in the direction of the Rossiya. He had a final stop to make before giving Joe his instructions. Two blocks away, he entered another electronics store and made a purchase.

***

Joe's eyes lit up when his special friend called out his new name and waved him close. "Joe, we must make this our secret. Can you keep a secret?" Joe's head bobbed as enthusiastically as before. "Good. I thought so." The man in the dark green cape and the colorful cap pulled out two small cell phones from a very deep pocket. One was placed in Joe's small palm. His eyes got bigger if that were possible.

"For, me?" he sheepishly asked.

"It comes with the job. Once finished, you and your mother can keep them both. The time-usage had been paid for the next two years. They're only usable within the Moscow area. Now here's what I want you to do." He pointed to the hotel doorway. "Whenever you see me leave the hotel, I'll walk toward you, turn around, and walk back to the hotel—then straight across the street. I'll stand by the telephone booth for two minutes, then walk back across the street. You watch for anyone— anyone that you think may be following me. They could follow, then as I turn, they may act suspicious or look confused as to where they were going. You'll know something is wrong when you see it happen. You follow me so far?"

The head hadn't stopped bobbing since Colby began his instructions. "Yes, Mr. Andrei, but what do I do if I think you're being followed?" He held out the folded phone.

"First, you flip open the phone like this," Mr. Andrei demonstrated. "You do know your numbers do you not?" Joe smiled and nodded. "Good. I thought a big fellow like you would." Joe's smile widened. "If you need to contact me, push the numbers 5984—and I'll answer. Can you remember that?"

"5984, 5984, 5984," Joe repeated. "I remember good, Mr. Andrei."

"I knew I could depend on you, Joe," Colby said, ruffling the young boy's hair. Slipping him a folded bill, he said once again, "This will be our little secret." Turning, he spoke over his shoulder. "Keep your eyes open for me. You could see me walk out of those doors at any minute."

***

This time of day, the hotel lobby was teeming with locals, including politicians, military types, and tourists from various countries. The hotel's numerous restaurants and bars were an attraction for the hungry and thirsty. Colby hesitated before the elevator, turned, and scanned the milling crowd. Anyone, or group of people, could be the assassin or associates of the Arctic Rose. No one matched the photos imprinted in his memory banks. But like him, they too could be in disguise. This wasn't going to be an easy assignment. Not now.

Colby held his bag of costumes in one hand, the cane in the other, stepped around the corner and entered the stairwell door. His day normally consisted of two periods of rigorous exercise, but circumstances of the past few days had precluded that effort. A good fast run upstairs to his eighteenth-floor room would be a good start. At the twelfth floor, he paused for a deep breath, gathered himself, and charged upward. *I can't avoid it any longer—I must begin my exercise routine tonight.*

Opening the door to the eighteenth floor, he glanced in both directions, swiftly strode to room 1809, listened for sounds or movement from inside, and inserted the electronic key. The adjoining room door was partially open, and he could hear his friends' voices. Kicking the door shut, he dropped the bag to the floor, tossed his coat and cane on the small desk, and sat dejectedly on the edge of the bed. He angrily threw the wig across the room and winced in pain as he tugged at the mustache and beard, then fell backward on the bed, his hands covering his face. There was a soft knock at the adjoining room door. "Not now!" he moaned aloud.

One eye opened when he heard the click and turning doorknob. A.T. walked in followed by L' Ami. "Is there something bothering you that we should be made aware of?" Arturo asked, hands on hips.

Rance hadn't yet looked up. "You don't listen very well, do you?"

Al walked to the bed and looked down. "No, we don't—not when a friend appears to be in need. Something's bugging you. So, damn it—get it out—come clean. We're all in this pile of horse manure together."

Rance got up and headed for the bathroom. "Let me take off several layers of makeup and feel as normal as possible—then we'll talk. One of you guys grab me a beer while I clean up. No. Make that two beers. I sure as hell need it. This day's been a mixed bag."

Al pointed to the TV. "Yeah, we're well aware of that."

A.T. was on his second beer and Al was attacking his whiskey with a vengeance when Rance stepped out of the bathroom wrapped in the hotel's white terry robe with the Russian pocket-crest. "Before I tell you about my day and my mood, what's this about the television?" He was fairly certain he knew.

L' Ami, sitting with one leg hanging over the chair's arm, leaned across and touched the cape lying on the desk. "Just before you arrived, we were watching the local newscast. The story was on all channels. A man who fits your description, by the way, became a hero that legends are made of." Colby was about to say something, but Arturo interrupted.

"You've changed your appearance somewhat by reversing the cape, changing hats, adding glasses, and that cane. But those moves to immediately subdue the three extortionists, one armed with a knife, was patently much—Rance Colby."

After a long swallow, Rance displayed both palms and shrugged his shoulders. "What could I do? I couldn't just sit there and allow that poor old lady to be bullied. So I reacted as I normally would have."

"No you didn't," Al firmly corrected him. "Up until this assignment, your first instinct would have been to safeguard the mission, and you would not have done anything to bring attention to yourself that might foolishly compromise that mission."

"Al's right. You know damn well he is," Arturo added.

From the grave look on their friend's face, the pulsating jaw muscles, and clenched fists, they became acutely aware that they may have gone too far with their criticism, although justified. Rance's sudden movement to stand and face them stiffened their backs. A beer bottle and whisky glass were quickly tabled. He remained standing, silently looking into each man's eyes, then turned and sat in the third chair brought in from the next room.

No one said a word. Rance's right elbow rested on the chair's arm, his fingers pressed his forehead. Looking up, he replied to their accusations. "You're both right, of course. For the first time since adulthood, I have concern for my safety. For my life. My success has always depended not only on my skills—but also on my ability to focus. Focus solely on the mission objective and not allow outside circumstances, like this morning's incident, to compromise the outcome."

L' Ami said, "It's this Molly. What's her last name? Isn't it? For the first time, you're looking forward to the future with someone other than the other two ugly guys in this room."

Rance admitted. "Her last name is Mac Winter. And yes, she's become my blind spot. Because of her, I can't see clearly anymore." He got up and looked out the window at the Russian 'White House' beyond the walled Kremlin. He turned and shook both fists. "And goddamn it, I don't want to be me anymore." He looked at his hands. "I don't want to use these hands for killing any more—just for making love." Grieving eyes searched the faces of his two best friends, pleading for understanding. Exhausted, he plopped into his chair. "I just want to be Adam Lee," he said, massaging his temples.

A phone ring broke the tension. Rance pointed to his cape. "Al, grab the cell phone in the right pocket and hand it to me." Flipping open the phone, he answered "Hello," and listened. "Yes, yes, it's working fine. Tell your mother hello for me." He hesitated, "But not about our secret."

Rance smiled for the first time. "Nothing to worry about—that was my new friend, Joe, checking in." He took the next several minutes to explain about Joe and his watchdog assignment.

"Did your headaches return today?" A.T. inquired.

"No. But as I sat watching a family pick apples in the park—my head began to throb and a brief flash of color startled me—but it disappeared as fast as it appeared." He looked at them both with a wishful expression. "Perhaps they're slowly dissipating."

L' Ami detected A.T.'s doubtful glance. "My friend," he said, as he opened the refrigerator, "what you need right now is a good stiff martini, a mouthful of olives, and to place your faith in your two friends."

"As much as it pains me to agree with this bib overall-clad Frenchman, he's right again," Arturo said. "We," pointing at Al, "recognized your *blind spot* long before your confession. That's one of the reasons we're both here."

Taking Al's suggestion, Rance mixed his martini. While L' Ami poured another Jack Daniel's and A.T. cracked open another beer, Rance voiced his appreciation for their loyalty and grew serious. "This mission is far too monumental for anyone's personal issues to jeopardize its successful completion. We are all expendable. We all understand that. From this moment on, barring these goddamn headaches that I cannot control, the only thing that matters is *the mission*. My focus will be entirely on you two and that ice bitch—the Arctic Rose. I hereby will my discipline to return." He clenched his teeth. "This I promise you." He pointed to A.T. "Debrief us. What have you accomplished?"

A.T. hooked his video camera into the television. "Glad to have you back with us," he said to Rance. Not expecting a reply, he dragged a chair next to the TV so he could point to the screen, pushed the ON button, and the video picture appeared. For the next half-hour, he narrated the entire tape, identifying his target's office buildings. When the camera zoomed in on the soldiers in the outdoor café, he elaborated.

"As I have said, not one of the targets appeared. However, it was at this point where I had the most success today. Considering the locations where each of the three guards are assigned within the Kremlin, I believe they would be most helpful if cultivated." He explained his reasoning.

Rance's eyes narrowed. He could envision future events where the soldiers could be used. "Good thinking, Arturo. They might prove to be most helpful. Pursue them. Win their confidence. But tomorrow, reverse your steps—and search out live bodies in those office buildings. It's imperative we make covert contact with clandestine CIA personnel and their local contacts. Al's team will tail them, once identified."

L' Ami adjusted the straps of his overalls and paced the floor, drink in hand, as he assumed his portion of the evening debriefing. "It's still too early for a full assessment of incoming targets, but they are arriving. Five have been positively identified as known assassins." He pointed to the floor. "Two are staying in this very hotel. The others are registered in three separate accommodations north of here: the Hotel Metropol Moscow, the Intourist Hotel, and the Radisson Slavjanskaya Hotel. Each man has a tail." He downed his drink and grinned. "One man is of particular interest. I'm told that he frequents Moscow regularly to visit a cocktail waitress working at the Hot Moscow Nights Lounge." Crossing his arms, he stood before Rance. "This man could help your focus. There's no doubt he'll be plying his charms there tonight." He glanced at A.T., then back to Rance. "What say you? Shall we horn in on his territory—apply competitive pressure, and see where the feathers fall? Should be an interesting diversion for us. Think of it as a little R&R."

Rance began to laugh just as a phone rang. He looked at Al and shook his head. "No, that's not Joe this time. That's my International GlobalPhone. Could only be General Brock. I'm long overdue reporting in. Hand it to me—it's in my left cape pocket." Al dug it out and tossed it across the room.

Colby got the first words in. "Yes, General dear, I miss you, too." He held the phone out for the others to hear, and to save his eardrums. "I know, I've been a bad boy, but I've been busy attempting to save the world—and your ass." He paused for a reply. Not forthcoming, he continued. "We're proceeding ahead as scheduled here. What's new at your end?"

General Rubin Brock was not amused by Colby's opening remarks, and what he had to reveal was too serious to allow himself to become distracted. "You need to find some way to get a message to my old friend, General Rutskoy. Do you think that's possible?"

"Piece of cake. Being shot at makes guys lifetime buddies. Besides, we may have stumbled upon a way to do just that," he said nodding to A.T., silently reminding himself of Arturo's contact with the three Kremlin soldiers. "Not only that, but I was going to devise a way to arrange a clandestine meeting with my flyboy buddy, myself." He listened while Brock demanded to know why. "No, I can't reveal the reason before I have the plan clear in my own mind. But I will tell you this. So far, other than my failed attempt to eliminate Rose, we've been on the defensive. We've been bound by the original *Overlay* planned timing. I'm going on the offensive again."

"Colby, goddamn it, you're going to give me a coronary yet" he bellowed.

"General, it must be early in the morning there. Pour another Scotch and have faith. Never fear, you'll be the third person to know my plans."

"Third person?"

Colby gave him a chance to settle down. "You go next, General. What's so important that it's keeping you up at night and making you so cranky?"

"You have to get a message to General Rutskoy—informing him that I had my study electronically swept and my sterile phone analyzed, and they're both clean. Rose's forehand knowledge concerning your flight to Greece came from his end. His end is dirty, and his position may be compromised."

"Roger on that. He'll be alerted within the next two days. What else is new?"

"Max Carlton had some disturbing news. He hired an ex-CIA agent, a good friend, to tail Alan Oakley. Approximately one-thirty yesterday morning, Oakley met with another man in a small park overlooking the Potomac. The ex-agent was unable to get close enough to hear the conversation because of all the teenagers necking in cars among a heavy stand of trees. He couldn't risk being accused of being a peeping tom and pounced upon by some local linebackers. But he did have a camera with a telescopic infrared lens for night photographs and captured both men clearly on film. I saw the pictures."

"Well, who was the other man?"

"None other than the Secretary of State, Thomas Cline."

Colby digested the information. "That's two strange bedfellows. Any idea of why those two would be meeting secretly?"

"Max has his suspicions. One scenario is that while that old bastard, Grayson, had a fit of conscience over saving your life and wanted you reprogrammed rather than sending you to guard dog heaven. Cline wanted you dead. And it was he that had Oakley drug the coffee. Right now, anything's speculation. Max will stay on it."

"That's most interesting. But right now I have a date at the Hot Moscow Nights Lounge," he winked at A.T. and Al. "Anything else?"

"You're incorrigible. Yes there is. Grayson's whereabouts may have been compromised. If the news gets out, it will no doubt affect Rose's *Overlay* schedule. She could strike at any time if she discovers that Grayson's dead. One of the men detained on his ship has escaped. It seems that his wife is pregnant and expecting any day now. We're searching for him and have her under surveillance. I'll keep you informed."

"All the more reason for me to put my offensive plan into operation. And don't ask, General. I'm not quite sure myself. Look. I promise to keep you in the loop. Once I have my meeting with Russia's Sky King— I'll get on my decoder ring, blow the secret whistle—and you'll know everything. Out." He flipped the phone closed and threw up his hands. "Let's go get a drink."

Chapter Nine

Moscow could become dark on a cloud-covered night, but not as pitch black as the long walkway from the lounge's cave-like entrance to the main room. Lights twinkled overhead, providing the illusion of stars. Although the threesome arrived at the same time, the plan was to split up and circulate. Once inside, they would locate various escape routes and the target. L' Ami had provided A.T. and Colby with a full description of Rose's hired man. He was tall and slim with greased black hair combed back into a four-inch ponytail. A pencil-thin mustache hovered above a pair of equally thin lips. Dark deep-set eyes accented a hawk-like nose with flared wide nostrils. He was known to wear black clothes with a white silk scarf about his throat to hide a hideous knife scar. Left-handed, his preferred weapon, an eight-inch stiletto, was Velcroed to the back of his left calf. His amorous attention to one waitress would identify his girlfriend.

When the giant Russian bouncer opened the door to the lounge, a furnace-like blast of heat stopped them in their tracks; a heavy oppressive cloud of cigarette smoke stung their eyes. The bouncer grinned and made a guttural growl. He seemed to get a kick out of patrons' first reaction to Hot Moscow Nights. Each man went his separate way. A.T. headed for the restroom to assess the possibility of a window exit, and Al mingled, eyes open for exit signs or an office door. Immediately spotting the target slouched in a chair at a table in front of the bar, Colby walked straight to a table next to him. The competition would soon begin. He was prepared. Dressed in a black leather biker's jacket and pants, he had utilized the crew cut wig and mustache disguise he had worn in the general's helicopter. Sunglasses were perched atop his head. He had hoped the swashbuckling outfit would attract the target's girlfriend, thus causing the planned competition. Arturo had taken a position at the bar directly in front of the tables, and Al sat quietly at a table behind the assassin.

The waitress was quickly identified. Whenever she walked past her friend, he would pat her rear; she would giggle and throw him a kiss. It was their little game. *Time to join the game.* Colby ordered a drink from her, as did L' Ami. Although not the most glamorous waitress in the lounge, nor the bustiest, her smallish, little girl features were framed with long golden curls, and the short-shorts exposed a pair of sculptured legs and derriere that Betty Grable would have envied. Obviously, the target was a leg-and-butt man.

"Hey there, sweet cheeks," Colby whispered aloud, "this is for you,"—he slipped a folded bill in her waistband, "because you're so pleasing on these tired eyes." She pulled back and began to frown until she saw the size of her tip.

Flashing a big smile, she flung a hip in his direction and purred, "Next time, the name's Olga, handsome." The customer's remark and her reaction had not gone unnoticed. When she passed the boyfriend, she received a swat instead of the customary pat. She spun around and spoke through her teeth. "Don't ever do that again. This job's all about tips. You show up here every three months." Her eyes became mere slits. "You don't own me," she spat and walked away. Mr. Ponytail turned and glared at her high-rolling biker. The man dressed in leather purposely avoided eye contact, instead choosing to watch couples bobbing and weaving to music on the dance floor. Colby could have acted on the stinging swat, an excuse to come to her rescue, but he had hoped to provoke the target into a fit of rage before he made his move.

L' Ami nodded a signal to A.T., then stood and slipped through the wave of pulsating dancers, intent on checking out the far corner office. Using a small gathering to hide his movements, he ducked into the unlocked room. Just as he had expected, there was a back door leading into an alley. After sliding the lock open, he exited the office unnoticed and returned to his table. Again, he nodded to Arturo, who in turn caught the biker's eye and nodded. The trap was set. Colby would ply the bait.

"Olga, sweetheart!" Colby shouted, holding up an empty glass in one hand and waving money in the other. "Your new benefactor is thirsty," he winked at the thin-lipped assassin, "and I'll come visit you every night, not just once every three months." Aware that Al was intently watching the man's every move, he shunned the boyfriend by turning his back, tempting him.

Olga approached Colby's table, skirting around the angry man's reach. L' Ami smiled when he saw the man's knuckles turn white as he gripped the arms of his chair. He was wound tight. Colby held out the bill, and just as Olga reached out, he snatched it away, grabbing hold of her wrist. One yank and she was in his lap. First startled, she gave a little squeal, but then laughed flirtingly when he whispered in her ear. Al yelled, "Now!" A.T. headed for the front entrance to alert the bouncer.

Colby lifted Olga out of the way, just in time to see the assassin jump to his feet, his chair flying backward. Enraged at being ignored by his girlfriend for a stranger, his bloodshot eyes flashed with hate. He broke a bottle on the tabletop and swung wildly at the man in leather. Colby stood his ground, moved his head, and easily ducked the blow. "Is that the best you have to offer? Who's your hairdresser, Pennzoil?" In the immediate area, tables were being turned over as people ran in fright.

"I'll tear out your heart, you mother…," he screamed, reaching down for his knife. Colby lashed out at his opponent, striking him in the right shin with his steel-toed biker boot, forcing him to grasp his raised leg with both hands. Colby stepped to the side and with the sole of his right boot, tore the ligaments and collapsed the knee of the planted leg, propelling the howling man backward into a group of chairs. Colby calmly stood his ground, smiling and gesturing—*Come to me*—with both hands.

Aware that A.T. was on his way with the giant bouncer in tow, it was time to fulfill their plan. The assassin snarled like a wounded dog. Tossing chairs aside, he crouched on two badly injured legs, a long stiletto in his left hand. Lunging, he made a wide sweeping motion. It came dangerously close as Colby leaned his head sideways; so close he felt the breeze. The move placed the would-be killer in a vulnerable position. The moment he swung and missed, Colby's powerful body blow crushed the brachial plexus nerve bundle under his left arm. Paralyzed, he lost all fight, his arm dangling helplessly, the knife suspended in limp fingers. He stood helpless among turned-over tables and chairs. "There he is!" A.T. shouted to the bouncer, pointing out the man with the knife. "He tried to kill his girlfriend and others, call the police! Lock him up!" In the confusion, Al and Colby disappeared into the crowd, through the office, and out into the alley to safety. Arturo slipped away and exited the front door, but not before he saw the assassin bludgeoned by the bouncer's club. That was one of Rose's hired thugs they wouldn't have to worry about.

***

All three men had had a long day. It was decided, amid yawns and stretches, that they would get a good night's sleep, what was left of it, and regroup in the morning over room service. Colby's GlobalPhone had a digital message. *'Lost sailor found. All is well.'*

Al asked the first question over morning coffee laced with a shot of Benedictine. "Now that we're fairly certain that *Overlay* is still on schedule, what is this offensive plan you teased General Brock about?"

Colby smiled and wiped his mouth with a napkin before answering. "I'm surprised you both waited this long to ask." He swallowed the last of his coffee and pointed to the decanter, motioning for Al to pour him another cup. "This is where Arturo's cultivating the friendship of those soldiers becomes so important." He paused. "Actually, it's crucial to the success of my plan." Locking eyes with A.T., he went on. "You must gain the confidence of the soldier who's the guard at the Russian 'White House." That's President Alexei Velichkin's residence, and also where General Rutskoy's office is located within the massive complex." Picking up the coffee cup, he stood and looked down at A.T. "I need that soldier to take a message to the general. It's vitally important that I meet with Rutskoy tomorrow—in the Church of The Twelve Apostles."

A.T. had a blank look on his face. "How in the hell do you propose I relay that message to a perfect stranger, a Russian soldier, no less? Hypnotism?"

"Isn't that what you do to the ladies? Is there a difference?" Arturo shook a finger at Rance but remained speechless. "No, my friend, I've got it all thought out. After you have them sufficiently juiced, take the man aside and explain that you're a student of military strategy and that you've long admired his general, General Rutskoy, and it would be worth a great deal of money to the soldier if he were able to arrange a brief meeting between you and the general."

"Why didn't you say that in the beginning?" Arturo said, rolling his eyes. "That should be easy."

"What's the point of all this?" L' Ami chimed in.

Rance noticed that both men's cups were empty, picked up the pitcher and provided refills. "You'll have to spice up your own." He sat in a chair away from the table and further explained. "Al, give me time. I'll get to the point of all this soon enough. Arturo, you have the guard tell General Rutskoy that Signor Pascucci is a friend of his aged Greek grandmother and would consider it a great honor to be able to say hello to him in Red Square tomorrow at noon, and to give the general a message from grandma. That will capture his attention. He'll understand."

"Okay. Let's assume that the guard accepts the small fortune offered, and Rutskoy shows up in Red Square. What then?"

For the next hour Rance explained his entire plan, as well as the message A.T. was to relay to the general. He instructed L' Ami to check in with his contacts as expected, and also to concentrate on the two suspected assassins staying at the hotel. Their movements needed to be monitored at all times. Rance intended to spend some time walking about the hotel grounds and lobby as bait, then take a stroll outside, and see if Joe spied a tail. He needed to discern if his identity had been compromised. Later, he'd look in on the church where tomorrow's meeting was to occur. They agreed to debrief at six o'clock back at the hotel.

***

When General Rutskoy's name was mentioned in the conversation, the soldier known laughingly as 'Anton the Thin Man' to his two comrades because of his lanky frame and ill-fitting uniform, raised his head in acknowledgment. "I'm posted one door down from our great general's office." He sat up straight in his outdoor café chair and puffed up his chest. "General Rutskoy never fails to speak to me when he arrives in the morning. I know him quite well," Anton announced proudly.

You're my man, Anton. A.T. prayed that the Thin Man would remain coherent enough to remember the message he was to deliver when the general arrived in the morning. Luckily, of the soldiers sucking down bottle after bottle of *piva*, Anton seemed the most conservative. He consumed far less and was the most passive of the three.

Unlike yesterday when the Italian left his new friends to go take pictures, this time he joked, laughed, and drank like a long-lost relative. Of course, buying the food and drinks endeared him in their alcohol- soaked hearts. In the late afternoon, when they had had enough and said their fond adieus, A.T. caught up with Anton. Placing a friendly arm around his shoulder, Arturo asked, "Valuable confidant of General Rutskoy, could I have a few minutes of your time?"

Anton took a step back and tucked his chin close to his chest. Peering down at the short, powerfully built Italian, he proudly nodded. A.T. went into his act. "I have become a great fan of your general after studying and reading the book, *Decisive Military Tactics by Famous Generals of the Past Century*. He ranks shoulder to shoulder with the most noted." He looked up at the soldier with puppy-dog eyes. "It would be the thrill of a lifetime to meet him, and since you two are such close buddies—could you ask him if he'd do you a favor and meet me tomorrow at noon in Red Square?"

Anton took another step back. He hadn't expected his bragging to become a burden. He pushed his cap back on his head, exposing a cluster of soft brown curls. As he was about to refuse, A.T. pulled a wad of bills from his pocket that would choke a horse and shoved it in Anton's open palm. Before he had an opportunity to reply, Arturo went into phase two of his ploy. "Besides, I'm a close friend of the general's aged grandmother—and she asked me to give him a message if I had the good fortune of talking with her famous beloved grandson."

The money was tempting. It would take him years to earn the amount he suspected was in the roll in his hand, and to have General Rutskoy beholden to him for such a favor could warrant a promotion as well.

What harm could it do? He squeezed the money in his grasp. "What message do you want given to my very close friend, the General?"

***

"L' Ami, Molly, and I are the only three people alive that have witnessed the real you," Arturo observed as he watched his friend remove his makeup, "and know just how ugly you really are." A shoe missed his baldhead by inches. A.T. grinned. "I hope your shooting aim is more accurate than your throwing arm."

Rance checked his watch. "What in the hell could be delaying Al? It's six forty-five." Arturo explained in detail his encounter with the soldier named Anton while Rance stripped and dressed in a light tan shirt and a comfortable pair of dark brown slacks. A.T. had yet to change from his gaudy tourist outfit. Rance secretly thought it matched his friend's outgoing personality.

The sound of the door latch opening in the adjoining room snapped both heads in that direction. Rance reached down for the 9mm strapped to his right calf. A.T. stood with his back flattened against the wall next to the open adjoining door. A reassuring voice filtered in from the next-door room. "Don't bother to get up, it's only *moi*—and Rance, put that Beretta away."

A.T. poked his head in and snarled at the Frenchman. "We were wondering what the hell had happened to you. You're late."

L' Ami shoved Arturo aside, grinning and holding up a fifth of whiskey. "Pardon me, gentlemen, but I had one devil of a time trying to find some JD." One arm made a wide sweeping arch. "I must have trudged all over this damn city. As it is, this is most likely the last bottle left in Moscow." He gestured toward Rance with his bottle hand. "We had better conclude this mission before I finish this, or it's guaranteed that I'll be in a nasty mood."

Knowing Alvin L' Ami as he did, taking him to task for his lack of discipline would be fruitless. When the chips were down, he could be counted on, even if it meant forfeiting his life. Even so, it grated on the ultra-disciplined, perfectionist, mission leader. "Pour yourself a stiff glass and report," Colby ordered in a tone obviously reflecting his annoyance with Al's lame excuse for being late. "We've waited long enough."

L' Ami filled his glass with ice and poured until the caramel-colored liquid touched the rim. He remained unperturbed by his friend's silent rebuke. Raising the glass, he toasted, "You're one hell-of-a task master—you are," then gestured with his glass to the hallway just outside.

"Fact is, I purchased the JD earlier in the day, and have spent the last hour and a half with my two confidants establishing an alternating team of round-the-clock guards, disguised as redecorating workmen, assigned to patrol the eighteenth floor. Of the two Rose associates registered at this hotel, one is a woman." He shook his head, answering Rance's silent question. "No, it's definitely not the ice bitch. This one's weight is pushing two hundred pounds. She was chosen for her role as a Russian cleaning woman. Not three hours ago, she was observed wearing a Rossiya Hotel uniform. Her male partner was dressed as a maintenance worker. Their ruse gives them easy access to any room, avoiding suspicion. My people have been alerted to their possible presence on the eighteenth floor, but not to our room numbers, nor to the reason why they should eliminate the two if they appear. They merely follow orders. No questions."

"Very good. Have there been any additional sightings of Rose's thugs?"

"Not as of today. So far we've been able to identify all we've marked and have them under twenty-four hour surveillance. Of course, any number could have slipped through our net of contacts. Moscow is ringed with a spider-web complex of metro stations. It's impossible to guarantee we've identified all of her assassins. We will, of course, continue our vigilance."

L' Ami took a long swallow, chewed on a chunk of ice, and again with glass in hand, one finger extended in Rance's direction, asked, "Now it's my turn to ask a question."

"It's most probably the same question I want answered," A.T. interrupted, walking to the refrigerator. He held up a beer, and Rance nodded, catching the bottle in midair.

Al pulled up on his overall chest pocket, leaned against the wall, slid down into a sitting position, and placed the glass between his feet. "Okay, now that we all have our drinks, debriefed and comfy, what's this offensive plan that has Brock so unnerved? Even though he hasn't a clue as to what you have in mind."

"That makes three of us," Arturo added.

Rance placed the bottle on the table and used both hands to demonstrate. "What are we doing here for the next ten days?" He paused. "I'll tell you what. We're waiting for Rose to make her move based on the *Overlay* timetable. The three of us are sitting on our duffs and at her mercy. She's playing the game and holding the only set of cards—and we're playing by her rules." He stood, grabbed the nearly empty bottle, and walked to the middle of the room. Downing the remaining swallows, he flipped it end over end to A.T. and folded his arms. Displaying a defiant posture, he explained. "We're changing the rules. We're destroying her timetable."

A.T. leaned forward, now sitting on the edge of his chair. "I like the aggressive move—but need details before I can offer an opinion."

"What do we know? We know the approximate date of the attempted assassination, who the players are, and who the target is." He raised a finger. "Since we cannot change the date of the hit or eliminate all the assassins—what is the one thing we can do?"

L' Ami jumped to his feet and shouted. "We remove the target! It will destroy the timing completely and confuse that bitch."

"I was about to say that," A.T. said with a shrug and a grin.

Sitting back in his chair, Rance explained the details. "When I meet tomorrow in the church with General Rutskoy, assuming he shows, I plan on taking him into confidence. He's practically a blood brother to Brock, trusts him, and believes me to be Brock's man. Of course I can't divulge the real reason behind the planned assassination of President Velichkin, but I can tell him what we know about the assassins and because of that—we're here to abort the catastrophe."

"What about Velichkin? Do you expect him to disappear at the whim of an American spy?" Al asked sarcastically.

"That part might not be so easy. There's every reason to anticipate that he'll believe his top general, and cooperate," Colby said.

"And if he refuses?"

"We go to plan B. We kidnap the Russian president without him."

A.T. slapped a palm to his shiny dome. "Oh, that's bizarre. Plan C presupposes that we have the option of a lifetime vacation of hard-time in Siberia or voluntarily submitting to a Russian firing squad."

Rance leaned across the table and placed a hand on A.T.'s shoulder. "Have I ever led you astray?"

A.T. squinted back. "Well…there were the times…"

"All right…all right. I knew I shouldn't have brought the subject up as soon as I said it. Let's move on." Al was holding a hand over his mouth and snickering. "You two, listen up." Rance smacked his hand on the table. "Our lives, as well as the president's, and maybe that of the general, rest on the successful outcome of this mission." He touched a finger to L' Ami's sleeve. "Al, see if one of your most trusted guys can lay hands on copies of an ancient and current set of blueprints to the president's residence and the entire complex of buildings. We need to quickly become familiar with all exits and entrances, who occupies which office, and any secret rooms and tunnels from the past. Rutskoy can brief us on placement of the guards and shifts."

"I was merely attempting to lighten the mood, old friend," A.T. interjected." Rance nodded his understanding. "If we can pull this off, it will completely destroy Rose's schedule, confuse the hell out of her, and force her to regroup." He looked Rance square in the eye. "And I suspect that we'll hightail it for China."

***

The short round man in the flowered vest and baggy shorts made a slow sweeping circle as he videotaped Red Square, including the tomb of Lenin and other famous Russians, and the magnificent nine domes of the Cathedral of St. Basil the Blessed. Completing the circle, his viewfinder went black. Lowering the camera to identify the obstruction, he found himself eye level with enough medals to sink a small boat. To prevent straining his neck, A.T. stepped back a few feet and peered up at the sternest-looking Russian face he had ever seen. Even his scowl, scowled. His bushy mustache quivered below a man-sized nose. Piercing blue eyes and the hand-on-hips posture definitely asked: *What the hell do you want with me, little man?*

Through clenched teeth, General Rutskoy growled. "You have a message from my sweet, aged grandma?"

Arturo swallowed, raised the camera, and pretended to take the general's picture so no one would notice his lips move. "Your sainted grandmother awaits your illustrious presence in the Church of The Twelve Apostles. She's there now."

"Convince me. Why in the hell should I choose to go to church, passing up a delicious lunch with a lady friend?"

"In Italy, we're taught from an early age to listen to our elderly grandmothers, and in your case," he lowered the camera, began to walk away, turned and added, "especially when the life of your president is at stake."

***

The poet Kropotkin strolled toward the fruit stand holding a bundle under his arm, turned, and walked back toward the Rossiya Hotel, quickly turned right and crossed the busy street. Watching the traffic, he stood by a telephone booth, waited a few minutes, and punched buttons on his cell phone. "He…helloo," came a tentative reply.

"It's me, Joe. Mr. Andrei. Like yesterday, you did a good job. No one followed me. Just wanted to be certain the phones were working. Keep up the good work."

Fifteen minutes later, Rance Colby had changed into the long black monk's robe that he had acquired at the costume store and was kneeling in prayer in the back row of the Church of The Twelve Apostles. The church reminded him of a huge ornate silent tomb. Gold leaf covered nearly every surface, colorful icons and lifelike statues stared down as if questioning his very presence. A deep breath filled his nostrils with perfumed incense. Empty pews cracked and snapped with age. With head bowed, Colby's ears remained alert to the sound of a shuffle or footstep. Five minutes into meditation, the distinct sound of boots on marble captured his attention. Barely raising his head from prayer, the general was soon in his peripheral vision. Rutskoy stopped halfway and looked in every direction, dismissing the monk in the rear, and slid into a pew.

Silently, the monk rose, walked down the aisle, and sat behind the general. "Thank you for coming grandson." Rutskoy's body stiffened. "No. Don't turn around just yet. Listen to what I have to say, then accompany me outside in the garden where we can talk freely."

Colby knelt down, placed his elbows on the general's backrest, and leaned forward. "As you know, I'm working for your friend, Rubin Brock; therefore you can trust me. If he were here, he'd verify everything I'm about to relay to you."

"But he is here," came a deep voice from directly behind. "You're not the only one that can operate in disguise—wiseass." He looked toward the altar, "Forgive me."

In frustration, Colby's chin rested on his chest. *I don't believe this. I don't need this. If he had been an assassin, my brains would have ruined Rutskoy's nice clean uniform.* He turned slowly, looking up into the laughing eyes of a totally satisfied General Rubin Brock, decked out in a Russian Colonel's uniform."

Brock leaned close to Colby's ear and whispered—*"Boo."*

Rutskoy was on his feet, reaching over and taking hold of the priest's arm. "I take it you know my new aide, Colonel Brocksky? We had better take this conversation outside, as you suggested, Father." Colby glared daggers at the American general as they walked down the aisle, through the huge wooden church doors and into a small, secluded garden enclosure. Still wearing his full beard and longhair wig, he yanked back the robe's hood in anger. They stood chest to chest and within an eyelash of each other when Colby's powerful shove staggered and surprised the general. "What the goddamn hell do you think you're doing here? How do you know you're not compromising this mission?" He stomped away, only to turn and angrily address the two surprised generals. First he pointed to Brock, then Rutskoy. "Whose harebrained idea was this? It's just like something the military mind would do."

General Rutskoy, not fully aware of the angry man's true identity and shocked at his treatment of an American general and close friend, stepped in between the two men. Gesturing with his hands for the priest to lower his voice, he explained. "After placing a call to Rubin's sterile line from a street-side phone booth, I discovered the reason behind why those shooters were in waiting for you at the island. My line was not bugged, as Rubin suspected. I discovered that my aide had eavesdropped and apparently sold the information to an interested party. Unfortunately, the man committed suicide before he could be confronted." He winked at his son's godfather. "Yes, most unfortunate. Unfortunate for him."

"That solves one mystery," Colby conceded, "but still doesn't explain what the hell you," he poked a finger on Brock's chest, "are doing in Moscow posing as a Russian Colonel?"

In an effort to save face in front of his friend and out of frustration, General Brock poked back. Colby inched forward, then smiled, well aware of the message behind the gesture and allowed the general his due. "Damn it, Colby, everything's riding on what happens next, and you were keeping me in the dark about this offensive you're planning. What did you expect me to do, sit back and guzzle Scotch?" He jabbed a thumb at his Russian friend. "Dmitry here picked me up late last night, just over the Finnish border." He offered his hand. "Let's get on with your plan; the general is willing to do whatever it takes to save Velichkin's life."

The priest shook the outstretched hand. "Okay. It seems that you're turning out to be an asset after all, instead of merely a pain in the ass." They both laughed. General Dmitry Rutskoy was still uncertain about their relationship and remained passive. Colby turned his attention to the Russian. "From the conversation, I assume that your friend here has already explained that a team of killers have been hired to assassinate President Alexei Velichkin in approximately nine days, give or take?" Rutskoy nodded the affirmative. "Well, since it's nearly impossible to find and eliminate all the hires, dozens have infiltrated the city, the plan is to remove the target."

Both generals' eyes widened. "Explain the word—*remove*," Rutskoy demanded in a suspicious tone.

Without hesitation, Colby answered, "Either you convince him to disappear for an extended, much-needed secret vacation—or we kidnap him. It's his choice. It's his life." He plunged each hand into large billowing sleeves and waited, attempting to read two very different puzzled expressions.

The Russian shut his eyes, opened them to glance skyward, and blew out a puff of breath. "My president is a proud and brave man. While I have his complete confidence, it won't be easy to convince him to run and hide." He pondered his words. "In fact, I'm certain that he could not be convinced." He threw up both hands in surrender. "He must be kidnapped and made to appear that he slipped away unnoticed for an announced vacation—to an unknown location." The general smiled. "Alexei is a widower, you know, and quite dashing."

The priest pulled the hood over his head. "It's agreed. You two have a nice lunch; I've got a kidnapping to plan. We meet again tonight. I'll outline everything in detail. You, General, will play a major role." Rutskoy tugged at his collar.

***

By mid-afternoon, Colby had returned to the hotel. Surging adrenalin hyped his senses. He felt invigorated; the game had begun in earnest. Al was out gathering blueprints and A.T. was sacrificing himself by drinking with his new soldier friends. It was an excellent opportunity for Colby to scout the office building where a key CIA operative was known to be functioning, in an attempt to discern their investigative activity into Rance Colby's whereabouts. The eighteenth-floor hallway was empty, except for five painters. The tall, green-caped, bearded eccentric poet wearing a colorfully embroidered cap drew stares from elevator passengers. He stared back over rose-colored, wire-rimmed glasses. In the lobby, Andrei Zakharov blended in, walking nonchalantly with cane in hand, toward the exit.

His thoughts were on the night's meeting with the two generals and his friends. Tonight, they would study the blueprints and formulate a plan to kidnap the President of Russia. Colby smiled at Joe and gave him a slight nod, turned, and proceeded back toward the hotel, then stopped, crossed the busy Moskvoretskaya Nab and stood by the telephone booth. The prescribed two-minute time was up; he wasn't being shadowed. A dozen steps away, the cell phone rang. "Mr. Andrei…I think there's an auto following you."

"Explain what you've seen, Joe. Give me details."

Joe took several deep breaths. This was the first time he'd reported a possible following, and he was nervous. "Ten minutes before you came out, I noticed a dark blue car parked across the street. I saw it because a police officer pulled along side and waved for them to move on. Cars are not to park there. When the car didn't move, the officer got out and talked for a minute or two, saluted the driver and drove off. The car remained." He stopped to catch his breath.

"Just take your time, Joe. You're doing just fine. Continue."

"Well…when you came out…Mr. Andrei, and began walking toward Mamma's fruit stand, the car pulled out, attempting to make a U-turn. But when you turned around, it pulled back to the curb. And just now, when you walked away from the booth, the car began to move slowly in your direction." Another pause. "I believe they are following you, Mr. Andrei! What shall I do?" he shouted excitedly into the phone.

"You've already done it, Joe. I'll do the rest. Thanks." Colby flipped the phone closed and smiled at his little friend's concerned enthusiasm.

Colby picked up the pace as he walked along the sidewalk paralleling the Moskova River. To his right was a steep landscaped bank leading down to a waterfront walkway, to his left, the slow cruising dark blue car. *They could be one of four entities. One, local police who have recognized me as the Coffee Shop hero. Two, Russian Mafia who want my kneecaps blown off. Three, CIA who want my head blown off. Four, Rose's goons who want my head blown off. One out of four isn't bad odds.*

Each time Colby increased his speed, the car accelerated. Windows on the side facing him were rolled down. He felt like a sitting duck in a shooting gallery. Quickly glancing to his right, he saw a number of sailboats and speedboats on the river, including a large slow-moving touring craft not less than six feet off the edge of the walkway. He made his decision. Vaulting over the pedestrian railing, he tumbled head over heels, then rolled down the embankment. Familiar spits of silenced weapons came from above. Clumps of turf burst around him. *Scratch those wanting to reward their hero.* Reaching the paved river-walkway, he sprinted toward the tour boat. Chunks of cement pelted his legs as he sprinted for safety of the boat. *Those shots are no longer coming from above—they're coming from the tour boat. Whoever they are, they have me surrounded.*

Running like a crazy-legged punt-returner, he managed to evade the shooter's aim, then dove for the tour boat's suspended metal roof. With an audible *oof*, Colby made a belly flop. He momentarily lost his wind, but instinctively rolled to his right just as three slugs tore through the roof where he had landed. Anticipating the shooter's move to the right,

Colby grasped the bar surrounding the roof, twisted his body and hands, swung off the side and into the boat. The momentum and powerful blow of both feet slamming into the man's chest drove him backward across the deck. It was then that Colby became aware of the wild screams of passengers.

Stunned but still gripping his pistol, the would-be killer shook off the solid blow. The weapon was in his raised hand, but before he could bring it down to squeeze the trigger, Colby leapt forward. Blocking the gun hand with his left, Colby maneuvered his right arm under the man's raised arm, then grasped his wrist. Using his own arm as leverage, Colby bent the man's arm back; the snapping bone sounded like a rifle shot. Before the cry of pain left his lips, Colby's claw-like fingers dug into his throat. In one quick forceful shove, he forced the back of the man's head into the railing. The man lay dead. Surprised, Colby whirled around to applause and shouts of, "It's the hero from the Coffee Shop!"

Colby had lost his cane, hat, and glasses in the altercation, and needed to escape his admirers. One glance to his left told him that the men in the car had sped away, not wishing to draw undue attention to themselves after the shooting, and that the coast was probably clear. The boat's captain, who had been threatened by the shooter, was again in command. Colby gestured for him to bring the boat close to the embankment. Once close enough, he jumped and scampered up the bank amid shouts of acclaim. He had to disappear and become someone else, fast.

Four blocks away, Colby entered one of Moscow's numerous Metro Stations. Picking one of three keys in his hand, he inserted it into the baggage locker. With bag in hand, he entered a communal restroom stall and became a middle-aged pregnant woman. The white headscarf tied tightly under his chin, hid his reddened face. Removing the mustache and beard without the proper solvent was always painful. He reminded himself to prepare for such an event from now on. Cape arms were knotted around his waist, the remainder folded to resemble a large belly, and both held secure with duct tape. A tattered, faded blue three-quarter length coat covered a gray peasant blouse and skirt. Scuffed high-top shoes and rolled-down white and red striped socks completed the outfit.

***

Genevieve, a short round tourist from America, whispered in her husband's ear. "Bill, look at that poor Russian woman. She's my age, and pregnant." She nodded sideways as the woman walked past. "She's carrying the baby so low and look at the way she waddles. Poor woman."

Colby smiled inwardly at the overheard comment. *And if I don't get to the room fast, I'll drop the baby in the lobby. The duct tape is coming loose.*

Following his normal procedure for changing disguises, he lifted the hotel house phone and punched room numbers. After several rings, the phone was picked up. "This isn't your grandma this time, sonny—it's your pregnant girlfriend. Brace yourself, lover boy. I'm on the way up."

L' Ami and Testaccio broke down, tears filling their eyes, laughing hysterically. Arturo composed himself sufficiently enough to point to Colby's legs and said, "Those rolled-down socks show off your hairy legs." Indignantly, Colby reminded him that women in many countries do not shave their legs.

"Nobody we know!" shouted both men in tandem.

The poor pregnant Russian woman took two steps toward the Italian and dove into his arms. Catching A.T. completely off guard, she kissed the top of his baldhead. Al fell back into a chair, wiping the tears from his eyes. Arturo, collecting his senses, placed both hands on Colby's waist and with a loud grunt, tossed him high into the air. Somersaulting as he hit the floor, Colby jumped up, spread his arms, grinned, rubbed his swollen-belly, and shyly said, "It's yours, you know."

A.T. shook his finger and was poised to respond, but Colby's expression changed, and he became dead serious. "Okay, enough of your distracting shenanigans, you two," he said, tongue-in-cheek. "We have a crucial meeting tonight. Let's begin our debriefing as I clean up and change into my new persona." L' Ami poured his usual, and A.T. cracked open two cold beers. Rance went first this time, explaining his meeting in the church with General Rutskoy, the surprising and annoying appearance of General Brock, their decision to kidnap the Russian president, and that his plan to check out the CIA Station Chief, John Campo, was aborted by his recent brush with death, resulting in a quick change of costume.

A.T. set his bottle on the table. "I can help you with Campo. Prior to meeting my comrades for lunch, I entered the building where he's headquartered on the second floor. Exploiting my Italian tourist gig, I was prepared to pretend that I had been told that this office was where my films could be developed in one hour. Instead, the outer office was empty. Two female voices echoed from a private office that I assumed was Campo's. Through the crack in the partially open door, I could see them lounging lazily while the boss was away." A quick swallow caused a pause in his report. "My ear for Russian is not as good as yours, but I was able to discern the gist of the conversation. They haven't seen their boss or any of his local agents in over a week. It seems that they all have been pulling alternating twelve-hour shifts at airports, train, bus, and metro stations watching for a man named Rance Colby. One woman said she had heard it was someone who escaped the reservation—whatever that meant. Campo's last phone message indicated he was mad as hell, and thought they were all on a wild goose chase. The man didn't exist, according to him."

"It would be too much to hope for—that everyone would believe as he does," Rance wished aloud. "Thanks for the Campo report. That crosses the CIA off my list of this afternoon's possible assassins. I have a sneaking suspicion that the local Russian police weren't involved, either." He downed his beer and tossed the empty to A.T. "That only leaves the Arctic Rose's men. If so, then I've been made. Andrei Zakharov is as good as dead, at least until the president's safe, and the assassins are eliminated. And I've got a plan to accomplish that." He nodded to L 'Ami. "That's where you and your contacts come in, but we'll discuss that after A.T. finishes his debriefing."

Arturo stood, stretched, and rubbed his ample girth. "Are we going to have the opportunity to eat before tonight's meeting?" The disgusted look on Rance's face encouraged him to move on. "As you are aware, I had my last visit with the three Kremlin soldiers. It was hilarious. When I approached their table, Anton jumped up so fast he tipped over his chair. He pointed to the insignia rank on his sleeve. One of his cronies shouted, 'My Italian friend, see our new sergeant. And he's buying.' "

With a straight face, A.T. continued. "I hadn't planned to stay long, but with the new sergeant buying, I couldn't easily refuse and hurt his feelings, now could I? After all, it was my money that made it all possible." He waited for a typical Colby response, but it never came. "Anton announced to his friends and his silent benefactor, that in addition to his new rank, he had a new assignment. It came at the direct request of his friend, General Rutskoy. 'I am now the personal guard posted outside President Velichkin's living quarters.' "

Rance smacked his palms together. "Great! That sly fox. General Rutskoy is setting the stage for the kidnapping. He doesn't waste any time." Now down to his shorts, Colby's ugly scars were visible. "Before I shave and shower, what do you have for us, Al?"

L' Ami held up one finger, stepped into the adjoining room and returned with two rolled-up sheets. He raised one, then the other. "This is as current a set of prints as we could find, and this is an old copy of a drawing that dates back to the late fourteenth century. I took the liberty of scrutinizing both." He held up the old, stained, and cracked set of drawings. "There are secret panels and passageways galore. Should be most helpful—if they haven't been sealed up."

"Let's hope they haven't. I'll take a peek prior to our meeting with the generals. You guys relax while I pretty up for the old folk. Arturo, you don't have to order dinner, our meeting host is taking care of everything—including refreshments."

Before stepping into the bathroom, Al stopped him at the door. "One last thing to report. My people have now identified nearly three dozen known assassins in the city as well as their resident locations. That includes the two staying at this hotel. They're poised to move whenever given the nod."

Rance smiled and gave Al a two-fingered salute. "We're nearly there. Nearly there."

***

"Yes, General Ruskey, your conference suite is prepared. Vodka, Scotch, whisky, a cooler filled with cold *piva*—and an assortment of cooked shrimp, cold cuts, breads, and of course caviar, await your party." The Rossiya Hotel manager placed a finger next to his nose. "And we haven't forgotten a box of exquisitely fresh Havana cigars."

Rutskoy turned and winked to his aide standing one-step behind and to his right. "As usual, Fyodor, my good friend, you have displayed impeccable taste, and will be handsomely rewarded." He placed a plain white envelope on the counter and slowly slid it across. "I can assume that the rooms on either side of my suite, directly above and below, are and will remain empty?" The manager discreetly slipped the envelope into his jacket pocket and closed his eyes, all the while smiling, and nodded that his distinguished guest was correct in his analysis.

General Rutskoy had just poured his aide a Scotch and himself vodka and was enjoying the aroma of a yet to-be-lit Cuban cigar when a knock on the door interrupted his pleasure. His aide raised a hand, indicating that he would get the door. The bow and click of heels, followed by, "Captain Alexander Khimki at your service, my Colonel," raised Brock's brow. Not waiting for an invitation, Captain Khimki elbowed his way in, immediately followed by a short heavyset bald man in a flowered vest and a tall, bearded man in overalls. Brock recognized the voice. Rutskoy jumped to his feet to protest. "Sit back down, we're old friends. I knew your sainted Greek grandmother, as well as your father confessor. Remember the Church of The Twelve Apostles?"

General Brock extended an arm in Rutskoy's direction and showed a palm. "Dmitry, this is the man," he raised a brow at the captain, "whom I had mentioned. He is here in Russia at my request. Once we intercepted the communiqué concerning the planned assassination on President Velichkin, he was sent for." *A small lie between friends never hurt anyone—especially when national security is at stake.* "A more skilled operator does not exist. I have complete faith in his abilities, and he's the man who saved my life when under fire in the desert a number of years back. You personally experienced his bravery in Greece."

The Russian's eyes scanned the captain from head to toe, then stood and extended his hand. "Yes, now that you mention it, I remember the military crew cut, the mustache, and the deep voice. Yet, he looks very much like my grandmother." Shaking the outstretched hand, he laughed.

"It must be the uniform that's different." He smacked Colby on the back and faced the others, spreading his arms wide. "Please. Partake of food and drink and let us be informal. Use first names. Call me Dmitry. And introduce your friends, Captain. Excuse me, Alex."

"The bearded gentleman, Al," he explained with a smile while massaging his shoulder, "is an old acquaintance—emphasis on the word *old*. The Italian bowling ball with muscles is called A.T.—among other names and deserves every one of them. Both men have, upon occasion, saved my life, as you have, Dmitry."

Dmitry stared at A.T., who was shoveling crackers and caviar into his mouth like a starving man. "You," he stabbed a finger at A.T. "I remember clearly. Where's your video camera, little man?"

He glanced over at Colby before answering. "It's in the shop being repaired. I believe that taking your picture broke the camera." He placed a mound of fish eggs on a cracker and smacked his lips.

The room went silent. General Rutskoy's jaw visibly tightened, then expanded into a wide grin. "I like you, little man," he said, walking toward the table spread with food. "Your eyes show no fear." Dmitry placed a large arm across A.T.'s shoulders, took the beer bottle from his hand, and walked him over to the bar. "No. No more of that wishy-washy *piva*. You and I drink vodka." A.T. looked back at Colby for help, but all he got in return was a grin and a shrug.

Brock pulled Colby aside, nodding at Al and A.T. "You didn't tell me about these two."

"General…Rubin, all I have to say is that without their expertise, I have no chance of survival or success. They're both invaluable to this mission—and like your friend there—they are not fully aware of our government's involvement." He had no intention of debating the situation, but rather walked away toward the door and turned to study the room. The suite's foyer was wide, the floor, marble. To the right and left were mirrored folding closet doors. The large combination conference living room was covered in extra-thick, white carpet. A good-sized kitchen was immediately to the right; the opposite side housed an equally large bathroom. Behind the fully stocked bar was a picture window three times the size of the one in Colby's room, exposing the entire Kremlin nighttime skyline. The windowpane featured one-way glass. Comfortable plush swivel chairs lined the long redwood conference table. The vaulted ceiling made the left wall the perfect location for his command center display. Satisfied, he asked L' Ami, "You do the honors?"

A portable electronic bug-sweeper appeared from deep within Al's overall pocket. General Rutskoy protested. He had been assured of their complete security. As Al went about his business, Colby addressed the general's comment. "Indulge me, Dmitry. I haven't lived this long—in a very dangerous profession—without taking every precaution."

They all watched in fascination as Al swept the room. "Clean," he announced. "Let's eat. And I'm as thirsty as a Russian bear." He looked over at Rutskoy. "But I'll stay with whiskey, if it's all the same to you?"

Both food and drink disappeared fast within the next half-hour. Small talk was abundant, but now was the time for business. "Don't get too comfortable in your chairs, gentlemen." Colby warned. "We'll be doing our planning on two feet. Al, A.T., would you mind removing the paintings from that wall, as well as the sofa and end tables? That's our command center area."

Using the conference room tabletop, Colby unrolled both charts that Al had brought. Rutskoy appeared surprised with the blueprint and drawing. Before the question was asked, Colby responded. "What can I tell you? We have friends in high places."

"These damn paintings are screwed down," Al complained.

Colby opened several conference room table drawers and found what he was looking for. Along with a plastic box of pushpins, he discovered a screwdriver. He flipped it to L' Ami.

While Colby proceeded to pin the current blueprint on the wall and the ancient drawing immediately above, he explained. "It's not possible to superimpose one over the other, so this will have to make do. Dmitry, dig through one of those drawers. There should be one or more laser pointers available." The general held up two. "Good. You keep one, I'll use the other."

They gathered in front of Colby's command center display. "Since you are the only person familiar with the layout of the president's private quarters—other than our brief review of the blueprint—please point out the entrance from the outer offices and his quarters, the master bedroom in particular."

A red dot ran along a hallway, traveled upward, then down, and circled a large room. "The door from the main office complex to the president's residence is well guarded—also two other entrances. Here and here." He used the laser beam to demonstrate. "Within his residence, the long hallway entrance to the master bedroom is always guarded."

A.T. nudged Al with his elbow. "And that's where the new Sergeant Anton is stationed, I venture to say."

"That's very perceptive, coming from a bald man whose head shines in my eyes," the Russian mocked.

Al elbowed A.T. back. "He got you that time," he whispered.

"Will you two guys put a sock in it, and that goes for you too, General—you're egging them on," Colby said.

Rutskoy looked at Brock for a translation. "What he said was to shut up—including you. And that your sense of humor was adding fuel to the fire." Rubin threw up his hands. "Oh hell, let's get on with this."

"Well said, Rubin," Colby observed, then pointed to the ancient drawing. "Al discovered a plethora of secret doors and passageways throughout the old building that the current structure was built directly on top of." The red dot made a circle around the president's master bedroom, then on the drawing above. "See the proximity of that old private dining hall and Velichkin's bedroom? If those old portals and passageways have not been sealed up, we may have a plan."

The Russian stepped forward for a closer look. He tapped his finger on the old drawing. "Could that be a subterranean passage beneath the bedroom?" Colby nodded. A strategy was being formulated.

"Yes, and as you can see, the president's bedroom fireplace is in the same approximate location as the dining room fireplace. With any luck, the secret door to the stairway down to the underground passage still exists." Colby's laser beam traced the passageway to where it exited on the bank of the Moskova River. Reaching up and touching the old drawing, he pointed out, "Here's our way into the residence. If it's not blocked—it tunnels under the Kremlin wall and will take us directly to Velichkin's bedroom."

General Brock, who had been silent up until now, offered his advice. "Look here...Alex, we have little time left to implement this charade and spirit him away. Critical questions must be asked and answered. Several elements must be developed simultaneously. Once we have a strategy, we'll need to work in shifts."

"You're absolutely correct...Rubin." Colby left the wall and picked up a cigar from the box resting on the conference table. Holding it under his nose, he deeply inhaled. "Gentlemen, I believe I can think more clearly puffing on a Cuban cigar washed down with liquid refreshment. How about you guys?" In his mind, he had already asked the questions—knew the answers—and had formed a strategy. Now it was only a matter of assigning responsibilities.

Strange bedfellows. Three Americans: the highest-ranking general, two civilian covert operators, one Italian ex-secret service agent, and a powerful and influential Russian General lounged comfortably in their plush swivel chairs drinking beer, Scotch, whisky, and vodka—planning to kidnap the President of Russia. The rich aroma of Cuban tobacco filled the room. The American in a Russian captain's uniform led the discussion.

Colby glanced at everyone individually and began. Pointing to both generals, he ordered, "Dmitry, Rubin, tonight if you have the opportunity, but tomorrow for certain, get into Velichkin's quarters. Search the bedroom for the secret panel. When you find it, make sure it's operative."

Rutskoy pointed to his watch. "It will be tomorrow. The president is already asleep."

Colby acknowledged the change of plan and nodded to A.T. "You and I will commandeer a small boat, and under cover of tonight's moonless night, investigate the entrance to the subterranean passageway. If it still exists."

General Rutskoy turned and pointed his laser at the old drawing. "At that point," he circled the spot, "where the entrance is reputed to be, is a cluster of large boulders and ancient shrubs." He faced Colby. "Chances are it's there."

L' Ami sat with his arms crossed, the cigar firmly clenched, his expression questioning, *What about me?*

"You, old friend, need to procure medical supplies, hospital equipment, and two nurses and a doctor. Three people who can play charades without asking questions and are willing to keep a secret."

"Hold on Alex. Why are we including others in an already dangerous venture?" General Brock demanded an answer.

Colby stood, stretched, paced back and forth, but did not reply directly. The answer would come soon enough. "No one has asked the crucial questions: Once we have Velichkin, what do we do with him? And how do we get him away from the residence? Where do we take him?" He waited. No one responded, so he continued. "He doesn't leave the premises. We don't take him away."

Rutskoy's jaw stuck out. "Explain!"

Explaining as he walked to the wall, Colby tapped the old drawing. "To the right of the stairs and just off of the passageway is a fairly large room. This will become his hospital room." They all began talking at once. He held up his hand until they became quiet. "Hear me out, then we can pick the plan apart.

"Assuming all elements are in place on the chosen night, the president will be sedated." He gestured toward Dmitry. "That will be your and Rubin's responsibility."

A very angry finger shook in Colby's direction. "President Velichkin's health cannot be compromised—in any way!"

"Dmitry, please hear me out. We're here to save your president, not to harm him. But after saying that, for the mission to succeed, it is imperative that he be sedated. Understand?"

"No. Not as yet. But I assume you will inform me."

"Once sedated, he will be carried through the secret passageway to the hospital room where he'll be attended today and night by a team of nurses and a doctor. When he awakens, you General Rutskoy, will be by his side to explain his condition. You'll tell him that he was suddenly taken by a fever and collapsed in his bedroom. That you found him on the floor and had him rushed to an obscure private clinic so that no one would be aware that the President of Russia was incapacitated. He will be, of course, given something that will keep him in a weakened state. Velichkin must believe that his condition is serious for this to work," he saw the general's concerned gaze, "but in no way have any residual side effects." Colby returned his attention to the group. "He will remain there until we have crushed the Arctic Rose and her assassins. Then he'll make a remarkable and complete recovery. His last shot of vitamins will again sedate him. When he wakes up, he'll be in his own bed—a safer man—but none the wiser."

L' Ami asked the question the others knew was coming. "What do we do with my three people? Must they be eliminated?"

Colby pondered the question. "At one time that would have been the standard protocol, but no longer. They will be provided a script for their part—blindfolded well before they are taken by boat to the passageway where they play their part, and again blindfolded before being transported to an undisclosed location." He looked at Brock. "To answer your question. You can see how valuable these outsiders are to our success. Of course they will again be sworn to secrecy before they leave the makeshift hospital—under the penalty of death. It will be made clear that if any of the three, at any time, ever disclose their part, all three will be disposed of."

"Sound strategy," A.T. noted, "but what about Rose and her team of assassins? How do they discover that the president's not in residence for them to trigger?"

Colby placed a hand on L' Ami's shoulder. "This man has the answer."

Al leaned back and looked up with a puzzled expression. "I do?"

"Yes," he said, taking his seat. "You control the local covert team of anti-assassins. At a prescribed date and time, perhaps two days from now at twelve noon—they do the world a favor and terminate all Rose's people—with the exception of one of the two in the Rossiya Hotel. We will take out the male and allow the other to live and report President Velichkin's whereabouts to her boss."

"You're going to let the, what did you call her, Arctic Rose, know where the president is located?" Rutskoy chewed on his cigar.

"That's correct. President Alexei Velichkin was observed entering a small exclusive, out-of-the-way hotel in a popular fishing village in the southern tip of Norway, called Stavanger."

"How could that be?" the Russian questioned, staring into Colby's eyes for an answer.

"Oh, he'll be there." Colby pointed to his chest. "You've never witnessed my impersonation of your president."

"He's laying his life on the line, and setting a trap for the ice bitch," A.T. explained.

For a split-second, the fake Russian captain appeared to slump in his chair and grasp his forehead. Recognizing the signs, Al and A.T. leapt from their chairs and rushed to their friend's side. The two generals looked on, both wearing deep frowns of concern. Colby waved them away, shook his head and slowly pushed himself up to his feet. "Sorry. It wasn't anything," he assured them, "just the aftermath of this afternoon's fray." He smiled at his two associates' looks of relief. "A.T. and I must be getting along. We have to find a boat and a passageway."

"It's dark along the river but be on guard. There are sentries posted in each tower," Rutskoy warned. Walking up to Colby, he embraced him with a typical Russian bear hug. "I'll return the compliment. I'm glad to have you on my side in this war with the terrorist, the ice bitch." Colby blushed. Everyone had a parting laugh.

Chapter Ten

He was cold, soaked to the skin, tired, and pissed. The overhanging tree was no shelter against the relentless heavy mist blowing off the Potomac River. The bench, normally illuminated by a decorative lamppost light, was dark. Alan Oakley, Special Projects Director of the CIA, had deliberately unscrewed the bulbs. Oakley hated his clandestine meetings with Secretary Thomas Cline, and the old SOB was half an hour late. *I should have killed the son of a bitch'en blackmailer three years ago, after he showed me those incriminating photos. I haven't been in a gay bar since. I was on that assignment, but he threatened to make it appear otherwise. And with his influence, he could, and would do it. Damn him!*

His ears picked up the sound of a car door closing, but it could have been one of the kids making out under the rolling stand of trees far to his left. Nevertheless, his hand fingered the grip of his shoulder-holstered weapon. *I could always claim that I thought he was a mugger, but that bastard probably has given orders for the release of those photos at the occurrence of an untimely death. I need to get them back. I'll play along.*

A loud whisper whipped his head around. "Oakley. Get the hell out of the rain. Follow me to my car. This way."

Following the dark outline of the slow-moving man, Oakley obeyed and thought to himself when he was ten feet from the black Lincoln: *Our surveillance tactics must have brushed off on him. He unscrewed the car's interior light bulb so it wouldn't come on when the car door was opened. Smart old shit.*

Oakley slipped into the passenger seat, pulled out a handkerchief and wiped his damp face. "What's so goddamned important that this couldn't wait until tomorrow?" he complained. His fingers again rested on the pistol grip. Staring at the hairless U.S. Secretary of State sitting in the dark next to him, he could never be certain of his motives and surely wouldn't put anything past this man. He remained alert.

Oakley was unable to see his face but felt his stinging words. "You're too impatient. That's one of the reasons that you'll never replace Director Carlton. You're a hothead who only looks out for himself." Cline blew his nose and took his time before continuing. "And I've got you by the short hairs—and don't you ever forget it." The CIA man squeezed the pistol grip, tempted to end his frustration here and now.

"Cut to the chase, Cline. What is it you want?" Oakley released his pistol grip and pulled out a pack of cigarettes, but before having a chance to extract a cigarette, Cline's hand smacked it away. "You know better. The lit end can be seen at a distance in the dark, even in this weather."

In a heartbeat, Oakley's weapon inched out of its holster. He held his breath and shoved it back. "And don't threaten me with petty theatrics." Cline laughed in his face. "Leave your playmate in its cradle. You don't have the balls. If I were to suddenly die under these circumstances, you'd be the prime suspect once the photos were released to the *Post* and Max Carlton. So sit back, relax, and tell me what's new with our boy, Rance Colby?"

"He isn't my boy. He belongs to you and President Grayson— wherever he's disappeared to." Bending over, he retrieved his pack of cigarettes, stuffed them in his inside pocket, and answered the question. "No one in the CIA, FBI, or the entire international security community has seen hide nor hair of your boy. It's like he's fallen off the face of the earth. Like he doesn't exist."

"Well, we know he exists—don't we? You tried to have him killed."

Oakley stared at the face of the man sitting next to him, attempting to make out his puffy bald features, and nodded. "Yes, and if I had been lucky, you and Grayson would have been sitting in that car when it went off that icy road instead of two of my men."

Choosing to ignore Oakley's wishful thinking, Thomas Cline asked the obvious question. "Brock's the only one to acknowledge seeing Colby months after the accident. And that one incident was with a drugged-up ex-soldier inside and outside the library that he suspected was Colby in disguise. Could it be that the guy was just a derelict druggy—and nothing more?"

"Look. From years back, you know him better than anyone else. He wasn't called the *Shadow Master* for no good reason. Which brings up a good question. If you're so hell-bent on having him eliminated, why in God's name did you try rehabilitating him in the first place? Why not just kill him and be done with it?"

Oakley could tell that the question was a source of irritation and hard for the secretary to answer. "That was President Grayson's call, not mine."

The cigarettes were burning a hole in the CIA man's pocket. He needed a drag in the worst way but wanted to end the meeting even more. "If you have doubts Colby's out there, and that his bones may be bleaching in a Colorado ravine—who in the hell is executing the *Overlay* schedule? And why?"

Secretary Thomas Cline, who had been staring straight ahead, reached to turn the ignition key. "If I had the answers to those mysteries, as well as knew where on God's earth Grayson was hiding, I wouldn't be forced to associate with the likes of you," he said, keeping the knowledge that the ex-president was on ice, literally—he chose to display ignorance.

"There's another snake in the library that's raised its ugly head," the secretary hissed his words. "As expected, President Rhoades' man, Steven Heywood, has been leaking information about our D Street

Library meetings. I've noted the two of them coming and going in the West Wing isolation room on various occasions, I'm certain Rhoades is now aware of our *Overlay* dilemma." Cline laughed aloud. "Although the coward wouldn't have the balls to do anything about it. The knowledge places him between a rock and a hard place."

He turned the key. "Get out. Stay on top of this disturbing Heywood situation. Find out where Rance Colby is, and that old bastard, Grayson—or I may get bored with you and expose your little hobby."

Oakley's jaws tightened until they hurt. As he opened the door of the darkened car interior, the click, whirl, click, whirl, click, whirl sound of a camera equipped with a telescopic infrared lens could be heard, but only by the figure clothed in a black rain poncho, hidden by a park shelter hundreds of yards away.

***

A.T. strained, dipping both oars deep into the still black waters of the Moskova River. He grumbled as his muscles bulged with each powerful pull. "We should have absconded with the boat with the motor." He thought better of his complaint. "No, don't say it. We need to remain unobserved," he muttered under his breath. They had rowed nearly a kilometer when Colby tapped A.T.'s shoulder and pointed to a cluster of boulders and brushes coming up on the left. Arturo dug in one oar and silently steered the boat toward the embankment. General Rutskoy's part in the night's conspiracy was to keep the guard in the closest tower engaged in conversation.

Stepping out of the boat, both men dragged it ashore. For the next twenty minutes, they probed each crevice and clump of foliage for a possible opening. They received nothing for their effort, but wet shoes caked with mud. In his frustration, A.T. angrily yanked at a large bush.

As it suddenly gave way, he tumbled backwards into the icy river. Realizing that noise would attract attention, Colby clamped a hand over his mouth to keep from laughing. Mad as hell, A.T. was professional enough to remain silent. He glared and refused his friend's extended hand.

Colby turned back toward A.T.'s source of irritation, and a quick glimpse of something metal glittered briefly as a dark cloud allowed the moon a momentary peek at Moscow. "Over here," he whispered, shining a small penlight beam behind a boulder. "There are four rusted hinges bolted into the edge of a fissure. Your bush hid what could be our passageway opening." He inserted his fingers and pulled. It refused to budge. "Come on, make yourself useful. You can dry off inside."

Arturo shoved Colby aside, wedged his fingers into the crack, placed his left foot on the rock next to it for leverage, and motioned for Colby to help. "One, two, three, pull." On the count of three, they pulled with muffled grunts. Nothing happened. Taking a deep breath, they tried again. This time there was movement. The ancient metal and leather hinges creaked in defiance, unwilling to cooperate, then finally surrendered. The opening was wide enough for even Arturo to squeeze through. To their surprise, a large rock had been split. The outside conformed to the natural cluster of boulders; the inside was flat, fitted with several leather strap handles to pull and seal the entrance. The foliage effectively hid the rock doorway. The large bush A.T. had torn loose was meant to remain attached so that when the entrance was closed, the bush would move with it, effectively hiding the access.

Two rotted straps broke as they partially closed the entrance. That was one repair that would have to be made. "Damn if we haven't entered spider city," A.T. observed as flashlights were turned on. His beam illuminated hundreds of webs clinging to what appeared to be a well-engineered tunnel leading from the river into the direction of the Kremlin Wall. The ceiling was semicircular in design. Walls and ceiling were hewn smooth; gravel lined the floor. It was wide and tall enough to accommodate a person on horseback. Continuing his observation, A.T. said, "I wish these walls could talk. What tales they'd tell of sexual intrigue and political espionage."

Colby kept walking and flashing his light in all directions. "Knowing you as I do, you'd probably plant a flower garden down here." He stopped and pointed the beam to the ceiling. "Look. You can make out the foundation of the wall above."

"There's not enough sunlight," A.T. complained.

"Sunlight for what?"

"My flower garden."

Colby ignored the Italian. "Look up ahead. There's a room and a winding staircase chiseled out of rock leading up into what hopefully must be, if I remember the drawing correctly, the president's master bedroom." Entering the large room, he noted that Arturo's beam lit up a huge carved wooden door to their left.

A.T. bent over and swung one arm back and forth. "Monster behind door, master."

Colby overlooked the comment, denying his own sense of warped humor to avoid a loss of focus. "Try the door, Igor." He hated himself for caving. "That could be our hospital room. We can store all the supplies in here," he concluded, shining his light from corner to corner. "A small refrigerator for food and perishable medical supplies, a microwave to heat the food, a cabinet for bed linens, cots for the players and whatever else we need to pull this off. Of course, we'd have to clean up both rooms and string wires from upstairs to supply electricity."

"L' Ami can tap into an outlet in Velichkin's room without it being noticed," A.T. said. "And don't forget a Port-A-Potty."

The lift of a rusted latch and a stout shoulder sprang the door open, revealing a small room that would soon be transformed into the president's secluded hospital room. General Rutskoy would explain the lack of amenities, blaming it on the clandestine facility. In a constant sleep-like state, the Russian President would never suspect.

Flashing his beam and stomping the floor of the enclosed room, Colby noted, "This is perfect. The walls are smooth, though covered in webs, and the floor is finished with slate." He quickly walked out, his head throbbing. The enclosure was a painful reminder of the clinic where Cline and Grayson had him committed.

"Let's see where the narrow winding staircase leads, Igor." Both flashlights lit the way. As they ascended, Colby occasionally stopped to kick chips of rock and small mounds of gravel off the steps. "Be certain to have Al clear the litter. We wouldn't want the general falling off while carrying his president—or we'd have done the bitch's work for her."

As the stairway narrowed, the webs thickened. "I've always hated spiders," A.T. commented, tearing away webs that clung to his face and neck. The last turn exposed a wide ledge; the steps ended abruptly.

"There's the entrance to the bedroom." Colby aimed his beam on a solid black sheet of metal. An area approximately ten feet wide and six feet high had been chiseled out of the rock wall; the thick sheet metal blocked the way through the opening. "If I'm correct, A.T., that's the backside of a massive fireplace. A lever in the bedroom must activate a mechanism that raises the back of the fireplace. Let's hope that the two generals can locate the lever, and that it's still operational."

"Wait," A.T. grabbed Colby's arm. "Look," his beam zeroed in on a three-foot long lever above and to the right. "I bet that if we pulled it down, the secret door would open. They needed a way to close and open it from this side." He brushed away the webs. "We had better alert Al to be up here at the same time the generals are ready to carry the president out just in case they don't find the inside lever. The three of them will have to coordinate their efforts." As they turned to leave, A.T. placed his hand on his friend's shoulder. "What's wrong, big guy? You look as though someone had hit you below the belt."

Colby took a deep breath and admitted, "That boat trip—it's a reminder of being on the ocean when my family drowned—I felt the same sensation when we were on the boat in Cairo. The feeling is real." Arturo remained silent.

***

As planned, everything would fall into place in two days. General Rutskoy and his American accomplice would discover the lever that would trigger the mechanism opening the secret doorway. Assuming it could be found—and worked. If not, L' Ami would be behind the fireplace to help—they assumed. Those in L' Ami's employment were poised to execute dozens of assassins like clockwork at noon on day two, assuming that they, too, weren't eliminated—or caught in the act. On the evening of day one, tomorrow, L' Ami, two nurses and a doctor, would have barged all the necessary equipment and supplies down the river, under cover of darkness. The rooms would have been cleaned, electricity strung, and the players fully made aware of their participation in the charade. Assuming he could make the necessary number of trips to haul goods without losing a boatload or alerting a tower guard and accomplish it all in one night and two days' time. General Rutskoy, on the morning of day two, would enter Velichkin's bedroom after the president retired, and armed with an aerosol can of chloroform, put him under. Assuming the guard did not sound an alarm after becoming suspicious of the president's absence later that morning, and that the general did not fall downstairs with his patient. It was Colby and Arturo's responsibility to take out the male assassin disguised as a maintenance man at the hotel, and in some way, make the female assassin believe that she had escaped with the knowledge President Velichkin was no longer in Moscow, but rather incognito and en route to Stavanger, Norway. Assuming that Colby's life-threatening risky plan worked—otherwise he would be a dead man. All of this in two days. And the entire strategy depended on every piece of the puzzle falling in place. Finally, there would be General Rutskoy's perilous dash across the skies with his passenger, President Alexei Velichkin, alias Rance Colby—and his anticipated showdown with the Arctic Rose. *Assuming* all went as planned.

***

"What the hell do you mean, I can't see Rubin? I mean, General Brock."

The attractive brunette lieutenant remained seated and calm behind her desk outside the Joint Chief's office. She took one slender finger, placed it in the middle of her thin turtle-framed glasses, slid them to the end of her nose, and fluttered her lashes. "Director, he's not available. He's indisposed for an undetermined period of time." She shoved her glasses in place, ignored his glare, and returned to the computer. Red-faced, Max turned and stormed off. He had always disliked what he called Pentagon types—even beautiful brunettes, though he had to admit, in her case, he could make an exception. *I wonder if she likes to sail?* Max Carlton's chauffeured car sped back to Langley; he looked forward to a most interesting appointment.

***

Ice clincked in the glass of Scotch held by the man slumped in the chair before the Director of the CIA. Everything about him screamed *crumpled*—from an uncombed head of bushy black curls to every stitch of clothes on his back. His scuffed leather shoes were crossed at the ankles. A wrinkled all-weather trench coat was haphazardly thrown over the adjoining chair. It made the celebrated Colombo coat appear to have just come off the rack. Even his face looked crumpled. Shining black eyes peeked through deep rolls of age lines. Despite his appearance, or perhaps because of it, Sam DeCorssi had been the agency's crack surveillance man, until a sniper's bullet shattered a hip and ended his government career. The director, from time to time, had provided Sam with private assignments. This was one of them.

Sam smiled and flipped two undeveloped rolls of film onto Max's desk. A raspy voice asked, "Do you want to have your lab boys develop the evidence, or me?"

Max shoved them back toward the ex-agent. "You'd better. This is entirely between the two of us. Were they both there, as we suspected?"

"Cline and Oakley—just as you called it, boss. The photo prints will bear out their early morning parley, but I've got something even better for you." He leaned over and yanked on his coat, fumbling for something in a pocket. "You got a tape player handy?" he asked, tossing a cassette to his old boss. While Carlton dug in his desk drawer for a small recorder-player, DeCorssi explained. "When Oakley entered the car, he cracked the window on his side about six inches anticipating having a cigarette at some point during their conversation." He laughed, thinking of what had happened when he did decide to light up. "I hadn't expected to have this kind of luck but came prepared for every opportunity."

Max still hadn't found the player. "Cut to the chase. What kind of luck?"

"The exposed window was all I needed for my trusty long-range eavesdropper to perform its duty. I've got most of their palaver on tape. And the conversation's a doozy, boss." Carlton found the palm-sized recorder-player, inserted the tiny cassette, refilled Sam's glass and his own, then sat back and listened intently. Although the reception tended to be garbled in parts, he smiled at the revelation.

***

L' Ami had been successful in acquiring a retired doctor. Although a veterinarian, he had extensive medical training and was confident he could pull off the charade. One nurse was also retired; the other had played a nurse in a stage play and was quite convincing. All three had agreed to the unusual circumstances of being blindfolded before and after the gig, and of the ominous death threat should anyone reveal the events of their activity. The Frenchman from America held his breath, hoping that Rutskoy would not discover that the doctor was really a vet, and that he managed to keep the romantic Italian gardener away from the busty actress. Local black-market contacts provided the necessary medical supplies and drugs. The players furnished their own uniforms. Four folding cots would do for sleeping in the outer room, plus card table and chairs, and a large folding metal-frame hospital bed that would be the president's place of residence until word had come that he was safe—assuming Rance Colby succeeded. Everything had been loaded, along with a Port-A-Potty, mini-refrigerator, microwave oven, a store of food and liquids, electrical supplies, heart monitor, IV pole, and typical hospital room amenities.

The plan was for Rance and Arturo to accompany Al on his trips to secure the site well after dark. L' Ami's third trip would be with the three blindfolded accomplices. Everyone would pitch in to prepare the hospital room for the president's arrival. The outer room would be cleaned last. Battery-powered floodlights would illuminate the areas until the morning when Al could enter Velichkin's bedroom. He would tie into the upstairs power after General Rutskoy brought down the drugged body. Since the president would be in a continual state of artificial slumber, a private bathroom would be unnecessary. He'd be allowed to relieve himself with waste bags. Not the best of circumstances, but under present conditions and time constraints, a full-size bathroom facility was out of the question. They were forced to compromise. After discovering the lever to open the secret entrance, it had been decided that the generals would not take the time to locate the inside lever. L' Ami and the doctor would open it when they heard a rap on the metal door. It would come at approximately six- thirty tomorrow morning. Immediately after the president had been secured and General Rutskoy had made a brief appearance explaining Velichkin's condition, where he was, and why, Rutskoy would meet Colby at a predetermined remote site for their breakneck flight to Stavanger, Norway. They'd stop just long enough at the Finnish border to drop off General Rubin Brock for his covert flight back to Washington. Timing was essential for A.T. and Colby to remove the male hotel assassin and use Colby as bait to pass on false information for the female killer to report to the Arctic Rose concerning President Velichkin's unannounced trip to the Norwegian fishing village.

***

"But my General," the new sergeant meekly protested, "the order is to remain at my post until relieved at seven o'clock." He swallowed hard, his knees shook, and his eyes pleaded for understanding.

General Rutskoy grinned at his aide, walked over to the nervous guard, placed an arm over his shoulder and squeezed. "Your first name is Anton, isn't it?" A quick nod affirmed the fact. "And who is it that issues your orders, Sergeant?" the general asked, still tightly gripping the man's shoulder.

"You, sir," came the weak reply.

"And didn't I reward you for the information you provided concerning my sainted grandmother?" Again a nod. "So now I'm doing you yet another favor. I have an early private meeting with our president, so I'm assuming responsibility for his safety. You are hereby relieved of your duty. Go." He released the sergeant and gave him a shove.

Anton gave the aide a sheepish glance and quickly left.

A bright red thick carpet muffled their footsteps. Approaching the bedroom's huge hand-carved double doors at the end of the long hallway, Rutskoy motioned with his head. Brock understood. He was to remain on guard outside until summoned. The Russian tightened his grip on the doorknob, turned it slowly, and eased the door open. He paused and held his breath. The only sound from inside was heavy breathing. President Velichkin's sleep remained undisturbed. Rutskoy gasped when the president's breathing became irregular after one spritz of chloroform. He was about to panic, but then breathing returned to normal. At the sound of a prearranged knock, Brock entered, turned, and locked the door.

"Rubin, give your people the signal while I make Alexie presentable." General Brock took a poker, leaned into the oversized fireplace, and banged on the back panel. The kidnapping of the Russian president had begun.

***

"I don't like this one goddamn bit!" A.T. complained bitterly. "If Al were here, he'd have a freakin' coronary. You're setting yourself up. One wrong move and you're dead."

Colby responded to his friend's concerns. "That's why I've got my favorite Italian hiding in the next room—to see to it that I stay alive. If it'll make you feel more comfortable, let's go over the scenario. We take care of our guy just prior to noon—when the others are eliminated. Then we request our favorite maid from housekeeping by asking for the chubby brunette named Maria. My room door will be open a crack as we discuss the fact that Alexei Velichkin slipped out of Moscow incognito last night for a discreet rendezvous in Stavanger, Norway."

Arturo stood and walked to the window and checked his watch. The killings would begin in less than two hours. Gazing at the walled compound, he thought of the president, unaware of his own kidnapping and hidden in an ancient crypt below his residence. Without turning, he again registered his concern. "You're purposely going to let her shoot you. You know she won't leave here, even though she has information essential to her boss, without making that attempt."

Colby opened his shirt and pulled on the fabric beneath. "My ultralight First Defense bulletproof dry suit top, and bottom will provide me the necessary protection."

"What's to protect your head and your good looks?" He threw up his hands, turned and glared at his friend. "If that's what you think, you're a dead man."

Colby pointed to a chair. "Have a seat. I know you mean well. You have a better idea?" A.T. remained silent. "Besides, if she aims her weapon anyplace but my chest—you have my permission to blow her head off." He thought for a second and continued. "Come to think of it, to make her hit convincing, just nick her in the arm as she turns to flee. Then wail like a banshee that I've been murdered."

On edge, both men jumped when the phone rang. A.T. was closest to the phone. "Yes?" He listened intently for three minutes, Colby sitting impatiently. "Good. I'll give him the message." Rance's eyes silently asked—*well?*"

"That was L' Ami. He wishes you good luck."

"Yes. Yes. What else did he say? Did all go as planned?"

"President Velichkin is in the hospital bed for a long sleep. The only problem was opening the secret exit. Al and the doc had to both hang on the lever before it would budge. Brock kicked the hell out of it until the damn thing finally broke loose. It was a tense few moments. The president appeared to buy Rutskoy's story, but probably will never remember the conversation. The old boy's back at the Kremlin, making excuses for the president's absence. Upon occasion, he's been known to disappear unannounced for a few day's tryst, so the general believes he'll sell the idea. He'll meet you as scheduled."

Colby looked pleased, but before he had time to relax, Arturo continued. "Al also said that he had received a cell-phone message from one of his contacts at our hotel. Our man is on the twelfth floor, pretending to work on a hall air conditioner vent. He's been systematically working his way, room to room, in search of you, it's suspected. There's no time to waste; we better take care of him now—then phone and wait for Maria's entrance, and if you survive, assume your Velichkin disguise."

Arturo took the elevator down to the twelfth floor. Colby, dressed as the Russian captain, ran down the stairs. They approached the large muscular man in a gray hotel uniform from opposite ends of the floor. Noticing A.T. first, the assassin then sensed someone behind him when the exit door slammed shut. Spinning around, his dark eyes raged with hatred. An instinct honed from years as a professional assassin alerted him that his life was in danger. The soldier's slow deliberate walk and the look in his eyes said it all. He had witnessed *that look* dozens of times before and had always been the victor. A chill ran up his spine. That look had also been in the eyes of the short bald man now behind him. The assassin ran fingers through his thick black bushy hair. This time something was different; he could feel it.

As the Russian soldier closed the distance between them, Arturo shouted a warning. "Don't move a muscle!"

The shout had a mind clearing effect on the assassin, snapping him out of a moment of indecision. His right hand dove into a deep uniform pocket. A Russian-made 9mm Makarov appeared, but before he could raise it in firing position, Colby spun on one foot. The other foot whipped the gun from the would-be shooter's hand. Staggering backward, the assassin fell to one knee, grasping the knife concealed under a pant leg. Placing his back to the wall, he flashed the blade back and forth, threatening them both. His only chance was to kill the soldier and take his chances fighting hand-to-hand with the shorter man. The knife flipped in his hand. Grabbing the weapon by the blade, he was prepared to fling it at Colby. When his arm drew back, A.T.'s knife sailed through the air, embedding itself deep into the killer's massive chest. The assassin's knife fell to the carpet. A look of disbelief crossed his face as he sucked in a deep breath and looked down at the protruding handle. The powerfully built man grunted as he yanked the knife free. A look of puzzlement skewed his features as he stared at the blade's missing tip. Arturo frowned at Colby, shook his head, and waved him away.

A.T. raised a finger and glanced at his friend. "Count to six, and it'll be over."

Colby was about to demand an explanation when the assassin let out an ungodly roar and tore at his chest with both hands. Blood erupted from his mouth in a gush. Dark eyes rolled back, he fell to his knees and over onto his face. The killer was dead.

It was Colby's turn to look puzzled. Before he could ask, A.T. explained as they lifted the man and headed for a laundry chute to dispose of the body. "It's one of my inventions. That particular knife has a barbed explosive tip. When pulled out, the tip breaks off and remains in the subject. Within six seconds, the charge explodes. You witnessed it's devastating effect." As the body fell down the chute, he went on. "Handsome here was my Guinea Pig. That was the first time it's ever been used. Effective, uh?"

Colby continued shaking his head. "It certainly is—but killing still isn't easy—even though the man deserved it."

"Don't look at this," he motioned to the chute, "as a killing. Look at it as a saving gesture. He's dead, and we've saved the lives of all those he would have killed in the future—had he lived past this day."

Rance slapped A.T. on the back and laughed. "Well, that's a convincing theory, but it won't hold up in court." He looked at both ends of the hallway. "We've been lucky. This floor's void of people for the moment. Let's head back and phone for Maria."

***

Workers in the Langley office building went about their duties with only mild interest in the large twenty-by-sixteen-by-twelve shiny black box, surrounded by workstation cubicles. All four sides were made of bulletproof one-way glass. Occupants could see out, but no one could see in. Magnetic vibration currents surged through the walls, ceiling and floor, making electronic eavesdropping impossible. A self-contained combination air conditioner, purifier, and circulator were attached to the twelve-foot glass ceiling. To the far right of the room and behind the massive onyx-top conference table was a large rear-screen projector monitor, and at the opposite end was a large television screen that could, with the flip of any number of switches and display photos from a selection of orbiting spy satellites.

"You asked to see me?" Alan Oakley spoke into an electronic voice analyzer while pressing a red button outside the black glass door. Four men sat inside. They could see him, but he had no idea who was there besides his boss, CIA Director Max Carlton.

"Enter," Max said, pressing the door release button under the edge of the table. A buzzer sounded, and the Special Projects Director stepped in. The door swiftly closed behind him, and the latch snapped shut. At first he hadn't noticed the two armed Marine MP's standing inside at parade rest on either side of the door. His eyes scanned the grim faces of three members of the D Street Library group: General Craig Tomasic, Chief of Army Intelligence, Senator James Cochran, Chairman of the Foreign Intelligence Committee, and Matthew Johnson, Secretary of Defense. Sensing the two men behind, he turned and glanced quickly at the Marines and then to Director Carlton.

Oakley motioned to his rear. "This is most unorthodox. What are they here for?"

The startling reply rode on a monotone voice. "They're your escorts for your long vacation to Kansas—Leavenworth, Kansas."

Alan Oakley took a step back and stuttered. "What…what…are you talking about? Surely you jest." His mouth remained open as he waited for the director to reply. All sorts of scenarios flashed through his head. Finally he blurted out, "If it's the Michaels' suicide—I told you I had nothing to do with that—although I was on the grounds outside the home when I heard the shots." He pleaded with both hands. "I admitted that."

Carlton's tone of voice hadn't changed. He pointed to the row of chairs opposite the three seated men. "Pick a chair." Cochran, who sat opposite Oakley, leaned over, and shoved a pot of steaming coffee across the onyx top. Oakley shook his head, refused the offer, and stared at his boss with a frightened expression, waiting for an answer.

"This has nothing to do with the unfortunate event at the Michaels. Forensic experts have determined without a doubt that poor Lester shot his wife and then took his own life. That case is closed. Your case is just now beginning." Oakley stirred in his chair, glanced back at the Marines, and appeared to be about to stand. This time Carlton's voice was loud and commanding. "Stay right where you are. We have much to discuss." He pressed the buzzer and the door latch clicked open. "Fellows, take up your post outside, will you please. I'll call you when you're needed." The Marines stepped outside, and the door swung shut.

Max Carlton swiveled his chair, exposing the full view of the rear screen projector monitor behind him. He pushed a button and a photo of Alan Oakley emerging from Secretary Thomas Cline's car filled the screen. "Where in the goddamn hell did you get that picture?" Oakley shouted, slamming his fist on the table, demanding to know.

Remaining silent, Carlton pressed the button four more times. Oakley was furious. He shoved himself away from the table and was about to jump to his feet when another image appeared. It was of him dancing with another man at a gay bar. Alan Oakley collapsed in his chair. He gasped. "Did that bastard Cline send you that?"

"No. The negatives and prints mysteriously disappeared from the secretary's wall safe while he slept—and he's yet unaware of the theft." He laughed to himself. "Can't imagine how that happened."

Oakley was now on his feet, poking a finger in the direction of the large screen. "That old son-of-a-bitch was blackmailing me. He threatened to send copies to the *Post* and the CIA if I didn't go along with his plan." His finger still wagged. "I was undercover at that time, damn it! I'm not gay!"

Carlton's hand waved his irate associate back to his seat. "I'm fully aware of that fact, Oakley. Although I have no respect for you personally, I can vouch that you were undercover during the time those photos were taken. That's not a problem for you anymore. Prints, slides, and negatives will be destroyed. No. You have another and graver dilemma." He keyed up a small tape recorder-player from the back credenza and placed it on the tabletop. Appearing completely bewildered, Oakley slumped in his chair.

Max Carlton placed a finger on the play button and pressed. Tomasic, Cochran, and Johnson sat mesmerized by the recorded discussion between the Secretary of State of the United States and the Special Projects Director of the CIA. When it was heard that Oakley admitted to the killing of the two agents, four sets of eyes tore him apart. Dejected and mentally exhausted, Oakley stared at the table's reflection, a beaten man.

"Oakley! Look at me!" Carlton ordered before any of the others could react. They appeared to be in a state of disbelief. How could two of their own trusted D Street Library members be guilty of such a crime? Oakley's gaze reluctantly rose to meet that of his angry boss. "You should get the full punishment you deserve, but if you agree to cooperate—my recommendation to the AG would carry weight. He may waive the death penalty and perhaps shorten your Leavenworth visit by a few years."

Oakley's voice was barely heard, his eyes downcast. "What is it you want of me?"

"Along with your testimony," he pointed to the tape player, "and his own words, we may have enough to accuse and indict Thomas Cline for conspiracy to murder. I'm certain the AG would want additional charges added for an undisputable case to take down a popular Secretary of State. For your next meeting with your friend, you'll be wired."

Oakley's eyes brightened for a second as he envisioned being set free—and not placed in the Marine's immediate custody. But the vision quickly faded when Carlton added, "Until then, your every move will be monitored, and if it's suspected you are about to run—you'll be terminated on the spot. Am I clearly understood"? Oakley's head fell to his chest.

None of the other men had spoken a word. Earlier, by mutual consent, they had agreed to remain silent and allow the director to conduct the interrogation. Max's eyes shifted to the athletically built black man, James Cochran. His arms and elbows lay on the table, both fists tightly clenched, jaw muscles twitching. Max was just as angry as Jim and fought to control his own emotions. Cochran appeared ready to pounce on the man across the table, but the piercing look in the director's eyes eased the tension. Oakley would have a difficult time explaining his imbrued condition to his fellow conspirator.

"There's the unexpected death of ex-President Grayson." He paused a moment to look at each face. "If he is indeed dead. We only have Cline's word for that, and he's yet to disclose the body's location—only to say he's on ice." He smacked his palm down, "And that's where I want *him*."

Max Carlton pressed the door release. A Marine opened the door and poked his head inside. "Yes, sir?"

"Escort Mr. Oakley out of the building, but first relieve him of his CIA credentials and weapon." He glared at his one-time associate. "You damned well better remember—you'll be under twenty-four hour surveillance—so stay close where you can be reached at a moment's notice. Don't even think about alerting Cline. And remember the alternative. Termination." He waved him away with the back of his hand and a look of utter contempt.

The moment the door clicked shut, General Tomasic swung his chair to face the director. "What have you learned about the chief's sudden disappearance?"

Carlton's grim features loosened slightly. "Brock's wife was reached in Arizona. Off and on, for the last four months, she's spent most of the time attending to her aged mother who refuses to enter an assisted living home. Mrs. Brock knows nothing of her husband's recent activities but did suggest that he had been hoping to sneak away for a week's fishing in Canada. She had no idea where in Canada. My Canadian counterpart has been alerted, but as of this morning, he's had no luck finding the general's whereabouts."

Matthew Johnson reached for the coffee pot while offering an opinion. "He may well be on a fishing trip. God knows he deserves some down time—but with a situation like this, with the world in possible turmoil—it's not a viable assumption."

Standing to signal the end of the meeting, the director dropped a bombshell. "A cryptic message was intercepted by our Mid-Eastern team suggesting that the assassinated Israeli Defense Minister has been observed alive, or someone resembling his description. We have no idea how many know of the rumor—but if substantiated—all hell will break loose in the Middle East. The implication of his being alive would light the match setting Israel afire."

"And conceivably, forcing the United States into war," the Secretary of Defense warned.

Chapter Eleven

A call had been placed. The call returned. Maria was on her way to Andrei Zakharov's room and should arrive in four minutes. The outer door had been purposely left open, allowing for a one-foot gap. A.T. was out of sight, next to the adjoining room door. Colby stood at the back of the room, facing the Kremlin skyline, noting the second hand of his watch. In exactly four minutes time, he nodded; it was the signal for the Italian to begin his report of President Velichkin's secret visit out of the country.

It was necessary for A.T. to raise his voice; he was purposely positioned across the room to ensure that the maid wouldn't miss a word, pretending that he had just entered the room. "Rance, I just received a phone call. President Velichkin is no longer in Moscow. My sources inform me that without anyone's knowledge, he slipped out of Russia late last night on his way to a fishing village in Norway called Stavanger. Unknowingly, he saved his own life. There won't be an assassination in Moscow tomorrow, as that bitch had planned." He forced a laugh.

Turning, now facing his room door, Rance asked the obvious questions. "Is he meeting a woman? Did you learn the name of the hotel where he's staying?"

A. T. adopted a lecherous tone. "He's a bachelor and has been known to disappear from time to time for a little R & R. It's rumored that a female is always present, although it appears that it's someone different each time." He stepped toward the adjoining room door. "It's suspected he's booked under an assumed name at a small discreet inn called the Norwegian Crown." Opening the door, he shouted, "I'll get on the horn and see what else I can learn!" He slammed the door shut, kept his hand on the knob, and reopened it a crack. His free handheld a ready pistol.

The next few moments moved as if in slow motion. "The *Overlay* schedule may have been temporally scuttled—but Velichkin will yet die!" the maid cried out from just inside the door. Her hand instantly appeared from under her apron. She held a gun. Aiming it with both hands at Colby's chest, she squeezed the trigger and screamed, "But you will die now!"

Just prior to the explosion and impact, Colby had taken a deep breath and held it. The slug hit its mark. His body was whiplashed against the portable wet bar with such force that it overturned, glasses shattering against the back wall. As his limp body slumped to the floor and the female assassin turned to flee, Arturo managed to squeeze off one shot. She made a shrill cry, stumbled back against the doorframe, and grabbed her blood-splattered shoulder. With her gun hand hanging by her side, the maid called Maria risked a likely second life-threatening hit for one final look at her kill—then dashed into the hallway screaming with laughter.

"Rance! Rance! Can you hear me? Are you alright?" Arturo shouted as he ran and bent over his unconscious friend.

Adam Lee, at age sixteen, thought he had mastered his father's instructions to the letter—that was until he decided to attempt a martial arts move that he had secretly invented and thought perfected. Halfway through Adam's new move, the heel of Master Lee's palm shot out as if spring loaded, hitting his young son's chest. The impact lifted Adam off his feet and propelled him through the air onto his backside. The blow had expelled all the air in his lungs. Gasping for breath, he attempted to focus his eyes on the concerned face of his adopted father. "Father. Father," he whispered, his chest heaving in an effort to swallow air, "you…hit me hard. I'm sorry…I thought I was well prepared. What….?"

Arturo interrupted his delirious friend. "I'm not your father. It's me, Mr. Trash Pile," he said, splashing water on Rance Colby's ash- colored face. He tore open the shirt to observe the spot of impact. A flattened lead slug was caught in the fabric folds of the protective vest and had not penetrated Colby's chest. "You'll have one hell of a bruise and maybe a cracked rib, but you'll survive, old friend. That was a crazy stunt you pulled," he chastised, while dabbing Colby's lips with L' Ami's whiskey. Holding a shot glass, he suggested the prone man take a sip.

Colby, with A.T.'s help, managed to sit up. "Where's my father?" he asked, still in a daze. His next words were concern for the success of the pretense. "Do you think she bought it? Did she get away okay?" He massaged his chest and gulped down another shot of JD.

Arturo's deep frown said volumes. "You didn't kill her?" Colby asked, grabbing A.T.'s shirtsleeve.

"No. I merely wounded the bitch. Hit her in the shoulder." He locked eyes with the other. "You know who that woman really was?"

Confused, still thinking of Master Lee, but curious, Colby slowly shook his head waiting for the answer that he already anticipated.

"I may be all wet, but from her almost hysterical reaction to what she believed she had accomplished—the death of her nemesis, and her mention of the *Overlay* schedule—I'd say you had a visit from the ice bitch herself. Maria, the woman who cleaned our rooms everyday, is none other that the Arctic Rose." He helped Rance to his feet. "But what bothers me is, with access to our rooms, why she never attempted to plant bugs or kill you earlier?"

Sitting on the corner of the bed, Colby offered an explanation. "She probably figured that we'd electronically sweep the rooms several times a day, and if discovered, she would be the logical one to interrogate. She wouldn't chance ending her ability to maintain surveillance, and by terminating me earlier, the opportunity to learn our plans to eliminate her and her band of assassins would have been lost."

He stood, did a few knee bends, and with feet planted, twisted his body from side to side. Claiming himself fit, he pointed to the closet. "It's time to become President Alexei Velichkin and fly away to Norway for my next meeting with the Arctic Rose." He grinned and said, "She, too, is a master of disguise, wouldn't you say? A slim, muscle-toned woman fooled us all when she became a short, hefty, nondescript maid."

One brow went up as Colby chuckled silently. *I could have sworn that my father was here.*

*****

Prior to leaving the hotel, Rance had received a report from L' Ami that the president was resting quietly, completely oblivious to his current situation. Before leaving Velichkin's side, General Rutskoy sent a message: "Come now. Let's fly."

Rance Colby said good-bye to A.T., listened to the instructions to be careful, and stepped into the street disguised as the Russian captain. A hailed cab took him within two blocks of the helicopter rendezvous spot. Two bags contained the disguises that would transform him into the President of Russia. That, he'd accomplish on board the craft.

Circling the idle craft from the backside, Colby approached it with caution. Well hidden in an opening surrounded by tall trees, he could make out its huge rotators that hung low like a wounded bird's wings. From his current position, he was unable to discern movement from inside. Hefting one bag over his left shoulder and securing the strap of the second with his left hand, Colby slowly advanced with the 9mm Beretta, firmly held in his right. Once alongside, he was about to flip the hatch, when it suddenly opened. Startled, he jumped back, pistol ready.

General Brock laughed aloud. "You wouldn't shoot an old general with a glass of Scotch in his hand, would you now?"

"Damn you! You're lucky you're not sporting a hole between those bushy brows." Colby shouted back, angry as hell. "I'd hate to be the one to drop your sorry ass off at the Pentagon. Though I don't foresee too many tears. Put down that goddamn glass and grab my bags."

Brock had hauled in the last bag and Colby was about to stow away his gun when a twig snapped. Spinning around and falling to a prone shooting-position, Colby's eyes frantically searched the brush and trees.

"I give up. Don't shoot," came a familiar voice from behind a tree. "I'll go aboard quietly."

Getting to his feet, Colby bristled. "Damn it Testaccio, as if I didn't have enough on my mind. What the hell are you doing here?" He thought for a second and shook a pointed finger. "You followed me." A.T. knew when he had stepped over the line; his friend never called him by his last name. This time, he'd have to do something drastic if he were to have his way.

"I'm coming with you on this mission to watch your back. There's no telling how many accomplices that bitch will have with her." Before Colby had a chance to say no, A.T. went on. "There's only one way that you can keep me off that flying piece of tin, and that's to do it physically." He walked slowly toward his friend, his stare never leaving Colby's eyes. "You'll probably win—but you'll sure as hell know you were in a dog fight. And you'll have to use that whole bag of makeup to cover the bruises and swollen nose and eyes." He stopped directly in front of Colby. "What's it going to be? Am I coming on board, or are you going to shoot me here and now?" Hands on hips, determined, he waited for a reply.

The two generals were amused by the conversation. "How can you turn down an offer like that? Make up your mind, my friend. We'll be airborne in one minute!" shouted Rutskoy, laughing boisterously.

Rance squinted at the two faces peering down at him from the helicopter, then to his expressionless Italian friend, trying his darndest to look innocent. Placing both hands over his eyes, then throwing his arms into the air, Colby burst into laughter. "All right, Trash Pile, get your ass in the craft. Didn't you hear the man? We leave in one minute." As they both climbed in, Colby silently agreed with Arturo's logic. *He's right, as usual. There's no telling what trap she's conjuring up for President Alexei Velichkin.*

General Rutskoy flipped switches. Lights flashed on the direct vision and overhead control panels. Huge sleeping rotators whined to life, then gathered speed. Suddenly Rutskoy shouted over the engine noise. He roared. "Look. Look at the late-edition newspaper headlines!" pointing to a large monitor screen. It was written in Russian, so he translated for General Brock and A.T.'s benefit. He read the headline first, then the sub-headline.

Killing Epidemic Claims Lives of
International Assassins in Moscow

At least thirty-six known and suspected international assassins were found murdered in the streets of Moscow. Apparent organized and calculated termination began at noon today. Although government officials deny knowledge of the incident, a reliable source asserts MLS forces involved in...

General Rutskoy turned off the screen and offered an explanation as he lifted the craft and headed north. "Our security people will find a way to take responsibility for what your Mr. L' Ami accomplished. No one will investigate the killings. Who would care, as long as the world has been rid of such trash?" He turned, looked in A.T.'s direction, and humorously added. "No offense, Mr. Trash Pile." Everyone laughed except Arturo. "It will be a coup in their feathered cap—as you Americans say."

"What's the MLS?" Brock asked.

"That's short for Mother Land Security, named after your own Homeland Security. The goddamned terrorists are everywhere today."

Arturo, making himself comfortable among all the stored gear, broke into the one-way conversation. "Might I remind you that today there are three dozen less of them to be concerned about." Everyone nodded in agreement and sat silently, pondering personal thoughts. It was another dark moonless night. Perfect, so reckoned the pilot as he opened up the throttles to full speed, prepared to fly low over Russia, Finland, Sweden and into Norway to avoid radar detection. First stop would be in Finland to drop off General Brock.

Rance, like A.T., took a short but much needed nap. Somewhat refreshed, Colby went about the task of becoming President Velichkin. Occupying two of the rear seats, with the president's photo and magnified mirror-light suspended before him, he determined what was needed to transform himself. Their faces were basically the same shape, his jaw slightly more square, but when the president's black mustache and goatee were applied, the difference would be negligible. Velichkin's eyes were deeper set, but shadowing would accomplish the needed effect. His hollowed cheeks could be handled by muscle control and sucking in his cheeks when not in conversation. Turning blue eyes into dark brown would be no problem with contacts. Temporary black dye would suffice, and with mousse, Colby would slick his hair back to match that of the infirmed-kidnapped president. In little less than two hours, President Alexei Velichkin appeared.

Raising his voice an octave, Rance Colby shouted instructions in Russian. "Damn it, General! Turn this craft around immediately. Take me back to the Kremlin! Enough of this nonsense!"

The voice and command startled Rutskoy. Flipping on the interior lights, he whipped his head around. Dumbfounded at what he witnessed, the shock caused him to lose temporary control of the helicopter.

Pulling out of a dive, he shouted over his shoulder. "By Lenin's beard, you nearly gave me a heart attack! Alexei's own mother wouldn't know you from him—even if she wanted to—which she wouldn't. She remains a died-in-the-wool communist."

"Then I take it that my appearance would fool anyone who does not know the president intimately?"

"Without a doubt!"

Satisfied, Colby opened the large bag and laid out a set of clothes purchased to complete the disguise, including black wingtip shoes, a long black cashmere coat, matching wide-brim hat, white silk scarf, and large oval rose-tinted sunglasses. Uncomfortable but necessary, under it all, he would wear a lightweight bulletproof dry suit. A.T.'s orders. He decided to delay dressing until after Brock was dropped off and they were over the Baltic Sea between Sweden and Norway.

Colby would have welcomed crashing among the gear like A.T. but had to be careful not to undo all his hard work. As it was, it would be necessary to touch up the makeup job before they set down in Stavanger. Sitting upright, he laid his head back and closed his eyes. For the first time in memory, he sensed fear on a mission. It wasn't specifically the danger to him that churned his gut, which felt foreign to him; it was the fear that he might not return to Molly's embrace and their anticipated future together. Arturo and Al had been right. Love for her now made him vulnerable. Colby opened his eyes and turned his head toward his friend, snoring in the corner of the craft. A hint of a smile crossed his face before he shut his eyes. A second element of fear nagged at his being—the sudden, yet temporary blackouts that rendered him helpless and any associate—Arturo, vulnerable. He would never forgive himself if this weakness were the cause of his friend's death. Sleep came and so did *the dreams*. Those horrible nightmare dreams of losing his loving family that had so confused him months ago. At times, in a melancholy mood, he wrestled with the concept of who he really was. Deep inside, he was convinced of the reality that he was both Adam Lee and Rance Colby, and that the ex-president had programmed him into believing otherwise. One isolated thought clawed at his sanity. What if he was really the college professor that lost his family and was programmed to believe he was Adam Lee and Rance Colby? No. He would convince himself. How could he suddenly become this expert covert *Shadow Master* with friends like A.T. and L' Ami? The craft's abrupt descent broke his dream-like state. Finland was straight ahead.

Before General Rubin Brock left the helicopter, Colby agreed to report in once he had uncovered Arctic Rose's whereabouts. Likewise, Brock would brief him on what had been happening stateside since his departure. The general had originally made arrangements with an old admiral friend, one eager to fill the late Admiral Lester Michaels' position, to covertly authorize an aircraft carrier-based fighter plane to secretly whisk him to Washington. In the meantime, he'd concoct a story as to why he had been out-of-pocket for nearly a week.

***

Colby and Arturo jumped down from the beached helicopter. Time was critical; it was imperative that Rutskoy lift off immediately before his unmarked craft was spotted. They had pushed the envelope, skimming treetops and waves to avoid four different countries' radar systems in their dash from Russia. The two remaining passengers voiced concern. General Rutskoy was dog-tired. Everyone had had the opportunity to sleep except the pilot, and it was now early morning on the coast of Norway. "Once I cross the Russian border, I'll set down and catnap," Rutskoy promised. "Then I have to visit my president to be certain he's being kept safe and comfortable." Tossing down the last bag, he added. "You two watch each other's back. I wish you good hunting. And understand this. You both are welcome in my country at any time—as my personal guest. Russia can never repay you for what you both have sacrificed to save its president's life—though very few will ever know." He threw them a snappy salute, slammed the hatch, and lifted off.

The two men scampered up the bank from a sandy cove and waved to the black dot on the horizon. "That's one hell of a man," A.T. thought out loud.

"And so is my general. They're two shiny steel peas in a cast iron pod," Colby observed, straightening his wide-brimmed hat. "You have the name of my inn?"

"The Norwegian Crown."

"That's it. It's located at the tip of the village, directly across the street from the fishermen's wharf, canning warehouses, and ship-repairing facility." Glancing at his watch, he shook his head. "It's too early to check into the inn, and the shops won't be open for another few hours for you to purchase a change of clothes." A.T., in his haste to follow Rance, neglected to pack a bag. "From my brief information concerning Stavanger, there was mention of a sailor's rest home in a converted warehouse close to the Norwegian Crown."

"Sailor's rest home?"

Colby couldn't help from laughing. "Don't get yourself in an uproar, my Italian friend. It's nothing personal, just a thought. The location would be convenient." A.T. nodded, but his brow remained in a deep frown. They walked through a grouping of tall grass until reaching a two-lane blacktop road. "We'd better split up," Rance suggested. "It looks as though the town buildings begin approximately a kilometer from here." From a rocky knoll they could view the entire area—a picturesque blend of low-lying mountains, rolling plains, scenic islands, rushing waterfalls, and the Stavanger harbor alive with fishing boats of all sizes, plus one giant commercial cruise ship. Colby breathed in the fresh salt air and peered up at the swooping sea birds overhead. "Seems peaceful—but I wouldn't want to spend my last days here."

"You mean being buried here," Arturo said in a foreboding tone.

"You said what I couldn't bring myself to say." Rance pointed in the direction of town. "I'll start walking. Wait until you can't see me anymore, then follow. I'm stopping at the first café I see and have breakfast. I would imagine they open early around here."

"Sounds like a plan," A.T. said. "If your café is the only one open, I'll join you. Rest assured that I'll sit as far away as possible from the peacockish-looking dude with the flamboyant cashmere hat." He raised a finger to be heard. "And don't forget the trouble you got yourself into at the last coffee shop you frequented."

Colby tugged at his brim and looked over the top of his rose-colored glasses but didn't respond. Six paces away, he turned. "Without being observed, meet me in Mr. Lomonosov's room at noon." Turning away, he threw a last dart over his shoulder. "Who am I kidding, you'll fit in perfectly with all the other fishy-smelling old timers wandering aimlessly around the dock."

With his back turned, Rance was unable to see the infamous Italian gesture made by his friend. But a grin appeared as he imagined the worst.

***

She ran to pick up the phone, not so much to answer it, but to stop the ringing. Mrs. Brock's mother had finally fallen asleep. She was surprised and pleased to hear his voice. "Hi honey, it's me. How's your mother doing?"

The conversation was typical of a husband and wife who hadn't seen each other for a period of time. Years of experience had programmed her not to question her husband's prior whereabouts, considering his sensitive position within the government. It wasn't unusual for him to leave on a covert assignment without notice, and she trusted him implicitly. General Brock was calling from his study on the scrambled line. Having just swept the room for bugs, a common practice when out of town for any period of time, he was satisfied that eavesdropping was not possible from his end. But they both had to assume the Arizona line could be jeopardized.

"Dear, Max Carlton called and inquired about mother, and he wanted me to ask you to phone him the moment you got back from your Canadian fishing trip. I believe it's important, he sounded upset."

He couldn't help but say it. "Good girl." She had given him his alibi for being away from Washington. "Have to run now. I'll call Max as soon as we hang up. Give my love to mother." He paused. "I've missed you—and you're in my prayers, too. Talk to you later my love."

Brock hung up, then dialed Carlton's private number. Although not fully rested, he had napped off and on while zipping across the ocean and was alert of mind.

"This better be important and fast; I have an early morning meeting," came the aggravated voice of the CIA director. "What?"

"I'm pleased to hear your normal happy disposition, Mr. Director."

"Brock!" he shouted into the receiver. The general held his away from his ear. "Where in hell have you been these past days? Your disappearance is the subject of this morning's meeting." The general tried to explain, but Carlton wouldn't let him. "And don't tell me, at a time like this, you felt like going fishing."

As controlled as he could be, Brock answered in a soft voice. "Max. Max, old friend—that's precisely where I've been—in Canada. I needed to wash the cobwebs from my mind. And damned if it didn't work." His voice grew in strength. "I feel refreshed and raring to go back to work. What's new? What's next?"

"Goddamn it, General, all hell's breaking loose! We uncovered our CIA mole—as well as a murderer. Two West Wing members of our D Street Library Group are under surveillance. An ex-president remains missing. The Middle East is about to explode and go up in smoke. Then there's the question of whether Colby is alive or has actually perished in the wilds of the Colorado mountains." He blew out a breath. "Other than your untimely disappearance, everything's normal around here." Yanking on his drooping mustache, he blurted out, "And did you hear what happened in Moscow? Three dozen assassins were assassinated at noon yesterday! The newspapers are having a field day, calling it an *epidemic of killings*. What the hell is going on?"

Brock was forced to stifle his humorous tendencies. "Now Max, control yourself. Remember your blood pressure. As far as the Moscow incident goes—that event, I would suspect, pleases you—pleases everyone around the world. The other situations are more serious. I have the ear of the Israeli Ambassador. Keep your shorts on; I'll be in your office in two hours."

"No, make it our glass isolation room outside my office—in one hour."

***

A smorgasbord home-style breakfast was just what Rance Colby needed to begin a day of unknown consequences. He had to laugh. *If stares could bore holes, I'd look like a Swiss cheese.* The stranger in the wide-brimmed hat caused quite a stir at the café. There hadn't been that much excitement since the 1966 World Exposition was held in Stavanger. A nonchalant quick glance at A.T. sitting in the back of the room said it all. A.T. could hardly contain himself—stuffing his mouth with eggs and sausage so he wouldn't laugh out loud.

Turning the corner from the restaurant, Colby came upon a four-lane street paralleling the harbor. The scene reminded him of a typical New England fishing village, a mixture of modern and old-town architecture. He marveled at the V-peaked storefronts, each painted a different bright color. Stavanger was famous for its canned sardines, so it seemed appropriate that blocks of buildings were squished together like packed sardines topped with tall, narrow, peaked, red-shingled roofs. Horse-drawn carriages were being readied for the early morning tourists. One block later, he stood in front of the Norwegian Crown, a white two-story inn trimmed in black and gold. But he wasn't ready to walk up the steps to the wide verandah. He had to make one important stop. The inn's back alleyway.

The Norwegian Crown was on the corner, which made access to the dark alley convenient. Unnoticed, Colby slipped into the shadows and shoved the smaller bag snuggly behind a large garbage bin. It was nearly empty, which meant that no pick-up would disturb his bag that day. Satisfied, he walked out of the alley and around to the front, and up the inn's steps. Once inside, he was startled by the lobby's interior décor. It was like stepping into an old western bordello, or what he thought one would look like. Red and gold glared at any arriving resident. Just to the right of the check-in desk was a circular staircase leading to the second floor. A massive sparkling crystal chandelier hung down from a high ceiling and lit the way. Where the thick blood-red carpet ended, the flocked red and gold patterned wallpaper began. Gold colored crown molding, a piano, an equally bizarre-shaped red and gold sofa completed the astonishing ambience.

Colby's wide-eyed expression wasn't lost on the short thin man behind the reservation desk. His thin lips disappeared in a wide smile, while peering over wire-framed glasses held in place by a long slim pointed nose. Red arm-garters and a matching pair of red suspenders were the frosting on the Norwegian Crown's cake. The stranger was about to approach the desk when the room to his immediate left caught his eye. But it was the elderly woman that captured his attention. She sat at a long cherry-wood bar, her gnarled hands wrapped around what looked suspiciously like a giant margarita. The only thing missing from her regal-blue chiffon dress was a crown. *She does look like royalty. Must be the Norwegian Queen Grandmother staying at the Norwegian Crown.*

Soft coughs coming from the little man at the front desk broke Colby's concentration. Walking forward, he announced, "The name's Pavel Lomonosov—that's with four O's—my good man." He tapped a finger on the open guest register. "You must have my reservation in there."

The good man knew every name in that book, and he had never heard of a Pavel Lomonosov, but the inn was nearly empty, and he wasn't about to lose a paying customer. So he lied. "Yes Mr. Lomonosov, we have a suite reserved for you facing the beautiful…"

"No. No, my good man," Lomonosov interrupted. "I want a room facing the alleyway. I am a writer and need solitude, not distracting touristy views."

Good man's eyebrows went up and his hooded eyes folded back. "But of course. You are our honored guest. As you wish, a room bathed in solitude," he said handing over a golden key. "Will that be…"

Before he had an opportunity to mention a credit card would be necessary or a cash advance, the strange guest snatched the key from his hand and threw a wad of bills on the gold-colored marble desktop.

"Here, this should be sufficient for a week's stay, and a handsome gratuity for your troubles." The desk clerk stood speechless as his newest guest tugged at his wide brim, picked up his bag, and stomped up the staircase to his isolated room. Halfway up, he paused and glanced back in the direction of the bar and shook his head. *No. That couldn't be her. She's good, but not that good—and she couldn't have gotten here before me—she would first have had that shoulder taken care of before heading for Stavanger and her target.*

***

Israeli Amvassador Abe Rubinstein sat stone-faced in the middle of the large sofa, his arms crossed. His friend, General Brock, and CIA Director Max Carlton leaned forward facing him, perched on the edge of their chairs. The posh Northern Virginia hotel was a CIA safe house and the site of a critical meeting with the ambassador. If he accepted Brock's suggestion, an armed conflict between the Israelis and the Arab world would be averted.

"General, my government complied with your earlier recommendation by faking the death of our Defense Minister—who is now in hiding." He unlocked his arms, placed both hands on his knees and pushed back to study the general's face. "And now you want him to be permanently housed in America?"

"The rumor that your minister has been sighted alive is spreading like wildfire throughout the Middle East—though unsubstantiated. We have not received a report that he has compromised his position, so we believe that someone resembling him was sighted. And that provides us with the basis of my suggestion." The two men locked eyes. "We want this man, or another resembling the minister, to come out into the open. Hopefully, this will quell the fire in the Arab's belly. Your government can claim mistaken identity. The minister will forever remain dead."

It was Carlton's turn to continue the scenario. "Covertly, the CIA will whisk him from his current hiding place to America where he'll be protected indefinitely. He'll be provided with a new name, identity, and substantial bank account. Even a slight change in his features, if necessary. In time, his family will be sent for. If he's the patriot you claim him to be—he'll be willing to sacrifice for his country's safety."

Ambassador Rubinstein's shoulders hunched forward, and a deep frown appeared, as if in agonizing thought. They sat in silence for several minutes. Brock and Carlton exchanged worried glances. Without a word, the ambassador stood and walked to the door, then turned. "Your logical solution to a complex and explosive situation is accepted. Contact me in twenty-four hours and we shall make all necessary arrangements." Before twisting the doorknob, he turned halfway around. "My country thanks you both."

Chapter Twelve

He clampted shut both eyes and stood completely still as the old and rickety fire escape shook and twisted under his weight. Rance Colby, minus the Velichkin makeup, dressed in a brown tweed sport jacket with leather elbow protectors, matching corduroyed pants, dark brown mock turtleneck pullover, high-topped suede shoes, and a brown suede golfer's cap—slowly made his way down the two-story rusted frame. Pausing long enough to quell his nerves, he proceeded to the large garbage bin. Reaching behind to retrieve the small bag, he felt around, briefly panicked, then discovered that it had slipped from its wedged position. Bag in hand, he turned the corner and walked up the hotel steps and entered the garish environment of the Norwegian Crown. His eyes gravitated left. Smiling, he spied the little old lady firmly gripping her drink with both hands. A man in his fifties sat next to her drinking coffee. *Must be her son making sure she doesn't slip off the stool.*

"Hey mate!" The husky shout gave the reservation clerk a start. Readjusting his crooked wire-rimmed glasses, he excused himself and promptly opened the ledger book. "The name's Dustin Deed—from the land down under—wishing a room for three days."

Inspecting the book, the skinny clerk peered over the rims at his energetic prospective guest. "You don't appear to have reservations, but we do have a few rooms available."

"Great, mate. I'm partial to room 222. (Lomonosov was in 220.) That's where me and the little Misses stayed on our honeymoon six years ago—bless her departed heart."

"Why certainly, sir. That room's available." He made a sad face. "I'm truly sorry for your loss."

Deed laughed. "She's not dead, mate. We were divorced six months after we married. Passed. Yes, you could say that—she passed on to some other fool just two months later." He slapped a palm down hard on the marble top. The little man jumped and dropped the key. His new guest tossed him the correct amount of cash and promptly bounded up the stairs.

Colby now had two rooms and two separate identities. One was bait for the Arctic Rose, the other, free to nose about in search for the woman with the tattooed ankle and a bandaged right shoulder.

***

"Don't give me cause to widen that string-bean nose," the short stocky man dressed in a well-worn navy jacket and wool knit cap growled.

"But I can't give you Mr. Lomonosov's room number. It's the law," the frightened desk clerk squeaked.

"I've got this here," he brandished a medium-sized brown envelope in front of the clerk, "package I was instructed to place in the Russian's hands." Leaning across the desktop, he managed to grab hold of both suspender straps and yanked him close. "I suggest that you get on the horn—and let the man decide. *Capisce?*"

The shaken clerk reached for the house phone, the angry sailor still gripping his suspenders. He nodded, hearing room 220's reply. "You may go up now," he whimpered, straightening his rumpled shirt.

Sixty seconds later, A.T. rapped on the door of room 220. "If that's an Italian lady of the evening, be forewarned, I'm promised, still a virgin, and saving myself for my wedding night. Other than that, come in," came the inside reply.

The door slammed shut. Arturo swaggered to the small refrigerator, opened the door and gasped. "No beer? Have you lost your mind?" He turned to face his friend and grinned. "You know I can't work without my beer…" Arturo halted in mid-sentence and studied Colby's latest disguise. "Thought you were that Russian…President Velichkin."

"It won't be long until word spreads that someone resembling the Russian President checked into the Norwegian Crown. Now that that's been established, I can roam the streets as Dustin Deed from Australia," he said, opening his arms wide. "At some point, later in the evening—I'll stroll around the downtown area as Pavel Lomonosov—and give everyone a good look. Hopefully, she'll take the bait." A finger pointed at A.T. "Of course, the salty old baldheaded sot will be somewhere close behind." He poked a thumb at the adjoining room door. "In case the accommodations at the rest home didn't suit you, plant your round hard body there for the next few nights. I own both rooms." A.T. snarled at the cheap shot, but knew it to be a sound idea. He nodded agreement and kicked the refrigerator.

***

Dustin Deed, smiling tourist from down under, had turned the heads of local ladies while admiring charming small wooden houses and polished cobblestone streets. As he had instructed A.T., he kept a watchful eye for a woman favoring her right shoulder or concealing an immobile right arm. Every store window reflection was scrutinized. Prior to leaving the inn, Arturo had accepted the room 222 offer. Colby decided to let him sleep, choosing instead to wake him when he again became Pavel Lomonosov.

Wide-brimmed hat snugly in place, Colby tapped on the adjoining room door. No response. He knocked harder. Sill no response. *Damn, he's a heavy sleeper.* Opening the door, he staggered back at the sight of a room that resembled a train wreck. Chairs and a table were overturned, the bed was ajar, and bedcovers twisted, one of the drapes hung lopsided, and the floor lamp was smashed. A closer look disclosed a blood-stained pillow. Arturo Testaccio was missing. And there was a bloody smudge on the exit doorframe.

"There was a terrible disturbance in room 222 next door to me! I came here for peace and solitude. Didn't you hear it?" Colby complained bitterly, attempting to pry what he could out of the timid desk clerk. A shrug of one shoulder was his only response. The flamboyant Russian threw up his arms and shouted as he left the inn. "If I were you, and thank God I'm not, I'd check out that room!"

He had to get his emotions under control to think clearly, so he sat in a rocker on the verandah. *They could have taken A.T. anywhere.* His eyes scanned the dozens of huge warehouses at the edge of the harbor. *It would be like looking for a single noodle in a pot of Italian meatballs and spaghetti. My best bet is to continue as though I know or suspect nothing—go for my stroll and let them find me. I'll do a little trolling and see what I catch. When I do, I'll find Arturo.* Stepping down the stairs, he had one last agonizing thought. *Hopefully, alive.*

***

A red and yellow glow streaked across the dark-blue sky as the setting sun slowly disappeared. Tall lampposts lined the street with gentle halos as darkness closed upon the waterfront. One block down in the middle of the main drag, people gathered to hear a fiddler perform and watch his two young children dance.

Colby circled the gathering, his eyes darting from one woman to another, ever mindful that one or more of Rose's assassins could be among the crowd. He remained on the edge, aware that close quarters could mean a knife in the kidneys. A nun was standing behind the dancing siblings. She was dressed in a traditional black habit; a half-length cloak hung over her shoulders, her left hand deep within a shoulder bag. Odd. Rose is also an expert in disguises, he recalled. The cloak could hide a wounded shoulder, and the left hand could be clutching a gun. The nun's eyes were not centered on the activity before her; they searched the applauding crowd, as Colby did. Not wishing to create a scene, especially concerning a nun, he decided on another form of action. Keeping a low profile, he moved slowly to his right until he was four rows behind her.

Raising his voice, but not so loud as to bring attention to himself, Colby called out the name—"Megara Perrakis." Everyone's concentration was on the two tykes keeping beat to their father's music. No one took heed, with the exception of the nun. Her head whipped around. The fixed smiling face puffed up by the tight uncomfortable high starched collar remained impassive, but those eyes—those icy eyes flared with burning hatred. There was no doubt. Rance Colby was staring into the cold eyes of the notorious and deadly Arctic Rose.

Rance shouted as he shoved aside a group of frightened tourists, "Look out! Run!" Rose spun around, her left hand remaining in the raised bag, prepared to fire with no regard for the people standing between her and her hated target. Miraculously, no one was hit. Fabric from the bag burst and fluttered in the air as the all too familiar *spit* of the silencer perked Colby's ears. As the bag and weapon were aimed, he instinctively twisted sideways, avoiding a direct hit. The slug tore through his coat and shirt, glancing off the bulletproof beneath. By the time Colby gathered himself; his assailant had lifted her skirt and dashed through the startled crowd toward the dock and rows of warehouses. In his effort to pursue, he bumped into the little dancing girl, knocking her to the ground. Picking her up and dusting off a scraped knee, he apologized and slipped her father a handful of bills. There was no sense in trailing after her, she had since long disappeared into one of the ware-houses.

Once he changed clothes, he would systematically check out each building, one by one. "Excuse me, sir," said a timid voice. The short man wearing a cowboy hat and three cameras hanging round a thick neck pulled on Colby's sleeve. "I saw what happened," he poked at the bullet hole, "and saw what building that nun ran into." He gestured with his head in the direction of the harbor. "It's that old rundown building to the right of the Royal Sardine Canning Factory—the one with the model ship hanging outside. We," he pointed at his wife, "toured it three days ago. They rebuild ships' hulls there. It was closed down yesterday. For at least a week, we were told." Colby patted the man on the back, smiled at his wife, and thanked them both. Then he took off at a fast pace for the inn to change his clothes, arm himself, and start his search of ware-houses for A.T. and Rose—beginning with the closed shipbuilding shanty.

***

Colby had exchanged the president's attire that apparently hadn't fooled Rose for black crepe-soled shoes, black trousers and knit pullover, and a tight-fitting waist-length black jacket. The 9mm was strapped in a holster under his left arm, another but smaller pistol Velcroed behind his right calf. A stiletto was hidden at his back, attached to his belt. He would move more freely now and blend in with the shadows of an already pitch-black night. Slipping down the side entrance, avoiding the skittish little man at the front desk, he wore the wide-brimmed hat and cashmere coat to escape prying eyes while crossing the street. Once on the docks, he'd shed the hat and coat and slip on a black knit cap.

She has to know I'm coming. That can't be avoided—but perhaps I can surprise her in some way. The determined man in black had time to think about the past few hours as he silently scampered over the time-worn wooden platforms. Three feet above water level, they served as a sidewalk attaching each warehouse, one to another, the entire length of the harbor. He now realized two things: Rose might not have known that he wasn't President Velichkin, and A. T.'s appearance at the inn may have given him away. If she had wanted his friend dead, they would have found his body in the room. She was using him for bait. Arturo must be alive. But in what shape, he did not wish to speculate. He hadn't given up without a fight. The condition of the room attested to that.

Three buildings away, he climbed over the edge of the walk and worked his way along two-by-fours that were nailed to each piling just above the water. Bending over slightly, he remained below the wooden walkway. At the corner of the old shipbuilder's shack, he peeked over the edge. No guards. They must all be stationed inside. Squatting down, he could make out a wooden framework beneath the building. The moon had come out and the shining reflection on the water made it possible to view the structure. Perhaps this could be the surprise. Carefully stepping from one wooden crossbar to another, first testing its strength, he made his way to what appeared to be a series of trapdoors leading into the building from below. Using his palm, he pushed upward on the closest one. He cringed as it squeaked in protest. This is what he was afraid of. Hand over hand, foot over foot, he made his way to the trapdoor in the far left-hand corner. It refused to budge. Placing his shoulder and back under the door, he lifted up. It gave, slightly and silently. Pushing up with all his strength, it opened as coils of thick rope lying on top slid off to one side. He held his breath. No sound from inside. Climbing in, he could now hear muffled voices. As his eyes adjusted to the darkness and diffused interior light, he realized that he was inside a fenced-off, block-

and-tackle storage area. To his right was a metal- framed stairway leading up to a catwalk circling the entire building. He was still unable to make out the words, but it sounded like both male and female voices.

Much to his surprise, the rickety suspended stairway managed to hold his weight without squeaking or swaying. As he approached the catwalk, his view of the interior of the building improved. Rows of panes of glass encircled the structure one-third of the way from the top; the bottom two-thirds consisted of aged wood planks. A combination of moonlight filtering in and a yet identifiable source of light bathed the huge workroom below in a surrealistic haze. Scraps of wood were piled throughout, and longer pieces stood on end against the walls. Hand and electric tools were neatly stored. Several smaller boat hulls lay on wooden horses. Overhead, two large hulls were suspended by ropes. And there, just below the far-hanging hull was a bloodied Arturo, sitting in a chair, hands tied behind his back, and wrapped with heavy chains.

Straining for a better look, he suddenly yanked his head back as a female voice shouted. "Colby! Knowing of your reputation—you've probably found a way in by now!" He could barely make out her silhouette standing next to a giant lathe. Though there was movement to both her left and right, there were no visible signs of others. But they were there. No doubt. "Come out in the open, or your baldheaded friend dies before your eyes." Colby knew she would do as she threatened. Rose was ruthless. To his frustration, from the position he occupied, he had no clear shot at the Arctic Rose or any of her assassins.

Arturo, although weakened by a merciless beating, managed to raise his head, and cry out. "Forget me! Complete your mission! Kill the bitch!"

His impassioned plea was met by a muzzle flash. The slug sliced through the upper and outer part of A.T.'s shoulder, propelling him backwards in the chair. Over his grunted pain, Rose screamed. "Now he's repaid for shooting me in the shoulder!" Colby gritted his teeth, stifling an outcry of explosive curses that would expose his position.

"Now, Karl, now!" She shouted a command. Two hands appeared from within the shadows and grasped a cord. A mighty tug released the right-hand side of the massive wooden ship's hull, dangling directly above the prone Italian. It swung down, swaying back and forth, held only by two remaining left-hand ropes. "Come out or the other side will be pulled free, and baldly will be crushed!"

There was no choice but to make an appearance, but Colby had an idea. "All right. Hold on. You win; give me time to get down." Walking across the catwalk to the middle of the warehouse, he paused. "I'll swing down on one of these ropes. Hold your fire." Vulnerable, in the open, he stepped over a wooden railing and reached for a rope. Unknown to Rose and her associates, it was the cord that would release the other hanging hull's left-hand ropes. There could be no wasted movement; A.T.'s life depended on perfect timing.

Yanking on the release cord with one hand, he grabbed another rope with the other. He had noticed beforehand that the second rope was attached to a beam on the far side of the building. The instant the hull swung loose, its momentum carried it toward the other dangling hull. Colby pushed off, holding the other rope. The impact of the second hull smashing into the first, along with the driving pressure of his feet shoving it forward, magnified the splintering collision. The first hull thrust to the side and away from the helpless body, shattered into thousands of pieces of wood raining down upon Rose and her thugs. Colby could only pray that his friend had somehow survived the shower. His hull hung intact, swaying above the scene. Momentarily stunned by the blow of his body coming in contact with the ship's hull, he had managed to cling to the rope. It seemed like an eternity before he could untangle himself from the displaced ship's rigging. A pair of welder's gloves, picked up from the catwalk before making his swing, assisted in the fast slide down the prickly-feeling thick rope.

Dropping down, he quickly rolled to his left, extracting the 9mm, and assumed an attack position. There were no shouts or gunshots, and no Arctic Rose. And Arturo was nowhere to be found. Cautious, he circled the wreckage. His eyes closed in frustration as he heard words seeping up through timeworn planks below his feet. "He's lost a lot of blood—but that's no concern—because he'll be sacrificed at midnight tonight where hundreds of lives were forfeited thousands of years ago." Over the racing motor of a boat heading away from the docks, the same insane laughter he had heard as she ran down the hotel hallway after being shot again rang in his ears.

Rose and her people must have escaped through one of the trapdoors into a waiting boat. *He'll be sacrificed where lives were forfeited thousands of years ago.* Colby's computer-like mind raced through all the data he had accumulated about Stavanger, Norway. "That's it!" he shouted aloud, smacking his palms together. "Pulpit Rock!" Racing for the front door, he shouted triumphantly, thrusting a fist into the air. "They're heading for Pulpit Rock, where historians say ancient sacrifices were performed." Glancing at his watch, he had less than two hours to get into position, save Arturo, and terminate Rose and her assassins. *Hold on old friend—I'm on my way.*

***

Rance could visualize the typed words on the display screen. It stated that Preikestolen, Pulpit Rock, was two hours by foot. He swiped, for the lack of a better word, a small, fully gassed, two-man fishing boat that had been docked two slips away. Following the wake of Rose's boat with its large noisy motor, he could approach, staying well out of sight, without detection. For the next hour, staying closer to the shoreline than the larger craft, he zigzagged from one fiord to the next. Small islands dotted the seascape. Low-lying mountains appeared like dark mounds on either side of a narrow waterway. Trees blanketing their tops turned into sparse clumps of vegetation as masses of rock began to dominate rugged mountainsides. Idling the small motor, he marveled at the outcrop of the jagged formation called Pulpit Rock. Moonlight illuminated the ominous slice of black rock that rose over six hundred meters above the sea. According to his data, the flat surface jutting out into space was an approximate twenty-five meter square plateau. That would be where Rose threatened to kill Arturo Testaccio. The larger fishing boat had just disappeared behind the bend when Colby made his risky decision. They would be taking the trail to the top. It was a long upward walk. He would take a shortcut up the sheer seaward side of Pulpit Rock and surprise them when they arrived at the top.

He cut the motor and drifted toward the rocky edge of the imposing cliff. Leaping from the boat to a low-lying boulder, Colby secured a line around a jutting rock, then scampered over a collection of rocks to the base of the sheer six-hundred meter-high cliff. The moon's glow worked to his benefit. Foot and handholds were visible. Taking a deep breath and straightening his jacket, the man in black proceeded to climb up-ward. *Never look down,* he reminded himself. The climb was fairly easy until halfway up where the handholds became scarce, and farther apart. Stretching to reach a small crevice to his left, he held on with one hand as his body's momentum swung in midair, then back far enough to the right to reach up and wedge fingers into another slice in the rock face. With a mighty effort and strained, aching arm muscles, Colby managed to repeat the exhausting process and now clung six feet from the top. Voices could be heard in the distance. The assassins carrying Arturo to his death had nearly reached the plateau. One final swing lifted one foot over the ledge. Arching his body, he flipped over, quickly rolling into a shadowed hollow to the far side of the plateau. Pulling the knit cap over his face to mask the moon's glare, he lay perfectly still. The black hulk of his body blended with the darkened rocky landscape. He could see the silhouettes of four men approach the Pulpit Rock summit—one carried Arturo over his shoulder. A.T. was dumped unceremoniously in the middle, the painful groan reaching Colby's ears. *At least he's still alive.*

Motionless, he visualized three basic moves. Slowly moving to a kneeling position, he hesitated, then sprang into action, sprinting toward the two standing at the plateau's edge, peering off into the distance. Before the remaining two thugs knew of his presence, and with a powerful burst of energy, Colby leapt into the air, both feet extended. The impact thrust both men headlong over the edge. Twisting his body, he landed face down. Watching the movements of the others, he sprang to his feet just as one man lunged forward with an arm extended. Sidestepping, the knife missed him by inches. Before the attacker had the opportunity to turn, the man in black took one-step forward and spun in the air, his heel swinging around to shatter the man's spine. While airborne, Colby's right hand grabbed the stiletto. By the time both feet touched ground, the knife, flung underhanded, plunged deep into the fourth man's throat. His automatic weapon had been trained on the badly beaten man but moved slightly for a clear shot at the moving intruder. Dying reflex caused a squeeze of the trigger; spraying rounds cut into the hard surface, barely missing A.T. Slivers of rock showered the only man who remained standing, one slicing his right cheek. In the space of one minute, four men had lost their lives.

"Are you still with me?" Colby asked, kneeling next to his friend.

A.T. groaned and attempted to move. Through a badly swollen mouth he coughed an answer. "Am I still alive—or in hell with you?"

"You must be alive; you sound ornery as ever." Placing a hand on his friend's chest as a comforting gesture, he added, "Don't move. You've lost a lot of blood." Aware that Rose was anchored somewhere below, he reassured Arturo of his return. "Stay put. I have to leave you; I hear that bitch trying to start the engines." Cranking sputtering sounds echoed from far below.

"I'll make it," A.T. gasped, struggling to push himself up. "Just help me...to a sitting position." He took a shaking finger and touched a line of blood trickling down his friend's cheek. Colby made A.T. as comfortable as possible, patted him on the back, and dashed for the Pulpit Rock's edge.

Rance Colby was never a diver. Although not intimidated by heights, he preferred to jump. Hurling himself into open space, he yelled aloud. "Nooooooooooo!" Straightening his legs, one arm grasped his body, the other's elbow pressed against his chest; fingers of that hand tightly held his nose. Both eyes were shut tight, teeth clenched. In the daylight, the water rushing up to meet him would have been clear turquoise; tonight it was jet black. The impact nearly buckled his knees as he plunged deeper within the icy sea. After experiencing a momentary blackout, he kicked his feet and struggled, clawing at the water to pull himself to the surface. Finally, he broke free, sucking in the night air.

Treading water, he searched the surroundings to find his bearings. Again, he heard the sound of engines turning over, but no ignition. She was having trouble getting them to turn over. Perhaps the commercial fishing vessel was out of gas—or maybe she just didn't know what needed to be done. Powerful strokes brought him closer to the grinding of the engines. A small pilot light inside the wheelhouse lit the way. Again he treaded quietly, his head just above water level, alert to any movement on deck. The grinding had stopped. All was silent except for gentle waves slapping against the boat's hull. Taking a calculated risk that the bow was unmanned, Colby swam in that direction. Once flexible joints were now stiffening from the water's chill. He had to get out or suffer the possible consequences of hypothermia, but the Arctic Rose wouldn't be that considerate. She wanted him dead, one way or another.

Both hands gripped the bow's railing. Commanding all his remaining strength, Colby pulled down, lifting his body from the sea. One leg was over the rail; he paused, anticipating a reaction from his enemy. No movement. No sound. Squinting, he could barely see inside the dimly lit wheelhouse. Quickly scanning the area, he spied the auxiliary fuel tank directly above the engine housing. About to jump down to the deck, a muzzle flashed from the stern. A slug shattered the wooden rail next to his hand. Instinctively, he tumbled backward, pulling his Berretta. Managing to get one shot off, the boat exploded, propelling Colby into the air. His aim was true; he had hit the exposed fuel tank. Knocked unconscious by the concussion, his body descended into the chilling depths of an uncaring sea. Shocked awake by the cold, Colby peered up into darkness. His mind screamed in silence. *Where are they? My wife, children—my mother and father!* Frantically, he forced his trembling body upward. Breaking surface, he gasped aloud, his eyes darted in every direction. "Nancy! Joel! Karen! Mom! Dad! Where are you?"

In panic, he dove into the black depths time after time—surfacing and shouting in vain for his lost family. Bobbing helplessly against the rocks at the base of Pulpit Rock cliff, he was beginning to lose strength. Slipping for the second time beneath the surface in an unconscious death wish to join his loved ones, a hand roughly grabbed his collar. He was being pulled up and across the jagged rocks; sharp edges dug into his torso. A blow from a rock smacking the side of his head jarred his senses. In a daze, he coughed up a mouthful of water and groaned. "What—what's going on?"

"It's me, Arturo. Colby, are you okay? I can't do this by myself," the weakened voice pleaded. Panting heavily, his one good hand released the nearly drowned man. Sitting lopsided on a boulder, breathing was difficult, but he continued. "You're having …one of your spells…it's not real. You're…Rance Colby…boy wonder. Think."

Colby, resting on his back, leaned his head back and looked up. There in the glow of a bright moon was a badly beaten face, trying desperately to display a grin, with only mild success. One eye was completely closed, deep purple in color; the other struggled to remain open. Both lips were swollen; the corner of his mouth was torn. Caked blood filled one nostril, as well as the left ear. His baldhead was a mass of deep scalp wounds. Wheezing breath indicated a punctured lung— perhaps from a broken rib, or more.

Colby hadn't moved, but now able to speak, he asked, "How in the hell did you make it down here in your condition? You look like death warmed over."

"Thanks…for the compliment." He tried to laugh but moaned from the pain. "I had to. Stumbled…mostly. I had no choice. I was given the job of watching your back…remember?"

"I saw the small pool of blood where you were tied up back at the shipyard." Colby rolled over and sat up. "How's the shoulder where that slippery bitch shot you?"

"She may have a sharp tongue—but fortunately her aim is off." He grabbed his right shoulder with the free hand. "The bullet went through the shoulder muscle without hitting bone. It'll be in good shape to do some pruning in a few days." Shaking his head to focus, he asked the next obvious question. "What in the hell happened to the bitch?"

"She went down with the ship," Colby announced, staggering to his feet. "Or should I say—up with the ship? She was onboard when it exploded. Luckily, her aim was off when she shot at me. The mission's over—and now we have to get you to a hospital. Stay put. I'll find my boat, get you on board and to a hospital. In no time—you'll be in tip-top pruning condition." Crawling over the rocks and boulders toward where the boat was tied, he caught his breath and said—"And I've got two calls to make: one to L' Amia, and one to Brock."

Chapter Thirteen

Hospital corridors were deserted this time of night. Dressed in a doctor's white smock, Colby slipped into a private room, placed a hand on the sleeping man's chest and whispered, "Don't bother to get up; it's only me." Local authorities had bought the injured man's tale of being mugged in the forest on the outskirts of town. Outraged that a tourist had been so badly beaten, they ordered the hospital to provide him with the best of care.

A.T., a mass of bandages, stirred, opened his good eye, and stuck out his tongue, making a razzing sound. "Good," Rance said. "Does that mean you're ready to go chase girls tonight?" Another wet razzing spray.

Highly sedated, he managed to whisper back. "I thought that…you had phone calls…to make."

"Made one. Al said that General Rutskoy was ecstatic, sending his highest regards for your complete recovery. President Velichkin returned to his room without ever knowing that he had not left the premises. He was so appreciative of what the general had done for him, he awarded the old boy with the papers to a once state-owned mountain villa overlooking a private, fully stocked lake. He's invited you, L' Ami, and me to go fishing with him." Rance pulled a chair close to the bed. "Both the doctor and nurses were blindfolded and ferried to safety. Rather than risk being discovered on the river with the hospital equipment, Al chose to dump everything into the Moskva River. If it ever surfaces, no one will ever suspect where it came from. Al and I made a pact that sometime within the next two months, you, he, and I will get together for a huge retirement celebration."

A.T. nodded, grinned, and winced. Colby stood up and placed an envelope on his friend's chest. "Here's a first class ticket to Rome. You're on your own from there." Leaning over he placed his lips close to A.T.'s ear. "You saved my life again. I love you like a brother. Later, bro."

***

General Rubin Brock had been away from his study when Rance had first called, prior to visiting Testaccio at the hospital. He needed to get through to the general, declare the mission a success, and arrange passage home. A quiet phone booth with a burnt-out light bulb on the edge of town was perfect. Someone picked up the receiver but said nothing. "General, are you there?" Colby questioned, a deep frown forming.

Silence. Then Brock growled into the phone. "Hold your damn horses—I've just spilled a perfectly good shot of Scotch. There. Okay, who in the hell is this?"

"The Arctic Rose is dead." Silence.

"You did it! My boy, you did it! This calls for another shot—no, make that a double shot."

"We're fine if you're interested. And I'm not your boy," Rance twisted the knife. "President Velichkin's alive and still president. Your buddy Rutskoy's a hero. Al's on the way home, and Arturo Testaccio's resting comfortably in the hospital."

"The hospital?"

"It's a long story. I'll provide you with a detailed briefing once you get me home. This is the next subject. Transportation."

"Yes, yes, my boy. Do you think you can find your way to where you dropped me off in Finland? My admiral friend will arrange a fighter to pick you up and wing you home."

301

"They don't call me the *Shadow Master* for nothing. Belay that. The *Retired Shadow Master*. And I'm still not *your boy*." Ignoring the last comment, Brock gave Rance a transportation time frame to work with, and then excitedly blurted out his own news of the day.

"All the pieces of the puzzle have now fallen in place. The Middle East tinderbox has been defused—but can only be explained one-on-one." He took a swallow of the double and went on. "President Rhoades will hold a press conference at nine this morning, announcing the replacement of Secretary of State Thomas Cline—who was killed late last night—riding in the same car as the deceased CIA Special Projects Director, Alan Oakley."

Rance let out a long whistle. "Damn, I'd like to hear an explanation for that event. Convenient. Great timing."

Silence. "Yea, wasn't it? Max Carlton had Oakley wired in hopes to obtain additional evidence on Cline. Oakley agreed, expecting a lighter sentence for his part in the deaths of the two agents that were taking their package—*you*—to Colorado. Against Cline's better judgment, he allowed Oakley to pick him up late last night at a designated location. Oakley claimed to have important information that just couldn't wait. Max listened in on the wire's transmission. During the conversation, Oakley managed to get Cline to disclose the whereabouts of Grayson's body. The director immediately dispatched people to recover the ex-president and release the crewmen on board his cruiser." Brock's pause was lengthy.

Impatient, Colby asked, "Is that it? How were they killed?"

"I was coming to that part. Had to run it over in my mind once again.

Max heard Oakley say something about *'getting their just rewards'* as he pulled out onto I-66. Their car was halfway into the crossover when it was hit broadside by a heavily loaded oncoming eighteen-wheeler. Both men were instantly killed. Considering Oakley's *'just rewards'* comment—Max believes that he committed suicide, taking Cline with him—rather than spending years in prison looking over his shoulder."

Colby interrupted. "Either that—or the CIA sacrificed a perfectly good eighteen-wheeler."

"That thought has crossed my mind, too. Especially since they both could have threatened to blackmail us into letting them go. Either one could have blown the whistle on this *Overlay* mission. Guess we'll never know if it was an accident or something sinister.

"This brings me to the subject of another death. Rance Colby's."

That raised both Colby's eyebrows. "Run that by me again."

"It's reported that three hunters were out after rabbit—and while chasing one through a ravine dense with thickets—they discovered a decomposed body with no identification. The location was in the general vicinity of the agent's crash site. Colorado authorities have concluded that the dead man is, in fact, the remains of the missing third man from the crash scene. Rance Colby is officially dead. You no longer exist."

Colby absorbed the information before answering. "That puts a whole new spin on things. Rose is dead, Velichkin is alive, the head of China is safe, as well as the Israelis. The *Overlay* project is dead—and so is Rance Colby." He glanced over at the harbor. The horizon was beginning to brighten. It was a new day. "And that makes me a free man." His mind wandered for a moment to his introduction to those in the general's group. "Members of the D Street Library are dropping like flies."

"That brings me to the final subject. President Willard P. Rhoades. We know that Steven Haywood was his mole in the group. Rhoades, even though he was aware of the *project,* could not expose it or us—or suffer international consequences. Now that it's over, I'm certain he'll agree to forget the incident—if the D Street Library Group disbands.

Which we will agree to." The general downed his Scotch. "I'll expect to see you in my study two evenings from now."

"I'll be there. And remember—you said that if successful—I could ask, and you would grant me *any* favor. I intend to collect."

Brock heard a click, then a dial tone. "Hello," he stabbed the ON button. "Hello! Colby! Damn that independent…!"

***

It was Wednesday evening, the day of the week that Molly MacWinter always frequented The Blue Heron Bar & Grill hoping to see her mystery man walk through the door. This evening the bar lacked its normal rowdy crowd, although you could always count on the same three men manning the booth opposite the far end of the counter. Besides Molly, another woman three stools down, and a young man to her right, there was no one else seated at the bar rail. Molly thought she had heard the door open, but a quick glance at the mirrored bar's reflection proved her wrong. It was then that she heard a soft whisper, "Hey, babe." Her eyes were riveted on the reflection. A squeal of delight caught in her throat. The other woman leapt off her stool and shouted.

"You dirty bastard!" she screamed, banishing a revolver, and pointing it directly at Rance Colby.

Taking three steps toward the wild-eyed woman holding the gun in her left hand, he noticed that her right arm was cradled inside her black leather jacket, the zipper pulled halfway down. "You're a smooth talker, Rose," he observed, noticing the tattoo on her ankle.

"And you're a dead man, Colby," she snarled, her small icy-eyes flashing with hatred.

He took another step. "Funny, I was told that very same thing three nights ago."

Before he could move, the crazed woman with the spiked black hair squeezed the trigger. Molly screamed as her future crumbled to the barroom floor. Colby let out a grunt and grabbed his left thigh. Rose stepped away from the stool, intent on placing another burning slug into the man who was responsible for wiping out her assassination ring—had ruined her plans to involve Israel in a Mid-Eastern war—single handedly saved the life of the President of Russia and had nearly killed her. "I survived the blast," she cackled. "As you did, I dove in the water just as you hit the fuel tank." She raised the weapon. "I clung to debris with my good arm," she cried out, waving her left gun hand.

Rose's concentration was on the man in a sitting position clutching his bleeding thigh. She hadn't noticed the tall brunette slip off her stool. Rance did, his eyes shouted—*"No Mac! No!"*

Sensing movement, Rose turned as Mac's left foot slashed out, kicking the revolver into the air. It skidded along the floor, coming to a rest in front of the booth housing the three startled regulars. Mac's fluid movement spun her on the ball of that left foot, her long right leg circled high above the shorter woman, and with crushing power, came down, snapping Rose's collarbone. Rose collapsed in excruciating pain. Mac ran to Rance's side.

He was more in shock seeing Mac handle the professional killer with ease than he was from the wound. Acknowledging his puzzlement, she simply said, "I'm a third-degree black belt. I guess I forgot to tell you that"

"Damn," he laughed, "I sure could have used your talent a few days ago." He looked down at his pant leg. "She ruined a perfectly good pair of slacks. But I have her to thank for providing me with matching thigh wounds."

Unknown to the two on the floor, Rose had regained her wits, and reached under her skirt for a backup weapon. She screamed, "Your bitch dies…" She never finished her decree; a shot rang out from the bar. Rose staggered to her feet, stiffened her body, and pitched forward. Finally, the Arctic Rose was dead.

"I was a cop before buying this bar." The barrel-chested owner held out his hand with the gun. "I'll take care of this—you three carry the body out into the alley, and dump it in the far corner next to the trash bin. After I lock up, I'll call a cop buddy and report finding a stiff. It happens. In time, it'll all be forgotten." He turned his attention to the wounded man. "How about you, buddy? Can you two make it home? You need an ambulance?"

Rance waved him off. "No. Thanks for your help and concern. All the medical supplies I'll ever need are available a short cab ride from here. It's a flesh wound; the slug went clean through." He looked up into the most beautiful eyes he had ever seen. "Help me up, babe. We'll grab a cab. I've been fanaticizing seeing you traipse around my townhouse wearing nothing but one of my shirts."

He whistled aloud and looked toward the ceiling. "A.T. was right—she was a poor shot. But it was because she was forced to use her left hand. His shot had crippled her right arm." Shaking his head, he continued. "Rose, dressed as a maid, must have heard me mention your name at the Rossiya Hotel—looked you up—and followed you here." Mac held the door as he hopped through. Leaning against the building, he started laughing.

"What's to laugh about? Want to share it with me?"

He shook his head in wonderment. "If her aim had been better, it would sure have spoiled a fun-filled evening." Mac laughed with him, leaned over, and kissed his cheek.

"I've been waiting for this evening all my life," she admitted. "And later…much later, I want to hear all about your adventure."

As the cab the bartender had called pulled up to the curb, Rance nodded agreement. "Later…I'll tell all. I have much to confess. And over two martinis—with marinated queen olives—we'll discuss a *favor* owed us by Uncle Sam."

Once inside the cab, she hugged him tight, planted a warm kiss on his ready lips, held him close, and whispered, "I love you." Right now, she wanted him all to herself. Anything else would have to wait.

Epilogue

The magical sounds of the world's greatest tenors reverberated through tall Roman column trees, weaved around stands of dark green olive trees, finally finding its way up rolling hills dotted with a rainbow of colors. Fragrances of flowers of every description excited the senses. Giant pots filled with freshly cut bouquets lined the huge patio overlooking the valley below, as well as every room in the ancient, red-tiled roof villa. Giggles of two young ladies tending to their wounded patron's every wish, wearing gardening aprons over flower-print off-the-shoulder blouses, brightened the early afternoon lighthearted mood—and good-natured laughter of friends enjoying each other's company made the threesome's retirement a blessing.

Still feeling the effects of the formidable beating at the hands of the Arctic Rose's thugs, Arturo Testaccio settled into a cushioned lounger and raised his wine glass. "Here's to a long and pleasant retirement. Rance, or whatever you now call yourself, you once said: 'We have enough cash stashed away for several lifetimes.' And with the booty we were rewarded for our latest caper—saving the world—we now have enough for a few more lifetimes." He glanced longingly back toward the patio's majestic archways, past the huge opened carved doors and into the high-ceilinged villa. "Now I can complete work to fully restore this ancient legend of a structure." An area where a large study, library, and second master bedroom once stood a hundred years ago remained in a ruined state.

A.T. motioned for one of his gardeners to plump a pillow resting behind his back, then looking at Rance, tapped his head. "How about you, old friend, any more demons in the night or daytime flashes of light?"

Rance returned his question with a frown. "I haven't given it a thought until you brought up the subject." He turned and smiled at Mac before answering. "No. All my thoughts have been pleasant ones," he reported, giving Mac's hand a squeeze. "That imaginary, drug-induced, programmed memory drowned forever in the sea below Pulpit Rock. Apparently, the shock of nearly losing my own life in the deep jolted me into reality. I haven't experienced an episode in two months."

L' Ami, attired in his patented bib overalls, leaned against a large patio column, a glass of ice in one hand, a half-full bottle of JD in the other. Seated in a chair next to him, looking up admiringly, was the well-tanned next-door neighbor. The beautiful widow owned the adjoining villa and acreage. Her dark eyes flashed with amusement at the three friend's playful banter. From time to time, Al reached down and tugged her long shiny black ponytail producing a sexy deep-throated laugh and kisses blown in his direction. Days later when Rance and Max were ready to say good-bye, L' Ami, with a gleam in his eye and an arm around the widow's waist, would announce that he had decided to take A.T. up on his offer to stay as long as he wished. Alvin L' Ami diverted his attention from the widow, as she walked to the lavatory, long enough to ask Rance a question that had been bugging him. "Now that I'm aware of all the elements of *Overlay*—why did the old bastard, Clifford Grayson, employ the Arctic Rose in the first place?"

"From what I gathered from Brock, the ex-president had become not only senile, but also obsessed with those he believed to be his enemies while he was in office—Israel, Russia, China—and wanted the Israelis destroyed and the heads of Russia and China assassinated."

Later that evening, two lovers lay quietly listening to soothing night sounds, enjoying the cool mountain breeze—and each other's tender caresses. Stars twinkled in the velvety-black sky outside the opened French doors leading to the balcony of their bedroom. Wrapped in each other's arms, snug in a large soft featherbed, they whispered of plans for the future. "You have wonderful friends, my darling," Mac said, kissing Rance's cheek.

"We've placed our lives on the line for one another many a time." He hesitated before going on. "Just look what A.T. endured for me," he sighed. "Thank God it's over now. All over. We all have new lives." He began to laugh. "And it looks like L' Ami found a new friend and admirer."

"More than a new friend," Mac observed. "It wouldn't surprise me if he permanently became Arturo's next-door neighbor."

From Rance's pensive expression, she knew that his mind had wandered elsewhere. "You appear to be miles away. Anything wrong?"

"No—not really. I just remembered that I failed to ask Al if he had given Joe the cell phone that I had promised. Just before leaving for Norway—I gave him a box with a second phone and some cash to give Joe—along with my good wishes and thanks for a job well done. The boy's keen eye may have saved my life." Rance paused and smiled. "General Rutskoy plans on taking the youngster under his wing and making certain he goes to the best of schools."

"Joe? Boy?"

"It's a short part of a long story." He nestled his head next to hers, one arm encircling her waist.

Pulling herself out from under Rance's arm, she propped up on one elbow. "Which reminds me of the subject our Italian host briefly touched on this afternoon. Your name. We're all wondering what you'll call yourself now that Rance Colby is officially dead."

He sat up and gave her a—*Does it really matter?*—kind of look.

"Don't give me that innocent look, mister. What will I call myself? Mrs. Colby? Mrs. Lee? Or, Mrs. Deed?

Instead of an answer, he laughed and gave her another tender peck. "I thought we'd decide where we wanted to live first," he teased, knowing that she deserved a reply. "Remember, General Brock's *favor* was that we could choose a location anywhere in the world, and he would make arrangements for the purchase of land and house in our name." He leaned over and kissed one breast, then looked her in the eye. "Where will it be? A villa like A.T.'s on the coast of France? A deserted island in the Pacific? Our own mountain and chalet in New Mexico?"

She squinted in revolt, pulled the thick quilted bedcover to her neck, and returned his gaze. "First the name. Then we can take our time researching where we want to spend the rest of our lives together. I assume the *favor* has no time limit?"

"Only if he passes away before we make our decision," he answered.

"I've seen him on television, and he looks as healthy as a horse. Now what will Mrs. What's-Her-Name be called?"

From her somber expression, he knew that she was serious. "Well, I could go with the name Master Lee bestowed on me. Adam Lee." He considered his answer for a moment, then added, "However, to tell you the truth, I kind of like the name I gave myself in Stavanger disguised as the Australian rogue—Dustin Deed." He threw up his hands. "Oh hell, it doesn't make any difference to me—you pick a name."

Exasperated, she rolled on top of the love of her life and whispered in his ear. "You're a picaresque-kind of character!"

"Yeah, I guess I am. Kiss me anyway."

About the Author

W.R. Park, author, columnist, teacher, lecturer, past president of three advertising agencies, William R. Park, Sr. has served as a consultant to some of America's largest and most successful companies and introduced at conferences as one of America's leading advertising authorities. As a nationally known and respected advertising executive for forty-two years, he has written thousands of newspaper/print ads and TV/radio scripts.

Winner of national awards in print and television, his popular 'Ad Pulse' monthly column appeared in Modern Retailer Magazine in the '70s and again in Publishers' Auxiliary in the '90s. In addition, his articles have appeared in Editor & Publisher, The Best Times Magazine, Route 66 Magazine, Atlanta Journal, Kansas City Star, and various nationwide daily newspapers.

W.R. Park's fifteen published novels have been read and reviewed by a host of bestselling authors comparing his work to some of the most talented suspense-thriller writers.

W.R. Park is a Member of International Thrillers Writers, Inc.

COMING SOON!

THE SHADOW MASTER SERIES
THE PROPHECY
(a.k.a. The Dacian Resurgence)
BOOK 2

BY

W.R. PARK

In 105 A.D., swords of Roman soldiers slaughtered Dacian warriors as women and children hid in fear, in a grotto below the fortified outpost. A prophecy uttered by a high priest nearly 2,000 years ago is catalyst for a 21st century threat of global proportions.

Once again, the Dacian flag with a wolf's head and a dragon's body is unfurled. Dacian She-Wolf descendants dedicated to world domination are responsible for deaths of powerful men worldwide. A plot unfolds so devious that even Rance Colby could never have anticipated…

**For more information
visit: www.SpeakingVolumes.us**